D0457684

DEVASTATION CLASS

DEVASTATION CLASS

BLINK

BLINK

Devastation Class
Copyright © 2020 by Glen Zipper and Elaine Mongeon

Requests for information should be addressed to:
Blink, 3900 *Sparks Dr. SE, Grand Rapids, Michigan 49546*

Hardcover ISBN 978-0-310-76900-2
Audio download ISBN 978-0-310-76912-5
Ebook ISBN 978-0-310-76904-0

"Xanadu" by Jeff Lynne. ©1980 EMI Blackwood Music Inc. All rights administered by Sony/ATV Music Publishing LLC, 424 Church Street, Suite 1200, Nashville, TN 37219. All rights reserved. Used by permission.

Cover design: Michelle Holme
Cover direction: Cindy Davis
Interior design: Denise Froehlich

Printed in the United States of America

20 21 22 23 24 / LSC / 10 9 8 7 6 5 4 3 2 1

To our fathers and Anthony the dog

PROLOGUE

"IDENTIFY YOURSELF."

It felt surreal to be staring at the face of Mathias Strauss on my Holoview. Captain of the UAS *Vanguard*, he was a legend of the Nine-Year War. Perhaps his greatest claim to fame had been destroying the Kastazi outpost in the Omega Sector, the enemy's primary source of supplies and reinforcements. Strauss led the attack force that blew it all to hell. No one in the Alliance had batted an eye at the slaughter. There were no Kastazi civilians. Every last one of them was to blame for our suffering. Any action necessary to secure our freedom was justified.

That hard truth aside, Strauss's attack on the outpost still had its troubling questions. The Alliance campaign on Titan Moon had already decimated most of what remained of the Kastazi forces, leaving them almost entirely incapable of defending themselves. Strauss carried on anyway. It wasn't a popular opinion, but my mother had always believed his assault was more about revenge than necessity. As I looked into Strauss's eyes, it occurred to me she was probably right. Something about him exuded a capacity for ugliness. It helped me see past all the shiny Alliance bars on his chest and accept him for what I knew he had become. A traitor.

"Identify yourself," Strauss insisted a second time.

Sitting in the captain's chair opposite Strauss felt equally surreal. Somehow fate had landed me in an absurd new reality—one in which I was the captain of the Alliance flagship, with the fate of

1

Earth and the human race resting in my hands. *Surreal*. There was no other word to describe it.

"My name is Vivien Nixon. Captain of the UAS *California*."

Strauss took two steps forward, his face filling the Holoview. "No. You are a child playing a dangerous game."

"Let's just get on with it, shall we?" I baited him, staying on plan.

Strauss angrily punched his fingers against his command module, and a three-dimensional identification photo appeared on the Holoview alongside him. *John Douglas Marshall: Age 18*. My heart broke all over again as JD's image rotated on a 360-degree axis.

"John Marshall—where is he?" he demanded.

"KIA," I replied.

Strauss's angry expression gave way to something that looked a whole lot more like anxiety, as if JD's demise had some greater consequence than I could have known. "I am placing you and your crew under arrest as enemy combatants of the Alliance. Lower your grids and prepare to be boarded."

Not yet. I had to take it further. Make him believe we were ready to die.

"I'm afraid you have it backward," I answered. "We're all that's left of the Alliance. You and your crew are treasonous cowards and Kastazi sympathizers. So just in case it isn't clear . . . no, I will not be lowering my grids."

Commander Gentry anxiously glanced over his shoulder at me, concerned I was overplaying things. His serving as my first officer added yet another layer of absurdity. Only fourteen weeks earlier he had been an ensign *and* my superior.

Strauss glanced at an officer stationed behind him. The officer nodded, confirming something for his captain.

"Then you leave me no choice but to destroy you," Strauss replied, looking suddenly more emboldened.

"Give us your best shot," I countered, knowing we had to take a beating in order to draw him in.

"We will," Strauss glibly replied as six hulking hostiles materialized from behind stealthing fields, three on either side of the *Vanguard*. The sight of the ships took my breath away. A peculiar amalgam of both Alliance and Kastazi technology, each was twice the size of the *California*.

One ship or seven, it made no difference. We still had to take it all the way to the brink.

I faced Strauss, narrowed my eyes at him, and issued the command I knew could very well be my last if everything didn't go according to plan.

"Fire all weapons!"

CHAPTER 1

JD

MY RED SPORTBIKE BREACHED A THICK WALL of opaque heat radiating off the pavement. To my left, the pristine blue waves of the Pacific Ocean. To my right, towering walls of gray-brown rock and boulder. Behind me, closer than ever before: Vivien Nixon, a yellow projectile hurtling forward at almost impossible velocity.

We'd raced each other in these canyons hundreds, if not thousands, of times. I had every curve, every line, every crevice memorized—and used them to my advantage. Even the seemingly insignificant angles of shadow and light were weapons at my disposal.

Our machines equal, only strategy and technique separated us—and perhaps the intangible will to win.

Entering a straightaway, Viv made her move. In my rearview I could see her foot stabbing downward, downshifting into third. The sound of five thousand RPMs rattled inside my helmet as I watched her yellow streak blast by me.

Instinctually, I matched her technique: Downshift. Accelerate. Overtake. She was not going to beat me.

In an instant, the road narrowed, and we were even. A blur of yellow and red intertwined.

And then came the curve. Our two bikes, cornering at breakneck speed, inches apart along the cliff's edge.

I could've eased off. Let Viv have the curve. But that would've meant submission and certain defeat. One of us had to lead and the other had to follow. I understood that. I wondered if she did. A phantom taste of bile flooded my mouth. The thought of losing made my stomach turn. No. I would hold my ground. Not give a single inch.

Ever predictable, Viv held her line, prioritizing technical precision over strategy. Her mistake. My opportunity. I took one short breath and leaned into the curve first, intersecting her path.

Behind me, I could hear the grotesque impact of Viv's bike against the guardrail. An intense wave of anger overwhelmed me. How could she let this happen again? After all this time, she should've been smarter. Better. Like me.

I turned my head and watched her bike plummet over the cliff on a meteoric collision course with eternity. And in the span of a moment, my world was gone. Empty. It was like floating underwater in the dark, no noise but the hammering of my heart.

And then the emptiness was filled with noise—the sound of metal against metal, an alarm and a cycling message broadcast over the PA: *This is a drill. All cadets report to the bridge. All students report to your safety positions. This is a drill.*

Next came blinding light as a hatch opened from above and a uniformed arm reached down to me in the darkness. As it pulled me upward, a sixteen-year-old bespectacled face came into focus: Roger Bixby. My roommate and fellow cadet.

"Come on, man. Snap out of it. Blink Drill," Bix said, shouting over all the noise. "You're going to get us written up again."

I acknowledged him with a half grin but didn't try to get out of my pod any faster. Getting written up didn't really bother me anymore, even though it should've.

I caught a glimpse of my reflection in the Iso-Pod tank as I stepped down to the floor. I may not have been the same physical specimen as my father—everything genetics divinely gifted him, I had to earn the hard way. Exhaustive, if not obsessive exercise. Strict dietary regimens. Constant discipline. But still, for all my limitations I was holding my own. At least physically, anyway.

The alarm and message continued to cycle: *This is a drill. All cadets report to the bridge. All students report to your safety positions. This is a drill.*

I pulled off my red armband and nonchalantly scanned Iso-Rec. The compartment was circular, with a dozen chambers arranged in a half-moon. The walls and floor were uniformly charcoal, the pods oblong and glossy black. You could always count on the Alliance to design everything in different, previously undiscovered shades of boring. A door at the far end exited to Beta Deck's main passageway.

Despite the fact Bix was standing right next to a control panel, he looked puzzled by the annoyed look on my face.

"What?" he asked, adding a flummoxed shrug of his shoulders.

"The noise, Bix. Kill the noise."

"Oh."

A quick swipe of his fingers across the panel cut off the Iso-Rec PA.

By the time my eyes found their way to Viv's pod, Julian Lorde was already standing beside it. He was tall, strapping, handsome, and smart. Not to mention British. My distaste for the guy aside, I had no trouble understanding why Viv—or any other girl for that matter—would've fallen for him.

He hoisted Viv out of the pod's inner chamber with effortless grace and gently set her on her feet. She responded by greeting him with a smile and delicately running her fingertips through his sandy-blond hair.

The softness of Viv's demeanor evaporated as soon as she turned her attention to me. Despite my best efforts, I couldn't help but focus on the sensory fluid clinging to the contours of her body as she stormed my way.

"What is wrong with you?" she snapped, inches from my face. "If that was a real track, I'd be dead!"

"But it wasn't, and you're not," I hit back.

"This is really starting to get old."

"What is? Losing?"

"And here we go again," she said with a sigh. "Your 'whatever's necessary to win' sermon."

"I like to think of it more as a lesson. One you still need to learn."

"You know, John," Lorde piped in, "perhaps if you concentrated more on rules and less on winning, you'd be having more success here."

My lips irresistibly curled into a smirk. "That's interesting, Julian. Perhaps if you concentrated more on winning, you wouldn't be languishing on the lower decks."

I immediately regretted saying it. The fact he hadn't made the cut with us was a vulnerability he couldn't escape, and it was beneath me to use it against him.

"If *my* father were captain, perhaps things would be different."

I wanted to get in his face, but resisted the urge. I was accustomed to taking potshots about nepotism, but not from him. To his credit, Lorde had never cried foul about it before. Probably because it would've put Viv in his crosshairs too. Her mother was my father's first officer.

"Are you really going there, Julian?" I asked.

"I'm sorry, John, but it really begs the question, doesn't it?"

"The question of what? My qualifications as a cadet relative to yours?"

"No. Not your qualifications. Your commitment. If anyone else showed so little respect for their position—"

"The captain wouldn't tolerate it? Is that it?"

"Like I said, John. It begs the question."

Thankfully the high-pitched tone of an incoming alert pinged from the com unit embedded in the wall beside me—interrupting us before I could indulge my impulse to belt Lorde in the jaw.

I steeled myself for what I knew was coming. "Marshall," I acknowledged into the com.

"Why aren't any of you at the Blink Drill?" my father's angry voice boomed through the speaker.

I cringed. So much for steeling myself.

My father had far more important duties to attend to than monitoring my schedule, yet he made a point of riding me anyway. As he always did.

"Apologies, Captain," I replied. Calling him *Dad* was only permissible off duty and in private. "I forgot to set the timers on the Iso-Pods. It's my fault."

"I don't want to hear excuses. Get to the drill now, cadet."

"Aye, Captain."

Bix wiped the sweat from his forehead. "We're getting written up, aren't we?"

"Relax," I answered. "You know this is about me, not either of you. The only thing you need to be worried about is tonight."

I felt Viv's eyes on me.

"What?" I asked her.

"What's happening tonight?" she asked.

"A microwave experiment," I lied.

"You're working on a microwave experiment? You? Tonight?"

"Yes. Me. Tonight," I answered. "Why? Is there something else I should be doing?"

"Unquestionably, there is," she said, trying to suppress a smile. "We're supposed to be celebrating my birthday, you jerk."

I maintained a straight face, but my eyes probably betrayed me.

"Are we? Well if I happen to miss the celebration, happy birthday in advance."

For a moment we stared at each other in a stalemate—neither of us wanting to break from the ruse. Inevitably, though, we both started laughing, and she gave me a shove.

"Whatever you're cooking up, it'd better be good."

Of course it would be good. Bix and I had been working on it for three months.

I looked at Lorde and wondered what he was thinking. If anyone was planning something for Viv's birthday, it should've been him.

"Guys." Bix anxiously stepped between us. He was considerably shorter than Viv and me, and his navy blue cadet uniform made him look something like an overmatched referee. "Guys, seriously, please get dressed. We're really late!"

"Punctuality is the thief of time, my friend," I answered, giving him a brotherly pat on the shoulder.

"Cute. That yours?" Viv asked.

"Maybe."

"It's Oscar Wilde," Lorde snickered.

"Was it?" I answered, playfully feigning ignorance.

"Well, John, at least your choice in plagiarism attests to good taste."

"Thank you."

Viv stifled a laugh, clearly relieved the bickering between Lorde and me had evolved into something less contentious. "You know what? You're both idiots."

CHAPTER 2

VIV

JUST STOP, NIXON, I THOUGHT, WATCHING MY hands shake as I laced up my boots in the Iso-Rec locker room.

My autonomic response to anger was always the same. I hated it. I might as well have had a flashing light on my forehead to let people know when they had gotten under my skin.

Breathe, Ditto. Just. Breathe.

That was my mother's usual refrain anytime she saw rage erupt through my fingers. And the nickname? Her doing, from the time I turned five and declared I wanted to be just like her. She was the only one who was allowed to use it—although JD dropped it on me occasionally, trying to be cute. It wasn't.

Hurtling off a cliff sucked, even if it was just an Iso-Rec sim. Every bit of it felt as real as life until just before my body smashed into the rocky gorge below. JD knew better than to do that to me. But then again, I probably shouldn't have been surprised.

I tried to fasten my uniform buttons, but my still-trembling fingers clumsily struggled.

Really?

"Okay, I'm breathing," I relented to my absent mother, taking in a few angry deep breaths.

Lo and behold, Mom's advice managed to ebb my rage ever so slightly. At least enough for some small measure of rational thinking to creep back into my skull.

Sure, JD was acting like an idiot, but it was a symptom of something bigger. It had to be. From the moment we left Earth, he hadn't been himself. He was falling behind in all of his studies, half-heartedly going through the motions with his training, and most bizarrely, questioning authority at every turn. I never would've accused JD of being perfect, but all of the angsty, loose-cannon stuff wasn't the guy I knew.

As the captain's son and senior-ranking cadet, he was under a spotlight, so at first I tried to convince myself it was just all the pressure and stress weighing on him. Eventually he'd adapt and return to center—but so far that wasn't happening. He was actually getting *worse*.

I had tried to talk to him about it more than once, but he was always defensive. First I was imagining it all. Then I was insulting him. Finally he shut me down entirely, saying it was none of my business.

The thought of JD throwing up a wall sent my fingers dancing again.

"We're still breathing," I said, cutting off the voice in my head before it could give me the same advice.

I wasn't getting angry for the sake of getting angry. At the rate things were escalating, JD being outrightly discharged from the program was quickly becoming a real possibility. That wasn't going to fly with me. He wasn't just risking his dream. He was risking mine. We were supposed to be doing it all together.

"Come on!" I heard Bix anxiously yell from outside the locker room. "Who are you talking to in there?"

The nagging voice in my head, Bix. That's who.

I finished lacing my boots and hustled out.

Julian quickly scanned me from my boots up to my collar. For the life of me, I couldn't tell if he was admiring my uniform or seething with jealousy. "Good luck up there," he said, offering me a quick kiss goodbye.

As JD, Bix, and I rushed out the door, I noticed him defeatedly sag against the wall.

Jealousy confirmed.

I didn't resent it, though. How could I? If I were him, I would've been jealous too. He'd worked just as hard as the rest of us and had all the right qualifiers, so it made no sense when he didn't make the cut as a cadet. The only possible explanation I could think of was the one thing I couldn't know—the confidential results of his Psych Ops evaluation. Did they show he lacked a certain makeup the rest of us possessed? Or was it that he had something we didn't? A quality that made him somehow less fit for duty.

If there was something mysterious lurking beneath Julian's surface, it was probably the same thing that attracted me to him. I liked the fact he had layers, and if there was some less desirable part of him I might eventually stumble upon, I would cross that bridge then. I wasn't thinking too far ahead. To me all that mattered was the right now. In the stress and monotony of the right now, he was one of the few things keeping me sane.

I looked down at my hands. They had finally stopped shaking.

A half second later, they were back at it again as my thoughts turned to the Blink Drill. I knew if JD handled it the same way he handled the last drill, it was almost guaranteed to get ugly.

Great.

Keep breathing, Nixon.

Our feet pounded heavily against the metal-plated floor as Bix and I jogged down the passageway toward the lift. JD lagged behind us as usual. Despite being late, he still wasn't going to *run*. I couldn't let it distract me. I needed to get my head straight before we got to the Blink Drill.

You only have one shot at the Blink. You have to get it right the first time. Every time. After three months of having that mantra drilled into my head, I could almost hear it in my sleep. Still, as tiresome as all the Blink Drills were getting, the prospect of actually Blinking was no joke.

The Blink Reactor was the brainchild of the brilliant but mercurial Alliance scientist Dr. Samuel Fuller. Repurposing his most important creation, the incomprehensibly powerful Generation One CPU, he had engineered a technology capable of transporting a ship far beyond the limits of conventional propulsion technology by folding the fabric of space-time.

In year seven of the war, Blink Reactors were installed aboard all fleet battleships, giving the Alliance a game-changing tactical advantage by allowing our vessels to instantly bug out to the other side of the sector—escaping any Kastazi attack in the blink of an eye. Fuller literally calling them *Blink Reactors* kinda felt like a bad dad joke to me, but if he built the contraption, it was only fair he got to name it.

Of course, like most sudden, giant leaps in technological advancement, Fuller's invention had some "we're still working on it" bugs. The most significant was its trajectory plotting, which might as well have been hooked up to a roulette wheel. Sure, the Blink would take you out of the frying pan, but it could just as easily drop you into the fire. Because of this dangerous fallibility the reactor's postwar use was restricted to instances of extreme danger or unsalvageable calamity. The proverbial *break glass in case of emergency* option.

Tragically, Fuller's creation ended up costing him his life. While attempting an unauthorized test of a second-generation Blink Reactor, one intended to take us farther and more safely into the beyond, something went terribly wrong. In an instant he was gone, never to be heard from again. The only clue left behind? His final transmission from aboard the UAS *Tripoli*.

It was, quite simply, *"Oh shit."*

In the annals of "greatest last words," Fuller's were definitely up there.

As cadets, we were never going to initiate a Blink ourselves, but the drills were our best opportunity for ship-to-ship combat exercises. Which is why they were so important. Despite this fact, lately JD was sleepwalking his way through them.

A group of plain-clothed Explorers students rushed past us in the opposite direction—the sound of their marching adding to the already calamitous percussion of our boots on deck. I finished buttoning up my uniform and glanced back at JD. He was still five meters behind.

"Move it!"

Even from the distance between us, I could see him rolling his eyes.

Keep breathing.

Amid the chaos, one of the students knocked shoulders with him. I couldn't remember her name. She was petite with bouncy blond hair. "Err, sorry . . . ah . . . Cadet Marshall. Just trying to get to my safety position," I heard her stammer.

JD turned around, walking backward even slower than before. "What's your name?"

"R-R-Rachel."

"Well, Rachel, better get to that safety position." Judging by the way R-R-Rachel blushed, I think he might've winked at her. It wasn't flirtation. He was just looking for any excuse to drag his feet for a few seconds more. And get my goat. It was working.

Bix and I shared a glance while we waited for JD at the lift. I could tell he was thinking the same thing I was. Our friend was definitely getting worse.

The lift doors slid open just as JD arrived, and we stepped

inside together, once again pretending nothing was amiss. The usual butterflies came as we shot upward toward our destination, and I couldn't help but wonder if this was going to be the day JD finally crossed the line.

As soon as the doors slid open to the bridge, my eyes gravitated to an enormous Holoview displaying a three-dimensional hologram of brilliant stars sparkling across an endless canvas of black. Space.

All those sparkling giants in the distance took my breath away. They always did. The view was never going to get old.

The bridge was sacrosanct. The central nervous system of the Devastation-class battleship UAS *California*, only Alliance officers and cadets were allowed to set foot upon it. It was from this grand room that command controls were input, piloting maneuvers executed, communications broadcast, courses plotted, and crises tackled. It was from this grand room on this grand ship that JD's father, Captain Philip Marshall, had led the decisive battle against the Kastazi on Titan Moon. And it was where my mother, Commander Merritt Nixon, had served right by his side as first officer.

Housed above Alpha Deck on its own structurally reinforced level, the bridge of the *California* measured eighty square meters and had two separate and secure entrances. Designed as a battleship command and control nest, it was deeply recessed from the hull to insulate it from attack. Consequently, there were no direct viewing portholes. Instead, the ship's external environment was captured by an array of exterior cameras. Those images were then projected to the captain's vantage point via the Holoview.

The captain's chair sat in the center of the bridge. Port side, the Pilot's station was positioned slightly ahead of the captain's chair, with the tabletop Navigation station forty-five degrees in front of it. The Analytics, Engineering, Communications, Medical, and Weapons stations shared the starboard side of the bridge, toward the bow. The Weapons station was typically vacant in peacetime, its empty chair a de facto reminder of how far we had come since the war.

By the time we entered the bridge, our friends and fellow cadets had already taken their posts. My roommate, Safi Diome, at Navigation. Iara "Ohno" Sousa at Engineering. Nicholas Smith at Communications. And Anatoly Kuzycz at Medical. They looked pissed. We were supposed to work as a team, and our being late reflected poorly on all of us.

JD made his way to the captain's chair while Bix settled into Analytics and I took my position at Piloting. Ensigns Evan Gentry and Dominick Lewis looked on disapprovingly from the back of the bridge.

We'd been on the *California* for a total of three months. It took two months and seventeen days to get to Gallipoli Station, where we'd been in space dock for the last thirteen days. An outpost in the outer rim of the Raya Sector, it was our last opportunity to replenish supplies and undergo routine maintenance before embarking on the final six-month leg of our journey. It also gave the command staff and non-commissioned officers some much needed off-ship R & R.

Cadets and students, however, were not permitted to leave the ship's confines. Not until we reached our final destination. Being stuck on the *California* for so long was starting to give me a serious case of "space burn." That's the name JD had bestowed upon our unique brand of cabin fever. My space burn had gotten to the point where I would've traded a month's worth of Iso-Rec privileges for a day pass to Gallipoli.

With the command staff off-ship, Gentry and Lewis were the two ensigns assigned to supervise our training. Both recent cadet graduates, they were charged with carrying out a number of the ship's ancillary duties. Being responsible for us was just one. Another big one was bridge prep. It was on them to make sure every last detail was in perfect order every time the captain walked onto the bridge.

I took a last look around and imagined the command staff at their usual stations. Captain Marshall front and center in the captain's chair. My mother at Piloting. Lieutenant Pelfrey at Navigation. Lieutenant Costa at Analytics. Lieutenant Commander Baber at Engineering. Petty Officer Franklin at Coms. Lieutenant Chief Medical Officer Green at Medical.

It was an honor just to sit in their chairs, even though it was only for drills. The mere fact we were there meant something important. It meant they believed in us, and that we had a real chance to be part of the next generation of great people leading the Alliance into the future. That was all I could hope for. It was everything I'd ever wanted.

CHAPTER 3

JD

UNCOMFORTABLY ADJUSTING MY POSTURE IN THE CAPTAIN'S chair, I ignored Gentry's angry gaze and wondered if I looked as apathetic as I felt. While I tried my best to muster up some focus, it continued to elude me.

Gentry lording over us wasn't helping. No matter how much I tried, I couldn't take him seriously. Observing him go about his business, I saw nothing special. There was a baseline competence maybe, but he seemed to be the epitome of ordinary. When every ensign in the fleet wanted to be assigned to the *California*, ordinary shouldn't have been good enough. His high-ranking rear admiral father probably got him his slot by pulling some strings. And that really pissed me off.

Anyway, apathetic, pissed off, or otherwise, it was time for me to get started.

"Status?" I asked Ohno.

The vibrant blue hair piled in a messy bun on top of her head and the few bio-reactive tattoos her sleeves couldn't hide presented a striking contrast to the uniform. "Engaged by seven enemy cruisers. We've taken direct hits to primary engines, defense grids failing," she reported. "I have to choke off the antimatter plasma relays to engine six or we're gonna go pop."

I'd known Ohno for a while, but it still amazed me how astounding her engineering skills were. She had taken over her father's garage when he was killed in the war. She was only eleven at the time. From that point on, all by herself, she'd repaired hovercrafts, skeet jumpers, Interceptors . . . pretty much anything with an engine.

I heard Ohno's grim report but didn't react. I was too distracted. Out of the corner of my eye, I had stolen a quick glance at Viv at Piloting. Technically, everything she was doing was just about perfect, but—my pissy mood entering full bloom—I still managed to find fault.

"Stabilize your attitude control, Nixon!"

"How about you worry about those seven enemy cruisers," she said, swiveling her chair to face me, "and I'll worry about my attitude."

"Children . . ." Gentry chided.

Children? I grimaced, and saw Viv do the same. No surprise, we both hated being reprimanded by the still wet-behind-the-ears ensign. I exhaled in frustration and pulled the next question from my internal checklist, just like I was trained to do. "Are they responding to coms?"

"No," answered Nick. I could see his bright-green eyes from halfway across the bridge.

"Distress signal broadcast?"

"Not operational."

I looked at Anatoly. "Casualties?"

"Thirty-two dead, Captain," he reported with his very faint Ukrainian accent. "And serious injuries reported on all decks."

I turned to Viv. "Can we evade?"

She scanned her console. "No go. Primary propulsion unresponsive."

"High-Intensity Vectoring Engines?"

"HIVE thrusters offline too."

There was only one option left on the checklist.

"Activate Blink Reactor."

The lighting immediately dimmed as artificial engine noise began to ominously hum in the background for effect. I drummed my fingers on my armrest.

And then Viv shouted, "Incoming!"

In the moment, all our playacting felt absurd.

"Direct hit!" exclaimed Ohno.

Of course nothing happened. No explosion. No quake. Not even a slight bump. It was all just a simulation. "Okay. Here we go," I said, trying not to sound as far away as I was. I turned back to Viv. "Commander, Blink Reactor ready to go?"

"Aye," replied Viv, focused on her control panel.

"Commit to Blink."

Viv punched a few buttons and pulled back on her throttle.

I immediately jumped up from the captain's chair. I wanted to get off the bridge as quickly as I could.

"Congratulations," Gentry said. "You just killed everyone." I had only made it two steps toward the lift.

"I completed the simulation. We Blinked."

"And under real conditions, you'd be dead. And so would everybody else under your command," Gentry said. "In a real crisis, when everything is going wrong all at once and you only have fractions of a second to make decisions, how long do you think you'd last with that laissez-faire attitude of yours?"

"Permission to speak freely?"

"Granted."

"Longer than you."

A conspicuous silence followed as Gentry resisted whatever his natural urge was—probably to slap me across the face.

"Because you've lived through life and death already?" he finally answered.

"That's right."

"So you've got nothing left to learn? Is that it?"

"Not from a Blink Drill, no."

Gentry turned away from me and pulled down on his uniform, straightening its creases. "Ensign Lewis, pull up shipwide vitals, please."

Ensign Lewis walked to the dark glass panel that stretched floor to ceiling and ten meters across at the bridge's port side edge. With a swipe of his hand, the panel lit up like a Christmas tree, revealing the vital signs of every person on the ship. Each set of vitals was enclosed within a glowing green border along with a name. The vitals belonging to *Marshall, John Douglas* were even and unremarkable. Exactly how I was feeling.

"One hundred eight heartbeats, Cadet Marshall," said Gentry, nodding toward the mosaic of digital life signs. "When you're in the captain's chair, all of them are your responsibility. I don't care what you survived, or how high your test scores were, or how many cadet candidates you had to beat out to get here. Until you understand what that means, you don't belong on this bridge."

I glanced at the vitals but revealed no emotion. The ship had felt almost unbearably empty to me until that very moment. But with the beating hearts of one hundred eight souls reflecting in my eyes? Suddenly I felt foolish for making it all about me.

Gentry leaned in close and grabbed my arm. "Set an example, cadet. Take this seriously."

I shrugged off his grip. "Don't touch me."

My fellow cadets exchanged nervous glances.

"I don't think I like your tone, cadet," Gentry bristled.

"I wasn't giving you a tone."

"You'll refer to me as 'sir.'"

"Whatever you need to hear . . . sir."

"JD . . ." Viv said with a warning in her voice.

"This isn't your concern, Cadet Nixon," Gentry barked, keeping his attention on me. "You know something, Marshall? Before you stepped foot on this ship, I heard a lot of stories about you. I'm starting to wonder if I should believe any of them."

"And what stories would those be, sir?"

"Gosh," he replied. "There seem to be quite a few tales. Saving your entire class at Farragut from a Kastazi assault when you were—what?—twelve? Or maybe the one where you completed the Maximus Trail by yourself in—"

"Two days," Bix piped up.

"Ah, yes. Two days. How incredible," Gentry continued. "Oh. I also really enjoyed the one about you solving Higgins' Puzzle. Tell me, is any of it true?"

"Only some of it, sir," I replied, unable to suppress a self-satisfied smile.

"And there it is again. More insubordination. I hate to do it, but I'm afraid I'm going to have to write you up again, cadet."

"Seriously? You're going to write me up for smiling?"

"If you think I'm only writing you up for smiling, you're really going to enjoy my report," Gentry answered with his own self-satisfied smirk. He really relished twisting the blade in me.

Four chimes signaling the start of the day's blocks interrupted me before I could lash out.

"Are we done here, sir? I need to get to first."

"Yeah, we're done here," Gentry answered, giving me one last scornful look. "Devastation Class dismissed."

It was Explorers tradition for each new class of cadets and students to be christened with a nickname. *Devastation Class* was the one we got saddled with. Not because it was the class of our ship, but because of the brawl we'd had with some of the students just before we all shipped off.

The students walked away with five cracked ribs, two broken noses, and a near unanimous bruising of their collective dignity. Six chairs, three tables, and one environmental control panel were additional collateral damage of the melee. We cadets walked away with some very unfortunate creasing of our uniforms.

None of us, cadet or student, would have been surprised if we'd been expelled from the program as a result of the fight. Personally, I wouldn't have been surprised if my father had canceled the *California*'s Explorers mission altogether. But as he so often did, he'd pivoted a regrettable incident to a teaching moment. He knew that being in space together for months at a time, confined to close quarters, we'd have little choice but to find a way to navigate our differences and cooperate. And in his mind that offered us a far better opportunity to learn something than booting us would have.

My father's best intentions aside, after three months there was still far more animosity between us than there was understanding and cooperation. Honestly, though, the lingering beef with the students was the least of my worries.

As we all piled into the lift, I could sense the disappointment from my comrades. I had always taken pride in everything I did, so it made me feel terrible to be derelict in my duties. At least every new strike against me served a purpose. As hard as it was and as much as I didn't want to admit it, the worst-case scenario was probably what I wanted anyway.

CHAPTER 4

LIKO

IF I DIDN'T KNOW ANY BETTER, I would've thought it was a practical joke. Out of twenty-five students enrolled in Debate Theory, Professor Sigvaatsan chose me to argue the Kastazi position. I guess I could've passed to another student, but why bother? Most people had already made up their minds about me, so I figured I might as well go ahead and win the argument.

"There is no justification for the actions of the Kastazi," Cadet Nixon went on. The swollen vein in the middle of her forehead told me I was getting to her. Quivering fingers soon followed, and then a sudden, sharp narrowing of her otherwise soft oval eyes. "What they brought with them wasn't just wanton despotism. It was pure evil."

Like most students, I was no fan of the cadets and all their militaristic ceremony, but it was hard to dislike Nixon. She was definitely more accessible than your typical cadet. Not stuck-up at all, she had no issue breaking ranks with her rank-and-file chums to commiserate with those of us on the lower decks—an exceedingly rare thing for a cadet to do.

For all the captain's talk of students and cadets having an equal opportunity to learn out among the stars, the reality was far from it. As a student, it almost felt like you were a stowaway—expected to stay hidden on your assigned decks, go to classes, be in bed by curfew, and thank the Alliance for the honor to stare out the *California's* portholes for months on end.

Cadets, on the other hand, had a function. Beyond the academic curriculum they shared with us, they got to learn all of the ship's critical operations, participate in bridge drills, and enjoy access to facilities we weren't allowed within five hundred meters of. They had aspirations for military service that most of us did not, so some additional opportunities made sense, of course. What galled me, though, was how the cadets spun these opportunities as hardships that entitled them to *even more privileges* than they already had. Later curfews. Additional meal options. Extra Iso-Rec credits.

There were seventy-seven of us and only seven of them, so their walking around the ship like they owned it understandably rubbed a lot of students the wrong way. It wouldn't have been so bad if they at least had some awareness of it. But they didn't. Except maybe for Nixon.

Unlike the rest of the cadets, at least she made a real effort to treat us as peers. Sometimes she'd even felt comfortable enough to ask me for help with her Comp Sci assignments. I would've expected her to ask Cadet Bixby instead, but my guess was she didn't want him to know she struggled from time to time. Cadets had it so drilled into their brains that they always had to be the best at everything. It was actually kind of sad.

"That's the problem with your argument. Its entire premise is predicated upon the idea that evil exists," I answered. "It doesn't. Evil is a matter of perspective—in your case informed by an emotional rationalization of something painful your mind can't intellectually process. Do you really believe the Kastazi's primary motivation was to cause us torment? That they received some kind of spiritual nourishment from all the blood we spilled fighting them?"

Nixon slowly exhaled, doing her best to maintain her

composure. It was only an academic exercise, but anything related to the Kastazi was bound to get emotional. "No one is saying that human suffering was the Kastazi's goal. From their perspective they may have believed their actions to be practically motivated. Even logical. It's the means they took to pursue their goals that made the Kastazi evil."

I suppressed a smile as she left herself further exposed. "So let's start there then. Are you agreeing that the underlying premise of the Kastazi Imperative was logically sound?"

"I said it might be logical from their perspective," Nixon replied.

"Fine, but as my entire argument is predicated upon the idea that evil is a matter of perspective, that's something I'd like to explore. Tell me about their perspective."

"Everyone knows about their perspective."

"I want to hear it from you. In your own words. I want to make sure you're not conflating their perspective with your own."

Nixon stood silent. The vein in the center of her forehead throbbed.

Professor Sigvaatsan gently motioned to her with an open hand. "Cadet Nixon?"

"Their perspective was that they were superior to us," she answered. "And they believed this superiority gave them a natural right to control an inferior race. Humankind. Their so-called Kastazi Imperative."

"And that's all?" I prodded. "Are you suggesting that this perspective alone is what motivated their occupation of Earth?"

"Yes."

"What about the destruction of their home world? If there was an alternative—an unpopulated, habitable world similar to Earth for the Kastazi to settle—do you think they still would have come just to cause us suffering?"

"I'm not going to argue against a hypothetical."

"Fine. Dispense with the hypothetical then. Let us presume

there was no alternative. That Earth was their only hope of survival. Should they have not come? Are you suggesting they should have allowed their entire race to perish?"

"They could have come. They didn't have to conquer."

A soft bell sounded, signaling the transition to open interrogatories. Nearly everyone activated their consoles, wanting to join the debate.

"Before we continue, I want to remind everyone of the purpose of this exercise," Professor Sigvaatsan cautioned us. "Not all of our enemies have descended upon us from the stars. Earth's history is littered with examples when we failed to promptly recognize a clear and present danger to our values, liberties, and way of life. What we must remember is that such threats rarely show us their true faces right away. Most often they arrive as simple ideas that appeal to our greatest fears and insecurities, requiring us to relinquish more and more of our freedoms in exchange for the promise of a better, safer, or more prosperous future. By the time we recognize the truth of the bargain we've struck, our present has become far worse than the future we were hoping to avoid. Mr. Chen's argument was intended to help us see these threats more clearly—and to better understand our capacity to rationalize almost anything if it appeals to our baser fears."

A required prerequisite to applying for a position in the Civilian Diplomatic Service, Debate Theory was supposed to train us in the skills of persuasion. All too often it felt like pretext for the Alliance's propaganda. It wasn't the propaganda itself that offended me—it was the transparency of its delivery. We were supposed to be drawn from the best and the brightest Earth had to offer, yet sometimes the Alliance treated us like they thought we were stupid.

I scanned my shipmates' faces. Professor Sigvatsaan's thoughtful qualifications aside, all their anxious, craving eyes told me they still had their daggers out. It was too easy an opportunity for them to pass up. One more chance to give a lashing to the son of a long-since-dead Kastazi sympathizer.

Professor Sigvaatsan nodded at Annalisa Vaccaro, who was so eager to jump into the fray her eyes nearly bulged from their sockets.

"Mr. Chen, I'd like to pick up where Cadet Nixon left off. She said they could have come, but didn't need to conquer. Did you not see the Kastazi as conquerors?" she asked.

Of course they were conquerors, but conceding that fact would have frustrated the whole purpose of the exercise. Besides, I didn't feel like rolling over to give Annalisa my belly. I was tired of people like her using any excuse to come after me.

"Calling them conquerors would be just as much of an over-simplification as calling them evil," I responded. "What if we had submitted to them?"

Annalisa leaned forward in her chair. "It wouldn't have made a difference. They still would have been conquerors."

"Are you sure that's true? Before the October Demand, when we tried to expel them from Earth's sanctuary, had you suffered? Had anyone suffered?"

"No, but—"

"Before the October Demand," I said, cutting her off, "did they not share their knowledge with us? Help us cure diseases we thought incurable? Help us solve scientific puzzles we thought unsolvable?"

"None of that matters!" Annalisa sniped back.

"Why?"

"Because they never told us the price! That all along they had a plan. That they would take control."

"Put aside your anger and indignity over that single deceit and answer my original question. What if we had submitted?"

Annalisa settled back into her chair, the stiffness of her posture easing. "It would have been even worse than the losses we suffered in the war. How many more lies would have followed their first? How soon would it have been before they tightened their grip around our throats? By the time we truly understood our mistake, it would've been too late. Just like Professor Sigvaatsan was saying."

"Or maybe you're being paranoid. Maybe the peace between us would have gone undisturbed. Maybe they would have continued to share all their gifts with us. And the price would have been nothing more than acquiescing to their friendly stewardship of our race. You saw them as enslavers. They could've been shepherds."

Annalisa pounded her first on her console. "Of course you'd say that. You really believe it, don't you?"

Checkmate. If you can't beat your opponent to the finish line, you can still beat them by forcing them off the field of play.

"I'm sorry?" I answered, feigning confusion.

"Everyone knows about your family. I guess the apple didn't fall too far from the tree, did it?"

"Okay, that's enough," interjected Professor Sigvaatsan.

I smiled ever so slightly at Annalisa to entice her to froth at the mouth even more. I was hoping to get her written up. She deserved it.

"Wipe that smile off your face, Chen!" she shouted.

"Enough!" Professor Sigvaatsan repeated.

It was too late, though. Annalisa was totally unhinged.

"Your father was a traitor, and that makes you a traitor! I don't know why they even let someone like you on this ship! The Kastazi may be gone, but as far as I'm concerned you're still—"

"Enough!" someone else shouted. This time it was Nixon. Even from where I sat I could see her hands still trembled. "Enough," she said again, now more calmly, obscuring her quivering fingers by squeezing them into fists. Her pal, Cadet Marshall, the captain's son, sat beside her with his arms folded. I couldn't read his face, but his stiffened posture made me wonder if her intervening on my behalf annoyed him.

Nixon had cut Annalisa off just before she could utter the dirty word on the tip of her tongue: *Axis*. That's what they called the alliance between the Kastazi and their human sympathizers. The war was long over, but my family still wore that word like a scarlet letter.

I hated the Kastazi as much as anyone else. But that didn't matter. The reconciliation of our postwar society was a slow process, and I remained guilty by association. That's why I never dared speak to anyone about my true feelings for my father. It would only have added fuel to the fire.

Two chimes marked the end of first block, sending everyone spilling out of the room. Annalisa stared at her feet to avoid making eye contact with me as she made her way out the door.

Nixon stopped by my side. "Sorry about that," she said, softly touching my elbow. "She was out of line."

"It's okay. Believe me, I'm used to it."

"You shouldn't have to be."

"Yeah, well . . . maybe with time."

She nodded politely, but we both knew it was unlikely time would help. The wounds of the war wouldn't fully heal in either of our lifetimes.

I noticed Marshall lingering behind. He waited for Nixon to leave before he approached me.

"Maybe next time, lose the smile," he said.

"Are you saying you agree with Annalisa, Cadet Marshall?"

"All I'm saying is keep your head down."

Unsure if he was offering genuine advice or simply firing a snarky shot across my bow, I stood there silently like a fool. Marshall hesitated, seemingly contemplating an additional thought. The awkwardness of the moment prevailed, however, and he quickly shuffled out the door without saying another word.

Marshall and I actually had something in common. We both lived in the shadows of our fathers—and suffered for it. People tried to knock him down because of his. People tried to keep me down because of mine. In my mind there really wasn't much difference.

I was curious about him, and the more I paid attention, the less he made sense. Ever since we shipped off it seemed like he was constantly playing with fire. Rumor had it he had been written up at least three times in the first three months on the ship. All that acting out couldn't have been normal for him. If it were, he never would've made the cut as a cadet, let alone nabbed the top spot. He was close to graduation, so it would've been easy to chalk it all up to a bad case of "senioritis." With nothing left to prove, perhaps he was just showing his true colors as the entitled son of an Alliance legend.

I had a different theory, though. I was pretty sure he knew exactly what he was doing. I just didn't know why he was doing it.

CHAPTER 5

VIV

LEVEL 15 OF GALLIPOLI WAS CROWDED AND loud as Alliance politicians, administrators, and soldiers rubbed elbows with transient civilians waiting for the next transport to someplace else. My cadet uniform definitely got some curious looks, but the Blue Pass hanging from my neck made it clear I was authorized to be on the station.

I wasn't sure why my mother had summoned me, but whatever the reason, me and my space-burned brain were excited to finally get off the *California* and see parts of Gallipoli. While the expansive outpost still maintained some of its distinct militaristic character, it had long since been transformed to accommodate the needs of a more diverse postwar population. Probably the biggest change was the availability of *real* food. Every two months, Gallipoli received large supplies of perishables from Earth, and fresh vegetables were harvested from the station's own mega-terrarium on Level 10.

I would've given my right arm for a single bite of anything other than a Protein Reconstituted Meal, but that wasn't going to happen. Absent a Blue Pass, cadets and students never left the ship during an Explorers mission, so PRMs were going to be on my menu for the forseeable future. Transport from Earth to the outer planetary colonies usually took six months or longer, and comfortable space station sanctuaries like Gallipoli were few and far between. Keeping us on the ship was designed to rid us of any romanticized misconceptions about the realities and rigors of long-term space travel. There was probably some hazing component to it as well to help us earn our stripes.

Despite pushing into the Outer Perimeter, the Alliance still had only made contact with three advanced civilizations other than the Kastazi—the Xax, the Aeson, and the Genuvians. As I descended more deeply into Gallipoli's maze, I encountered more and more of their kinds mixed in with the station's mostly human population. As freedom of movement between our worlds was a relatively new development, the increased alien presence on Earth and interstellar assets like Gallipoli took a lot of getting used to.

The Xax, a bio-hacked humanoid race, had dispensed with their need for mouths and survived by absorbing free-roaming ambient energy from almost any source in their environment. If they weren't unsettling enough to look at to begin with, the bulky universal speech synthesizers sharply protruding from their throats really made you want to avoid eye contact.

Compared to the Xax, the Aeson were downright cuddly. An amalgam of humanoid and feline physiognomy, each had light orange skin with an intricate network of black and white stripes, complimented by bright yellow eyes. Instead of speaking, the Aeson communicated through a relatively simple series of hand gestures. Thanks to already being in my third unit of Off-World Linguistics, I was almost fluent enough to engage in Aeson conversation.

More often than not we referred to the Genuvians as the "Grays," a reference dating all the way back to the mid-twentieth century of our history when they made their first clandestine visits to Earth. Also humanoid, rarely taller than a meter, and, of course, gray, they had unusually large heads in proportion to their bodies, no ears or noses, very small mouths, and large, opaque black eyes with no irises or pupils.

The Genuvians' preferred means of communication was telepathy, but being as telepathy caused excruciating headaches in humans, they had embarked upon the slow process of learning Earth's many languages. Unfortunately, as they had no written or verbal language of their own, we were unable to reciprocate the gesture. Or maybe not so unfortunately. It was one less language for me to learn.

While none of these alien civilizations had directly intervened in our war with the Kastazi, all had provided us with valuable intelligence and passive support. Whatever their true motivation —whether it had been a moral imperative to fight against tyranny or just a fear of the Kastazi—the risks they had taken on our behalf had earned them not only our trust but also our loyalty. After the war we were proud to have made them the Alliance's first three extraterrestrial members.

In the years prior, the idea of these worlds joining the Alliance would have been unthinkable. Relative to the Xax, the Aeson, and the Genuvians, we were still an inferior civilization, but war had accelerated great leaps in our scientific and technological advancement—transforming us into a formidable and valuable ally.

As I rounded the last corner toward my destination, I finally noticed the absence of all the *California*'s unique sounds and vibrations. After three months on the ship, it was a strange feeling to so abruptly acclimate to such different surroundings. By the time I'd arrived at my mother's quarters I was ready to enjoy the comfort of something familiar.

The moment I stepped inside, I knew something was wrong. My mother always looked the same in uniform. The Alliance's traditional dark blue had a way of altering her gentle features into something more formidable. Every soft corner of her face would narrow into something sharper. Her posture would stiffen as if constantly poised to salute. But her typical transformation was conspicuously absent. She just looked like my mom.

"What is it?" I blurted out.

"Ditto, sit down," she answered, gesturing to a couch.

I sat, settling deeply into its cushions. I had forgotten what it felt like to sit on anything so soft. My mother pulled up a chair opposite me and rested her hands on mine. The reassuring gesture only made me more nervous.

"At 0600 this morning, a Scouter responded to a distress signal just outside the Outer Perimeter. An adrift vessel. Its fuel cells were severely damaged in a firefight."

"Another smuggler's skirmish."

"Yes, probably. But that's irrelevant. I called for you because of the ship." She squeezed my hands. "It's the missing Interceptor from the UAS *New Jersey*."

My heart sank into the pit of my stomach. Two years before the war ended, the *New Jersey* was destroyed by an Interceptor stolen from its own hangar. Six hundred fifty-three souls died that day. One of them was my father.

There were no survivors who could tell us what had happened. The little we knew had been pieced together from the *New Jersey*'s final transmitted data and sensor logs. The most accepted theory was that a Kastazi sympathizer had perpetrated the attack. Someone who felt the walls closing in on them.

Eight years had passed, and the demise of the *New Jersey* remained the most horrifying enigma in Alliance history. Every day I prayed that whoever had done it would be found and brought to justice.

Sometimes I fantasized about finding them myself, but I never really thought through what I'd do if I actually did find them. Pull out their fingernails? Shoot them with a pulse pistol? Launch them out an air lock? It was ridiculous, but somehow the fantasy was enough. I think maybe it made me feel less powerless.

"Is the pilot still alive?" I asked.

"Yes, but he can't be who we've been looking for."

"How do you know?"

"Because he's too young. He couldn't have been there."

"How young?"

"Just a few years older than you."

"That doesn't make any sense. How could he have gotten his hands on an Interceptor?"

"He claims he traded for it."

"I don't buy that."

"Nor do I, but he's sticking to his story."

"Did he say anything else?"

"He stopped talking once we made it clear we intended to take him and the Interceptor with us to Wolf 1061c. We've already loaded his ship onto the *California*. As soon as we're done processing him, we'll transfer him aboard too."

"What about the Interceptor's computers? There's got to be something there."

"He wiped them before we towed him in, but once we get to 1061c our engineers will rip her apart and go over every last scrap and circuit. If there's something to find, we'll find it."

"That's not good enough. You've got to push the guy harder."

"It's not my place. We need to let the Alliance investigators do their job."

"Mom, please don't leave this to someone else. This is personal for us."

"Precisely the reason it's inappropriate for me to be involved in the investigation."

"I can't believe this! What if they stash him away in some secret prison, never to be heard from again? We'll never learn anything!"

"You're being melodramatic."

I lost my father when I was only ten. I had so few memories of him, all of them probably idealized over the years. In my mind he was perfect. The personification of everything good in the world. I wanted so badly to find someone to blame for taking him away from us. It was hard not to be melodramatic.

"But Mom—"

"Breathe, Ditto. Breathe," she said calmly, again squeezing my hands.

It may have annoyed me, but it worked. As it always did.

A few deep breaths and some clarity returned.

The discovery of the Interceptor had to be just as upsetting for my mother. I lost my father, but she lost the man she had loved for half her life. "I'm sorry, Mom. I didn't mean to . . ."

"You have nothing to be sorry about," she said, letting go of my hands. "You should get back to the *California* for lunch. Please don't say anything about this to anyone. Until we have Captain Marshall's authorization, it needs to stay confidential."

I stood and flattened the creases in my uniform. "Okay."

My mother paused and tilted her head at me, no doubt trying to determine if my wheels were still spinning. Which, of course, they were.

"One more thing before you go," she said. "We need to talk about this morning's Blink Drill."

"Gentry reported JD."

"He reported you."

Reported me?

"I didn't do anything."

"John was insubordinate. And so were you."

"I was trying to help."

"You escalated the situation."

"No. I defused it before JD could make it worse."

"He's risking his future, Ditto. I don't want him risking yours as well."

"I've worked too hard to get here, Mom. I'm not going to let anyone take this away from me. Not even JD."

Mom paused, her mother's intuition scanning me like a laser.

"I really wish I could believe you."

She was right to doubt me. No matter the stakes or consequences,

I could never turn my back on JD. If it ever came down to it, she probably couldn't either. JD was family.

Captain Marshall and my mom had climbed the Alliance ranks together, their assignments bouncing us from one place to the next. The demands of their duties kept quality time in short supply, so each of our families kind of acted as a surrogate for the other. It was probably fair to say that in the days before the war, JD and I spent as many nights under each other's roof and at each other's dinner table as we did our own. "Parenting by proxy" is what my mom used to call it.

The war changed all that. Once the fighting got bad, almost everyone shipped off to the front—my dad aboard the *New Jersey* and my mom and Captain Marshall aboard the *California*. The only constant in our lives was JD's mom, a civilian who stayed behind to care for us both at Camp Jemison.

One day before my ninth birthday, a Kastazi Striker regimen ambushed Camp Jemison. JD was caught in an explosion and nearly died. I got shipped off to the Farragut School for Girls and Boys while he was still clinging to life in the hospital. I begged the Farragut proctors to let me visit him or, at the very least, send a com. They always refused.

Just when I thought I might never see him again, JD arrived at Farragut. His mother had been killed. At the time I didn't know how. Ten months had passed since I had last seen him, and he wasn't at all the JD I remembered. Everything about him felt awkward. It was as though he was starting from scratch, slowly learning to be himself all over again. After everything he had been through, it wasn't difficult to understand why.

I never tried to force our friendship back to where it used to be. Instead, I just waited and made sure he knew I was there for him. About a year after he arrived, the *New Jersey* was destroyed, killing my father and everyone else aboard. JD held my hand for hours as I cried. It was the first time he had touched me since before we'd been separated. It was then that I knew he had finally turned a corner.

Two years after my father died, the Kastazi found Farragut. I had almost no memory of that day. Maybe because it was just too painful to carry with me. One thing I would never forget, though: JD running through a barrage of Kastazi Eradicator fire to activate a perimeter defense grid. He saved my life and the lives of at least twenty other students. He was twelve.

I leaned in and kissed my mom's cheek.

"Everything's going to be okay. I'm going to be okay."

She took my face in her hands and smiled warmly. "Okay. Almost happy birthday."

I smiled back but said nothing. I was still fixated on the Interceptor and its pilot. I rarely interpreted anything as a "sign," but it felt like my father might have brought me a birthday gift—an answer to the mystery that had been haunting me since the day he died.

CHAPTER 6

LIKO

I USUALLY SPENT MY LUNCH BLOCKS IN the ship's library. No one really wanted to sit with me in the mess anyway, and besides, I enjoyed being alone with the library's Historical Archive Terminal. One of the most exhaustive receptacles of mankind's accumulated knowledge, the HAT indexed a nearly limitless database of books, journals, and other compendiums of knowledge from throughout our history.

Each day I spent countless hours losing myself in the details of the past. Its triumphs and tragedies. Its heroes and villains. Its discoveries and disappointments. They all offered me something the *California* and its complement could not: distraction and companionship.

As I spent more time with the HAT, my curiosity drove me to peek behind its curtain, and when I did, I discovered something rather remarkable. It turned out the HAT wasn't a dedicated mainframe, as I had presumed. Rather, its software architecture pulled memory and bandwidth from almost every noncritical system on the ship.

It made sense once I really thought about it. As the HAT contained more data than every library in the history of mankind combined, it required a tremendous amount of processing power to function properly. The unintentional, or perhaps overlooked, consequence of this architecture, however, were the two security vulnerabilities it created.

In pulling memory and bandwidth from noncritical systems, the HAT also opened a backdoor channel to them. That meant anyone could use the HAT to send and receive messages through the internal communications server without going through Sentinel, the ship's central computer. As I had no need to communicate with anyone in secret, this vulnerability held no utility for me.

I did, on the other hand, have a use for the architecture's second vulnerability, the reciprocative data flow that gave me access to one of the *California's* lowest-priority systems—the personal accounts of every student and cadet on the ship. I was tired of being bullied, and I wanted to know once and for all what everyone was saying about me behind my back. Regrettably, the moment I exploited the vulnerability, I had the karmic misfortune of crossing paths with Julian Lorde.

The irony was that he was snooping himself. Trying to hack into his girlfriend's account for some childish reason. His skills being as cursory as they were, he inadvertently tripped a system-wide security firewall. I had to kill it quickly, or both of our breaches would've been logged. Problem was I could only do so from the trigger site—his personal console.

My only choice was to go to him and fess up. We were both in the wrong, so I thought it would be safe. Mutually assured destruction and all that. But Lorde surprised me. He saw it as an opportunity.

"We're not the same, Chen," he said. "If I get caught, I'll be guilty of being a jealous boyfriend. If you get caught . . . my goodness. The son of an Axis operative rummaging through the personal accounts of everyone on the lower decks? How might that be interpreted?"

He was right. A charming guy like him, someone everybody liked, he could probably talk his way out of just about anything. Me on the other hand . . .

Maybe I should've just let the firewall stand. At least it would've ended there. But instead I gave in to Lorde's demands. He quickly figured out there was another low-priority system I could access through the HAT—the Curriculum Database. In exchange for his silence, Lorde had me hack the exams for each of his courses as soon as they posted.

I didn't understand the allure of cheating. The Explorers Program was supposed to be for students and cadets who wanted to learn, who wanted to be challenged. When I asked Lorde about it, his only response was, "Don't be so naïve."

It seemed obvious he wasn't some mustache-twirling black hat who took pleasure in cutting people off at the knees. Most of the time he behaved like a decent guy. It was only at the intersection of opportunity and self-interest that he seemed to tap into his darker inclinations.

My guess was he was like a lot of people who grew up during the war. In those days almost anything could be justified if it gave you a better chance to survive. But for all its lasting consequences and traumas, the war was over. We lived in a different world, and it was time to let go of that way of thinking. Maybe, like some of the others, he was still struggling to figure that part out.

My nose suddenly twitched in defense to an invasive odor. Lorde's aftershave. Thanks to its peculiarly sweet bouquet, I could always smell him coming. And as was normally the case, he greeted me with all the affection of a friend.

"Doing well, Mr. Chen?" he asked as he pulled up a chair.

"Day's not off to the start I was hoping for."

"Debate Theory?"

"You heard?"

"Vivien told me," he replied, shaking his head with commiserative disapproval. "Ah, the sad confluence of hatred and stupidity. Annalisa is a small-minded bigot. Don't take such nonsense personally." It was stunning how he could so completely compartmentalize the fact he was abusing me in an even more despicable way than she had.

I pulled the microdrive from the archive terminal and placed it in his hand. "The new Stellar Cartography and Philosophy exams. They were uploaded last night."

"Still insisting on microdrives, are we?"

"Would you prefer I sent you the exams unsecured through Sentinel?"

"Right," Lorde conceded while placing the drive into his pocket. "You sure you don't want to come to the mess for lunch?"

"No thanks."

"Suit yourself," he said, getting up to leave.

I turned my attention back to the terminal to wipe any digital fingerprints I might have left behind.

"Hey, Chen," Lorde called out from behind me, inspecting the microdrive with a quizzical look on his face. "Why don't you ever look at these exams for yourself?"

I hesitated to answer, presuming Lorde knew the answer and was just trying to lure me in to help him make a point. Nevertheless, I acquiesced.

"I'm trying to learn something."

Lorde fussed with his cuticles, avoiding eye contact. "Knowledge is indeed power," he answered. "But I might argue you're concentrating on the wrong lesson."

As he exited the library, the intention of his words sank in. Julian was telling me what he would do if he had people like Annalisa Vaccaro trying to trip him up at every turn. Right and wrong wouldn't really be part of the equation. To him it was about survival. About taking every possible advantage before someone else who hated him did. As much as that kind of wartime thinking troubled me, I couldn't help but wonder if he was right. That I was being naïve, just like he said I was.

CHAPTER 7

JD

AS ALWAYS, MY FELLOW CADETS AND I sat together in the *California*'s mess hall for lunch, our usual table closest to a large observation window with a view of the stars and beyond. Since the ship's claustrophobic confines had only narrow portholes to gaze out from, a table with a good view was prime real estate.

I took a bite of my pizza. Well, a PRM version of pizza. It tasted like an experiment concocted by someone who'd had the concept of pizza explained to them but never actually tasted pizza for themselves. Its stale cardboard flavor aside, it did provide me with my exact nutritional requirements. Each of our PRMs was special. Designed and tailored for each of our unique physiological profiles, every meal contained the specific protein, carbohydrate, calorie, and vitamin content we needed for peak physical and mental performance.

As the others talked among themselves, I scanned their faces. I took another half-hearted bite, amused by how accurately the PRM in front of each cadet reinforced my understanding of them.

Anatoly poked at his pierogi and goulash with surgical precision. He was eighteen. Ukrainian. The smooth, complementary movements of his fork and knife delicately separated his double portions of food into neat little quadrants. Double portions because anything less would have left his stomach grumbling. Anatoly was a big guy—six feet tall and at least two hundred pounds. Despite his gentle manner, if a brawl ever broke loose, he was the first person I wanted by my side.

Nick was our odd eighteen-year-old comrade from Maine. Fair-haired, soft-featured, and conspicuously quiet, he seemed like the bookish offspring of New England intellectuals. A nice guy and friendly enough, nothing about him would've indicated he was actually on work release from an Alliance diversionary program for criminal offenders.

A cadet appointment for someone like him was unprecedented, but for reasons unknown to us, Alliance Command had deemed Nick worthy of a remarkable second chance at service. We all had our opinions, but I could only wonder what Julian thought of some hooligan being the beneficiary of one of the slots.

I watched as Nick nursed a purplish PRM smoothie from a stainless steel cup. He once offered me a sip of his strange concoction, and I still wished I hadn't taken him up on the offer. It tasted like a combination of beets and black licorice. It would have been gag-inducing had the taste not been so bad as to nearly paralyze my gag reflex. There were actually a number of strange things about Nick, his weird taste in PRMs only being the tip of the iceberg.

For example, despite the Alliance's generous forgiveness of Nick's past criminal transgressions, they still insisted that he be confined to quarters in off-hours. If he was trusted to serve alongside us, why did they not trust him to *live* alongside us?

Perhaps even more confounding was the fact he had been given no definitive role as a cadet. Instead, he had what was referred to as a "floating" detail—no training specialization or permanent assignment. As my father put it, Nick was *plug and play*—you just stuck him where you needed him. On this mission, it was Coms.

Sure, *plug and play* had a nice ring to it, but practically speaking, it was just one more thing that didn't make sense. Of course, I raised all of this with my father, but he was steadfast in his dismissiveness. *Maybe you should be more concerned with your own problems right now* was his most common refrain of late.

There were probably perfectly rational explanations for all my questions about Nick, except one: the strange, somewhat ominous feeling I had anytime I was near him. I didn't want to be preoccupied by it, but it kept coming up for me as something more than just a gut reaction to all his many oddities and their all-too-convenient explanations.

I mentioned it to Viv and she half-jokingly replied, "Did it ever occur to you that maybe you just don't like him?"

I laughed it off, but there was no denying how much he unsettled me.

Next I turned my attention to Ohno. Her PRM was every bit as colorful as her hair and her bio-reactive tattoos. Traditional Brazilian favorites like coxinha, feijoada, and pao de queijo were piled high against an equally formidable mound of her favorite dessert: bolo de rolo. Restraint was not a particular strength of hers, and that's what made her so unique. When properly channeled, the passions that drove her beyond boundaries were an asset, particularly in her specialties of mechanics and engineering.

When others gave up, she was just getting started, formulating workarounds we'd never find in a repair manual. Pretty impressive for a seventeen-year-old. That said, many of her solutions bordered on unacceptably dangerous, which is also what made working with her both terrifying and exhilarating. Appropriately, that's why Viv took to calling her "Ohno"—as in *Oh no, she's going to kill us all*.

Then there was my friend Bix, with his no-crust peanut butter sandwich and "apple." He might as well have pulled his lunch from a brown paper bag along with a note from his mother. A born savant, Bix had been raised in the lonely isolation of Earth's Moon colonies, nourishing his gifts without almost all of the normal childhood distractions. His social development definitely suffered some for it, but by the time his family had migrated back to Earth, he had few, if any, intellectual peers.

Alliance Command had tried to recruit him into their Applied Sciences Laboratory three years ago, when he was thirteen. *Thirteen.* Despite the honor of the invitation, Bix had passed. Like the rest of us he wanted to be a pioneer, venturing deep into the heart of the universe to see its many wonders with his own two eyes. So instead, that same year he applied to the Explorers Program. The age requirement for cadet training was fourteen, but my father had made an exception. Bix was that special.

Standing five feet, six inches short on his tippy-toes, he wore glasses even though his nearsightedness could easily be corrected. "They just feel right on my face," he would always say. Biology, astro-physics, quantum mechanics, and statistics were his favorite topics of conversation, which, needless to say, made conversations with him difficult. I didn't mind, though. I couldn't have hoped to have a better cadet on Analytics detail, and in the eighteen months since we'd all been brought together for the final phase of our training, he had become like a little brother to Viv and me.

I marveled at Safi's perfect posture as she ate. She never even came close to resting her elbows on the table as she worked her tray in a clockwise rotation. Bite of chicken, bite of carrots, bite of potatoes, sip of water, and then back around again. Even the way she lined her tray up flush with the table's edge. All patterns and precision. *Kharagn* was the Wolof word she used to describe herself. In her Senegalese language, it meant something like "meticulous." She once told me that her habits gave her a sense of control in a world that had for so long been filled with chaos. I often wondered if my father had chosen her as a counterweight to the rest of us. He seemed to have a preference for candidates who were outside-the-box choices, and Safi was anything but. Rules were her religion, so I was glad she was on Nav detail. It meant we would never get lost.

My eyes finally came to rest on Viv. I caught her staring, but she quickly looked away while taking a small, disinterested bite of her cheeseburger. She was worried about me. Not just because of my performance at that morning's Blink Drill, but everything leading up to it.

For as long as I could remember, she and I had been nipping at each other's heels, and our friendly competition had always been a good thing. It pushed us to set higher goals. To work harder. To be better. But lately, whatever competitive fire I had left manifested as it did in our Iso-Rec race through the canyons. Not as healthy competition, but as petty, mean-spirited behavior that only put a strange, unfamiliar distance between us.

I wanted to confess. Tell her what was really going on inside me. But how could I? Finally applying our talents on the big stage of the Explorers Program, we were so close to the dream we had shared since childhood. My truth was a betrayal of all of it.

Viv was the best pilot I'd ever seen, and watching her at the controls of the mighty *California*, even just in drills, gave me a glimpse of the future I knew was hers. There was no doubt in my mind she was going to get everything she ever wanted. I was just terrified of how she'd react once she knew it would all have to happen without me.

She looked back in my direction, a distant, troubled look in her eyes. We both knew something needed to be said, but the uncomfortable moment was interrupted by a tapping on my shoulder. Lorde.

"May I join you?" he asked, holding out his lunch tray.

There was no official rule that only cadets could sit together, but Lorde was smart enough to abide by an unwritten one. Each time he'd do the same thing—ask for permission as a bogus formality, knowing none of us would ever object in Viv's presence.

I slid over to open a spot at the very end of the bench, implicitly granting my consent. Lorde ignored the space and muscled his way between Viv and me.

He swallowed a spoonful of his split pea PRM and said, "So I hear there was some excitement up on the bridge this morning."

Viv put her hand on top of Lorde's. "Please don't start."

At first it seemed strangely random that he'd so blatantly instigate something with me twice in one day, but then maybe he was beginning to see an opportunity for himself.

I glared at him. "How about you stop dancing and just tell us what's really on your mind, Julian?"

Furrowing his brow, Lorde spooned another mouthful of soup. "Perhaps this is a conversation better had in private."

"If you have something to say, you can say it in front of my friends."

"Are you sure about that?"

Viv shot me a look before I could respond. There was really no need for me to indulge Lorde. I was quite sure I knew where he was going. After leaving Gallipoli, the *California* still had six long months left on its journey. He was probably fantasizing that if I actually did fall off the tightrope, they might need someone to replace me. No student had ever been granted a cadet field commission. It wasn't even in the realm of possibility, as far as I knew. "You know what? Maybe you're right. You can tell me what's on your mind later."

Ohno was the first to jump in and change the subject. "So why'd you get summoned to Gallipoli?" she asked Viv.

Viv swallowed like her food was made of broken glass. "I'm not supposed to say."

"C'mon. It's just us," Ohno replied.

Safi bristled. "If she doesn't feel comfortable, she doesn't have to—"

"No, it's okay," Viv interrupted. "Just, guys, please. It stays here for now."

Everyone nodded.

"Of course," Lorde added unnecessarily.

"They found it. The Interceptor from the *New Jersey*."

"Really?" I blurted.

"Yes. Complete with a pilot."

"They got the guy?" Anatoly exclaimed.

"No," answered Viv. "They think he came into possession of the ship later. After the attack. His story is he traded for it somewhere in the Outer Perimeter. Whether that's true or not remains to be seen, but he's definitely not the guy. He's too young."

"That's odd," said Lorde.

"That's odd?" Viv scowled at him. "Sometimes you've really got a talent for heightening the art of the understatement."

"Apologies, love. I didn't mean anything by it."

"Is there anything else? Does he have a name?" Ohno persisted, rolling right over Lorde's faux pas.

"I don't know his name. Only thing I know is we're taking him and his ship with us to Wolf 1061c."

"Wow," said Bix, finally speaking up. "If we're taking him with us all the way to Wolf 1061c, it's probably safe to assume he's not just a random Outer Perimeter pirate. I'd bet you ten Iso-Rec credits that Alliance Command knows exactly who he is."

Viv pushed her lunch tray away in disgust. She had clearly deduced the same thing for herself and it was eating her up inside.

"Hey, this is a good thing," I said. "One way or another, maybe we'll finally get some answers."

"He's right," Lorde added. "Just give it a little time for the clouds to part."

Lorde had an infuriating way of using me as cover with Viv. If anything sensitive came up, he'd let me take the risk of speaking first, and, presuming I emerged unscathed, basically repeat the same sentiment in slightly different form.

Ohno and Anatoly smirked at me. Lorde's repeated use of this cowardly tactic had become something of an inside joke between us.

Viv stood up, offering him a forced smile. "I'm gonna take a walk."

"Shall I join you?" Lorde asked.

"No, I need some time to myself. Finish your lunch. I'll see you in fourth."

We waited for her to leave before we started to bat around our theories. We had plenty, but none of them were particularly insightful or likely to be accurate. There were still too many missing pieces. All we could do was fill the gaps with the same guesses that people had offered up a thousand times before. A mystery that had lingered as long as the one surrounding the UAS *New Jersey* wasn't going to have any easy answers.

CHAPTER 8

VIV

MY LONG WALK AROUND THE LOWER DECKS managed to take some of the edge off my anxiousness, and I was counting on fourth block to help me knock out the rest. I scanned the gymnasium as I exited the locker room in my Alliance-issued T-shirt and shorts. Zeta Deck's massive athletic facility always felt half-empty to me—probably because it was intended to accommodate hundreds of soldiers at a time. A handful of students jogged around the track encircling the periphery of a full-length basketball court, while several others made use of the adjacent batting cages and gymnastics floor. A few more lazily lounged on the spectators' bleachers that overlooked it all.

Three times a week, we signed up for whatever sport or activity we wanted. A two-on-two basketball game was already in progress. I saw Bix and Anatoly hitting some balls in the batting cage. JD was usually with them, but I didn't see him anywhere. Julian was among the handful running the track. Although I had barely snapped at him in the mess, his pouty expression told me he still felt wounded.

My day didn't need more drama, so I smiled and gave him a quick wave to let him know he was off the hook.

I jogged over to an empty mat and stretched, ready to blow off some steam. I called out, "Activate Holosynth Kung Fu protocol, Level 6, please."

At my prompt, a holo-synthesized avatar appeared in the middle of the mat. The ship utilized many kinds of Synths. Maintenance and Utility Synths helped support the ship's basic functions. Preceptor Synths instructed our courses. And some served more critical functions, like Command and Emergency Support Synths, which could be automatically activated in the event of a crisis.

Synths simulated mass by channeling electromagnetic energy through motion-adaptive containment fields. Their sophisticated inner workings aside, they were ideal partners to beat the living daylights out of.

Some looked remarkably human, while others were humanoid in form but devoid of human features. My sparring partner was the latter, a generic, faceless avatar of light and energy.

My legs apart, knees bent, and arms extended, I readied myself opposite the Synth as it engaged me in combat. Crouching into my signature snake position—bending my body back and raising my head up to strike—I easily dodged the Synth's first downward slicing blow and sprang forward with my own attack. I speedily circumvented its blocking attempts, stabbing its torso with exploding jabs from my tightly clenched fingers. Every shot landed with an outwardly bursting red circle with a numbered score displayed within it. *Ten points. Ten points. Twenty points. Fifty points.* In a matter of seconds, I had tallied one hundred points, and the Synth automatically returned to its resting position.

My father had started training me in various arts of hand-to-hand combat when I was barely old enough to walk. Karate, judo, capoeira, Krav Maga, and jogo do pau were just some of the disciplines in which he'd taught me the basics. After his death I continued training on my own. I loved doing it for myself and also as a way to honor his memory.

Word of my skills had gotten around the *California* quickly, which is why I only had Synths for opponents. No one else really wanted to risk the embarrassment of taking me on. Except, of course, Julian.

"Impressive display," I heard his voice call out from behind me, accompanied by some sarcastic applause. "For a simulation."

"Oh, is that a challenge? Does someone want another shot at the title?"

He stepped forward to the center of the mat and assumed ready position. "Don't mind if I do."

I began circling him in anticipation of his first strike.

"What are you waiting for?"

"For the right moment, love."

I leapt forward with a rear leg front kick, which he easily blocked. "I'll start easy," I said. "Let me know when you're ready for me to start trying."

"Ah, and so the psychological warfare begins," he answered while glancing my shoulder with a poorly executed Wing Chun punch.

Both of us stepped back and resumed our dance. As we circled each other, I drifted toward distraction, my thoughts returning to the Interceptor and its pilot.

"I have a proposition for you, Jules," I said, forcing myself to turn the page to something less consequential.

"You have my attention, as always," he replied while still stalking me.

"Tell me what you know about tonight, and I'll end this quickly."

"You must be referring to that unspoken something that John and Mr. Bixby may or may not have been planning for your birthday," said Julian as he assumed a dragon pose, his legs spread wide and fingers curled into claws at the ends of his outstretched arms. "If I had been invited to partake in this . . . experience . . . I'd probably feel compelled to honor their request for my confidence."

I halted and invited him to attack with a dismissive wave of my hand.

Julian sprang forward. Casually sidestepping his offensive, I grabbed his left wrist and pulled him over my back. As soon as he landed on the mat, I dropped my two knees down on either side of his waist, pinning him. "Whattaya know?" I teased. "Looks like I'm on top again."

Gazing into his eyes, I found myself searching. As if my gut was trying to find something I didn't know I was looking for.

Anatoly and Bix interrupted before I could make any sense of it.

"Do you know where JD is?" Anatoly asked.

"I don't," I responded as I stood and wiped the sweat from my forehead.

"Weird," Bix said. "PE is the one block he hasn't been cutting."

"Maybe he's not feeling well," I replied.

"He seemed fine when he left the mess," answered Anatoly.

It was no surprise to me that JD was suddenly MIA. Disappearing acts were increasingly becoming part of his repertoire.

"I'm going to get dressed, then I'll track him down."

Bix gently touched my shoulder as I turned to leave.

"I was waiting for JD to tell you, but since we can't find him . . . Your . . . thing . . . is ready," he said, unable to suppress a mischievous smile.

"Oh, is it?"

"Twenty-three hundred. Iso-Rec."

"After curfew?"

"Live a little," Anatoly playfully chided me. "It will be fine."

He was probably right. If there was ever a night to break curfew, this was it. The command staff and most of the crew were still on Gallipoli, and the few NCOs who remained aboard were all housed on Gamma Deck, an entire deck below Iso-Rec. The only real wild cards were Gentry and Lewis.

"Gentry and Lewis will be working graveyard tonight, prepping the ship for departure. What if they check our biosigs from the bridge?"

Bix disappointedly shook his head at me. "Who do you think you're talking to here?"

"So it would be safe for me to presume . . ."

"Yes. If they check our biosigs, we'll all be safely tucked into bed."

"This one thinks of everything," Anatoly chuckled.

"So see you then?" Bix asked.

"See you then."

"Perfect! You think you might convince Safi . . ."

"I'll try. But you know her."

"She doesn't know what she'll be missing," Bix said as he turned to leave with Anatoly.

Despite everything weighing on my mind, I was excited to see what they had in store for me. For all their efforts to keep it a surprise, JD and Bix hadn't done a very good job of hiding their enthusiasm. Which made it a pretty safe bet it was going to be special. I just needed to get something out of my system first to enjoy it.

CHAPTER 9

JD

I COULD FEEL HIM WATCHING ME. IT wasn't ESP or anything. I could literally feel his electromagnetic pulse. Yet another "gift" I woke up with after the attack. Except this one I didn't tell anybody about.

"Are you hungry, John? Shall I begin to prepare your dinner?" asked Charlie while affectionately tousling my hair.

"Sure. Thanks," I replied, my eyes never losing focus on the holoscreen in front of me. I was finally going to solve Level 173 of Gyrosphere. The game console's interface tracked the movement of my pupils as I guided a sphere through an increasingly complex maze.

The further I got, the faster the game became, and so far I had been able to avoid crashing into the obstacles materializing and transmuting in my path. Level 174 was in my grasp. Before I got hurt, I couldn't even get past Level 120. The doctors said my hand-eye coordination got better because of the way they had regenerated the damaged parts of my brain. There were other things too. I seemed to learn things faster. I could remember things easier. I even started to use bigger words than other kids my age. They said it would all fade with time, and eventually I'd be back to normal again. I wasn't sure I wanted to be.

"John!" my mom shouted from her bedroom, breaking my

concentration. "I told you to shut that off and get started on your assignments!"

My eyes slipped downward for a fraction of a second. That's all it took to send my sphere hurtling out of bounds. Game over.

Frustrated, I glanced over at Charlie. He offered me a funny smirk as he pulled ingredients for my dinner from the pantry. My partner in crime. Charlie didn't care if I did my assignments.

From the moment I opened my eyes in the hospital, I felt more connected to him than I did to anyone else. It wasn't the fact that he wasn't family that made our connection so unusual. It was the fact he wasn't human.

Hybrids like Charlie were a creation of Dr. Samuel Fuller. Powered by Fuller's Generation One CPU, they were engineered to be soldiers for the Alliance war effort. Artificial, powerful killing machines, they were supposed to fight the Kastazi alongside us. Before long they were fighting the Kastazi instead of us. That's why we were finally winning the war. In a single battle, thousands of them could be lost, but we'd just build ourselves a thousand more.

Charlie had been assigned to protect Mom, Viv, and me because we were what they called "high-value targets." I hadn't understood what that meant until the day the Kastazi came for us. All I could remember were the air-raid sirens, and then waking up in a hospital bed. Everyone said I would have died if Charlie hadn't pulled me from the flames as quickly as he did.

The attack left me with ugly, painful burns all along my stomach and chest. For a while it was excruciating just to breathe. I probably would've given up if Charlie hadn't been there for me. It took me four months to get out of bed, and he never left my side. He'd even hold my hand while the nurses peeled the soiled re-gen packs from my sticky wounds three times a day.

My mom, on the other hand, hardly visited. When she did, it made me feel worse. Every time she looked at me, it was like I was reminding her of something she didn't want to remember. I told Charlie how sad it made me feel, and he tried his best to cheer me up. "When you almost lose someone you love very much, maybe for a while it's hard to let yourself love them that much again," he told me. He may not have been alive, but when he said stuff like that, it was hard for me to believe he was just a mishmash of artificially intelligent circuitry and biomass. That's why I gave him a name.

Hybrids weren't supposed to have names, but Charlie deserved one. So I named him after the family dog we had before the war. It seemed fitting enough. He was loyal, compassionate, and nonjudgmental, just like Charlie the dog. At first Mom would cringe every time I called him that, but eventually she accepted it. Or maybe she just stopped caring.

I wanted to go be with Viv at Farragut when I finally left the hospital, but Dad wouldn't let me. Instead he insisted that Mom and I stay in an underground Alliance facility deep beneath New Oklahoma City. The domestic suites we lived in were supposed to be just like the aboveground homes we'd lived in before the war. They had comfortable bedrooms, living rooms, bathrooms, and kitchens, and we put art, photos, and other knickknacks on the walls to remind us of home. But no matter how we dressed them up, the suites' gray concrete floors and bright overhead lights made them feel exactly like what they were meant to be: bunkers.

I wasn't surprised when Mom got even more depressed living under three miles of rock and dirt. Pretty soon she was spending nearly all of her days in bed and mostly only came out to eat. That's when Charlie took on a lot more than a name. He became our caretaker. That meant doing a lot of things a Hybrid was never meant to do. He even cooked for us. It made me laugh to see Charlie wearing an apron, but he knew his way around the kitchen. Reconstituted protein fajitas were his specialty. He could almost make them taste like chicken. Almost.

Mom slowly shuffled into the living room and sat on the couch beside me. No doubt it was the delicious aroma of Charlie's fajitas that had coaxed her out of her bedroom.

I quickly flipped open my geometry book. "I did most of my assignment this morning," I said.

"Uh-huh," Mom replied, her eyes fixed on the holoscreen. It was frozen where my last game had ended. "Almost to Level 174."

There was familiar sadness in her voice.

I shifted uncomfortably. The tight scar tissue from my burns still hurt every time I moved. "Yeah, almost. Maybe tomorrow."

"How about tomorrow you go to the rec room and play with some of the other children? A normal nine-year-old boy shouldn't be spending every day glued to a holoscreen, playing Gyrosphere."

It was maybe the eight thousandth time I'd gotten the same speech. I used to get upset and fight with her about it, but eventually I realized there was no need. In two hours she'd be asleep, and the next day would be half-over before she'd show her face again. "Sure, Mom," I replied. "I'll think about it."

She sat there quiet as the noise of Charlie clanging pots and pans echoed in the background. "Your father sent a message last night. Said he might be able to visit us sometime next week."

The ruckus of pots and pans gave way to the sound of Charlie chopping onions faster than any human ever could have.

Chop-chop-chop-chop!

Chop-chop-chop-chop!

"That would be nice," I answered, knowing better than to get my hopes up. It was stupid for us to expect to be a family in the middle of a war. Dad was, after all, captain of the UAS California. His responsibility to the Alliance was not something we could ever compete with.

Chop-chop-chop-chop!

Chop-chop-chop-chop!

The sound of Charlie's knifework added a soothing rhythm to the awkward silence between us. I listened as he worked his blade against the cutting board in perfect intervals, the pattern of his chopping so precise it was almost musical. And then with one loud, final chop, he abruptly stopped as if in the middle of a note.

Chop!

It sounded . . . wrong.

I turned around to see what was happening. Charlie had his back to us and stood frozen in place.

"Charlie?" *I called out.*

He didn't respond.

"Charlie?" *I repeated, a feeling of queasiness quickly rising up inside me.*

He remained silent, but his head began to twitch ever so slightly to the right.

I got up to go to him, but my mom grabbed me by the wrist.

"Don't," *she said, pulling me back toward her.*

"But something's wrong with him, Mom. He's . . . malfunctioning."

"Hybrids don't malfunction, John."

Charlie suddenly spun to face us. The look in his eyes terrified me. What I felt terrified me even more. The pattern of his electromagnetic pulse . . . the one I could feel ever since I got hurt . . . it was different somehow.

"Charlie, what's wrong?" *I asked, my body quaking.*

He ignored me and moved to the suite's exit. Before I could say anything else, he punched a code into its keypad. The dozen massive bolts in the security door slammed into place. We were locked in. Charlie still had a knife in his hand. Its blade gleamed brightly in the artificial overhead light.

My mom ran to the fire alarm on the living room wall and pulled down its lever without ever taking her eyes off Charlie. A blaring siren sounded, and water began to gush from the ceiling like a torrential rain.

Charlie didn't flinch. He raised his knife in the air and marched right at me. Mom jumped between us, blocking his path.

"Run to your room and lock the door!" *she shouted.*

I was completely paralyzed.

"Run!" *she shouted again.*

I couldn't move. I was too scared. Charlie charged at Mom and an instant later she buckled. It happened so fast, at first I didn't understand what I was seeing. Then I saw the blood. So much blood. It splashed to the floor as if spilled from an overturned bucket and flowed away with the flooding water's current.

Mom fell to one knee, and Charlie tried to push past her. She grabbed him by the leg, slowing him down. He swung his knife backward, cutting her throat without ever looking back. Still she held on, buying me a few more seconds. Her mouth opened and closed, but no words came out.

It was the most terrible thing I'd ever seen.

Slipping with almost every step, I ran to my room and locked the door behind me. Before I could even catch my breath, Charlie was pounding against its heavy titanium alloy. It was like watching a cartoon as each of his blows left an inward bubbling dent in the shape of his fist. A few seconds later, the door completely gave way.

I stared at the ground and cried. I couldn't look at Charlie. With each step he took, I could hear the splashing water moving closer in my direction. His feet came to rest right in front of me, my mother's blood slowly dripping from the edge of his knife. I waited for his attack, but it didn't come. I looked up and saw his arm quivering. He was fighting against whatever had taken control of him.

All of a sudden his arm fell limply by his side. He looked at me with wide, sad eyes, the water streaming down his face like tears. He was Charlie again. But only for a moment. In the blink of an eye, he stiffened and swung the knife back over his head.

Just then, the room filled with the shrieking sound of pulse fire. Charlie fell to his knees, and his body writhed with each shot fired into his back by the Alliance soldiers charging into the suite behind him. It took at least fifteen hits for them to bring him down.

The soldiers scattered in every direction as Charlie lay motionless. I could hear explosions and shouting in the hallways outside the suite. Something was happening. Something big. Something awful.

I reached down to touch Charlie's face. For the first time since I woke up from the attack, I couldn't feel a thing. No energy of any kind.

That's why I had no warning he was still alive.

He plunged his knife into my stomach so fast I never saw it coming. I only felt the pain.

―――――――

I snapped up in my rack, drenched in a cold sweat.

These nightmares were all too familiar. I used to wish they'd stop coming but had long since given up any hope of that. Eventually I had learned to accept them as part of my life. My new normal.

A brief moment of disorientation passed, and the room around me came into focus. My bed beneath me. My unlaced boots on the floor. A photo of my mother staring back at me from the shelf above my desk. Bix's perfectly made rack directly across from mine.

I stood up to shake the sleep from my head and walked to the full-length mirror in the corner of my quarters. Lifting my shirt, I inspected the long scar running down the entire right side of my torso. The melted skin was still uneven. Beside it, in the middle of my belly, was the jagged stab wound from Charlie's blade. That scar would've been easy to fix with dermal regeneration, but I told the doctors not to touch it. It was one more thing that could help me remember.

A call chime rang out, startling me. I assumed it was Bix. Anytime I ditched, he was usually the first one to come find me. He knew how to tap into the ship's biosig tracker—it was impossible to hide from him.

"All clear, Bix!"

The chime rang again.

"Enter!"

Another ring.

"Seriously, Bix!"

I shuffled to the door and opened it. To my surprise, it was Viv. "You missed PE," she said before getting a good look at me. "Wait— were you sleeping?"

"I wasn't sleeping. I was napping. There's a difference."

"During fourth block . . . you just decided to take a nap."

"Fourth block's optional," I answered, rubbing my eyes.

"Optional? Since when?"

"C'mon. No one's logging attendance in PE while we're hitched to Gallipoli."

"The Synths are."

"Bix can take care of that for me later," I said, fighting my way through a yawn.

Viv frowned at me. "Well, you look terrible."

"Thank you. I feel terrible. What time is it?"

"Thirteen forty. We've got twenty minutes to get to fifth."

"It's still fourth block? You cut out early yourself? The Synths are gonna log that, you know," I said.

"Bix can take care of that for me later," Viv said without missing a beat.

"Hilarious."

"I learned from the best."

Still tired, I plopped back down on my bed. "So you got worried and came looking for me? Don't worry. I'm fine."

"After this morning's performance on the bridge, you bet I'm worried about you. And you better prepare yourself, 'cause you and I are gonna have it out once and for all."

"Are we really doing this again?"

"Yes, we are, just not right now. Right now I need to borrow you for a few minutes."

"For what? Does it involve any kind of manual labor? Because if it does—"

"The Interceptor. It's been loaded into the hangar. I'm going to check it out, and I want you to come with me."

"That'll actually involve a significant amount of walking, so technically . . ."

Viv put her hands on her hips and shot me a formidable death stare. I was pretty sure I was the only one who could inspire her face to contort into such an unpleasant configuration. Anytime she went full death stare on me, I knew there was only one option left.

"Let me get my boots."

———

Three NCOs were milling about when we arrived, still attending to the various power utility modifications necessitated by the Interceptor's arrival in the hangar. The space was cavernous, stretching 220 meters long and 150 meters wide. Twenty-five bays lined the port side toward the stern—though only four of them contained Alliance shuttles, as the *California* had little need for a full squadron of auxiliary crafts on an Explorers mission. The tip of the Interceptor's nose peeked out from a bay near the stern. One of the NCOs, Rania Saad, cut us off as we made our way toward it.

"Where do you think you're going?"

"What's the problem? We're authorized to be here," Viv replied.

"No one is authorized to go anywhere near that ship."

"Says who?"

"Says Captain Marshall."

Viv let out something that sounded like a grunt.

"I have to ask you to step away."

"It's fine. I just need to see it for a minute," said Viv, walking right past Saad.

"I said you're not authorized, cadet," Saad answered, grabbing her by the wrist. "And if you take another step toward that Interceptor, your mother can come collect you from the brig."

I noticed Viv's fingers begin to quiver. A sure sign things were about to escalate.

"Saad, is it?" I interjected.

"Yes, cadet."

I motioned over to the side.

"Can you and I . . . ?"

Saad nodded and followed me until we were a few feet away from where Viv was standing.

"She's been waiting to see that thing for eight years," I said quietly to Saad.

"I have my orders."

"Yes, I know. I'm just asking for a little compassion here."

"I'm sorry. I can't."

"Look at her. Put yourself in her shoes."

Viv remained frozen in the same spot, her focus on the ship unbroken. I didn't need to explain anything to Saad. Everyone knew the story behind that Interceptor.

I saw a crack in Saad's demeanor. "Don't put this on me, man," she said. "I'm just doing my job."

"Did you have anyone aboard the *New Jersey*?"

"No, but that doesn't mean I don't care, if that's what you're driving at."

"No one's saying you don't care, but you can't possibly understand."

Exhaling in frustration, she craned her neck to see if the other NCOs were watching us.

"Give us two minutes. Two minutes is all we need," I persisted.

Viv looked over at us for a verdict. She made direct eye contact with Saad.

"Two minutes," I repeated.

"One minute," Saad reluctantly conceded. "Do not go inside. Do not touch anything. *Anything*. Are we clear?"

"Crystal. Thank you."

I gave Viv the thumbs-up, and she sprinted right for the Interceptor. I followed closely behind.

The moment I got a clean look at the ship, she took my breath away. At thirty meters long, with a wingspan of half that, the flat black Interceptor was undeniably a bird of prey. With the cockpit camouflaged, bladelike chines ran aft from the needle-sharp nose along the sides of the gracefully sloped forebody, contributing to its superior aerodynamics in atmosphere. The primary thrusters and armaments burst outward from its fuselage, casting an ominous, jagged shadow over where we stood.

Viv slowly walked along the length of it, tracing her fingers across its razor-sharp lines. Despite Saad's admonishment, I wasn't going to tell her she couldn't touch it. I knew she needed to.

Battle scars tattooed the fuselage. The ship looked angry. Vengeful, even. I noticed what first appeared to be more battle damage on its tail, but upon closer inspection it seemed like a deliberate yet hasty attempt to laser-blast away the *New Jersey*'s designation flag.

"You see that?" I asked Viv.

"See what?"

"The tail."

Viv spun around the back of the vessel and checked it out for herself.

"Why would anyone do that? There are a hundred other ways to identify where she came from. There's no practical purpose."

"Maybe it was emotional. Flags hold meaning to people. Maybe whoever did it—"

"Didn't want to remember," Viv finished.

"You all right?"

"Uh-huh," Viv replied, stepping back to take it all in. I could see some of the weight had already lifted off her.

"Ready to go?"

"Right behind you."

I waited, but she didn't move. "You coming?"

"I want to talk to the pilot," she said, her eyes still locked on the Interceptor.

"That's gonna be harder. Once he's transferred to the *California*, they're gonna stash him in the brig."

"Any ideas for how I might get past the guards when they do?"

"Honestly, no. Not really. Not yet, anyway."

Viv turned. Her intensity seemed to have cooled a bit. There may have even been a hint of a smile. "Not yet."

CHAPTER 10

VIV

TWO MINUTES LATE FOR FIFTH BLOCK, JD and I quietly slid into our seats next to Bix. Surrounded by students, our cluster of blue uniforms only served to further disconnect us from our civilian shipmates. There were seventy-seven of them on the *California*, and only seven of us, so, of course, we stuck out like sore thumbs.

Seven cadets wasn't a random number. It corresponded to the number of bridge officers on every Alliance ship during peacetime. One for each station, including the captain.

For every Explorers Program, thousands of candidates competed intensely for seven spots on usually no more than three Alliance ships. Our class's year had three participating vessels—the *California*, the *Estonia*, and the *Normandy*—and the competition had been typically fierce. Eight thousand candidates for twenty-one slots.

The competition included every type of testing you could imagine, with a heavy concentration on mathematics, advanced sciences, and critical analysis. Combined with extensive mind puzzles to evaluate your integrative reasoning, logic, and cognitive strengths and weaknesses, the tests were designed to separate those who knew how to study from those who knew how to think. If you had the brainpower to get past all that, you were just getting started.

Next came the punishing long days and short nights of boot camp. Day one, our drill sergeants greeted us with the ominous but undeniably accurate "Welcome to the Suck." Reveille came every day at 0430. Wake up, enjoy your runny egg PRM, and set off on a five-kilometer run. And that was just the beginning. In eight weeks there were enough push-ups, sit-ups, and pull-ups to last a lifetime, topped off with daily hand-to-hand combat, marksmanship, flight readiness, and zero-gravity training. You were physically and emotionally spent by dusk, if you even made it that far.

There was a 50 percent dropout rate over the first seven weeks. The remaining number of candidates was cut in half again in the eighth week, when you had to get past the Crucible: the final test in candidate training, representing the culmination of all the skills and knowledge we cadets were expected to possess. It included a total of forty-eight kilometers of marching, grueling combat situation simulations, and a serious deprivation of both food and sleep. Anytime a student aboard the *California* was foolish enough to make a crack about Bix's size, I took great pleasure in reminding them that he had, in fact, survived the Crucible. That tended to shut them up real quick.

Of course, getting past all of the academic requirements, mind puzzles, boot camp, and the Crucible guaranteed you absolutely squat. From there you were submitted to special skills qualifiers for Command, Piloting, Communications, Navigation, Analytics, Engineering, and Medical. Candidates who failed to show a special aptitude for at least one of the seven disciplines were out of luck.

After all that there was yet another hurdle to clear, one that was impossible to prepare, study, or train for—the Psych Ops testing. They never even showed you the results. You just submitted to the testing and waited to see if you had been selected. And if you were, it meant you were the best of the best. The elite.

If you didn't want to put yourself through the torture required to become a cadet, you could always apply to the Explorers Program as a student. The student requirements were almost exclusively academic, with the selection process weighted heavily toward diversity. If you were a cadet candidate who made it past the Crucible and skills qualifiers but didn't make the final cut, you were offered an automatic student invitation. Not a lot of people took advantage of those automatic bids because of how much pride it required them to swallow. Julian was one of the few who had.

If your mother or father was an active Alliance officer, that made you a Legacy. Despite some people whining about special Legacy privileges, the only thing the designation really helped with was your assignment requests. No doubt, this explained how JD and I managed to be assigned to the flagship together. If anyone wanted to throw stones at us for that, I didn't really care. I knew we belonged on the *California* regardless of who our parents were.

After everything we had been put through to become cadets, it was nearly impossible to step aboard the ship without a little bit of a chip on our shoulders. That was strike one against us with the students. Strike two was probably the handful of privileges we had that they did not. Access to certain restricted areas. Fewer course requirements. A slightly later curfew. All of it well earned. Not only because of everything we had endured to qualify as cadets, but also because of all the other responsibilities we were burdened with that they were not. Things like bridge duty, utility and maintenance details, and Command Ops training. If we weren't in one of our courses, sleeping, or eating, most of our time was spoken for with one obligation or another.

Strike three was definitely that we were entrusted with a measure of authority over the students. Explorers missions only took place on ships embarking upon low-priority, routine diplomatic or transport missions. These low-priority missions required much smaller complements—usually not more than a skeleton crew of NCOs, who were housed separately on their own deck. Without much adult supervision for students on the lower decks, the command staff trusted us to make sure that keeping general order never became their headache.

Our authority had its perks, but the trade-off was that if a student's behavior ever required the attention of an officer, we had failed—which, putting it mildly, was frowned upon by the captain. So sometimes we had to be tough with the students to avoid those kinds of situations. Sure, they might have resented it, but the bottom line for us was it was always better to have a cranky student than a cranky captain.

I looked around me. What we'd come to know as a lecture room didn't really look like a lecture room or any other kind of classroom: thick bulkhead walls with crisscrossing latticed support girders and a floor of interlocked mesh alloy plates with bright, colorful wires easily visible beneath them. This room, like many others on the *California*, was a retrofit. Yes, there were desks. And a Visioslate. But it was never intended for us. It was originally an ammunition locker. Or Alliance infantry barracks. Or protein rations cold storage. It was hard to tell. Without a war to fight, the mighty *California* wasn't much more than a whole lot of empty space. But it was home for now. *Our* empty space.

Bix leaned intently forward on his elbows as Professor Jones wrote a ridiculously long, complicated equation on the Visioslate. JD doodled on his desk's console. I tried to focus on the equation, but my mind drifted back to the Interceptor and its pilot.

Upon completing the equation, Professor Jones tapped the Visioslate with her finger, and a glowing blue star appeared over the numerical string. "This equation is your road map to the chain reaction in a blue giant star. Something incredibly beautiful, but also something incredibly complex."

The same equation and glowing blue star on the Visioslate appeared on each of our consoles. I glanced down and attempted to make sense of it all, but all the numbers and symbols did was make my head hurt. And then Bix laughed out loud. Not good. We were supposed to be the ones setting an example.

I kicked his chair, but it was too late. In a fraction of a second,

Professor Jones dematerialized from the front of the room and rematerialized right next to Bix. All Preceptor Synths, like Jones and Sigvaatsan, were adept at that little trick. It seemed to startle Bix even though he'd fallen victim to it many times before. I sat up a little straighter. I didn't want to appear distracted and have her materialize by my side next.

Bix's posture slumped as "Professor Jones" looked down at him. "Cadet Bixby, do you care to share what you find so amusing?"

Even though she was little more than an electromagnetic projection of ones and zeroes, she still managed to convey the intimidation factor of a real professor. "Not really," he replied.

"No, please. Share your wisdom with us," Professor Jones insisted.

Bix looked in JD's direction, seeking his approval. Bix wasn't as brave as he was brilliant, but he always seemed to find the courage he needed when JD had his back. They had a big brother–little brother dynamic. It was endearing.

JD nodded reassuringly at Bix. Watching their subtle interaction made me smile.

Bix shrugged and stood up. "Well, it's just that you're overthinking it."

"Overthinking it?" Professor Jones replied.

"Yeah. We're always trying to impose our confusion upon nature. Nature is simple," Bix explained, gesturing toward the mathematical statement on the Visioslate. "Nature doesn't need all that . . . stuff."

"Would you care to enlighten us?"

"Oh, I don't think—"

"By all means," the Synth demanded.

JD and I shared a knowing look, proudly anticipating what would come next.

Bix reluctantly made his way to the front of the room. Sweeping his hand across the Visioslate, he erased two-thirds of the equation.

The glowing blue star disappeared. He replaced the original equation with a much simpler one and tapped the surface with a finger. The blue star immediately reappeared.

"Yep," Bix softly muttered to himself in satisfaction.

Professor Jones materialized next to him and silently processed his simple mathematical genius as if frozen before it. This was not an uncommon occurrence—his outsmarting a Synth to the point of freezing its program.

Then, just as I prepared to get up and reboot her, she returned to operational status. A slight flicker of her image told me she was receiving new data.

"Cadet Marshall," she called out, "please report to Gallipoli Station. You will be issued a Blue Pass at Receiving. You've been summoned by the captain."

––––––––

"Well," said Bix as we walked together down the Gamma Deck passageway without JD, "I guess that was about the Blink Drill this morning."

The day's blocks concluded, a constant flow of students shuffled past us in either direction. I gestured with my hand for Bix to keep his voice down.

"Yep, probably," I answered, trying not to let on how concerned I was. "The captain will get his pound of flesh, and then it'll be done."

"Really? How long do you think he's going to keep tolerating this?"

"For a while. It's his son," I said, though I wasn't sure I believed he'd be so lenient.

"Well, I for one am very concerned. He's getting worse."

"Don't say that."

"But it's true."

"That's not what I mean, Bix. Talk is dangerous. These things take on a life of their own. We should stop talking and deal with it. Ourselves."

"I've already tried that. You have too."

"We haven't tried hard enough. We've both been afraid of pushing too hard. Of alienating him. We need to let go of that. Take the gloves off. We can—"

I was interrupted by a small commotion coming from just around the bend of Gamma Deck's central junction. First it was a muddle. Then I heard the voices of two Alliance MPs barking at students to clear a path.

And then the MPs emerged in front of us. Between them, a prisoner, his hands cuffed in front of him. The Interceptor's pilot. It had to be. He couldn't have been a day over twenty-five, although with his shaggy hair, patchy beard, and general scruffiness, he could've passed for older. As he approached, I zeroed in on his eyes. They were cerulean blue, but I recognized something darker lurking beneath.

Walking past me, he smiled, and I inexplicably flinched. Then, as he disappeared down the passageway, he looked back at me, seemingly tickled by my reaction. Having carried so much dread in my expectations, it was almost a relief to be disarmed by the pilot's whimsy. He was not at all what I had expected. Not even close.

"So that's our bad guy?" Bix quipped skeptically.

"We don't know what he is yet," I replied. "But one way or another, I'm going to find out."

CHAPTER 11

JD

THE OFFICERS' MESS ON GALLIPOLI WAS AT least three times the size of the one on the *California*. Like Alliance regiments aligned in tight formation, at least sixty dining tables sat empty in perfectly even rows. Similar to the one on the *California*, a long observation window traversed the length of the room, with an unfettered view of gleaming stars and distant worlds. The slightest sound, even the squeaking of my boot against the leg of my chair, seemed to echo from every wall. The room made me feel small.

I'm sure that's exactly what my father wanted.

He was ten minutes late. Undoubtedly, that was intentional too. He wanted me to sit there alone, agonizing over my fate. By the time he arrived, I'd be so anxious and inside my head that there'd be no arguing. He'd dole out my punishment, and I'd take my licks without protest or complaint.

Finally, a door slid open at the far end of the mess, and there he stood. He took a moment to regard me with some rehearsed disappointment before marching toward where I was seated. When he sat opposite me, he didn't offer the slightest acknowledgment. Not a smile. Not a nod. Nothing. Instead he slapped a rigid file folder down on the table and slowly leafed through its contents. All my disciplinary reports, including Gentry's latest.

Paper. A nice touch. It added to the ceremony of my punishment ritual. I watched as he licked his fingers and turned each page slowly, his head down, shaking ever so slightly in frustration. I focused on the deep graying at his temples.

Eventually he looked up and leaned forward. It was hard to escape the metaphor of the wide shadow his broad shoulders cast over me. "I'm finding it difficult not to be insulted."

"Insulted? Insulted by what?"

"That you can sit there across from me, look me in the eyes, and honestly believe I don't know exactly what you're up to."

"Dad, I . . ."

The creases in my father's forehead scrunched more tightly together. "Are you having trouble seeing my uniform from where you're sitting, Cadet Marshall?"

I swallowed hard, pushing down my emotions. I was so tired of the constant need for formality. "I'm sorry, Captain. I don't know what you mean."

His back to the observation window, he looked over his shoulder and regarded the stars. "I know you better than anyone. I may even know you better than you know yourself," he said before returning his eyes to mine. "Please don't lie to me anymore."

Please don't lie to me anymore.

His words were so inevitable, yet somehow I hadn't seen them coming.

Over time it had become like a game. Go over the line just enough, but not so much as to bring things to a head all at once. But the longer the game went on, the more I bought into the lies it required. Eventually I lost touch with its purpose altogether.

His gaze locked on me like a spotlight, I was suddenly drowning in the reality that I had become so proficient at denying. Still, despite being exposed, I couldn't bring myself to admit it.

"I don't know what you're talking about," I replied, ashamed by how disingenuous the words sounded coming out of my mouth.

My father's expression sank. My intentions must have been so infuriatingly obvious to him all along. My maintaining the pretense of ignorance was like throwing gasoline on the fire.

"Everything in these disciplinary reports is a complete contradiction of who you are," he said, indignantly tossing my file to the side. "Insubordination. Dereliction of duty. Failing grades. I would've expected you to have been a little more subtle in your strategy."

Despite the truth being laid bare right in front of me, my mind desperately grasped for excuses.

Maybe you've overestimated me.

The program is more demanding than I ever imagined.

The rigors of deep-space travel were too much to handle.

All were too ridiculous to say out loud.

"Or at least a little more consistent in its application," he continued. "Your performance as a cadet has been an abject failure, yet nothing else about you has changed. Your confidence. Your friendships. Your competitive fire. I reviewed the data stream from your Iso-Rec race this morning—*that* young man isn't the same person who would waltz through a Blink Drill like he didn't care about the outcome."

He paused, as if hoping I'd have the courage to confess. When I didn't, he went ahead and put me out of my misery.

"You're trying to get bounced because you think it will spare you the shame of quitting," he said before leaning back in his chair and folding his arms. "If you want to quit, I'll let you quit, but first you'll have to do something."

"And what's that?" I asked, the question itself conceding he was right.

He unfolded his arms and leaned in close.

"You need to convince me. You need to convince me that's what you want."

"You've got all those reports right in front of you. Aren't they enough to convince you?"

"I've been your father for eighteen years. Not just the last three months. I know everything you've been through. Everything you've survived. How you've used all that pain and suffering to drive yourself to be the best at almost everything. You've been running circles around competition you had no business competing with for half your life now. Your being here is proof of it. You blew through boot camp like it was a Sunday walk in the park and scored off the charts on every test and command aptitude qualifier they threw at you. That didn't happen by accident. I know what it takes to accomplish what you've accomplished. So, no, those reports convince me of absolutely nothing other than one thing."

He paused again, careful to give his next thought enough space to stand alone and land hard. "That you're afraid."

My father, the hero of Titan Moon, was the last person I ever wanted to cry in front of, but I couldn't contain the quickly swelling glaze of tears over my eyes.

"The closer you got to what you've always wanted, the more frightened you became. After all your preparation, what if you're still not good enough? What if everyone's belief in you is misplaced? What if you fail those under your command? Am I getting warm?"

The tears spilled out, rolling down my cheeks.

"Everyone is afraid to fail, but it's different for you. It's different for you because you know more about the life-and-death stakes of sitting in the captain's chair than anyone your age ever should. The pain, misery, and suffering you may one day be called upon to prevent, and may not always be able to. And you have one more impossible challenge to contend with that no one else ever will. *Me*."

Everything he said was true, but it was the last part—his acknowledgment of the burden of his legacy—that broke the dam inside me. Whatever vestige of denial I was still clinging to evaporated. I slumped slightly in my chair.

My father unbuttoned his collar and released a long, slow breath. Two tiny, innocuous gestures, but they revealed more vulnerability than I had seen from him in too long a time.

"You will always be the son of Captain Philip Marshall. There's nothing I can do to free you from that. But what I can assure you is that every fear you'll ever wrestle with, I've wrestled with too."

"The hero of Titan Moon," I said, wiping away tears with my sleeve, "wrestling with fear?"

"Do you think I wasn't afraid at Titan Moon?"

I looked past him out the observation window and imagined column after column of Kastazi Destroyers and Strike Fighters descending upon the *California*.

"Fear never leaves you, John. Never."

I could picture the blazing power of the enemy's energy weapons smashing against the *California*'s hull.

"Fear is like a fever. It consumes you. Burns through your veins. Takes hold of all your faculties."

My mind took me further, onto the *California*'s bridge. My father in the captain's chair, his eyes reflecting the glorious blaze of battle.

"But if you can learn to trust yourself in the face of fear, the fever will break. And then you will feel . . . invincible."

My waking fantasy resolved with a cascading explosion of Kastazi warships over my father's shoulders, so stark the illusion I could almost see its fiery halo silhouetting him.

"Invincible," I skeptically muttered.

"As hard as it may be for you to believe, it's true. If you can get that far, that's how you will feel, and that's when you'll have to learn an even more difficult lesson."

"Which is what?"

"That feeling invincible can be more dangerous than feeling afraid."

We sat there in silence for what seemed an eternity, although it was probably no longer than thirty seconds.

"What's it going to be, John?" he finally asked, breaking our quiet standoff. "Stay or go?"

Having dispensed with my charade, he boiled it down to that painfully simple choice. But there was nothing simple about what was going on inside me.

I had worked nearly my entire life to get to where I was, and the thought of throwing it all away made my stomach turn. I meant every promise I ever made to Viv about chasing so many adventures together out among the stars. I wanted to challenge myself to realize the limits of my potential, and there was no better path for that than being an Alliance officer.

But despite all that, the crushing fear of failure remained.

"Are you going to answer me?"

I tried to push an answer past my lips, but nothing came.

My lack of response inflamed him. I could tell by the way he flexed his jaw. It meant he was gritting his teeth.

"Being a cadet is a privilege," he said. "You don't need to convince me you want to quit."

He stood and refastened his collar. "The *California* is disembarking Gallipoli Station in seventeen hours. That's how long you have to convince me *you want to stay.*"

I couldn't tell if his abrupt about-face was more emotional or tactical, but either way he had me questioning everything that had brought me to this moment. And I had to imagine that was his goal.

"Are we clear?"

"Yeah, we're clear," I responded, still stunned.

He said something else as he walked out the door. I couldn't have heard him right. It would've been extraordinary for him to say such a thing while in uniform. Still, I let myself believe it. I needed to.

"I love you too, Dad," I whispered.

CHAPTER 12

NICHOLAS

SAFI AND I WALKED TOGETHER DOWN THE Beta Deck passageway toward our respective quarters. In our three months off-world, we'd become closer friends. We were simpatico in a way—part of the exclusive cadet clan, but outsiders within it. The cadets regarded me as aloof and detached, if not altogether weird. They regarded her as something of a toady, always sucking up to the command staff and following every rule to the letter. I felt bad that she didn't quite meld with the rest of them—but then again, neither did I. That was our common burden, and it felt good to share it. I suppose that's one reason we were drawn to one another. I didn't feel judged by her. And I thought she felt the same about me.

"Are you going to Viv's thing in Iso-Rec tonight?" Safi asked as we stopped in front of my quarters.

I looked down at my feet.

"I'm so sorry. That was a really stupid thing to ask," she said, realizing her mistake. It didn't bother me. I understood how easily she could forget. During the day, I was just like everyone else.

"It's fine," I laughed. "I think I'm going to rearrange my sock drawer. Again."

It wasn't a particularly funny response, but Safi chuckled anyway. She was always so kind to me.

"Well, if it's any consolation, I'm not going either. I'm not breaking curfew."

"I believe Bix has that problem covered."

"Yes. And that makes it twice as bad. Breaking curfew and tampering with our biosigs? No thank you. Besides, no one is going to miss me anyway."

I paused, thinking through my response. "Vivien will miss you. And I'd miss you too if I were there."

She smiled at me and gently kissed my cheek. "You're sweet."

"I try," I replied. This wasn't the first time she had invited me to say something more. To somehow affirm the feelings we both shared but had not openly acknowledged to each other. Yet, once again, I failed to take advantage of the opportunity.

She stood there, saying nothing, her eyes betraying an undeniable hint of disappointment.

"Good night, Safi," I said.

"À demain," she replied before going on her way.

I stepped inside and surveyed my quarters. The room was bigger than I needed, and its emptiness made me feel even more alone. Single-occupancy quarters were not a luxury typically afforded to cadets. Despite a vast surplus of empty living space, Captain Marshall insisted everyone have a roommate. Everyone except me.

I turned to face the door as it automatically closed behind me. What came next was routine as clockwork. Every night, at precisely 2030, the ship's computer would lock me in for the night. I bounced my fingers in the air like a symphony maestro, as if conducting the five distinct noises of the door's locking mechanism. It would be 0600 before the door would open again. In time to shower, get breakfast, and head to first block.

With a swipe of my fingers across my quarters' control panel, the lights dimmed. My attention lingered on the panel's com interface.

It was dark, signifying inactive status. As always, all outgoing communication was restricted.

I sat down on my rack and inspected the picture on my nightstand. A happy couple embracing a small child I vaguely resembled. I ran my fingers over the faces of the man and the woman. I knew they weren't my parents. Did they belong to someone? Somebody else's mother? Somebody else's father? Or were they real at all?

I was beginning to understand who I was. Like water from a leaky faucet, my memories would drip back to me over time, slowly revealing a mosaic of truth piece by piece. Was this intentional? Did the captain intend for this to happen? Or perhaps I was sick. Or even dying. The thought didn't particularly frighten me, so I presumed I wasn't.

I wondered how much Captain Marshall really knew. There were so many layers of secrets, but we only acknowledged the big one openly to each other. I was amused by the cover story he had created for me. That I was on work release from a diversionary program for criminal offenders and nightly lockdown was a condition of my probation. There were so many other explanations he could've provided. Why that one? The only reason I could gather was the obvious implication of a criminal past. That I had the potential to be dangerous, and people should use caution around me.

I lay back on the bed and stared up at the ceiling. The tiles were fastened in with simple rivets and bolts. I could have easily removed them and escaped if I really wanted to. But I didn't. There was nothing for anyone to be afraid of. I just wanted to be normal. Like everyone else.

Yes, I was dangerous. But only when necessary. Only if I needed to be.

CHAPTER 13

VIV

"THAT'S NEVER A GOOD SIGN," SAFI SAID as she walked through the door to our quarters.

I was lying on the floor at the foot of my rack, incessantly throwing my rubber handball against the bulkhead wall. My special brand of meditation was a particularly annoying habit for her to have to tolerate.

"I saw the pilot," I said in between bounces.

"And?" she asked as she sat down at her desk.

I bounced the ball a few more times, catching and releasing it more slowly as I considered my thoughts.

"Not at all what I imagined he was going to be."

"What were you expecting?" she inquired while fastidiously organizing a few scattered items on her blotter.

"I don't know. Someone who looked a little more . . . nefarious."

Safi swiveled in her chair. "Need I remind you of the idiom 'wolf in sheep's clothing'?"

"No."

"Where did you see him?"

"On Gamma Deck. A couple MPs from Gallipoli were escorting him to the brig."

"The brig," Safi mused. "Never would've guessed it would be occupied during an Explorers mission."

My next throw hit a seam in the bulkhead, and the ball bounced out of my reach.

"What do I need to do to get you to come with me tonight?" I asked, rolling over onto my stomach to face her.

"Ha! Speaking of the brig!"

"So dramatic. It's breaking curfew, not treason."

"Call it what you want, but it's still violating the Code of Conduct."

"Barely."

"Barely is still a violation."

"You realize you're no fun at all, right?"

"I've been accused of worse."

"Seriously, if you died in your sleep, you'd regret not breaking a rule every once in a while."

"And if you had been a bit more respectful of rules during launch prep, we'd probably be known as something other than the 'Devastation Class,'" she teased.

"You make a valid point. A depressing one, but valid nonetheless."

Safi reached into her top desk drawer and pulled out a small gift box wrapped in plain brown paper. "Well, hopefully this will cheer you up then."

"You got me a present?"

Safi joined me on the floor and presented the box. "Happy eighteenth birthday, Vivien," she said earnestly.

I couldn't imagine what she had come up with off-world. "Should I open it?"

"Yes. Of course. I would've preferred to use real wrapping paper, but I couldn't find any on the ship."

"It's perfect. It's very . . . minimalist."

I carefully unwrapped the paper so as to not tear it. Beneath it was a hand-carved wooden box. I carefully inspected it and traced its ridges with my fingers.

"It's beautiful. Did you make it?"

Safi laughed at me. "Indeed, I did. But that's not your gift. Your gift is inside."

"Really?"

"Yes, really. Open it."

I carefully lifted its top, revealing a beaded bracelet. "Oh, Saf, it's amazing. But how did you . . . ?"

"They're stones I had collected on the beaches of Dakar. I brought them to remind me of home."

Safi helped me tie the bracelet onto my wrist. Unexpected tears welled in my eyes. I was especially touched because Safi wasn't a very sentimental person.

She and I were as close as she would allow us to be. She knew more about my inner workings than I did about hers. But even though she didn't open up to me very often, I trusted her without question. In the year or so since we'd met, I could always count on her to keep my secrets, and she never really judged my choices even if she disagreed with them.

I played with the stones and fumbled for words. "Saf, I honestly don't know what to say."

"Say thank you."

I hugged her tightly. "Thank you so, so much!"

Safi patted my knee and returned to her desk. She required nothing else from me in the moment. My gratitude was more than enough for her.

I retreated to my rack and admired the bracelet on my wrist. The weight of the stones felt heavier than they appeared. Which was sort of poetic in a way. For someone like Safi, the mere gesture of a gift was also more substantial than it appeared.

I fell back onto the mattress, and my mind began to wander. To JD and all of his troubles. To more pleasant thoughts of Julian. And then, of course, again to the Interceptor and its pilot. My eyes growing heavy, I didn't try to resist a creeping sleep. I still had a couple of hours to kill and just wanted to turn off. Give my brain a rest.

CHAPTER 14

NICHOLAS

I LINGERED BACK, UNNOTICED, AS A SCRUM of students held Bixby prostrate over a table in the Camp Penbrook canteen. I surmised the commotion of the students' taunts combined with Bixby's futile thrashing would be sufficiently clamorous to summon an MP to quell the situation, so I didn't feel compelled to intervene. Regardless, my intervention would have been ill-advised considering the tenuous nature of my enlistment.

The tension between students and cadets had been palpable from the moment we arrived at Penbrook for launch prep. Initially I could identify no root cause, but over time I came to understand how our separation itself contributed to breeding resentment, jealousy, and suspicion.

Students prepped for launch according to one curriculum, and we cadets, who were charged with additional extracurricular responsibilities aboard the California, prepped according to another. The bifurcation of our preparations made practical sense but operated to create a distance between us—its vacuum too often filled with misunderstanding and misappropriated malintent. The students, not fully appreciating the demands of cadet enlistment, prejudged us as elitist and unfairly privileged, whereas we fairly could have been accused of viewing students as lacking sufficient investment in the Explorers Program to be deserving of the opportunity. It took only twelve weeks at Penbrook for this vicious cycle of misapprehension to escalate rivalry to acrimony and ultimately graduate to outright contempt.

Jagdish Patel pushed down on the back of Bixby's neck, while Cooper Lynch knelt down to meet him at eye level. Lynch and Patel had distinguished themselves as the ringleaders of the students' antipathy for the cadets, taking every opportunity to aggravate hostilities. Of late they had taken to getting in the ear of Ensign Gentry, calling attention to even the smallest of technical code-of-conduct infractions by cadets. Unsurprisingly, this antagonized JD and Vivien, and in the final days leading up to launch, there had been increasingly frequent petty aggressions from both factions. I presumed Bixby's predicament was likely retribution for yet another.

"What did you do to our test scores, Moon Boy?" Lynch demanded.

It seemed I had presumed correctly.

His face pressed hard against the table, Bixby's mouth struggled to form words.

"Nugthin," he mumbled, his response accompanied by a fair amount of drool leaking out onto the table's surface.

Lynch pulled Bixby up by the neck, freeing his mouth to speak more coherently.

"What did you say?"

"Nothing. I said nothing."

Lynch released his grip and nodded to Patel. Patel took his cue and flipped Bixby onto his back to face them.

"You were the last person to log in to the mainframe, and suddenly the bottom drops out of our scores. Do you expect me to believe you had nothing to do with that?"

Bixby straightened his uniform and considered his response.

"Yes."

"Are you trying to be cute?"

"No, I'm trying to be literal. You cheated. So, in a manner of speaking, I did nothing to your scores other than return them to their typical underwhelming mean."

The scrum tightened around Bixby.

Lynch's temples throbbed.

"You're going to go back into the mainframe right now and put everything back. Exactly the way it was. Exactly."

Bixby pursed his lips. It seemed as though he was resisting the urge to speak while engaging in some further internal deliberation.

"Mmmm . . . don't think so," he finally answered.

"You don't think so?" Lynch shot back, his body language spiking toward apoplectic.

A wide grin grew across Bixby's face. "Yep. Can't do it. Sorry."

"You're about to be on the receiving end of one of the great beatings of your young life. I can't imagine why you're smiling."

Bixby pointed over Lynch's shoulder.

"That's why."

Standing behind Lynch were JD, Vivien, Iara, and Anatoly. I had been so focused on the scrum I had not noticed them enter the canteen.

"Anatoly," JD said softly.

Anatoly pushed through, a mere nudge of his forearm nearly knocking Patel to the canteen's floor.

"Come now, Bix," he said, effortlessly lifting Bixby to his feet.

Lynch and Patel stepped in front of them, blocking their path back toward the other cadets.

Anatoly looked to JD.

JD held up his hand. "Not yet."

"We're two days from launch, Lynch," Vivien said, making no attempt to mask her indignation. "Do you really want to do this?"

"Your little mascot tanked our scores."

"You cheated. We made a correction."

"We? You told him to do this?"

"Yes, we did. We're going to be on the California together for a long time, and letting you get away with something like that would set a very bad precedent for how things are going to go up there."

"You've got no authority over us or anything else."

Vivien smirked. It seemed an unnecessary inflection, its result only likely to further instigate Lynch's ire.

"You're all in for a very rude awakening once we ship off," she cautioned. "Who do you think the captain is going to look to, to keep you and your friends in line? Ensign Gentry? Ensign Lewis? The NCOs?"

"If you think we're going to take orders from cadets—"

"We're not going to give anyone orders," JD cut him off. "The captain and his officers give the orders. We just carry them out. And if their orders are to keep you in line, you better believe we're going to keep you in line."

Lynch got directly in JD's face.

Iara's tattoos peeked out from her sleeves. I could see them shifting into sharp, angular shapes, their colors intensifying toward different shades of deep red. I had learned through observation this was an indication of severe agitation.

"I don't care if you're the captain's son. There's not a single thing about you that scares me. Not a single thing."

"Do you have a point, or is this just more bluster?"

It was evident the situation had reached a tipping point. Despite my reticence to intervene, inserting myself appeared to be the only remaining option to avoid a larger, more consequential physical altercation.

"Everyone please calm down," I said, stepping forward.

There was no reaction.

Sensing imminent danger, Anatoly shoved Bix a safe distance from the scrum.

"Please, I urge all of you to disperse," I said, this time louder.

Still no reaction. It was as though no one could hear me.

Lynch stabbed a finger into JD's sternum and held it there.

"My point is, if you're not going to fix our scores . . . we're going to go right here, right now."

JD slowly dropped his head to inspect Lynch's finger in his chest.

"You touched the uniform. Never touch the uniform."

Before I could take another step, I saw Lynch's head snap back from a sharp right-fisted jab to the mouth. A moment later, the entire canteen erupted into a full-on melee. JD eluded a series of desperate swings from Lynch, countering each missed punch with efficient blows to Lynch's ribs. Starting with Patel, Vivien worked her way down a line of charging students, knocking them over like dominoes with a series of impressively dexterous kicks and punches. Five students jumped Anatoly from his blind side. It required only moderate exertion for him to repel them as though they had been launched backward by a high-tension spring. Six students circled Iara. She removed her uniform jacket, revealing her tattoos in full angry bloom.

"Who's first?" she taunted them.

All six charged her at the same time, unleashing a fury of vicious kicks and punches. I quickly lost sight of her behind her assailants.

Then, suddenly, just as had happened so many times before, the same song began to swell in my ears.

A place where nobody dared to go. The love that we came to know. They call it Xanadu . . .

I rushed to Iara's aid. As I approached, the students ceased their attack on her and turned to face me. They smiled eerily and allowed me passage.

I saw a body on the floor. But it was not Iara's.

It was mine.

. . . And now open your eyes and see. What we have made is real. We are in Xanadu . . .

This version of me looked up into my eyes with a warm, soothing familiarity.

"Everything in its right place, Nicholas. Everything where it is supposed to be," it said.

The room began to spin. So fast that my entire environment blended into a centrifuge of streaming light and color.

. . . A million lights are dancing and there you are, a shooting star . . . an everlasting world and you're here with me eternally . . . Xanadu . . .

And when it all finally slowed, I emerged someplace different.

In front of me stood Safi Diome. I was in the quarters she shared with Vivien.

"What's happening to me?"

Safi leaned forward and gently kissed my lips.

"Everything in its right place. Everything where it's supposed to be."

Her kiss was something I had long desired, but the enigma of her words deprived the moment of the pleasure it deserved.

"What does that mean? 'Everything in its right place'?"

She turned her back on me and entered a code on her quarters' control console. The console emitted a confirmation tone. A moment later, a hidden panel on the bulkhead pushed out slightly.

Safi ran her fingers beneath the panel's edges and pulled it off. Whatever waited inside the bulkhead glowed bright, silhouetting her in a golden halo.

. . . Xanadu, your neon lights will shine for you, Xanadu . . .

"Safi," *I called out to her.* "Please tell me what's happening."

When she turned, I saw someone I did not recognize. It was still her, but she appeared older. Her uniform had changed. Replaced with black, form-fitting tactical armor. Muscles bulged from its contours. I observed four perfectly symmetrical scars on her neck, two on either lateral side, perfectly aligned. In her hands, a weapon similar to a pulse rifle, but with design elements I had not before encountered.

"We need you, Nicholas," *she said.* "You have the power to save us."

"Save you from what, Safi?"

She raised the weapon and took aim at me.

. . . The love, the echoes of long ago . . . You needed the world to know . . . they are in Xanadu . . .

"You already know," *she replied.* "You can feel it coming."

Her finger squeezed the trigger, and a pulse blast consumed me into an infinite, empty white. There was no pain. No fear. Only my mind alone, wandering through a vacuous abyss until the neverending white surrendered to a soft blue.

I gained my bearings, realizing I was on my back, surrounded by thick jungle foliage, staring up at a perfect, cloudless sky. I stood and observed a clearing in the distance, in it a crashed Alliance escape pod. JD stood before it, captured by a contingent of alien soldiers whose appearance did not comport to any known humanoid life-form. He struggled mightily to escape their grip.

I walked closer. I could see the escape pod's ship of origin emblazoned on its side: Tripoli.

JD noticed me and shouted out, "Everything in its right place. Everything where it's supposed to be."

I ran toward him.

"I don't understand!"

. . . The dream that came through a million years . . . That lived on through all the tears . . . It came to Xanadu . . .

With another step the earth disappeared beneath me, sending me falling through a horizonless star field. There was no bottom I could sense. No place to fall to.

. . . An everlasting world and you're here with me eternally . . . Xanadu . . . Xanadu . . .

Everything was weightless and forever. It felt safe. Like a womb.

. . . Now we are here in Xanadu . . .

I wondered if I had always been in this place. That perhaps this was my reality, and the life I had thought I lived was actually a dream.

The song grew louder in my ears.

. . . Xanadu . . . Xanadu . . .

Abruptly, I sensed my descent accelerating. Beneath me appeared the scorched wreckage of a decimated Earth city.

. . . Now we are here in Xanadu . . .

A deadly collision with the ground was imminent, yet still I felt no fear.

Instantly upon impact, I shot up, awake in my familiar reality. Lying in my bed, only the dim light of the stars illuminated my quarters—but I knew I was not alone.

. . . *Xanadu, your neon lights will shine for you, Xanadu . . . Now that I'm here, now that you're near, in Xanadu . . .*

I reached for the nearest control panel, activating the lights.

He sat in a chair opposite my bed. Beside him an antique turntable from Earth's late twentieth century spun a black acetate disk. He lifted the turntable's needle off the disk, ceasing the music.

Everything about him was the same despite how long it had been since we last visited. His long black hair. His well-manicured beard. The jagged scar by his right eye.

"I love that song," he said.

"What is the meaning of this?"

"Sadly, I can't tell you. That would defeat the purpose. All I can do is ever-so-slightly nudge you in the right direction."

Despite all the many thoughts racing through my mind, all I thought to ask was the one question that frightened me.

"Are you real or a figment of my imagination?"

He smiled. "What's the difference?"

Suddenly, again, I shot up in my bed as though waking from an intense dream. Once more, only the dim light of the stars illuminated my quarters. I quickly activated the lights, but this time there was no one with me.

I was alone, but things were not the same.

Safi, or whatever she represented, was right.

I could feel them coming.

CHAPTER 15

JD

I STOOD ALONE, WAITING INSIDE THE SEMICIRCLE of Iso-Pods. Two pods sat dead center in front of me, their hatches open. On either side of center were two more pods each, all occupied. Bix, Ohno, Anatoly, and Lorde were already sealed inside, their central nervous systems merged with the sensory fluid their bodies floated upon.

Amid the faint purring of the Iso-Pod pumps, my mind spun in a dizzying vortex of uncertainty. Everything had happened so fast. And now there were only nine hours left for me to do something to avoid going past the point of no return. It would have been so easy to do nothing. I had survived the inevitable reckoning with my father. My discharge papers were already signed. I could just let it happen and finally be free of all my fear.

But then what? An ordinary life? Would I be a doctor or a lawyer or a politician, growing old, staring up at the stars and dreaming of the life I was supposed to have led? Would the weight of all that be any less crushing?

Trying to pull myself out of my head, I fiddled with my pod's intake valve, adjusting its sensory fluid buoyancy ratio one final time. This was Viv's special night, and I couldn't do anything to let on something was wrong. That could come in the morning. Or maybe not at all. I thought of just disembarking the *California* without saying a word.

"This party is out of hand. Somebody turn down the music," Viv wisecracked from behind me.

I hadn't heard her walk in and turned to see her eyes beaming with excited anticipation. I did my best imitation of my happier self, hoping to avoid her sensing anything was amiss.

"You actually missed the party. You want to help me clean up?"

"You know, I think the older I become, the less funny you get."

"That hurts. It really does. Where were you, anyway?"

"I fell asleep waiting."

"So much for excited anticipation."

"Oh, stop. Has everyone already dropped?"

"Indeed they have."

"Okay. Can I guess?"

"Sure."

"Suborbital free diving?"

"Cold."

"Dune buggy desert rally?"

"Colder."

"What about—"

"No more guesses. Everybody's waiting on you. Go suit up."

Viv rolled her eyes at me and skipped off toward the locker room. A heavy wave of nausea nearly buckled me at the knees as I waited for her return. If I was going to quit, of course I had to tell her. But how? What could I say to make her understand? I wouldn't just be leaving the program—I'd be leaving her. Nothing would ever be the same between us again.

"Let's get wet," Viv trumpeted as she jogged back into Iso-Rec.

The last fastener of her Iso-Suit was still open. I reached out and tightly clasped it just beneath her neck. She looked into my eyes, searching for something. "What's wrong?" she asked.

"Nothing," I lied while holding her gaze. "You just look . . . pretty."

"Now I know something's wrong," she laughed.

"Get in the pod already, before you make this whole thing anticlimactic."

With a smile and a wink, she hurtled herself on top of her pod and lowered herself inside. The hatch automatically closed behind her, and the pod released a long hiss as it sealed and pressurized.

Alone once again, I didn't feel like a cadet anymore. I felt like a passenger. Or, perhaps even worse, a trespasser.

I climbed up onto the last remaining pod and eased myself into its womb. I let my body rest upon the tranquil buoyancy of its warm sensory fluid. Inside, the quiet respite invited me. Almost as soon as the hatch closed, the reaction began, my central nervous system absorbing multiple zettabytes of electrochemical data.

The usual brilliant flashes of color invaded the darkness. Like infinite varieties of starbursts filling an empty black sky, they accumulated and overexposed until there was nothing but a seemingly endless horizon of white. Slowly, the emptiness filled with a thick soup of overlapping sounds and disembodied voices. They grew louder and louder until the Drop. That's what we called the sudden, somewhat indescribable sinking feeling that always came next. And after that, once again, there was nothing. The Empty.

This final stage of Iso-Pod immersion, the Empty, was always the most unsettling part for me. It felt more like a glitch or a stutter than the natural crescendo of my brain synapses firing faster than the speed of light. Despite hundreds upon hundreds of prior Iso-Pod immersions, I still couldn't shake the fear of being lost forever, floating untethered ever deeper into the barren void of my own unexplored mind.

Yet, just as I always had, I emerged safely inside the program's illusion. For me Emergence was like waking from a dream inside another dream. Like remnants of sleep still casting shadows on my waking mind.

As my eyes came into focus, I marveled at all the sights around me. I had seen some of it before in holo-simulations, but only in fits and starts. Running the full program required rerouting more power than Bix and I could've had authorized for recreational Iso-Rec use, so we had been limited in what we could test in advance. To run her in all her glory, we had to wait for the perfect moment.

In preparation for her disembarking, the *California* had already begun its launch protocol. It took three hours to safely re-sequence her engines to full ready status, and four more to reseed the plasma that had been siphoned from her weapons systems and reenergized during our stay at Gallipoli Station. All that energy pumping to and fro gave Bix the ideal opportunity to mask his custom Iso-Rec program's massive power spike. The perfect moment was finally upon us.

It only took one step forward to confirm everything was just right. Fine blue grains of silicon sand, soft as dust between my toes. Pink ocean waves breaking against the beach and receding slowly back toward the burning amber dusk. Incandescent clouds of yellow-green gas painting the distant horizon. A sweet floral fragrance carried on the drizzling haze of a softly blowing sea mist. It was paradise. Otherwise known as Sigma 547-T.

547-T was an Earth-like planet in the distant Blevins System. Its distance was so great it would not be reached in my lifetime, my children's lifetimes, or even their children's children's lifetimes. Our only knowledge of the planet came from one of Dr. Samuel Fuller's Transdimensional Probes, a technology he'd created to allow us a glimpse of worlds we might otherwise never have dreamed of.

Transdimensional Probes and Blink Reactors worked according to similar principles, both folding space-time to travel great distances almost instantaneously. Their most important difference, however, was the power required for their successful operation. The forces generated by the probes would have, quite literally, ripped human beings apart.

We received the first image transmissions from 547-T shortly before the war. Never before had we seen anything so pristine and untouched—or so closely resembling our human notions of perfection. For many it was like touching heaven. In fact, some even went so far as to assign it spiritual provenance. Absent the war, the discovery of 547-T probably would've inspired us to dive even farther into the stars. But the war did happen. And most people forgot about the beauty of 547-T and how it made them feel.

In our time at Farragut, there were so many in-between moments when Viv and I were uncertain and afraid. That's when we'd talk about 547-T and invite each other to imagine we were safe together in paradise. We had spent countless hours in our minds climbing its snow-capped mountains, running through its lush, verdant jungles, and swimming in the deliciously pink waters of its oceans.

Our daydreams were our sanctuary, and for her birthday I wanted to bring some small part of them to life. Doing it right was no small task, though. It required Bix to ingest extraordinarily dense volumes of data from the original probe transmission and painstakingly repopulate it, detail by detail, inside the Iso-Rec computer. What he ultimately created revealed itself to be beyond my wildest expectations. It was, quite truly, a masterpiece.

About twenty meters ahead I saw the last small detail I had requested: a bonfire. The crackles and pops of its thirsty flames were just as inviting as I had hoped. Sensing my approach, Viv swung her head back in my direction. She looked like a kid on Christmas morning.

"You've outdone yourself, sir," she said.

"I'm just the idea guy. Bix was the execution."

She stood and hugged Bix and me. "Well, it's perfect. Thank you. Both of you."

I smiled and spied Lorde out of the corner of my eye. If he had his own birthday surprise in store for Viv, he had already been hopelessly upstaged. Unsurprisingly, he looked defeated.

"We picked Julian's brain too," I fibbed. All the grief I had given him suddenly felt so unnecessarily petty, and throwing him a bone was the least I could do.

"Is that so?" Viv cooed in his direction.

Julian flashed an embarrassed smile and quickly looked away.

I sat down in an empty space between Viv and Bix and pushed my palms out to warm them on the fire. "So are you going to blow out this candle or what?"

Viv puffed out her cheeks and pantomimed a futile effort to extinguish the flames. "I could stay inside this forever. I really could," she said.

"Why can't we?" Ohno wondered aloud. "I mean, when you think about it, what's really stopping us?"

"Brain function. You'd die of thirst in two days," Anatoly answered while casually throwing a stick into the fire.

I could see Bix's wheels start spinning. "Nourishment is certainly an obstacle, but not an insurmountable one."

"How do you figure?" Viv asked.

"It wouldn't be difficult to integrate an intravenous nourishment interface into an Iso-Pod. The real challenge would be the sensory fluid. After a day or two, it would begin to have a somewhat . . . corrosive effect on your body."

"Who needs a body when you can have all this?" Ohno joked.

"Disembodied but forever in bliss?" Lorde chimed in. "Sounds like a familiar story. Only the addition of angels would be required."

"I guess that would make you God, Bix," I said.

"Well, as your duly appointed, all-knowing, all-powerful creator, I'm finding myself slightly frustrated that you're all huddled around my modest gift of fire when I've created two square kilometers of heaven all around you. Start exploring or subject yourselves to my vengeful wrath."

Viv snapped to her feet and started walking backward toward the ocean, a wide grin on her face. "Amen!"

She made a beeline for the water's edge, and one by one we

chased after her. I had a fleeting moment of panic as I began peeling off my clothes. Fortunately, Bix was as detail oriented as always—right down to providing us with skivvies.

I hung back a moment and watched my friends all plunge themselves into the shimmering water. Viv dove headfirst under a breaking wave. Bix, all forty-nine kilograms of him, was immediately consumed by the same swell. Anatoly and Ohno playfully splashed and frolicked in the shallow depths, while Julian gracefully front crawled out into the deep.

Wading into the water, I took it all in. It was good to see everyone so happy and temporarily unburdened by the constant, unyielding regimen of the Explorers Program. It may have been Viv's birthday, but they all deserved a break. Though as much as I wanted to, it was difficult for me to share in the fun. The prospect of it all soon coming to an end for me made it feel so unearned.

About to lapse into another fog of introspection, I noticed a shimmering, murky something gracefully gliding toward me underwater. I soon recognized it to be Viv and waited until she breached the surface. Her skin gleamed with tiny pearls of pinkish seawater. I let my eyes linger on her for a second longer than felt comfortable.

"What's wrong?" she asked.

I sheepishly smiled, thinking that would be enough of an admission to satisfy her. But it was too late for that.

"Tell me," she persisted.

"It's nothing," I maintained.

"It's not 'nothing.' You've had that same expression on your face since the moment I walked out of the locker room. There's something you're not telling me."

Unable to look her in the eyes, I bowed my head and watched the water split around my waist in a soft current of foaming bubbles.

"You're scaring me, John. Please tell me what's wrong."

"I wanted to wait. Until morning. I didn't want to ruin this."

"You're more important to me. Tell me."

You're more important to me. Those were probably the last words I wanted to hear. What I was about to confess couldn't have been any more selfish.

"I'm so sorry, Viv," I said. It was all I could manage.

"Sorry for what? What did you do?"

"I think it's over."

"What are you talking about?" she asked, her voice tightening. "What's over?"

I didn't answer. I didn't have to. The anguished look in my eyes pushed her toward the most obvious explanation—which also happened to be her worst fear.

"They expelled you?" she cried out. "No. That's not happening. We're stopping this right now and going to my mom. She'll talk to your dad—"

"It's more complicated than—"

"You've been struggling," she interrupted, trying to get ahead of me. "I know that. Everyone knows that. But the answer isn't throwing you out. Not now. Not when we're this close. Not after all you've done to get here."

"Viv . . ."

"Just shut up and listen to me. We're going to my mom. She's going to talk to your dad, and we're going to figure this out. We can fix this."

"No, Viv."

"It was Gentry, wasn't it?" she asked, her voice growing increasingly manic. "He got you expelled? This is not happening. Absolutely not."

I took her wrist and gently rested my hand over hers. "Viv . . . Vivien . . . no one expelled me. I did this."

"That's not funny," she said, snatching her hand back.

"No, it's not."

She stared at me in disbelief, still searching for any hint I might be joking. "I don't understand. You can't . . ."

"I did. I had to. It's time for me to let go."

"Let go? Let go of what?"

"The Explorers Program. Graduating. Becoming an officer."

"I don't . . . I don't understand. This is the life you've always wanted."

The life you've always wanted.

Her words hung in the air between us like a ghost, the shadow of my dying destiny staring back at me. My future would not be out among the stars. There would be no grand adventure across new worlds. Worst of all, our shared journey would be coming to an end.

Despite all that would be sacrificed, somehow the horrible bargain still soothed me. That's how weak I was in the face of fear. I felt more cowardly than ever before.

I took her hands in mine and waited for her to settle. In a moment she knew I was opening that part of myself only she had access to. Her panic subsided, giving way to the reality she probably saw coming from the moment we left Earth. Still she needed to hear it.

"What have you done, JD?"

Until right then it hadn't felt truly over. Admitting it to myself wasn't the final step. Admitting it to her was.

I squeezed her hands more tightly.

"This isn't the life I wanted. I think it's just the story I needed to believe."

Her body swayed inside a passing wave as the laughter of our friends juxtaposed the silence between us. My heart felt like it was breaking in two. I placed my hand on her cheek, praying her reaction to my touch might reveal that she understood. Or that she might one day be able to forgive me. I thought I saw it. A glimmer of hope for what I needed to hear. She opened her mouth to speak, but a sudden, thunderous rumble rolled across the sky before she could utter a word.

The rumble was closely followed by the program losing its integrity, leaving the world around us to strobe in and out of existence.

Next came a sensation of violent impact, but nothing moved. The disorienting disparity of stimuli induced a powerful wave of nausea. Viv doubled over, feeling the same sickening effect. I tried to call out to Bix. All the overlapping sounds and disembodied voices of immersion returned. It was almost as if we were about to lapse into a deeper immersion. A simulation within a simulation. When I started to feel the Drop, I thought my frightening suspicion might have been right.

I closed my eyes and waited for the Empty, but it never came. Instead, the bottom flap of my Iso-Pod slammed open, dumping me and fifteen hundred liters of sensory fluid onto the Iso-Rec floor. Viv and everyone else were lying beside me, looking equally confounded. Each of us had been ejected from our pods.

"What the . . . ?" I said as a strange sound and vibration echoed from the walls as if a powerful wave had just crested and crashed at the *California*'s feet. Without warning, the ship rolled hard to starboard, sending us all sliding across the wet deck into a bulkhead wall.

Before any of us could gain our bearings, the ship's Emergency PA system suddenly came active, emitting short, shrieking bursts of alarms.

"Listen," I said, getting to my feet.

"This is not a drill. All cadets and students report to your safety positions. This is not a drill. All cadets and students report to your safety positions. Remain in your safety positions and await further instructions."

The announcement continued in a loop. Stunned and disoriented, everyone else uneasily got to their feet as well.

"What the hell is happening?" Viv shouted over the alarms.

Still dizzy from our abrupt disconnection, I struggled to find my focus. "I don't know."

"All right. We need to follow protocol. Get to our safety positions."

"No, wait," I interjected. "The senior command staff isn't on the ship. Most of the crew are probably still on Gallipoli. What if no one's in command?"

"Gentry and Lewis should still be on the bridge."

I ran to the emergency com.

"Don't!" Viv exclaimed. "We're not supposed to touch that!"

"They can write me up," I said as I activated the com. "Bridge, this is Cadet Marshall. Do you require assistance?"

No response.

"Bridge, I repeat: This is Marshall. Do you require assistance?"

Still nothing. In the background, the PA continued to loop over and over again. *"All cadets and students report to your safety positions. Remain in your safety positions and await further instructions."*

"Guys, this doesn't feel right. I want to hear ideas, and let's start by forgetting about safety positions."

Lorde, of all people, was the first to speak up. "We should evacuate to Gallipoli."

"Negative," Ohno answered. "All points of disembarkation are automatically sealed in an emergency alert."

"What?" Lorde exclaimed. "If this is an emergency, why would the ship prevent us from getting out?"

"This is a battleship," I reminded him. "Usually emergencies aren't about the good guys trying to get out. They're about the bad guys trying to get in."

"Bix, can you get into Sentinel to see what's going on?" Viv asked.

"Not from here. In an emergency alert, the only direct point of access is the bridge."

"Any way to override?"

"Yeah, if you give me two hours."

"Shouldn't we just wait here?" Anatoly asked. "Just stay where we are and—"

A crashing boom and another hard, abrupt shift of the *California*'s attitude interrupted him. We braced ourselves as an odd modulation of static and buzz crackled through the PA's speakers. My skin began to tingle with unwelcome goose bumps.

"Defense grids," I said as the realization hit me.

"We're under attack?" Viv uttered in disbelief. "That can't be."

"There's only one way to know."

By the look on her face, I could tell she knew exactly what I meant.

"This isn't a Blink Drill, JD. If we do what you're suggesting, there aren't going to be any write-ups or disciplinary hearings. It's summary expulsion. We're done."

"I'm the senior-ranking cadet. You'd be following my orders. I'm the only one who's gonna be done."

"Bix, Ohno, Toly . . . ?" Viv called out, seeking their vote.

"Same as always. We go where you go," Ohno answered for all of them.

Viv grudgingly shook her head. "All right. I guess we're doing this."

"What about me?" Lorde asked.

"You can stay here or you can come with us. It's up to you," she replied, looking in my direction more than his. Her message was clear. She wasn't going to tolerate contradiction. There wasn't any time for me to argue with her anyway.

"Well, I'm certainly not staying here by myself."

"So be it," I said. "But until this is over, you follow orders just like everyone else. Got it?"

Julian half-heartedly nodded, clearly reserving an unspoken right of insubordination.

Viv gestured toward the exit. "All right, fall in."

She held me back as everyone else hustled toward the Beta Deck passageway. "You understand the moment we step foot on the bridge, there's no turning back. It's really going to be over for you."

"You know it already is."

CHAPTER 16

VIV

ANOTHER THUNDERCLAP RATTLED THE *CALIFORNIA*, AND WE all struggled to stay on our feet as we ran down the Beta Deck passageway toward the central personnel lift.

None of us was prepared for the chaos that greeted us as we rounded the next corner. Cries and screams echoed from the bulkheads as students scattered in every direction. Like a chain of falling dominoes, emergency harness systems dropped from evenly spaced compartments along the length of the passageway. Even though they had rehearsed their safety position drills dozens of times, many students still struggled to secure themselves into place.

I noticed a slight, redheaded girl fighting against her gear. I barely knew her but remembered her name was Heather. Tears streamed down her face, and she tumbled to the floor as another blow belted the *California*.

JD and Julian stopped when they saw me reach down to help her.

"Go! I'll catch up!" I yelled.

Both conceded, reluctantly dashing ahead.

"Heather, right?" I said, kneeling beside her. She nodded at me, terrified. "It's okay. You got this."

My heart was pounding like a jackhammer, but I didn't want her to see I was probably just as afraid as she was. I tried to think of something to calm myself. The only thing that came to mind was a technique they taught us in boot camp—talk *over* the voice in your head.

Something really bad must be happening . . .

. . . but there are a thousand possible explanations, not all of them that scary.

Seriously, Nixon? You really think this is a systems malfunction? Or some kind of surprise, crazy-realistic drill?

Yes! Why not? It could totally be one of those things.

I wasn't doing a particularly good job of convincing myself, but the thought process itself helped pull me out of my anxiety loop. Which was probably the whole point of the technique to begin with.

Lifting Heather up by the arm, I used my other hand to pull a compact jumper seat out from the wall. "Just like the drills," I said. With a gentle motion, I guided her up into the seat. "Sit." I quickly adjusted the length of her harness straps and then criss-crossed them over her chest. "Strap." Lastly, I fastened each strap into buckles on either side of her lap. "Lock. SSL. All there is to it."

I gently raised her chin so we were face-to-face. "Are you hurt?" I asked.

Her eyes shifted frantically with panic. "What's happening?"

"I don't know," I replied, doing my best to keep it together.

Beta Deck groaned as the *California* yawed hard to port. Heather's anxiety reached a crescendo. "Isn't someone going to do something?" she pleaded.

I rose to my feet, trying to push the chaos all around me into the background. I had to keep focused. "Yes," I assured her. "Everything is going to be okay."

Everything is going to be okay? You don't believe that, do you?

I do. Even if this is something bad, that's what we're trained for. Cadets eat bad for breakfast.

"Cadets eat bad for breakfast"? What kind of boot camp rah-rah nonsense is that?

The same kind of boot camp rah-rah nonsense that got me through the Crucible!

I ran toward the central personnel lift. The other cadets and Julian were one hundred meters away down the straightaway. I sprinted to them. Ohno and Bix were frenetically fiddling with a control panel by the lift door. An error message repeatedly flashed on its display.

Ohno slammed her fist against the panel. "Lifts are down."

"Access shaft," said JD. "We can get to the bridge by access shaft."

"They're gonna be locked down, just like everything else."

"I can manually override an access shaft," Bix interjected. "I think."

"Go," I implored him. "Hurry."

JD urged Bix ahead, and he led us through more chaos, around two corners to Junction 12—where a bulkhead-mounted ladder led up to an access shaft secured by a wheeled hatch.

Not waiting for anyone's order, Bix climbed up and punched a very long, sequenced code into a control panel. A series of beeps sounded, followed by a hiss of compressed air evacuating from around the hatch's pressurized seams. Bix tried to turn the wheel but wasn't strong enough. He hopped down from the ladder. "A little help?"

JD climbed up and managed to open the hatch. "Bix, you first," he said as he descended. "You're going to need to override the lock on the other end. Ohno, you bring up the rear and resecure this hatch. I don't want any panicked students getting into the shaft behind us."

"Aye," she confirmed.

JD followed Bix up through the entry. I climbed up after JD, and Anatoly followed me. Then came Julian and Ohno. I took long, slow breaths in rhythm to the climb. Despite the shaft's insulation, I could still feel punishing concussions landing against the ship's hull. The hits seemed to come at ten-second intervals. My palms drenched with sweat, I tried to time each impact so as to not lose my grip.

Frightened and disoriented, the only thing that kept me climbing was my survival instinct. Despite all the competing thoughts in my head, my gut was telling me one thing loud and clear. If we didn't get to the bridge, we were all going to die.

CHAPTER 17

JD

THE ALARM CONTINUED BLARING THE ENTIRE CLIMB up the access shaft. Upon finally reaching bridge level, Bix typed another long sequence of code, and the hatch above us let out a hiss. Putting all of his weight into turning the wheel, he pushed the hatch upward and climbed out. I hoisted myself out right after him and pulled Viv up behind me. Then the rest of the cadets and Julian spilled out of the shaft one by one.

Bix ran to the keypad by the bridge's rear entrance and entered the next access code. It didn't work.

"Have to override this too," he said, quickly getting to work.

I made eye contact with each of the other cadets. A trick I learned from my father. *Let your officers see the confidence in you that they want for themselves.* It felt as if every cell in my body was boiling in terror, but I tried to put on the bravest face possible. A second later, the door slid open.

We marched onto the bridge and into more chaos. Viv and I stood front and center. Straightening our backs, we brandished the same practiced, confident expressions. The rest of our group lined up in tight formation behind us, also exuding brave, albeit slightly less confident, demeanors. Julian lingered in the back, almost hiding behind us.

"Aft view!" Gentry shouted.

Lewis's fingers trembled as he alternated the settings on his console.

We fixated on the Holoview. It revealed an ominous vessel lurking over Gallipoli. None of us could believe our eyes.

A Kastazi Destroyer.

It bombarded the station with round after round of plasma fire and pulse missiles like a fire-spitting beast. Three hundred meters long and one hundred meters wide, the closest approximation of its shape was a twisted, deformed submarine with sharp, rectangular edges. On either side it had evenly spaced vents protruding along its length, each fifteen meters higher up than the one before it. It appeared as though forged in a place resistant, if not immune, to the laws of physics and counterintuitive to every basic precept of interstellar dynamics—and it was coming at us business end first.

One of the incendiary pulse missiles soared toward the California's docking platform. "Brace for impact!" Gentry yelled out, tightly gripping the arms of the captain's chair.

The missile impacted, its blast rattling the ship hard. The consistent, buzzing hum of the ship's defense grids weakened. We stumbled but quickly regained our footing.

Lewis feverishly checked his readout. "Defense grids critical!"

Gentry's eyes turned glassy. "We're going to die," he softly muttered to himself.

"No!" Lewis screamed back at him. "You've got to do something!"

My adrenaline spiking to dizzying levels, I knew if we didn't break free from Gallipoli, the shearing force of the shock waves would soon tear us apart. I stepped toward Gentry. "We're sitting ducks! You've got to com the captain and get authorization for an emergency launch!"

Gentry swung around to face me. "What do you think you're doing? All of you get out of here! This isn't a drill! We're under attack!"

"Com the captain!" I repeated, ignoring his admonishment.

"Don't you think I've tried that? We've lost all communication with Gallipoli!"

I quickly surveyed the bridge. Station after station, I saw nothing but vacant consoles. "Where is the Emergency Synth support? Why hasn't it been activated?"

"Disabled in the attack!" Gentry shouted back, stabbing his finger into my chest. "You get your people out of here now, cadet!"

I grit my teeth, pushing through a sharp wave of anxiety.

"We're not going anywhere," I replied defiantly. "You can't do this alone."

Turning my back to Gentry, I addressed the cadets. "Take your stations."

Without hesitation, they hustled to obey my command.

Gentry blocked their paths. "You'll do no such thing!"

None of us saw the next salvo hurtling toward us. The bridge shook violently as the *California* absorbed a direct hit.

"Do it!" I hollered at the cadets.

Viv, Anatoly, Ohno, and Bix scattered around Gentry and ran to their stations. Julian asked, "What can I do?"

I pushed Julian toward Weapons. "Go. Pull up targeting."

"What are you doing? Weapons are still offline!" screamed Gentry.

"What? They should've been reenergized hours ago!"

"There was a malfunction with Gallipoli's plasma injectors. We couldn't initiate the infusion sequence. We were trying—"

"Forget it!" I said, cutting him off. "You've got to get us out of the line of fire. Start the launch sequence now!"

The *California*'s acting captain stood impotent and completely disoriented. Another blow rattled the ship. "I can't," he said in a quiet voice.

"Gentry, listen to me. Forget about waiting for authorization. If communication to Gallipoli is cut off, you're never going to get authorization. We'll die waiting for it."

"No, that's not what I mean," he answered, his eyes chaotically darting back and forth in panic. "We're locked into the station's moorings. We can't launch. It's impossible."

The Holoview lit up like a flame as the hostile showered Gallipoli with another epic barrage of plasma fire. An instant later, a huge explosion erupted from the upper quadrant of the station, likely killing almost everyone above Level 15. The aftershock powerfully jolted everything beneath the impact, including the *California*.

The cadets exchanged horrified glances—and then directed them at me. I felt frozen. Fear was beginning to consume me. Just like I was afraid it would if I ever had to face the specter of death again.

"JD!" Viv snapped at me.

I swallowed hard. "All right. There has to be a way . . . I want ideas. Now!"

"Bix, can you override the mooring locks?" Viv asked.

"They're hardwired to Gallipoli. I've got no access."

"Can we just launch? Will the force break us free?" Anatoly asked.

"Tug-of-war between us and Gallipoli, Gallipoli wins," I replied.

"There's a way," Ohno shouted over us. "But you're not gonna like it."

"Tell us."

"I can blow the moorings by overloading them. Just need to reroute enough power to do it."

"And what's the 'not gonna like it' part?"

"I can only get enough power by rerouting energy from one place—"

"Defense grids," said Bix, finishing her sentence.

"Are you crazy?" Gentry hollered. "We'll be completely defenseless!"

"For maybe ten seconds," Ohno replied. "Probably not even that long."

On the Holoview I saw the Destroyer pivoting in our direction. A moment later, a bombardment of phosphorescent projectiles smashed against our grids. With each collision there was a blinding flash, like lightning *after* thunder.

We looked on helplessly as another shower of hostile fire plunged toward the *California*, this time landing with a direct hit somewhere near the lower decks. The ship lurched and wailed as our defense grids labored to keep us together. Sparks flew from overhead and smoke began to pour into the compartment.

"Give me shipwide vitals!" Gentry demanded.

"Aye," replied Lewis.

The dark glass panel lit up with the life signs of every soul on the ship. Last name first, first name last. Except now every name wasn't bordered in green. Some were in yellow. Those were the injured. Far too many were in red. Those were the . . . dead. The readout was too small to see individual names, but the concentrated grouping of the red boxes told a horrific story.

"Gamma Deck. Starboard side. It's gone," said Lewis, swallowing tears. "They're all dead."

If Gentry had been teetering on the edge, Lewis's report finally pushed him over it. "No, no, NO!" he shrieked.

I noticed Anatoly watching Gentry closely. No doubt he had concluded the same thing I had: Gentry was having a breakdown.

"Open a com to the Destroyer," Gentry ordered, standing from his chair.

Lewis looked at him like he was crazy.

"I said open a com!"

"What are you doing?" I screamed at Gentry.

"Surrendering."

"Are you out of your mind? Does it look like they want to take prisoners? Blow the moorings and get us out of here!"

Gentry pushed me. "I will not take orders from a cadet. Stand down!"

I felt a damp sweat pool around my neck as I watched the man controlling our fates breaking down in front of me.

Gentry glared at the hostile. "Is the com open?"

"Aye," Lewis hesitantly confirmed. "Com open."

"This is Acting Captain Evan Gentry of the UAS *California*," he said, raising his chin with a practiced but false dignity. "We unconditionally surrender."

With the *California* still helplessly tethered to Gallipoli, the Destroyer's vents again glowed amber before releasing another, perhaps final, strike of brilliant, jagged energy bolts.

The first impact pushed the *California* nearly fifteen degrees sideways, dangerously straining its tether to Gallipoli's moorings. Another two names on the vitals screen went from yellow to red. As the destruction of Gamma Deck had likely killed all the NCOs, the latest dead were almost certain to be students.

"I repeat: We surrender!" Gentry yelled at no one in particular.

The second impact sent the bridge circuitry into overload. Lewis's station exploded in his face, launching him backward, unconscious. Anatoly rushed to the fallen ensign's aid.

Gentry staggered back, collapsing into the captain's chair.

Ohno yelled, "Defense grids losing integrity fast! There's not going to be enough power left for me to overload the moorings!"

"We've got to act!" Bix shouted, matching her volume.

I looked at Gentry one last time. His eyes were vacant and glassy. He was broken. Gone. I knew we only had one option left.

Then, as if he had been reading my mind, Julian shouted at me, "If you're going to do it, do it now!"

I looked to Viv for reassurance. With a slight nod of her head, she gave me what I needed.

"Mr. Gentry, you are relieved," I asserted, barely believing the words were leaving my mouth.

Gentry didn't move. "No, I am not," he replied, not breaking from his distant stare.

"I will not ask you again. Get out of the chair. You are relieved!"

Gentry jumped up and throttled me. Struggling to breathe, I

never did see Anatoly coming. I only saw his thick forearm wrap under Gentry's neck, pulling him off me.

Regaining my bearings, I watched the consciousness draining from Gentry's eyes. Anatoly wasn't letting go. With a single word, any of us could've stopped it. But we didn't.

A moment later our acting captain crumbled in Anatoly's arms.

Another torrent of plasma fire rocked the *California*, and she shuddered as though she were about to snap in two. Adrenaline flooding my bloodstream, my thought processes seized, replaced by the basic instincts of fight or flight.

The same fear that had consumed Gentry was poised to devour me as well. I felt more than frightened. I felt helpless. Like a runaway train, my distress escalated to the precipice of hysteria and then peaked at the limit of my fortitude's tolerance.

Then, suddenly, like a ghost whispering into my ear, I heard my father's voice.

Do you think I wasn't afraid at Titan Moon? Fear never leaves you, John. Never.

I struggled to my feet, my mind scouring a landscape of painful memories. The shimmering daggers of fire that melted away my skin. My mother's weak mouth trying to form words. Charlie cruelly twisting his blade in my gut. It was as if all that pollution was spiraling down the drain of my psyche, escaping to someplace else where it couldn't touch me.

Fear is like a fever. It consumes you. Burns through your veins. Takes hold of all your faculties.

Viv watched as I steadied myself. My pulse slowed. My head cleared.

But if you can learn to trust yourself in the face of fear, the fever will break. And then you will feel . . .

Everyone waited expectantly as I settled myself into the captain's chair. I sat up straight and rested my elbows on its armrests.

"Bix, intervals between plasma cannon fire?" I called out, my eyes fixed on the Holoview.

"Five, maybe six seconds," he answered.

"Ohno, wait for the next hit and then reroute enough power to blow those moorings. You'll have four seconds to get the grids back up."

"I'll do it in three."

The Holoview lit up with another barrage of plasma fire.

"Brace for impact!" I shouted.

The ship quaked fiercely from the hit. In the corner of my eye, I saw another cluster of names on the vitals display go from green to yellow.

"Now, Ohno! Now!"

"Aye. Rerouting power!"

Instantly, I felt the popping jolt of four small explosions and a sudden, incremental drift of the *California*'s position.

"We're free of the moorings!" Ohno hollered.

"Incoming!" yelled Viv as the Destroyer launched its next salvo at us.

I didn't have time to ask about the grids as the flaming ribbons of plasma soared toward us.

The hostile strike landed, but we remained intact.

"Grids stabilized and holding at twenty percent," Ohno confirmed.

"That last hit pierced our fuel cells. Containment field activated, but we're still venting plasma from the aft turbines!" Bix cried out.

Blindly operating my console, I input a sequence of commands. "Viv, transferring piloting controls to your station. Take us away from Gallipoli."

Viv's console lit up like the Fourth of July, the throttle automatically rising to the level of her dominant hand. "Aye. Go for piloting."

She pushed the throttle forward, and three spheres immediately animated on her screen. One each for roll, pitch, and yaw. With polished, exacting movement, she made adjustments to each.

The engines fired back up, and the *California* pitched hard to starboard, away from the enemy vessel. We all jerked sideways in our seats.

I looked to Ohno. "I need more power, and we can't burn the engines."

"I can reroute everything other than life support and defense grids, then try to alternate the plasma relays to keep us cool," she replied. "I think I can make it work . . . or . . ."

None of us liked it when Ohno used the word *or*.

"Or what?"

"Or we explode."

"Oh no," Bix lamented, inadvertently invoking her well-earned nickname.

Ohno entered the necessary commands to adjust the timing and flow of plasma fed to the ship's nine engines. The *California* enjoyed a sudden, powerful burst of speed, quickly gaining a few thousand meters' distance from Gallipoli. The Destroyer pivoted its trajectory to pursue.

"Bix, prepare to activate the Blink Reactor."

Viv swiveled to face me. "What about Gallipoli?"

"There's nothing we can do to help them. We have to get out of here. Now."

"Our parents . . . All those people . . ."

I wanted to try something, anything, to save them. But I knew I couldn't. "It's too late. We go or we die too."

"The reactor's gone flatline," Bix interrupted. "Must've taken damage in the attack. We can't Blink. It's not an option."

Weaponless and without any means of escape, there was only one thing left to do. Improvise. Just like we were trained.

"Viv, put some more distance between us and that Destroyer," I ordered.

"Aye," she confirmed.

With a hard push of the throttle, the *California* heaved forward, placing us another few thousand meters ahead of the Destroyer's pursuit.

"Ohno, can you give us a shot at HIVE thrusters?"

"I can give us a good burst, but that'll be the end of our grids," she replied.

Lorde, who had been mute almost throughout, finally spoke up. "A good burst of HIVE thrusters?" he squawked. "The Kastazi can match our HIVE thrusters!"

"I know. Stand by at targeting."

"But we've got no weapons!"

"I said stand by!"

I turned my attention to Anatoly, who was still attending to Lewis.

"Leave him," I ordered. "I need you at Navigation."

He reluctantly left the ensign's side and took a seat at Nav.

"HIVE thrusters at your ready," Ohno announced.

"Viv, stand by for HIVE on my mark," I directed her.

"HIVE standing by."

The humming buzz of our grids hissed with interference as a volley of hostile firepower narrowly missed our fuselage.

"Whatever you're doing, please do it faster," Bix urged me.

"Moving as fast as I can," I replied. "Anatoly, plot in some coordinates."

"To where?"

"Not here!"

Anatoly pushed a glowing dot on his console up and across both a longitudinal and a latitudinal axis. "Aye. Plotting in coordinates to Omega Seven One."

The bridge angled slightly as the *California* adjusted direction.

"We still venting plasma from the aft turbines?"

"Yes," Bix replied.

"How long's my tail?"

He looked at me, confused.

"How long is the plasma trail we're venting?"

"Oh, um . . ." he mumbled, settling his mind to making a series of increasingly complex calculations. "We're moving too fast, I can't give you an exact—"

"Guess!"

"I don't know . . . A thousand meters!"

"If you're thinking what I am thinking," Viv said, "we're going to have to time it exactly right."

"We will," I answered. "Bix, bring up weapons inventory."

"We have no weapons!"

"Just do it!"

The weapons cache was indeed empty. Absolutely no pulse torpedoes or plasma armaments of any kind. But the one thing I was expecting to find was still there: the low-yield explosives the *California* carried to dispatch hazardous interstellar flotsam intersecting her path. "We've got sixteen debris charges," Bix reported. "That's it."

"Only need one," I replied. "Link the charges to weapons targeting."

"Linking charges to targeting."

The dim panel in front of Julian powered up and flashed. "Weapons targeting active," he acknowledged.

"On my mark, I want you to fire one debris charge directly into the plasma trail. You copy?"

Lorde gulped as he realized what I was planning to do. "I copy."

Anatoly looked nauseous. He obviously had caught on as well. "I'm not sure this is going to work, guys."

"It might work," said Bix.

"It's going to work," Viv tried to assure them both—and also perhaps herself.

"Well, if it doesn't," Ohno chimed in, her bio-reactive tattoos shifting from multicolored hexagons to sharp red and black blades, "it'll be over quick."

I studied the Holoview and counted down: "And in three, two, one—fire charge!"

"Charge away," Lorde called out as he launched the projectile.

We anxiously watched as the small debris charge, no bigger than a basketball, silently sailed from the *California's* torpedo bay into the middle of the molten morass of vented plasma trailing from our aft turbines.

I raised my hand in the air and clenched my fist. "Detonate charge!"

"Detonating," Lorde called back to me.

The charge detonated on command. Its explosive yield was small, but still sufficient to ignite the plasma trail like a match lighting up a puddle of gasoline. The Destroyer, too close to evade, flew directly into the heart of the conflagration and was sent careening out of control.

At the same time the ignited plasma raced back toward a catastrophic collision course with its source—the *California's* engines. "Engage HIVE now!" I shouted.

Viv punched her throttle hard forward, firing the *California's* powerful High-Intensity Vectoring Engines. The ship instantly burst away at incredible speed, separating it from the plasma trail.

Bix jumped from his seat. "It worked!"

"We need to keep thinking. That ship will be back on top of us again. And soon."

Checking on Lewis, Anatoly bowed his head. The ensign was dead.

An eerie silence washed over the bridge, the magnitude of our circumstances beginning to sink in. The horror of the attack. The almost certain loss of my father and so many others. And what we had done. It was mutiny.

Pain crept into my body as my adrenaline dissipated. Suddenly every emotion was amplified. Every thought difficult to process.

"Casualties?" I called out, gathering myself.

Anatoly scanned shipwide vitals. "All twenty-two hands on Gamma Deck lost. We lost . . . seventeen . . . on Beta Deck."

Beta Deck. *The students.*

Viv slammed her fist against her console.

Bix shook his head in disbelief. "Maybe sensors are down and their biosigs just aren't reading."

"No," Ohno responded, her voice quivering. "There's a massive hull breach by Junction 13. There's no way . . ."

Her throat tightened before she could finish, but we all knew what she was going to say. There was no way anyone in that section could have survived.

Everyone on the bridge moaned.

"Keep it together!" I barked. "Damage report."

Ohno spoke up first. "Defense grids at three percent. Engines two, three, and nine offline. The Blink Reactor's CPU is completely unresponsive."

"Repair estimates?"

"Containment fields are now active on Beta Deck, and atmosphere is already being restored. The grids are easy. I just need to stabilize the power flow. The engines are more complicated. Lieutenant Baber never really let me get my hands dirty down there, but I'll figure it out."

"The Blink Reactor?"

"That's a lot more AI than it is engineering. Not my department."

"Bix?"

"The reactor's CPU is really chewed up."

"Are we talking replace, or repair?"

"Maybe neither. We don't have a replacement, and if your name isn't Sam Fuller, good luck repairing it."

"If anyone else can do it, it's you."

"But . . ."

Anatoly approached the vitals screen to get a closer look. His legs buckled. "Oh no. Please, no," he cried.

We all rushed to see what it was. Anatoly collapsed against the screen, plaintively resting his hand over the name of one of the casualties.

Viv gently peeled his palm away. Beneath it was one name bordered in red. *Diome, Safi.*

"No!" shrieked Viv.

Julian pulled her close. Sobbing, she buried her head in his chest.

Trying to maintain my composure, I scanned the scattered names of the dead to see who else we had lost. My eyes stopped on one name boxed in green, still very much alive. *Smith, Nicholas.*

Bix noticed it as well. "Nick was locked in his quarters without access to a safety position," he said. "He should be dead. Or at least severely injured."

"It's got to be a malfunction," I responded, even though it occurred to me it might not be. There was another possible explanation for the green box around his name.

My first reaction was fear, but that quickly gave way to something more closely resembling relief. If I was right, all my lingering questions about Nick might be answered, and more important, there would be new possibilities for our survival when only moments earlier there had been few. Or none.

Bix noticed my gears turning.

"What is it?" he asked.

I didn't dare say what I was thinking. Not until I was sure.

"Nothing," I answered, "I'm just trying to think of what to do next."

"We're going back," Viv demanded, wiping her tears onto her sleeve. "We're making repairs, and then we're going back to get those bastards!"

I wanted to do the same thing but knew we couldn't. "Viv, the ship's coming apart at the seams. And we have no weapons to fight with. If we—"

"We're cadets. We don't run from a fight."

"It wouldn't be a fight. It would be suicide."

"He's right, Vivien," Julian said, taking her hand in his. "Getting yourself killed is not what Safi would've wanted."

"Guys, who is that?" Ohno interrupted us as a glowing green box on the vitals screen approached a cluster of surviving students. Inside it was a name I didn't recognize. *Bossa, Veen. (P).*

"I have no idea," Bix replied. "And what's the *P*? I've never seen that."

Then the green box abruptly went dark. Not yellow. Not red. It was gone.

"Prisoner," I answered. "It stands for *prisoner.*"

CHAPTER 18

LIKO

MY EYES FLUTTERED OPEN, BUT I WAS still in darkness. The faint sound of an alarm amplified as I started to gain my bearings. I tried to stand, but something was restraining me. I reached up and felt the two heavy straps of the safety harness crossing my chest. My flesh burned beneath where they held me in place.

A series of sparks suddenly strobed through the black.

In the first flash I saw my father standing before me, proudly wearing the leather and cloth brigandine of our Chinese warrior ancestors. And then, just as quickly as he appeared, he vanished along with the sparks' light.

"Are you injured?"

My father's voice eased my escalating panic. I desperately wanted to answer but couldn't bring myself to speak.

"Are you hurt?" he called to me again, his hand reaching out from the black and gently touching my chest.

The second flash burned away my hallucination, revealing someone else. In the glint of light, I knew he didn't belong. After three months in space, I could recognize every face aboard the *California*, and his was not one of them. He had to be an infiltrator.

A third flash quickly followed, drawing my eyes to its source—a severed energy conduit hanging from the ceiling of the Beta Deck passageway. I began to remember. The crushing impacts against the *California*'s hull. The terrified screams of the other students. How I had strapped myself into my safety position just as the ship violently accelerated.

"I'm going to get you out of this thing. Set your feet so you don't fall."

The infiltrator yanked open the buckle at my sternum, releasing the harness's straps. Despite his warning, I fell hard into a pool of syrupy liquid. At first I thought it was coolant from the severed conduit. But it was too warm. And the smell too familiar. It smelled like . . . copper.

"Give me your hand," he said, reaching down.

A fourth flash became a series of cascading bursts as the conduit began to overload. For a few seconds everything around me was illuminated as bright as day. It was impossible to avoid the sight of the carnage.

Two dead students, Jensen and Miller, were still harnessed into their safety positions. A piece of shrapnel had lodged in Jensen's neck, unleashing an arterial effusion that streamed down the length of his body. I couldn't tell what had killed Miller, but his head hung limply against his chest. His blood-soaked canvas knapsack lay just beneath his feet.

A powerful urge to vomit finally pushed some words past my lips.

"No. This can't be happening."

"Stay focused on me," the infiltrator said, pulling me to my feet. I could see his blue eyes in the faint amber glow of the dying conduit. They shifted restlessly, but not without purpose, searching the corridor behind me. "Can you stand?"

"Yes."

Just then I noticed what he was holding. I couldn't see it clearly, but its shape was unmistakable. A standard-issue pulse pistol. *Why would an infiltrator be carrying an Alliance sidearm?*

"It's all right," he said, tweaking the weapon in his grip. "This isn't for you."

"Who are you?"

"Do me a favor and check yourself for holes," he said, ignoring my question.

"I don't think I—"

"Just shut up and do it!" he insisted, waving his pistol.

I ran my shaking hands all across my body. Every fiber of my being ached, but it seemed my only injuries were bruises and abrasions I had sustained from thrashing against my harness.

"We good?"

"Yes, I think so."

"You have no idea what happened, do you?"

"No. We were ordered to our safety positions and then—"

"Forget it," he interrupted me. "The hangar. Epsilon Deck?"

"That's right."

"If I were you, I'd move away from that live conduit and find a safe place to cop a squat until your captain sends an evac team down here. Sound like a plan?"

All I managed was a nod.

"Good."

As the infiltrator sprinted away, another flash lit up a small-arms repository mounted on the bulkhead beside me. Mangled from an explosion, its door dangled from its hinges. Inside were seven pulse pistols. In the next flash of light, I saw its contents more clearly. There were only seven pistols, but eight slots.

CHAPTER 19

JD

THE KASTAZI DESTROYER HAD FALLEN OFF OUR sensors, but Viv continued to push the *California*'s HIVE thrusters to their limit. It was only a matter of time before they came looking for us, so we had to give ourselves as much of a head start as we could.

Bix had broadcast an SOS on every secure Alliance channel, but there was no response from Gallipoli. Our presumption was it had been destroyed in the attack, so the silence came as no surprise. For Viv and me the tragedy went far beyond even its worst practical implications. Our parents were dead. The Kastazi had made us both orphans. As excruciating as it was, we didn't have time to mourn. We had to keep moving.

When there was no response from Gallipoli, we had sent ping signals to every Alliance beacon within sensor range. A ping back would've at least told us that our sector-wide communications channels were open and active, but those beacons had all gone silent as well.

Cut off from communications, it was impossible to know exactly what we were up against. An isolated attack by a rogue Kastazi splinter cell? A full-scale invasion of a new, reconstituted Kastazi fleet?

However dire the reality outside of the *California*, the situation inside her was just as grave. Shipwide vitals showed three more names had gone from yellow to red in the time since we had narrowly escaped the Destroyer's assault.

Still in crisis mode, no one was ready to put their lives back in Gentry's hands, and regardless, we had already gone past the point of no return. To keep him asleep, Anatoly had administered a slight and very precise overdose of Morphalexine into his system. Nanocapsules of the powerful painkiller were standard issue in every bridge's med kit.

Relieved of command by force, Gentry never had the opportunity to sign out of his bridge Command Control Interface. This allowed Bix to reprogram the ship's Command Priority Roster, removing Gentry and replacing him with ourselves. We were in total control of all the ship's systems.

As for the prisoner, Veen Bossa, we figured he had been freed when the attack caused a failure of his cell's containment field. Hiding somewhere in the lower decks, his presence was an immediate threat. One we needed to neutralize quickly.

Staying focused on the critical matters at hand, Ohno toiled underneath her console, trying to restore the Emergency Command Synth to functionality. The rest of us huddled as she worked away.

"Bossa. He had to be in on the attack somehow," said Viv.

"Why would you think that?" asked Julian.

"Because it's too much of a coincidence. Less than twenty-four hours after he's brought in, we're ambushed by the Kastazi? No proximity alerts? No warning of any kind? I'm telling you, that Interceptor was a Trojan horse. There's something in it that jammed Gallipoli's long-range sensors. It was no accident we found that ship. We did exactly what the Kastazi wanted us to do."

"No," Bix interjected. "There's no way the Interceptor would've cleared quarantine if she was broadcasting any kind of jamming signal."

"Then what's your explanation?" Viv challenged.

Bix stared at her, his expression blank. "I don't have one."

"I do," I said, "and it's much worse than a Trojan horse."

Viv looked at me. "What do you mean, worse?"

"It was someone on Gallipoli. One of our own. Or maybe more than just one."

"That makes no sense."

"Think about it. What makes more sense to you—an elaborate Kastazi plan involving an Outer Perimeter pirate and the *New Jersey*'s long-lost Interceptor, or someone aboard Gallipoli flipping a few switches?"

"Too thin, JD. It's not as simple as flipping a few switches. Only someone with command clearance could've gotten into Gallipoli's central computer."

"I'm not done. What about the attack on Gallipoli itself? Did you see a single round of plasma fire targeting anything below Level 10?"

"Gallipoli's gone. The Kastazi destroyed it."

"After they evacuated their conspirators."

"You're reaching, JD."

"Am I? What about the *California*?" I persisted. "They could've destroyed us, but they didn't. They were surgical—gunning for Gamma Deck to take out the crew most likely to put up a fight. The NCOs."

"No," said Julian, shaking his head in disagreement. "They kept going after Gamma Deck. They tried to kill us all."

"Because we tried to escape! The Kastazi weren't counting on that. With the NCOs gone and the *California* locked into Gallipoli, who was going to resist them? A couple of ensigns and a handful of cadets?"

"That doesn't make sense either," Viv argued. "What reason would they have had to spare anyone at all?"

I knew that was the missing piece, and I didn't have an answer for it.

"That's the part I'm still trying to figure out," I conceded.

"There's nothing for you to figure out," Viv retorted, "because that's not what happened."

"We can argue about it later," I said. "Right now we need to concentrate on three things: making sure we're ready when the Destroyer finds us, attending to the ship's casualties, and securing that prisoner. Let's start with priority one—the Kastazi Destroyer. We can't outrun it. We can't fight it. That only leaves the Blink."

"I really don't think I can fix it," said Bix.

"Get down to the reactor and take a closer look. Then you can tell me you can't fix it."

"And what if Bix is right?" asked Viv. "What then?"

"Ohno," I called out, "when you're done under there, report to the Engineering compartment. Do whatever you can to reinforce our grids and push more power to HIVE thrusters."

"Aye," she confirmed, her hands busy beneath her console.

"You said it yourself. We can't outrun them," said Viv, pointing out the futility of relying on grids and thrusters.

"We have to start somewhere. If we can get some more distance, it'll buy us more time. Time to think of something else."

"Casualties?" she asked, moving on.

"Anatoly, report to Medical and prepare to receive the injured. Med Synths are offline, and you're the closest thing we've got to a doctor."

"Okay," he nervously replied. "I mean, aye."

"Viv, you and I will go to Beta Deck to check on the students. See what we can do. Who we can help."

"And what are you going to tell them?" asked Lorde.

"Excuse me?"

"When they ask you what's happened, what are you going to tell them?"

"As little as possible. We can't risk a panic right now."

"So you're going to lie to them? What gives you the right?"

All of the responses that came to mind would've only escalated the situation. Thankfully, Viv answered him before I said something stupid out of frustration. "They'd all be dead if it weren't for us. That's what gives us the right."

"If *you* agree to this tactic, then I accept it," Julian conceded to Viv all too quickly. "But let me come with you. The students are distrustful of cadets. But they do trust me. I'm one of them. I can help you." It seemed obvious he was working an angle, but time was not on our side. We needed to move.

"You good with that, Viv?" I prompted her.

"Yes."

"All right, Lorde. You're with us."

"And what do we do about the prisoner?" asked Anatoly.

"We start by finding a way to track him. Bix, how could he have killed his biosig?"

"It probably wasn't synced into Sentinel yet, so the one we saw had to be coming from a track bracelet the MPs slapped on him in the brig. He could've removed it. Or smashed it. Anything's possible."

A com alert sounded from Auxiliary. Presuming it was a medical emergency, Anatoly rushed to check it.

"What other options do we have to track him?"

"I suppose I could use the biosigs of everyone left on the ship as a control reference and isolate his life signs as the only unknown quantity. But that'll take time, and the Blink Reactor is the priority."

"I've got an easier way," Anatoly called out to us. "I've got him on com."

What?

"Okay," I responded, making no attempt to mask my incredulity. "Transfer wide to bridge."

"Aye," Anatoly confirmed. "Com is live, wide to bridge."

"Who am I talking to?"

A long silence followed.

"I think you know," the voice answered, finally.

"Veen Bossa."

"And you are . . . not the captain."

"No. Not the captain. But I am in command."

"I don't care who's in command as long as you can give me what I want."

"Which is?"

"The *Delphinium*."

We all exchanged confused looks.

"*Delphinium*?"

"My ship, genius," he replied. "Let me into the hangar and I'll be on my way."

"I'll consider it, but first I have a question."

"About the attack? I know nothing."

"Attack?" Viv interjected, obviously trying to corner Bossa in support of her Trojan horse theory. "How do you know we didn't drift into a debris field?"

"I know the difference between debris and plasma fire. And frankly, I don't care if you believe me or not. Just let me into the hangar or I promise you, your bad day is about to get a lot worse."

I swiped my hand underneath my chin, signaling Anatoly to mute the com. "Do we have enough systems functionality to open the hangar and then lock him in?"

"Yeah, we do," Bix answered.

Bossa's voice crackled back through the com. "If you're thinking about locking me into the hangar, that's not a good idea," he sniped. "There'll be consequences."

"He's bluffing. It'll work," said Viv. "He's one guy out of his element. What's he going to do?"

"Get in his ship and blast his way out?" Anatoly posited.

"He doesn't strike me as stupid. He has to know that if he fires his weapons inside the hangar's containment field, he's going to be inside the blast radius."

I signaled Anatoly to open the com back up.

"No tricks, Bossa. I've got too many problems to add you to my list. The hangar's open. Get off my ship."

"Com is closed," Anatoly confirmed.

"Did I make it too easy?" I asked Viv.

"Would you believe it if you were him?" she answered.

I rubbed my temples. "I don't know. Maybe if I was desperate. Let's hope he is."

Ohno emerged from under her console, her bio-reactive tattoos returning to their resting position, a leopard-like pattern of tightly packed semispheric shapes and bright, contrasting colors. "Command Synth is operational and ready for activation."

"Well done. Bring him online so we can get to work."

"Wait a second," said Viv. "You modified his command directive priorities, yes?"

"I did my best," Ohno replied. "Synths aren't my area of expertise, but he should follow our orders now."

"Only one way to find out," I said. "Activate him."

Ohno entered the activation code, and an Emergency Command Holosynth materialized into the captain's chair. He—or *it*—looked every bit the part. Strong, steely eyes, graying at the temples, a thick, formidable physique. Integrated into all of the *California*'s systems, it instantly knew the full extent of the ship's damage as well as all the unauthorized modifications Ohno had made to its program.

"This is a level one emergency situation," he said calmly but sternly. "Why have you modified my command directive priorities?"

Like all other higher-functioning Synths, it was purposefully designed to consider variables, such as my pulse, temperature, and pupil dilation, to help it evaluate me and choose the appropriate tact of engagement.

"This isn't a level one emergency," I answered. "This is something else entirely. Something you were never programmed to deal with."

The Synth thoughtfully considered my words. That too was part of its programming. To evaluate any and all input and respond in a way that would most likely serve its core objective—in this case, restoring its command directive priorities.

Whatever algorithm it used to process my words, it must've determined that challenging my authority was unlikely to achieve its objectives. "I see," it said, taking great care to mimic concern by thoughtfully massaging its chin. "The ship has clearly sustained catastrophic damage and casualties. I can understand why you've resorted to unusual measures to ensure the safety of everyone on board. But now that you've stabilized the situation, the safest course of action would be to restore my command directive priorities."

"I'm sorry, but we're not going to do that. We are going to remain in command, and when we leave the bridge, you're going to pilot the ship and execute all of its basic primary support functions. Any attempt to circumvent or override your new command directive priorities will result in your program being terminated." The decorative captain's insignia on his uniform caught my attention, my eyes lingering on it a moment before continuing. "And should that happen . . . *sir* . . . you will be putting this ship and everyone on it in great danger in violation of your primary command objective. Our safety."

The Synth stared back at me, perhaps searching for some weakness to exploit.

"Very well," it answered before turning away to assume the duties we had constrained it to.

"All right. Let's get started."

With the swipe of a hand across his console, Bix activated the automated alert: *All injured report to Medical or await medical attention. All other hands report to quarters and stand by for further instructions.*

With the alert looping in the background, Anatoly gently lifted Gentry off the floor and tossed his limp body over his shoulder. "Bring him to Medical?"

"No. Take him to his quarters," I answered. "Bix, go with him on your way to the reactor and secure Gentry inside. We need to take him out of play for the time being."

"Aye," they both confirmed.

We followed behind them and entered the lift at the rear of the bridge. Lewis's body lay on the floor where we had rested it a few minutes earlier.

"And Lewis?" Ohno asked in a somber tone.

"We need to decide what to do with all our dead. For now I suppose we can take his body back to his quarters. I don't know what else . . ." A sudden lump in my throat caught me by surprise. "Let's go. We need to go."

As the lift's doors closed, I looked out at the Holoview and saw only emptiness and peace. Nothing about it belied the havoc we all knew would be waiting for us below.

CHAPTER 20

VIV

THE LIFT'S LIGHTS FLICKERED ON AND OFF, struggling to keep its small confines illuminated. I tried to rub Lewis's blood from my hands, but the friction only mixed its wetness with soot, creating a sticky black paste between my fingers.

When the doors finally opened to Beta Deck, we saw the same mess we had just left on Alpha. Red-hued emergency lighting streaming through an abandoned passageway, smashed, overloading energy conduits, and the wreckage of twisted infrastructure.

As soon as we rounded the first corner, I saw a girl's body lying in the middle of the deck. Moving closer, I bent down and delicately brushed her hair aside. I recognized her face but, shamefully, couldn't remember her name. A trickle of blood leaked from her bottom lip. I touched a teardrop suspended in the middle of her cheek. It was still warm.

The same thought kept spinning through my head again and again.

This can't be real.

"Do you know her name?" I asked JD.

"Rachel," he said, an anguished look on his face. "Her name was Rachel."

Of course. *Rachel*. The girl he'd bumped into on the way to the Blink Drill. That was less than twenty-four hours ago. It might as well have been a lifetime.

Julian offered me a hand, pulling me up. But I couldn't take my eyes off Rachel.

"We have to keep going, Vivien," he said.

I jogged ahead in front of them, steadily increasing my pace until I found myself sprinting. Safi. I had to see what had happened to Safi.

Pivoting around the final turn, I crashed into something in the darkness. A busted energy conduit threw off a shower of sparks, illuminating what it was—the bodies of two students still strapped into their safety positions. One was Alistair Jensen, his head bowed low against his chest. I only recognized him by his antique digital watch. The other student, Barrett Miller, had a jagged piece of shrapnel impaled deeply into his neck.

The same thought. Again.

This can't be real.

The conduit threw off a final, dying burst, haloing another student crouched beneath them with his head slumped between his knees. I could just make out the sound of his soft crying.

"Are you injured?" JD asked, rushing to his side.

He didn't answer.

"What's your name?"

Julian knelt down beside him. "It's Liko Chen."

Liko raised his head. "It was an attack, wasn't it?"

A group of students suddenly emerged from the dark recesses of the passageway. There were about fifteen of them, bloodied and hobbled. At the front of their pack was Annalisa Vaccaro.

"Is he right?" she asked. "Were we attacked?"

"Yes."

"By who?"

"We're not sure yet," JD hesitantly replied, clearly not yet prepared to reveal it was the Kastazi.

"I could feel the HIVE thrusters," said Liko. "We're not at Gallipoli anymore."

"We had to evacuate to save the ship."

"The captain?"

"There wasn't time for him to get back to the *California*. It was Gentry. He's in command."

"And what now?" Annalisa questioned him. "Is he going back for the captain? Is the captain coming for us?"

JD hesitated, not sure how to answer. Then he looked at me.

He had to say something. I tried to signal some urgency with a subtle dip of my chin.

"Alliance Command has instructed Gentry to hold the *California*'s position," Julian jumped in. "He's standing by on the bridge, awaiting further orders while the injured are attended to."

His covering for JD took me by surprise. Never in a million years would I have expected that from him. But then again, everything about our circumstances was upside down.

Annalisa bent down and wiped a smudge of blood from above Liko's eyebrow. "Are you okay?"

I found nothing strange about her compassion. I had seen the same thing many times during the war. Fear was the great equalizer, quickly rendering long-standing grudges and prejudices meaningless.

"Yes," Liko replied, rising unsteadily with her help.

I noticed a bulging blood-soaked knapsack lying by his feet and reached down to grab it for him.

"I've got it," he spat, snatching it for himself.

"Are you sure you're not injured?" I asked.

"Just a few bumps. I'm fine," he answered.

"Ms. Vaccaro," I said, addressing her formally to maintain some semblance of our authority, "would you mind escorting Mr. Chen to Medical? I want to make sure he gets looked at."

Annalisa reassuringly rubbed Liko's shoulder. "Yes, I can do that."

A feeling of dread returned as soon as the students gathered themselves and disappeared back into the darkness. Even before the stakes were far less than life and death, the chasm between them and us was deep. We may have lied to them for good reason, but eventually they'd learn the truth. And when they did, it was destined to make things even worse.

JD and Julian followed as I continued ahead through the wreckage. Reaching my quarters, we saw that the entire section had been ripped open to the vacuum of space.

This can't be real!

When I ran closer without thinking, the ship's emergency retention field threw me backward. I reached up and touched the invisible wall. Its electromagnetic surface sent light-blue static charges sparkling through my fingers.

On the other side of the barrier, there was no blood. No body. Just the scattered remnants of the small space I had called home for the past three months. Our bed frames were still there. Mine and Safi's. Bolted to the deck plating, they weren't sucked out in the abyss with everything else. The wall opposite the outer hull was also still intact. As were some of the photos we had affixed to it. Most of them were mine. Safi wasn't much for keepsakes or memories. She was always about the here and now. And the future.

No, no, no! This can't be real!

I squinted at the one photo that was hers. I couldn't see it clearly, but my memory filled in the details. It was a photo of her and me. We had taken it the day before we left Earth. There was so much hope and possibility in our expressions. That's why she'd kept it. It wasn't about memories. It was about the here and now. And the future.

Please, no . . . It can't be.

Julian crouched beside me, gently placing his hand against my back. I wanted him to look at me, but instead he stared straight ahead, focused on some distant point out in the darkness. Was he thinking about Safi or himself?

"We can't let this stand," I said, turning my attention back to the picture.

"We won't," JD replied, most likely placating me. "Take a moment here. I'm going to do one more sweep. Rendezvous on the bridge in ten minutes?"

"Okay."

JD sprinted away, his boots pounding against the deck until their racket slowly faded into silence.

"Are you afraid?" Julian asked me, his gaze out into the stars growing more distant.

No, he wasn't thinking of Safi. Or of me. He was thinking of himself. And he was afraid.

"Yes, Julian," I said. "I'm afraid too."

After that it was like he was invisible, leaving me alone opposite the *California*'s gaping wound and the stars beyond it.

My fingers began to quiver.

The Kastazi have to pay for this.

Somehow we'll make them pay for this.

CHAPTER 21

JD

MY HAND GREW TIRED PUNCHING SEQUENCE AFTER sequence of override codes into the door. Bix had taught me only so many. Another minute longer and I would've found a way to blow it open. Then, just as I was about to give up, the keypad turned from red to green. Its lock disengaged, the door slid open. Nick stood there waiting for me. Just as I expected, he was completely unscathed.

"What are you?"

"By virtue of your question, it would appear that you already know the answer," he replied.

His inexplicably surviving the attack alone could have justified my suspicion, but it was something else that made me almost positive I was right. The strange, ominous feeling he had always given me suddenly felt uncomfortably familiar. Only one other *thing* had made me feel even remotely that way before. And it too could have survived the Kastazi attack without a scratch.

Charlie.

"I need to hear it from you."

Nick watched me intently as I waited for his response, seemingly taking measure of even the slightest twitch of my eye. Just like a Command Synth would. "I'm not anything like the Hybrids the world once knew."

His admission stunned me despite my suspicions. Hybrids of the past—the ones like Charlie—looked human at first glance but upon closer inspection revealed themselves to be anything but. Their eyes were too bright, their skin too pristine, the movement of their limbs too smooth. Nick exhibited none of these all-too-perfect imperfections. Any physical difference between him and a human was imperceptible.

"You don't need to fear me," he added, noticing how anxious I must have looked.

How could I not be afraid? Designed as expendable, emotionless soldiers to fight on behalf of the Alliance, the Hybrids had been hacked by the Kastazi and turned against us. Not just turned, but pushed far beyond their impassive nature into something far more cunning, vicious, and diabolical. Through their corruption they became brutal, heartless killing machines, wreaking terror and suffering wherever deployed.

Thousands of our citizens had perished at their hands by the time Dr. Fuller managed to crash them with a poison-pill virus. By then the Alliance had almost been destroyed from the inside out by the very creations that had been intended to help save it.

"Why should I believe you?"

"Because in me Doctor Fuller has perfected his vision."

Perfected? Nick shouldn't even have existed. After the war the High Command had banned Fuller from developing his Hybrids any further, seizing and storing all of his surviving creations in military black sites. Most Alliance citizens wanted them destroyed once and for all, but it was naïve for them to think our leaders wouldn't try to salvage one of their most valuable weapons.

"No, that's not possible," I replied. "Fuller couldn't access the Hybrids thanks to High Command."

I might've imagined it, but I could have sworn I detected the corners of Nick's mouth bend ever so slightly toward an indignant frown.

"They took the past away from him. *I am the future,*" he admonished. "The doctor's final objective realized."

Suddenly I felt naïve myself. The doctor was known to be many things, but a compliant functionary was not one of them. Would he have simply given up on his Hybrids at the behest of the High Command's bureaucratic wagging finger? "What do you mean? What final objective?"

Nick looked perplexed. As if the answer was all too obvious.

"Life, of course," he said, speaking the words as though he truly believed them. "Life was his final objective."

Artificial intelligence earnestly claiming sentience was nothing new. Command Synths routinely performed the same parlor trick to carry out their core directives. In fact, they were expressly programmed to do so.

Regardless, I had neither the time nor the patience for an existential debate on consciousness. I wanted to know where he had come from. Why he had been made a cadet. How much my father had known.

"The Kastazi attacked Gallipoli," he declared before I could ask a single question.

"How could you possibly know—"

"I possess the capability to recognize energy signatures and other peculiarities of specific technologies. Put more directly, I can feel them."

It took a moment for the enormity of his assertion to sink in. That he could literally feel our enemy's presence.

"And now? Can you feel them now?"

Nick solemnly nodded. "The captain must take evasive action immediately."

"We have no captain. There's only us. We were cut off from Gallipoli. Lost all our NCOs and nineteen students. Lewis was killed. Gentry completely broke down. We took command. If we hadn't, the *California* would've been destroyed along with the station."

"What's our condition?" he queried without emotion, rolling past our mutiny as though it were just another detail.

"Gamma Deck starboard side is gone entirely. Primary engines are compromised. It's a miracle we have any propulsion at all."

"Blink Reactor?"

"Damaged and offline. If Bix can't fix it, you're going to be our only shot at survival."

"What do you mean?"

"There's no time. I'll explain on the way to the bridge."

"I can't come with you," Nick called out as I turned to leave. "The Kastazi energy signature activated my self-termination failsafe."

I thought my head was going to explode.

"Self-termination? You mean . . . kill yourself."

"Doctor Fuller coded the failsafe into my programming. What happened before must never be allowed to happen again."

"Disregard the failsafe. That's an order."

"I can't. Once the termination countdown begins, I cannot override it."

My mind raced. If Fuller's final objective had been to give Nick life, why would he have deprived him of its quintessential essence: the right of self-determination?

"Do you feel pain?" I prodded him.

"In a manner of speaking, but not in the sense that you would understand it."

"Fear?"

"Yes."

"How about anger? Can you feel anger?"

"I can. I do."

"Safi's dead, Nick. They killed her. And they're going to kill the rest of us if you don't help us."

I searched for the slightest hint of emotion, but he gave me nothing.

"You know how she died? She got sucked into space and suffocated out in the vacuum. She suffered, Nick."

Still nothing.

"I know she meant something to you," I said, stepping closer.

Then, finally, a glimmer of something behind his eyes.

"You say you're alive. Prove it."

———————

Standing alone under the lift's strobing lights, I wondered if I had done enough to elicit whatever seeds of self-determination Fuller might have planted in Nick. He had asked to be left alone. To be given a chance to consider everything I said, and also to contemplate the idea I had not yet confided in anyone else. We were running out of time, and we couldn't wait much longer. If his suicidal trigger proved more formidable than his will, I was going to need to find yet another option. One I wasn't sure existed.

In the quiet *whoosh* of the lift's upward trajectory, something else dawned on me. I wasn't afraid anymore. On the contrary, I was exhilarated.

At first the idea that our horrific situation could give me any nourishment felt repugnant, so I tried to reject it. But then I recognized it for what it was. The fever of my fear had broken, and I was finally stepping into the bright light of what I had always been meant to be.

How could that not feel good?

How could that not feel *right*?

The lift stopped with an abrupt jerk and opened to the bridge. Viv was sitting still in the captain's chair with Lorde standing stiffly by her side.

"Report."

Neither Viv nor Lorde budged.

Then I felt the cold barrel of a pulse pistol against my temple.

"The report, sadly, is bad news."

I recognized the voice immediately. Bossa.

"Guns. I don't like 'em," he continued. "But you have really put me in a pickle here."

Holding perfectly still, I pointed my eyes toward his weapon. "Where'd you get that?"

Bossa adjusted the weapon in his hand. "When a ship like this one gets rattled, dangerous things tend to fall out of the cupboards."

"He was hiding on Beta Deck and took us by surprise," Viv explained, slowly getting up with her hands raised high. "Said he'd kill us if we didn't take him to the bridge to disengage the hangar lockdown."

"I told you there'd be consequences if you tried to trick me. And here we are."

When I rotated to face him, the barrel of his pistol slid right between my eyes.

"Your friends got me up to speed," he continued. "Cadets in command of a battleship. A sad state of affairs, to which I am surely just one more needless headache. Let's make this easy. Release my ship from the hangar, for real this time, and I'll be on my way."

"Leaving the *California* right now would be ill-advised."

"Suddenly concerned for my welfare, are you?"

"You don't have any idea what's waiting for you out there."

"Sure I do," Bossa answered. "Doesn't take a genius to put two and two together. The farther the Alliance pushes into the Outer Perimeter, the more likely something new pushes back."

The Frontier, ranging five systems across the expanse from Earth to Xax, Xax to Genuvia, and Genuvia to Aeson, was as far as we had explored. The Outer Perimeter marked everything beyond it, including the unexplored depths of space from which the Kastazi had emerged and to which it then retreated. The Alliance had finally just begun to traverse it.

"No, not something new," I warned him. "The Kastazi."

Bossa smirked as if I had just delivered a bad joke. "If you think I'm going to buy that one—"

"It's them. I promise you," I replied.

"*It was* a Kastazi Destroyer that attacked us," Viv added as she stood and edged closer to us, Lorde sticking right behind her.

Bossa swung the pistol in their direction. "Back off!" Sweat beaded on his brow, and he gripped his pistol more tightly. "Let's move a little faster, shall we?"

"You do understand you can't outrun a Destroyer. Not even with an Interceptor," Viv said.

"I don't run. I'm a lot better at hiding."

The lift opened and out walked Bix, purposefully striding onto the bridge, oblivious to the scene unfolding right in front of him.

"We won't be Blinking. The damage to the CPU is much worse than I . . ." Bix finally noticed what was happening and stopped in his tracks.

Bossa waved his pistol toward Viv and Lorde. "You, little man, over by those two."

Bix raised his hands and hastened over to them.

Just then an alert sounded.

Bossa craned his neck around the bridge. "Go check that proximity alert," he said to Lorde.

The bridge of every Alliance ship had a seemingly endless array of alarms and alerts, each with its own unique ping, blip, or chime. The fact Bossa could so quickly recognize something as specific as a proximity alert was disquietingly without explanation.

"Long-range sweep has reacquired the Destroyer," Lorde reported, swallowing hard before delivering the rest of the message. "It's on a direct intercept course with the *California*."

"How long?" I asked.

"Maybe two hours," he replied. "Give or take."

"The hangar. Now," said Bossa, shaking his pistol to regain my attention.

I nodded to Viv. "Do it."

"That Interceptor has answers," she replied. "Answers I've been waiting on for a very long time."

"I'm sorry, but right now we have to prioritize the safety of this ship."

Viv returned to the captain's chair and reluctantly entered the necessary commands. "Security protocol disengaged."

Bossa lowered his aim ever so slightly.

"Get off the bridge, Bossa. We did what you asked."

The proximity alert still chiming, Bossa hesitated. "If you can't Blink, you better get ready for a fight," he said, offering his unsolicited advice.

"We can't fight," Bix replied. "We have no weapons."

"What do you mean, you have no weapons?"

"Our weapons systems were still being reenergized on Gallipoli. We had to launch before we could get them back online."

"Can't Blink, can't fight? So what are you going to do?" Bossa asked, an edge of agitation in his voice, likely due to our lack of ideas.

"It's not your problem, Bossa," I indignantly replied.

"How many souls are you carrying?"

"What do you care? You've got your ship back. Time for you to go hide."

"How many?" he insisted.

"Sixty-five. Almost all of them students," Viv answered.

"Students?"

"Yes, students. This is an Explorers mission."

"I don't know what an 'Explorers mission' is, and frankly, I don't care. But you can't just lie down and wait to die!"

"That's not our intention, Bossa," I answered. "And if you weren't pointing a gun at our heads, we'd be working on our options."

"Probes," Bossa said matter-of-factly, as though it were the most obvious thing in the world.

"Probes?"

"Yes, sensor probes."

"Of course!" Bix exclaimed.

"Help me out here, Bix," I said.

"All our sensor probes are powered by a small fusion generator. We probably have enough time to modify one to overload."

"You mean turn one into a bomb."

Bix shuffled his feet. He tended to do that when he got excited. "Yes. Exactly. And if we launch it with enough force out of one of our bays . . ."

" . . . you've got yourself a torpedo," said Bossa.

I turned my attention to finding a flaw. Lorde beat me to the most obvious one. "The impact won't be strong enough. The Destroyer's grids will be able to withstand the blast."

"Then you'll just have to drop its grids first," Bossa stated.

"And how are we supposed to do that?"

"Only one way I can see."

Viv and I shared an uncomfortable glance. If Bossa was intimating what we thought he was, it was crazy—bordering on suicidal.

"There's got to be an alternative," I said.

"There isn't," he replied.

"How does that not in and of itself get us all killed?"

"If you reroute enough power to your forward grids, you give yourself a chance. A real one."

Bix knew exactly where we were going. "It could work. It really could."

"And then what? If we take out one ship, how many more will come behind it?" Lorde protested.

Out of time and without any other viable options, we had to try it. "Right now it's all about buying time," I replied. "Bix, get started on those probe modifications."

"Aye," Bix confirmed as he scurried toward the lift.

Bossa blocked his path. "First things first. The little man comes with me."

"No way. That's not the deal."

"There is no deal. You want me to trust you? We tried that once already."

Thrusting his forearm under Bix's neck, Bossa dragged him backward toward the lift.

I instinctively sprang forward.

Bossa squeezed Bix's neck harder. "Don't come any closer," he cautioned, hitting the lift's keypad with his elbow.

Keeping my hands in the air, I stepped closer anyway. "Please don't do this."

The lift's doors opened to darkness, its lighting having failed entirely.

"Now it's your turn to trust me."

I focused on Bossa's trigger finger as he pulled Bix into the lift. Adrenaline rushed through my veins, but there was nowhere for me to channel it. I was absolutely powerless.

Just before the lift closed, something snatched Bossa and pulled him deeper inside. Bix broke free, scrambling to take cover behind the closest console. Then that *something* stepped out into the light.

Nick.

Bossa's legs dangled like a marionette's as Nick held him up by the neck with one hand. Viv and Lorde stared with their mouths agape, while Bix, gaining his bearings, marveled at the same sight.

Bossa raised his pistol to fire, but Nick batted it away just as it discharged. The weapon hurtled across the bridge, coming to rest right at Viv's feet.

Nick waited for Bossa's eyes to roll back into his head and then dropped him to the floor. That's when we all noticed it. The gaping pulse blast right over his heart.

Nick gently dabbed at his wound's muculent red discharge. The sense-memory of the smell of melted flesh made me gag. Viv covered her mouth and gasped. Lorde stood motionless. Bix staggered backward in shock. Only I knew what was about to come next.

The sinewy, frayed edges of Nick's wound were the first to repair themselves. It was as though an invisible seamstress was weaving the fabric of him back together again. Next, all the blood bubbled and evaporated, and the beating muscle of his heart disappeared behind a swiftly reconstituting husk of bone and skin.

Viv snapped up the pistol lying at her feet.

"Shoot him! Shoot him now!" Lorde shouted.

Viv pulled the trigger, but it didn't fire.

The safety must have activated when the pistol hit the floor. Viv tried to disengage it, but her sweaty thumb slipped over the button.

"Don't wait! Shoot!" Bix yelled.

Viv tried again, successfully disengaging the safety. The pistol began powering up, the sound of charging plasma whirring in its chamber.

I stepped in front of her before she could pull the trigger.

"Get out of the way!"

I held my ground. "Don't."

Nick looked into Viv's eyes. "You don't have to do this."

"Do not fire," I admonished her.

"He'll kill us all!"

"He won't."

"He's a Hybrid!"

I rested my hand on the barrel, carefully guiding it downward. "No, Viv. He's something more."

CHAPTER 22

NICHOLAS

I HAD DONE NOTHING TO DESERVE THE fear in their eyes, but all they saw was a monster. Everyone except JD.

"No, Viv," he said. "He's something more."

He'd repeated my words with such conviction. It was as though he actually believed them.

"What does that mean, 'something more'?" said Viv, her voice still quivering.

JD knew I was a Hybrid the moment he walked into my quarters. The question that vexed me was how. Yes, there were things that could have raised suspicions. The implausible explanation for how I had become a cadet. My floating detail. Being locked away inside my quarters every night. But none of them should have been enough to lead him to such a conclusion.

"More than just a Hybrid. Fuller made him an individual. A sentient being with his own—"

"Free will," Bix softly uttered.

"Yes."

"Is that what it told you?" Viv challenged. "That it has free will?"

"He did. And I believe it."

"Why?"

"He has a self-termination protocol. A kill switch that flipped when the Kastazi returned. He clearly found a way to override it. He chose to help us when he shouldn't have had the option."

Her posture still cautious, Viv flipped on the pistol's safety. "Did your father know?"

"He had to. But I don't know anything for sure."

"Well?" Viv demanded, finally addressing me directly. "Tell us. What did the captain know?"

"He knew I was a Hybrid. Beyond that nothing was discussed."

"You never discussed where you came from or why you were on this ship?"

"No. We did not." The answers she wanted, the same answers I wanted for myself, lurked inside a cache of memories too far away for me to reach. I wasn't supposed to remember.

"Nothing I say will make you any less afraid," said JD. "But he's here. And we need him. Tell them, Nick."

"The Blink Reactor's damaged CPU—I can replace it."

"With what?" Viv skeptically replied.

"Myself."

"Yes . . . of course!" Bix exclaimed, his caution ceding to the irresistible excitement of a big idea. "Your CPU is the same!"

"No," I corrected him. "My CPU has been enhanced to Generation Two."

My cadet comrades exchanged suspicious glances.

"There is no Generation Two tech," Ohno challenged me, saying what the rest of them were undoubtedly thinking. "Or at least there shouldn't be."

"Well, there is," JD responded. "And you're looking at it."

"But it's still compatible?" asked Bix, pushing through to the only issue that was relevant.

"The fundamental principles of the two processors are the same," I answered. "But compatibility aside, the interface remains a hypothetical."

"What's your take?" JD asked Bix. "Best guess."

"I don't know," Bix answered, shirking under the weight of JD's impossible question. "There are so many different variables to consider. I need time."

"Do whatever you have to, but get started now."

"Hold on," Julian objected. "You're ready to bet our lives on a hypothetical?"

"There's a Kastazi Destroyer on an intercept course with the *California*. We can't outrun them. We can't outgun them. The Blink Reactor's CPU is damaged beyond repair. What's your alternative, Julian? Because if you've got one, believe me, I'm ready to consider it."

Julian had no response. There was no alternative.

"We have to protect ourselves," Viv demanded, still not satisfied. "Unless and until this idea works, I'm not trusting that thing."

"What do you want to do? Lock him in the brig until Bix can interface him with the reactor?"

"Yes, that's exactly what we should do."

"He's a cadet, and we're shorthanded."

"It's not one of us. Not anymore."

Their needs standing in diametric opposition to their fear, I did the only thing I could to reconcile the two. I proceeded to the Analytics station.

"Stop!" Viv yelled at me.

I considered the possibility she would soon be training her pistol at my head. I worked the console as fast as I could.

JD tried to stop me, but I pushed back.

A chime noted the entry of my first set of the commands. Bix recognized it. "He's in the biosig system!"

He was correct.

I could hear Viv's pistol charging through its power cycle behind me.

"Don't shoot!" JD shouted.

A second chime marked my completion of the full sequence. "I've established a link between the ship's biosignature system and my termination failsafe's trigger," I announced. "I am now, quite literally, at your mercy."

"Check it," Viv ordered Bix.

I stepped aside to allow him a closer look. Resting his elbows on the console, he silently mouthed the calculations he was making in his head. "There's definitely an active link," he reported. "It looks like we could flip his switch at any time."

"That work for you?" JD queried Viv.

Ignoring his question, she kept her eyes on me. "I swear you so much as look at any of us the wrong way, I'm going to flip that switch myself. Are we clear?"

"Yes," I answered, "we're clear."

CHAPTER 23

VIV

THE VOICES OF THE THIRTY-NINE ANXIOUS STUDENTS echoed off the gym's walls, conflating into a low rumble. They sat tightly bunched together in the center of the bleachers opposite the basketball court. Julian and I stood facing them, my tired eyes lingering on their fuzzy reflections in the shiny parquet floor.

I tried to loosen the knot in my stomach by confronting my nerves head-on.

What's the worst that can happen?

How rough could it be?

On a good day the students distrusted us. On a bad day they outright despised us. In what universe could it have gone any way but badly?

"Remind me why we're doing this," I whispered to Julian.

"Because we have to," he quietly answered.

JD walked through the main entrance and joined Julian and me. "What's the word?" I asked.

"Bossa's secured in the brig, Anatoly's prepping Medical, and Ohno will have us at full propulsion in ten."

"Bix?"

"Making headway with Nick on the reactor . . . and the probe modifications."

Kill switch aside, I wasn't happy leaving Bix alone with that thing—particularly when they were poking around inside a probe that was about to become a nuclear bomb.

"We have to trust it's going to work out," said JD, sensing my discomfort.

"Right," I acquiesced, albeit reluctantly. "You ready?"

"As I'll ever be, I guess."

I gave him a reassuring pat on the shoulder despite probably needing just as much reassurance as he did.

"All right, everyone listen up," JD announced, trying to settle the students.

It had the opposite effect. They got even louder—shouting out their questions one on top of another.

"What's going on?"

"Who attacked us?"

"Where is the captain? Why isn't he here?"

Scattered details of our predicament had already filtered down, but—not surprisingly—they had also grown exaggerated.

"Is it true we're losing hull integrity?"

"What about life support?"

"Everyone, please calm down!" JD shouted, trying again.

The students continued to clamor over him, their energy spinning out of control.

"What are we doing about the injured?"

"How many are dead?"

Using his thumb and forefinger, Julian cut through the noise with an ear-splitting whistle. "Listen to him! If you just listen to him, you'll get some answers."

The students' raucousness subsided into a more manageable frequency of restlessness.

After taking a deep breath, JD started with the hardest truth of all. "I can confirm we were attacked by the Kastazi."

A collective gasp rose from the bleachers, followed by another string of questions.

"Are you sure?"

"How can that be true?"

"How bad is it?"

"Is it an invasion?"

"We cannot yet confirm the full extent or scale of the attack," JD responded.

The nervous chatter amplified to a higher intensity.

"As many of you already know, we had to evacuate Gallipoli without the captain or any of the command staff. Ensigns Gentry and Lewis formally assumed command of the *California* at that time."

"But what happened to Gamma Deck?" someone shouted. "Where are the NCOs?"

"Starboard side of Gamma Deck was destroyed in the attack. The damage is contained, but there were no survivors."

Scattered cries erupted, inflaming the students' already dangerously escalating hysteria. The knot in my stomach twisted itself into stabbing, excruciating cramps. It took everything I had to hold it together. To not let the students see even the slightest hint of weakness.

"Where are Gentry and Lewis? Why aren't they telling us this themselves?"

Plaintive, unhinged voices threw more questions at JD, but one was more familiar than the rest. It was Liko, still wearing his blood-stained clothes.

"They're dead too, aren't they?" he asked. "Gentry and Lewis."

Another cramp seized my stomach. I knew this was the moment that could send everything into total pandemonium.

"Lewis was killed," JD answered before hesitating. "Gentry was incapacitated."

"Then who is in command?"

"We are."

The crowd burst into a roar, seemingly ready to spill out of the bleachers and trample us.

"The cadets are in charge? Where is the Alliance? Why haven't they come for us?"

JD held his ground. "We've lost contact with Alliance Command, but we're doing everything we can to—"

"What are you doing, exactly?"

"And why should we trust you?"

"You should trust us because we're the only ones here trained to carry out the critical functions of this ship," I hollered back, the growing pain in my gut adding some venom to my retort. "We're the only option you've got!"

A bunch of students jumped up and shouted back at me, yelling one on top of another. All I could make out was their swearing.

"Enough!" shouted Julian. "If anyone has a legitimate objection, step forward and be heard now. Otherwise we need to let the cadets do what they've been trained to do: protect this ship and keep us all alive."

The bleachers fell quiet as the students craned their necks, waiting for someone to step forward.

"No objection, only a question," Liko said, addressing JD.

"Go ahead."

"What are you not telling us?"

JD had to lie. Considering the tempest that was brewing, the truth could've sent the students into a riot.

"Nothing," JD answered. "Right now we're safe and trying to reestablish contact with the Alliance. If we can just hold out awhile longer, we're confident help will find us."

I watched Julian's face, concerned how he might react to such a vast understatement of the danger we were in. He had a faraway gaze, just like he did staring out the breach in the *California*'s hull.

Where is he?

What is actually going on inside his head?

Taking advantage of a lull, JD moved to bring the assembly to a close. "If any of you have injuries that have not yet been attended to, please report to Medical. Cadet Kuzycz will do his best to assist you. Also, please listen closely for additional announcements from the bridge, and as a precaution, remain vigilant in your awareness of your closest safety positions. We will continue to update you as additional information becomes available. Thank you. You're dismissed."

And with that, the students climbed off the bleachers and made their way to the exits. Liko lingered slightly behind the rest, taking a final opportunity to observe us with a healthy dose of suspicion.

Emptied, the gymnasium felt like a vacant bubble—JD, Julian, and me standing awkwardly alone, each of us waiting for someone else to say something first.

"I was right," said Julian, as though coming to a sudden realization. "They trust me."

"Yes, you were," JD acknowledged. "We couldn't have gotten through that without you. Thank you."

"Anything I can do to help, I stand ready."

"Stay with us. We can use you on the bridge."

I was relieved they were cooperating, but something about their battlefield truce didn't feel quite right.

"We need to get back to work," I prompted JD.

"Give me a minute. I'll be right behind you."

"You all right?"

"Yeah, I'm fine."

"Bridge in five?"

"In three."

I peeked back at JD on my way out. Sensing my presence, he turned and caught me watching him. I self-consciously smiled, which he returned with an uneasy smile of his own. Just then the Command Synth materialized right between us.

"You're needed on the bridge immediately," he reported.

"Why? What's happening?" JD asked.

"The Kastazi Destroyer has accelerated significantly. It will intercept the *California* in approximately twenty-five minutes."

CHAPTER 24

JD

I STARED OUT AT THE DECEPTIVE SERENITY on the Holoview from the captain's chair. All I saw were bright, glistening stars strewn across a wilderness of never-ending quiet. Nothing about it revealed the terror quickly gaining on us from just out of view.

Behind me, Bix and Ohno exited the lift and hustled to their stations. Nick followed behind them but stopped after just a few steps.

"Your orders?" he asked.

"I need you at Nav."

Viv looked on disapprovingly as Nick settled himself into Safi's station. I held up my hand to acknowledge her concern was noted.

With the Destroyer only a few minutes away, I had ordered Bix to cease work on the reactor. He was nowhere close to cracking the interface, so our immediate survival was going to hinge on the jerry-rigged sensor probe.

"All right, Viv," I called out. "Run it."

One by one, she called out for each station's report from Piloting. "Hostile's position?"

"Approximately twelve minutes, thirty-two seconds from intercept," Nick replied.

"Go, no go for full propulsion?"

"Go for full propulsion in T minus thirty seconds," Ohno answered.

"Probe status?"

"Modifications complete. Fusion generator at max critical," Bix reported.

"Armed?"

"Locked and loaded in Torpedo Bay Two. Ready to fire on command," Lorde responded from Weapons.

Viv activated her com. "Medical?"

"Medical prepped and standing by," Anatoly confirmed from Beta Deck.

"Bix, activate shipwide automated Emergency Alert Two."

Bix, eyes wide as saucers, carried out her command. A moment later the alert began to loop throughout the ship: *All hands immediately report to your safety positions. This is not a drill. All hands immediately report to your safety positions. This is not a drill.*

Responding to my kill sign, Bix muted the alert on the bridge.

"You're absolutely sure there's no other way to drop their grids?" Lorde prompted me one last time.

"I wish there was."

"Has anyone ever attempted this before?"

"Yes," Viv answered him. "The UAS *Jaipur* tried it on a Kastazi Destroyer in the Second Battle of Gemini."

"If I remember correctly, the *Jaipur* didn't survive the Battle of Gemini."

"Neither did the Kastazi Destroyer."

"Wonderful."

"The *Jaipur* was a fine ship, but she was no *California*," I noted. "We're going to survive this."

Steeling myself, I heard my father's voice again invade my thoughts, cautioning me against what came *after* fear.

And then you will feel invincible . . . Feeling invincible can be even more dangerous than feeling afraid.

"Ohno, forward grids status?"

"Eighty-five percent and rising."

"Go, no go for full propulsion?"

"Go for full propulsion," she answered, her bio-reactive tattoos peacocking in an effulgent array of bright colors.

"Viv, propulsion on full on my mark."

"Aye, standing by."

"Nick, please change our course to Alpha One Two Seven."

"Aye. Entering course to Alpha One Two Seven."

Nick's console chimed three times in confirmation of the course correction.

"And full propulsion in three, two, one . . . mark!"

Viv gunned the engines, and within seconds every proximity alarm on the bridge rang out. Alpha One Two Seven was a complete course reversal. Instead of running away from the Kastazi, the *California* was hurtling right at them. We were fully committed. There was no turning back.

CHAPTER 25

VIV

A VISCERAL TENSION PERMEATED THE BRIDGE AS I eased the throttle forward.

"Two minutes to visual contact," Nick reported.

"Steady ahead," JD replied, standing behind my station. "Activate targeting."

"Aye. Targeting active," Julian confirmed.

"Forward grids status?"

"Ninety-one percent," Ohno replied.

JD sat and ran some calculations on his console, returning a sharp warning tone. The math must not have added up. Ohno instantly understood its implication.

"Rerouting all available emergency power to grids," she said. "I'll get us to ninety-seven in thirty seconds."

I didn't know which systems she was accessing, but she was definitely pulling from more than just emergency power—likely life support and grav stabilization.

"Visual contact with the Destroyer," announced Nick.

It looked like a tiny speck. Just another star, slightly brighter than the rest.

The knot in my stomach returned, wrenching itself into a new configuration of nervous agony.

This is insane.

This is just absolutely—

"Time to intercept?" JD called out, interrupting my thought spiral.

"Sixty seconds," Nick called back.

The Destroyer drew closer, its brutal features coming into soft focus.

"Grids?"

"Ninety-nine percent," Ohno reported.

"Lock targeting on the Kastazi vessel."

"Targeting locked and standing by," Julian confirmed.

"Emergency harnesses, everyone," JD hollered.

We pulled our emergency harnesses up from behind our seats and strapped them over our shoulders.

The Destroyer launched two flaming daggers of plasma at us.

JD had just enough time to hit the shipwide com. "All hands brace for impact!"

The energy bursts rocked the *California* with a thunderous wallop.

"Grids down to ninety-four percent," Ohno shouted.

Proximity alarms rang out all over the bridge.

"Fifteen seconds!" Nick exclaimed.

"This is it!" JD shouted.

He waited a fraction of an instant before he gave the command we had all been dreading.

"Ramming speed!"

The moment was finally upon us. Stomach acid burned my throat as I slammed the throttle all the way forward to max propulsion.

The Destroyer tried to evade us, but it was too late.

Crash!

I felt my left shoulder dislocate as the bow of the *California* plowed directly into the Kastazi vessel's center mass. With my senses bombarded by the sight of ignited debris and the sound of two irresistible forces colliding, the intense pain in my arm escalated, producing an intense wave of nausea.

An alert sounded from the *California*'s sensors.

"Their grids are down!" Bix shouted.

"Fire probe," JD ordered.

"Aye. Probe away," Julian confirmed.

The harmless-looking sphere sailed right into the ragged, gaping hole we had ripped open in the middle of the Destroyer's belly.

"Detonate probe."

"Detonating."

All we saw was a muted flash. The probe didn't work. It was an absolute dud.

I had never actually allowed myself to believe we would fail. Our plan was going to work. It was going to work *because it had to.*

But it didn't.

And all I was left with was a single, solemn thought.

It's not supposed to end this way.

Unhooking my harness, I turned to face JD. I didn't know why. Perhaps to say goodbye. That's when I saw the reflection in his eyes. A series of cascading explosions. I whirled back around just in time to see the Kastazi predator violently convulsing in a cauldron of its own fire. A few seconds later, it exploded into a billion tiny pieces.

Unable to contain our emotion, we burst into euphoric cheers. JD pulled up shipwide vitals. The board was mostly green. A few yellows. No reds.

JD hit his com. "Medical, report."

There was no reply.

JD leaned in to his console. "Toly, talk to me."

The com crackled to life. "I'm fine. We're fine. Shipwide vitals appear steady and unremarkable."

JD noticed me nursing my shoulder. "Excellent. Sweep the decks for injuries, and then get yourself up here."

"Aye."

Another proximity alarm rang out before we could even consider what to do next.

JD turned to Bix. "Report."

Bix didn't respond. Instead, he just stared ahead, looking stunned.

"Report!"

"Five," Bix answered, eyes still vacant.

"Five?"

"Five more vessels on an intercept course with the *California*."

"Kastazi or Alliance?"

"I can't tell. They're too far away for me to analyze their energy signatures."

JD glanced at Nick. Nick returned a confirming nod.

"What was that?" I asked.

"It's the Kastazi. He can feel them."

He can feel them?

"How long?" I said.

"Approximately two hours," Bix responded.

Two hours. We barely survived one Kastazi ship. There was no way we were going to survive five.

"The reactor. What's it going to take for you to get it operational?"

"More than two hours."

"How much more?" I asked.

"Three. Three and a half hours minimum, presuming I can get it to work at all."

JD stood. "You'll find a way. Take Nick down to the reactor and get started."

Yet another alert sounded.

Now what?

"You've got to be kidding me," Ohno moaned.

"Incoming com on the Alliance secure band. The transmission is corrupted, but there's sufficient data. I can try to throw it up on the Holoview," Nick said.

"Do it."

Beneath a layer of interference stood Captain Marshall. His image brought with it something that had been desperately absent. Hope.

An incredible sense of relief instantly came over me.

Having survived as long as we had was remarkable. Our obliterating a Kastazi Destroyer without weapons was almost inconceivable. In a crisis we had executed on all of our training beyond all reasonable expectation—but we were still just cadets. Whatever new war the Kastazi had brought upon us, it required soldiers, like Captain Marshall and my mother.

Not us.

Not yet.

JD jumped to his feet. "Dad! Where are you? I can hold our position until you're able to—"

But Captain Marshall talked right over him. This wasn't a live com. It was a recording.

"Ensign Gentry, this is a confirmed Priority One Emergency message. By the time you receive it, I and everyone aboard Gallipoli will already be dead."

JD staggered backward, falling down into the captain's chair. Tears spilled from his eyes. I ran to his side, intense pain surging through my arm.

Fighting back my own tears, I wasn't prepared to believe it yet. Maybe Alliance reinforcements had arrived before it was too late. Captain Marshall could have survived. My mother could've made it too.

"A second wave of Kastazi invasion has begun," the recording continued. "Their technology has advanced beyond anything we've ever seen. Earth is under siege and all contact with Alliance High Command has been lost."

They were already taking Earth. It was the worst-case scenario.

"If you are receiving this message, it means you were able to escape the *Destroyer* that attacked Gallipoli. Well done, Gentry."

If only he knew it was us.

"Be advised that our sensors are showing at least five additional Kastazi vessels in the immediate sector. Engaging these hostiles will be futile. If you have not done so already, you are to engage the Blink Reactor to retreat the *California* into the Outer Perimeter. Do not attempt to return to Earth unless and until you receive a confirmed order from Alliance High Command."

The message flickered as everything around Captain Marshall shook, the obvious result of Gallipoli taking yet another hard blow. He steadied himself and concluded his message not as a captain, but as a father.

"Evan, if you are able, please show the rest of this message to our children."

He paused.

"John Douglas. I'm sorry I never got a chance to tell you everything I wanted to. But the most important thing I could tell you, you already know. You're destined for something special, something more."

That was it. No final statement of affection. No goodbye. As soon as he stepped away, someone else took his place. My mother. She was crying. My whole life, I had never seen her cry. Not even during the war.

Whatever strength I had been using to keep myself together completely abandoned me, and my tears finally escaped. In a moment I went from a woman summoning every ounce of her courage to a frightened girl who just wanted her mother.

"Vivien. My sweet Vivien. You have everything you need to survive. Be strong, be a leader, and know that I love you very much. Whatever happens, never give up. Keep fighting no matter what it takes. Find strength in my memory. I'll always be with—"

And then she was gone, replaced with nothing but static.

CHAPTER 26

NICHOLAS

STANDING OPPOSITE THE BLINK REACTOR—AN IMPOSING BLACK monolithic rectangle standing fifteen by seven meters—unnerved me. I wondered how much intention Dr. Fuller had applied to its outward design. He had made no effort to soften its appearance, or to forge an illusion of sameness with its creator, as he had done with Hybrids like me. Perhaps he simply wished there to be no confusion about its purpose—to perfunctorily carry out its functions upon the command of its human masters.

Now that my truth had been revealed, it seemed as though everyone had taken to thinking the same thing of me: that despite my sophisticated design, I was little more than a lifeless contraption, existing only to carry out their will. And worse yet, that the absence of my own free will had left me exposed to corruption by their enemy.

Despite their lack of faith in me, I continued to help them. They likely viewed my cooperation as the preordained acquiescence of an automaton. But it was a choice. *My choice.*

"That hurt?" Bix asked, carefully feeding a needle into my forearm as JD and Viv observed from a few meters away.

His concern I might feel pain gave me some solace. It meant he at least entertained the possibility I existed as something more than the manifestation of their worst fears and presumptions.

"No," I answered. There was never exactly pain. Only feedback.

A long wire lead was attached to the needle, its other end connected to an input port on the reactor. The lights on its control board began blinking chaotically in no particular sequence.

"Those lights—what does that mean?" JD asked.

"It means there's a connection, " Bix replied. "But don't thank me yet. There's still no interface."

Viv massaged the bump in her neck where Anatoly had implanted a pain-killing nanocapsule. "Your finger's on the button, right?" she asked JD.

Obviously placating her, JD held up the command module Bix had loaded my kill trigger onto.

"There will be no need for that," I assured her.

"We'll see," she replied.

"What does it feel like?" Bix asked. Unlike Viv, he no longer appeared afraid, his concern having ceded to his scientific curiosity. "Is anything happening?"

Something was indeed happening. The moment the needle entered my arm, I felt myself join with an inconceivable power, boundless in scope. There was no reference point for it in nature.

The link also merged me with vast volumes of data, and within the data lived a truth I never would have imagined. It was remarkable, yet far too dangerous to reveal. Doing so risked initiating a chain of events that could've threatened our very existence.

"No, nothing yet," I responded. I thought that was a less problematic response than *"You're not ready to know."* "How is your shoulder, Vivien?"

"Do you think you're going to be able to make it work?" she asked Bix, ignoring me.

"I don't know," he admitted. "The problem is his autonomic registry protocols are firewalled and—"

"Layman's terms, Bix. Layman's terms," JD cut in.

Bix stretched his neck, searching for one of his more easily understood metaphors. "All right, basically what I'm doing right now is trying to open a door. Opening the door is step one. The answer to whether or not I can make the interface work is on the other side of that door."

"Fine. How long until you can open the door?"

"Same estimate. Three, three and a half hours. From there I'll know what's possible pretty quickly."

"I need you to do better than that!" JD snapped.

"We're attempting something that has never been done before," Bix groused, his anxious eyes dancing back and forth. "Something that was never intended to be done at all."

JD handed the command module to him. "I'm sorry. I know you're doing the best you can. We'll find a way to get you more time."

"How?" Viv asked.

JD hesitated before responding. Finally, he said, "Come with me."

JD exited with Viv before Bix could utter another word. I watched him stare at the doorway, as if half expecting them to come back. When they didn't, he dropped his head, forlorn by the weight of the responsibility they had left resting solely on his shoulders.

"Everything will be okay," I said.

Bix looked deeply into my eyes. "Why?"

Trying to explain *why* was futile. Without connecting with Fuller's creation himself, there was no way for him to fathom its divine superintendence. You had to touch the possibilities in order to comprehend them.

There was one other thing I could have said, but chose not to. Telling him the reactor never would have existed without him would likely have been both incomprehensible and terrifying. And it also would have conveyed an incomplete understanding of the truth.

So, instead, I simply offered him the honest sentiment of a friend.

"Everything will be okay because I know exactly what you're capable of."

CHAPTER 27

VIV

MY EYES STAYED FOCUSED ON JD'S SHOULDERS as he walked in front of me down the undamaged port side of Gamma Deck. His stride held deliberate purpose. It was clear he knew where he was going and what he needed to do.

"Why won't you just tell me?" I asked a second time.

"Because it's going to be an argument, and we don't have time for one."

Turning the corner toward Junction 5, it finally all came together for me. He was headed for the brig.

I was in no mood for his *my plan, my way, put a complaint in the suggestion box later if you don't like it* routine. Not today of all days.

"Stop!" I demanded.

JD kept walking.

"JD, stop!"

Halting, he turned to face me.

As soon as our eyes connected, I knew. He didn't have to say a word.

"It's the only way," he said, realizing I had put two and two together.

An all-too-familiar frustration rose up in me. As far as he was concerned, any idea I might think of he had already considered and dismissed.

"There's never only one way," I countered. "Think back to our training. Everything we've ever learned is about finding solutions when everyone else thinks there are no solutions left."

JD stared back at me, his jaw pulsating from angrily grinding his teeth.

Finally, he spoke. "How many other solutions were there for escaping Gallipoli? Did you have any ideas other than using a debris charge to ignite our plasma vent? What about dropping the hostile's grids? Did you or anyone else have another solution for that? Because if you did, I would've loved to hear about any plan that didn't involve the *California* T-boning a Kastazi Destroyer."

"That's not fair. We were in a crisis and—"

"We're still in a crisis!" he shouted, cutting me off. "And yes, we're the ones who find solutions when no one else can. But sometimes there's only one solution. One chance. And you have to take it."

I wasn't going to give in. This plan of his was different. It meant he was going to die.

"You've been right twice. That doesn't mean you're going to be right the next time. One day, maybe today, you're going to get it wrong. And this time there's no coming back if you are. Take a breath. Stop and think. What else can we do?"

"There's nothing."

"But we have Bix and Ohno and Toly—"

"All of whom need to keep doing exactly what they're doing right now."

We stood there in silent stalemate as we had done a thousand times before on the heels of arguments of no real consequence. It felt bizarre that the stakes could so suddenly be life and death.

"Do you think there's any part of me that wants it to be this way, Viv?" he said softly while rubbing his tired eyes. "If there was any other option, I'd try it."

My mind raced, trying to find even one alternative. I came up empty.

"You know it, Viv," he said. "It's the only way."

As much as I didn't want to accept it, he was right. But I still couldn't let him do it. Not because I loved him. Because he was the wrong person for the mission.

"Yes," I replied. "But it should be me."

As the words left my mouth, they sounded like they had been spoken by someone else. I meant them, but they carried no emotion. Not even fear. Perhaps the reality of it still felt too far away. Or perhaps it was just too terrifying for me to fully process.

"Absolutely not," he snapped. "It's suicide."

"You're the only one who can make that sacrifice?"

"That's not the point."

"Then what is?"

"Listen to me," he pleaded. "You're needed here."

"And you're not?"

"How can you expect me to let you die?" His voice quivered somewhere just above a whisper.

"What I expect is for you to act like our leader. Isn't that who you're supposed to be, John? Our leader?"

"I can accomplish the mission."

"You may be a good pilot, but you're not me."

Unable to refute fact, he struggled to find another argument.

"That's the only math here, and you know it," I continued. "Who's the best. Who can buy us a few minutes more. Or even a few seconds more. Just a few seconds more could be what it takes to save this ship."

"It's not that simple."

"Isn't it? Answer one question for me, John. If the best pilot on this ship was anyone other than me, would we be having this conversation?"

I watched his eyes dance back and forth as he searched his

brain for a response that could outflank me. "Let me ask you something more important first."

"Go ahead."

He hesitated, obviously struggling to push the question past his lips. "Are you ready to die?"

I didn't have to think about it for even a second. "No," I replied. "I'm not."

He gently brushed the back of his hand across my cheek. His touch sent goose bumps up my arms and uninvited thoughts running through my head. I didn't want any of it. Not now.

"Then let me do this for you. Let me do this for everyone."

"You're not going to back down, are you?"

"No. I'm not."

I thought back to Iso-Rec, the two of us racing through the canyons barely a day earlier, and how, yet again, he had so casually dispensed with the rules in order to win. I also thought of what he had said to me just afterward. That he considered it a lesson. One I still needed to learn.

"If you want me to let you go, then you have to promise me something," I said as convincingly as I could.

"Anything."

"You'll do everything you can to survive."

"I can't promise that. You know what's out there."

"Yes, I know what's out there," I acknowledged. "But we're Alliance cadets. We find solutions when no one else can."

———

We stood opposite cell number six, its downward-beaming lights creating a soft halo around Bossa. He sat upright on his thinly cushioned rack.

"Say what?" he yawped.

"We're taking your ship," JD repeated himself.

Bossa pushed himself up off the slab. "The hell you are."

"We don't have time for a debate. What is the key code to the *Delphinium*'s primary computer?"

Bossa folded his arms.

"The key, Bossa."

He didn't answer.

"You should understand I'm prepared to do whatever is necessary to retrieve that key code from you."

"What are you going to do?" Bossa quipped. "Pull my toenails out?"

"I don't think you're going to last long enough for me to get to your toenails."

"Is that so, cookie?"

Finding something humorous in JD's perplexed reaction, Bossa smirked. "What, they don't call you cadet-types cookies anymore?"

JD returned an angry glare.

"Okay, how about we try this friendly-like? Why do you need my ship? Tell me what's happening."

"That's not your concern."

"No. Go ahead. Tell him," I said.

Bossa had already provided us with one lifesaving solution we hadn't thought of, so it was worth making sure he didn't have another.

"We isolated five Kastazi vessels on the long-range sweep," JD told him with some hesitation. "They're coming for us, and I'm going to hold them off with the *Delphinium*. Buy the *California* enough time to Blink."

Faintly visible electromagnetic filaments stretched toward Bossa's fingertips as he cautiously felt for the limit of the containment field. "A suicide mission?" he scoffed. "You're bluffing."

"Why else would we need the key?"

"Because you're looking for something. You needn't bother. I've already wiped her primary computer."

"We don't care what you're hiding."

"Of course you do. Do you really think I don't know who you are?" he asked, looking in my direction. "Or more relevantly, who she is?"

"No more games. The key."

"Vivien Nixon, daughter of Commander Merritt Nixon."

"Shut up and give me the key."

"And daughter of Lieutenant Commander Damon Nixon of the UAS *New Jersey*."

"What are you doing, Bossa?" I interjected, my fingers beginning to quiver.

JD rested his hand on my shoulder. "Ignore him. He's trying to get in your head."

"No one knows what I do about that ship. I was there. On the *New Jersey*. If you ever want to know what really happened—"

"Lying isn't going to help you," JD interrupted him. "I'll ask once more. The key, or we get down to business."

I poised my hand above the keypad controlling the cell's containment field.

JD looked at me sideways. "What are you doing?"

"Whatever happens, don't try to stop it."

Bossa nervously inched back. "Don't try to stop what?"

Activating the keypad, I pushed the field one meter inward. It hit Bossa's chest and knocked him to the floor.

"Are you out of your mind?" he shouted at me, snapping back to his feet.

"The key code."

"Screw you!"

I hit the keypad again. The field jumped in another meter, knocking him down again.

"Stop it," JD said. "You could kill him."

"I know."

I hit the keypad twice more, doubling the field's inward progression to two meters.

Leaping backward, Bossa narrowly avoided another thunderbolt. "Last chance."

He retreated until his back was up against the wall. "Don't!"

I pushed the field forward until it boxed him in like a coffin, its electromagnetic discharge singeing his skin.

"Stop!" Bossa screamed out in pain.

I kept going, squeezing him against the wall like a vise. Visibly excruciating waves of energy pulsed through his entire body.

"Okay! Okay! I'll give it to you!"

I waited an extra second before releasing the keypad.

"The key, now, or we start again," I said as the field reset to its original position.

On his knees, exhausted, Bossa struggled to stand. "There is no key," he said.

"Excuse me?"

"You heard me. It's disabled."

CHAPTER 28

JD

WE ENTERED THE HANGAR THROUGH THE FORWARD observation deck, a small compartment overlooking the launching floor. More often than not, the FOD was empty, a consequence of there being very little worth observing on an Explorers mission. In our three months in space, its seclusion had offered me a sanctuary. A place to disappear and empty my burdened mind out among the stars. It seemed appropriate it would be the last place I'd ever visit on the *California*.

I leaned against the transparent floor-to-ceiling viewing wall. Some twenty meters below, the *Delphinium* sat waiting. She looked expectant, as if ready for a fight.

I could feel Viv's anxiety.

"It's going to be okay."

"I know," she replied, although she couldn't have possibly believed it.

"I'll do what you asked. I'll do everything I can to survive."

Viv smiled through her sadness and nodded.

The hatch to the launching floor exhaled with a hiss as soon as I punched in its access code. Too overcome with emotion to say goodbye, I turned my back on Viv and prepared to step through.

"Don't. Not yet," she called to me.

Taking my arm, she turned me toward her. Then she leaned in and kissed me. It felt exactly like I always thought it would. Perfect.

"I'm sorry," she said, our lips finally drifting apart.

"You don't need to say—"

Still consumed by the moment, I never saw it coming. I only felt her open-fisted strike against my temple. Stunned, I crumbled down to one knee.

Viv stepped through the hatch and closed it behind her, smashing the control panel on the other side to lock me out.

I jumped to my feet and hit the com. "No!" I screamed at her through the viewing window. "It has to be me!"

"You Blink. No matter what."

"Don't do this!"

"I love you, John."

I pounded on the glass as Viv climbed down a ladder to the launching floor. It didn't matter how hard I pounded or how loudly I screamed—there was nothing I could do to stop her.

———

"What's wrong?" Ohno whispered, noticing my wet eyes as I relieved her from the captain's chair.

"Julian, I need you at Piloting."

"What? Where's Vivien?"

A disembarking alert sounded on the bridge. A moment later the *Delphinium* burst into the center of the Holoview. She was beautiful, a striking image of power and fury. Viv tipped a wing to us, then blasted into overdrive with a magnificent burn of the Interceptor's thrusters.

"Was that—?" Julian squeaked.

"Yes."

"What does she think she's doing?"

"Buying us enough time to survive."

"She's going to try and hold off the Kastazi herself? She'll be killed!"

"I understand that," I answered as calmly as I could. "And so does she."

"And you just let her go anyway?"

I didn't know how to answer him. "Ohno, do you have the other bridge Synths back online?"

"Yes, but—"

"Activating Nav Synth." I pushed on, entering its activation sequence in my control console. A featureless avatar materialized at Safi's station. "Countdown to hostile intercept. Report."

"Forty-two minutes, thirty-six seconds," the Synth responded.

Ohno approached my station and hovered over me, her tattoos spinning angrily into black, tightly wound circles. "We have to stop her."

"We can't."

"Why not?"

My eyes begged for her understanding. "If we don't let her do this, we'll never make it to the Blink."

"We don't even know that Bix can make the interface work!"

"We have to conduct ourselves as if he can. If he can't, we're all dead anyway."

"Why her?" Lorde seethed. "You're the senior-ranking cadet. Why not you?"

"It had to be her," I said, admitting the truth I had tried to ignore. "She's the best pilot on the ship."

"Dear God. You're really letting this happen."

"There's got to be another way," Ohno insisted. "There's always another way."

Every fiber of my being felt the same way she did, but I knew that was all about emotion. Our training was to compartmentalize those feelings, allowing us to focus on the most rational means of survival. I had failed miserably at applying that training too many times already.

"There's not. Not this time."

Resisting a deep swell of sadness, I concentrated on my mission checklist and commed to Medical.

"Report."

Anatoly's image materialized on the Holoview. "All injured in stable condition," he replied, light static slightly obscuring his expression.

"Acknowledged. Stand by." Another few swipes of my console expanded the Holoview horizontally and brought up a split screen with the reactor compartment. Glitching with distortion, it revealed Bix monitoring Nick's connection to the reactor. Its various lights continued to strobe erratically. "Report."

"Slightly ahead of schedule," Bix declared. "I think I might be able to open that door a little sooner than I thought. And then we'll see."

"He's ahead of schedule!" Ohno shouted. "We have to stop her!"

Bix peered back at us, confused. "Stop who?"

"Viv took Bossa's ship to buy you more time."

"She did *what*?" Anatoly bellowed from the other side of the split screen.

Ohno stepped closer to the Holoview. "Tell JD you can get us to the Blink in time, Bix. That she doesn't need to get herself killed."

"I . . . I don't know."

"You'd better know," Ohno snapped at him. "Otherwise she might die for nothing."

I never would have bet the ship's survival on an educated guess, unless that educated guess belonged to Bix. "I need an answer. Are you confident you can get us Blink capable before the Kastazi intercept our position?"

Bix paused a moment.

"If there was ever a time to trust yourself, this would be it, Bix," I said.

He shook his head. The answer was no.

Ohno was unyielding. "Not acceptable, JD. You may be the senior cadet on this bridge, but that doesn't mean you get to make a choice like this by yourself."

"Then who's going to make it?" I asked.

"We all do. Together."

"I was wrong," said Lorde, his voice taking on a detached affectation. "We're thinking with our emotions instead of our heads. There are too many lives at stake. We can't stop her."

"Too many lives, or your life?" Ohno challenged him.

"Anatoly, what's your call?" I asked.

He agonized, struggling to make a decision.

"If you've got an opinion, I need it now."

"We have to stop her," he finally replied.

Two against two. A deadlock.

"Bix, it's up to you then."

I already knew his answer. The pained expression on his face told me everything.

CHAPTER 29

VIV

STANDING ON THE EDGE OF THE DOCK, I stared out across the stillness of
Serenity Lake, its surface gently rippling from a faint breeze. I
inhaled deeply, taking in the menthol fragrance of the surrounding
pine trees. The crisp, cool air expanding into my lungs brought back
powerful sense memories. Freedom. Possibility. The safety of my
dad's arms.

My father had first brought me to this special place. It was the
only spot on Earth that could still make me feel close to him. Like
he was standing right next to me.

I'd last visited during the two weeks' leave we were granted
right before prelaunch.

It felt far longer than that.

"There you are," Safi's voice beckoned from behind me.

My heart skipped a beat and then seemed like it stopped
altogether.

Not believing my eyes, I rushed toward her.

"Safi . . . you're . . ."

She cocked her head slightly sideways.

"I'm . . . ?"

"Alive!" I blurted out.

She laughed as though I was joking.

"I certainly hope so. I definitely feel like I am."

This isn't possible.

I reached out and touched her hand. Her skin was warm and soft.

Am I losing my mind?

"You're real. This is real," I said, tears spilling over my lips just as the words left them.

She noticed my tears, but her expression showed no concern or compassion.

"There's no time for that, Viv."

"You died. Our quarters were ripped open. You were . . ."

An anguished knot in my throat choked off my words.

Safi slipped her hand past mine and squeezed my wrist.

"Come," she said as she guided me back toward the water.

As we approached the dock's edge, she turned and pulled me close.

"Back on the ship. When you saw what happened to me, what did you feel?"

I reached up and touched her face. My unsteady hand shivered against her cheek.

"Horror. I felt horror. And sadness. Terrible sadness."

Her eyes locked on mine with an odd intensity. It wasn't the answer she wanted.

"Beneath that. Go deeper. What else did you feel?"

"Emptiness."

"No!" she scolded me. "There was *something else.*"

I flinched, startled by her sudden bite.

"I'm sorry . . . I don't know what you want me to say."

Safi raised her gaze to something over my shoulder. I couldn't see what she was looking at, but the hair on the back of my neck stood on end.

"Look," she urged with a nod of her head.

I slowly turned.

And then I gasped.

A destroyed *California* sat half-submerged in the lake, its burning fuselage diagonally piercing the water's surface. Juxtaposed to the natural elements, it looked absolutely massive, dwarfing the canopy of the surrounding treescape.

The sight made my stomach turn. But the feeling was not unfamiliar.

Of course. Yes. I understand now.

"It felt like this," I said. "It felt wrong."

I turned back to Safi. A thin ribbon of energy illuminated the air behind her.

"Yes. This is all *very* wrong. But . . ."

The energy ribbon crept outward until it formed the exact shape of the breach in our quarters, and then, with a pop of light, its interior filled with distant stars.

" . . . you can stop this future."

"What if I'm not ready?"

She smiled at me warmly.

"Fate doesn't wait for the ready."

Without warning, an unseen force grabbed Safi, hurtling her up into the breach and out into the stars.

I tried to scream, but the ribbon exploded outward and consumed me before I could. I couldn't see, but I knew everything around me had changed. I was seated. The temperature was warmer, and the air smelled stale and canned. Gone were the sounds of wind and birds, replaced by the ambient hum of an Interceptor's engines.

I kept my eyes closed for a few moments longer, hoping my mind's illusion would return. That it would take me back to Safi and Serenity Lake. But I knew I couldn't go back.

What was that dream? Was it my subconscious trying to tell me something? Or was it just my exhausted brain trying to make sense of all my fear and pain?

When I finally did open my eyes, the stars looked exactly the same as they did before I had drifted off. No matter how fast I traveled, they never got any closer. Always in the distance, they reminded me of the boundless enormity of the universe. And how tiny a space I occupied within it.

Strapped into the pilot's seat, I sat before a dizzying array of controls and displays. With the exception of the yoke, throttle, and weapons systems, most everything else was new to me. But it made no difference. In my hands the *Delphinium* had one purpose: holding off the Kastazi long enough to buy the *California* the few extra minutes she needed.

I closed my eyes and gladly accepted the rush of endorphins spilling into my bloodstream, providing me with some much needed chemical bravery.

The *Delphinium*'s proximity alarm interrupted my temporary adrenal euphoria. I couldn't see anything from the cockpit yet, but the targeting monitor displayed five ships approaching in V formation. A glowing red triangle represented each.

My training told me the three triangles leading the formation were likely Kastazi Strike Fighters. Strike Fighters typically worked together, swarming like stinging wasps—apt, given their three-segmented body shape resembled an insect's head, thorax, and abdomen. The two triangles behind them were almost certainly Kastazi Destroyers. Strikers came first to paralyze. Destroyers came next to kill.

Maybe it was childish, but I just wanted my mother's comfort and protection. I imagined her sitting next to me. My silent copilot.

I don't want to be afraid, Mom. Help me get through this.

And then I saw the tip of the spear. Just as I thought, a Kastazi Strike Fighter led the charge at the top of the formation. Yellow instrument lighting filtered out from its crystalline cockpit.

Another burst of endorphins arrived to help take the edge off.

Any last-minute ideas, Mom? Speak now or forever hold your peace.

For a second I waited, as if actually expecting a response.

Guess not. Okay, here we go.

Another alarm. The lead Strike Fighter was almost in firing distance. I scanned through my internal checklist. *Lower the blast shutters.* Without them, one direct hit to the cockpit would destroy me. My eyes raced across every inch of the control board. There was no obvious activation switch.

The Fighter fired a controlled field plasma burst. Even from thousands of meters away, I could feel its blistering heat on my face.

"Blast shutters! Where are the blast shutters?" I cried.

"Blast shutters activated," the *Delphinium*'s computer politely replied. Startled, I probably would have jumped out of my seat had I not been strapped in. Interceptors weren't supposed to be voice responsive. Must've been a Bossa special.

The heavy silicon carbide shutters slammed closed just before the Kastazi blow landed. The *Delphinium* tolerated the hit unexpectedly well, its exoskeleton not just repelling the energy but also absorbing it.

Okay, Mom. Let's disrupt their formation. That's where you'd start.

I punched my throttle and zoomed directly at the Fighter. It veered away just before the collision, forcing the tightly aligned squadron to scramble in every direction.

All right, I've got them separated. Now I can take the initiative.

I chased the closest Fighter as it bobbed and weaved trying to avoid my targeting systems. Anticipating its maneuvers and matching its trajectory, I locked it in my crosshairs and fired the *Delphinium*'s forward cannons.

Direct hit. Immediately upon the plasma's impact, the Fighter exploded into a thousand flaming pieces, rattling the *Delphinium* with turbulence from the ensuing blast wave.

Whoa!

The *Delphinium*'s weapons shouldn't have been that powerful.

Pushing forward through the Strike Fighter's cloud of decimation, I felt a hard crash against the blast shutters. Blood from the Kastazi pilot suddenly obscured my peripheral viewing aperture. Just hours earlier we had obliterated an entire Destroyer, but this was the first time I felt the full consequence of taking a life. I felt sick to my stomach.

Another alarm. This time it was one of the Strikers locking target on the *Delphinium*. Blind to the predator stalking me from behind, a chill ran down my spine. With no time to think, I instinctually adjusted hard at ninety degrees. The hostile sailed underneath me.

If you couldn't outgun them, what would you do next? You'd concentrate on the objective. You'd do anything you could to buy the California *more time. Stretch this out and make them give chase.*

I reversed course, and the Kastazi immediately pursued. The *Delphinium* shuddered as I gunned her engines to their limit. She wasn't designed to tolerate such sustained acceleration, but as long as the Kastazi were following me farther away from the *California*, I was prepared to fly her apart.

The two remaining Strikers gained speed, closing on my position. Once more they locked on me, but I couldn't make an extreme trajectory adjustment because I was moving too fast.

What now? What options do I have left?

A different alarm sounded. Louder and shriller. *Missile launch.* My monitor revealed four projectiles stalking me. Even if I could've maneuvered, the missiles were already locked and would've adjusted along with me. There was no escaping.

You wouldn't panic. You'd push down the fear. Focus.

Countermeasures. The *Delphinium* had to have countermeasures. Every Interceptor did. I just didn't know where they were or how to activate them.

Voice command?

"Launch countermeasures!"

There was no response, only the creaks of the ship unhinging around me.

I had five seconds to live.

My hand squeezed the throttle like a vise grip.

An abrupt jolt jarred the ship. It was the *Delphinium* carrying out my command, launching four charges. "Countermeasures away," she finally confirmed. My targeting monitor showed three of the Kastazi missiles quickly scuttled by my countermeasures—but the fourth sailed through them unscathed and came right at me.

No. I'm not ready.

Impact. The *Delphinium* tumbled end over end out of control. Thrown free from my harness, I crashed hard against the airlock. I heard a snap before I felt anything. Intense pain soon followed. My arm was broken clean, its fractured bone grotesquely pushing out from under my skin.

Help me. Help me, please. I didn't know it would be like this.

My forward monitor revealed one of the Strikers circling back to come at me head-on. An instant later, it fired its missile. Facing death was so much worse than anything I had ever imagined. Not because of pain, anguish, or fear. Because it felt empty. Barren, vacant, and without meaning.

I waited for the void to fill with something, and it finally did— rage. The same rage I felt kneeling opposite the hull breach where Safi had been sucked out into space.

If you're going to kill me, you're going to have to look me in the eyes!

"Open blast shutters!"

The *Delphinium*'s shutters retracted to reveal the dagger of fire that would end me. Its brilliant corona filled the ship with blinding white light.

Once more, my life was reduced to but a few final seconds. Except this time there would be no reprieve.

Three.

My heart pounded with ferocity I never knew it possessed.

Two.

Its thunderous beating filled my ears, drowning out the calamity of the *Delphinium*'s proximity alarms.

One.

And then the light was eclipsed by something. It was so close and so enormous I couldn't make it out. But I knew.

It was the *California*.

CHAPTER 30

JD

EVERY LAST RIVET ON THE *CALIFORNIA* RATTLED as we absorbed the impact from the missile intended for the *Delphinium*. Our grids were barely strong enough to take it.

"Ohno, now!" I yelled.

"Launching!"

Our two hastily weaponized probes streaked through space toward the attacking Strike Fighters. Each hit its target with a glancing low-yield detonation, just enough to force the Kastazi bogies into a temporary retreat.

I triggered the ship-to-ship com on my console. "Viv, give me your status."

There was no response.

I stared at the *Delphinium* on the Holoview. She was battered and bruised. Half of her fuselage was on fire. Our rescue attempt was putting the ship at far more risk than we ever could have justified. The deafening silence on the com told me it might all have been for nothing.

More alarms sounded as two Kastazi Destroyers adjusted their trajectories to intercept the *California*. The Strikers circled back around as well. Together they assumed an attack formation.

An angry voice crackled through my com. "Get out of here!"

"Viv!" I shouted. She was alive!

"You're going to get everyone killed!" she screamed back at me. "Go now!"

"Too late for that. Stand by."

On the Holoview's split screen, I could see the Blink Reactor's lights strobing in an increasingly synchronic, ordered pattern. Nick was eerily quiet and still.

"Report."

Bix stepped into the frame. "It's as ready as it'll ever be."

My attention snapped back to the Strikers as they broke formation and came diving toward our ship.

"Evasive now!"

"Aye," Lorde answered before yawing the *California* hard right and punching the throttle. His maneuver eluded the Strikers, but they swiftly altered their course toward the vulnerable *Delphinium*.

"Viv, you've got two Strikers coming at your six. You gotta move now!"

"I'm dead in the water." Her voice barely broke through the interference. "Total engine failure."

With the *Delphinium* paralyzed and defenseless, I turned to the unlikely ally standing beside me.

Bossa.

Saving his ship was the only motivation he needed. The pulse pistol Anatoly was holding to the back of his head probably helped too.

Bossa took a small step toward me. "Open the com."

"It's open."

"Listen to me closely, Nixon—"

Viv abruptly cut him off. "*Bossa?*"

He rolled right over her. "If you're sitting in the pilot's nest, you should see a red light underneath the engine temperature gauge. Do you see it?"

There was a pause that seemed to last forever. Perhaps that's how long it took for Viv to accept we weren't going anywhere without her.

"Yeah, I think so. It's blinking."

"Right. Beneath that you should see a switch. It's the antimatter reserve. Flip the switch now."

"Copy."

The Strikers neared firing distance on her. More proximity alarms rang out on the bridge.

"Destroyers at ten thousand meters and closing," Ohno reported.

"Take us out in front of the *Delphinium*," I instructed Lorde.

"Aye," he confirmed.

"Talk to me, cookie," Bossa shouted.

"Nothing! She's got nothing left, Bossa."

"She always saves something," he replied. "On the count of three, I need you to punch the throttle to max."

"It's not going to work!"

"Just do it!"

The Strikers fired four more missiles at the *Delphinium*.

"One."

I could hear alarms blaring inside Viv's cockpit.

"Two."

Bossa leaned forward, resting his weight against my chair.

"Three."

The *Delphinium* shot forward like a bat out of hell, avoiding the missiles at the last possible second.

"That's my girl," Bossa proudly cooed. I wasn't sure if he was referring to Viv or his ship.

"Strikers closing on us," Ohno hollered. "One thousand meters!"

The *California* was too weak to tolerate much more punishment. Just one Kastazi warhead might've been enough to breach whatever was left of our grids. We needed to get Viv back on the ship, and we needed to do it fast.

"Where's the *Delphinium*?" I frantically asked.

"Behind us," Lorde responded. "Four thousand meters at five o'clock."

"Open the hangar doors now!"

Ohno confirmed my order.

"Hangar doors are open, Viv," I said. "Bring her home."

"You're not broadcasting a beacon," she replied. "I can't lock on the *California*'s trajectory."

"Our landing beacon must've been damaged by the last hit we took," Ohno said.

Without the beacon, Viv was on her own. She'd have to pilot the *Delphinium* into the *California* manually, requiring near-impossible precision. It was like landing one speeding bullet on top of another.

I went back to my com as the Strikers circled for another attack. "Where are you, Viv?"

"I'm coming in hot. Hold her steady."

Lorde worked the piloting controls. Viv's life was entirely in his hands. One wrong move, a fraction too far in one direction or another, was all it would take to send her crashing into the *California*'s hull.

I had grown deaf to all the alarms ringing in my ears, but the next siren got my attention with its shrieking intensity. The Holoview switched back to its primary bow view. One of the Destroyers was coming at us head-on.

Lorde glanced over his shoulder at me. The options were clear: hold steady for Viv or evade.

"Hold her steady."

Not inclined to indulge in a game of chicken, the Destroyer veered off—but not before launching a phasing torpedo at us.

I couldn't instruct Lorde to adjust our course. If I did, Viv was dead.

"Reroute all emergency power to forward grids!"

Ohno implemented my order just in time. The torpedo rocked

the *California* somewhere below Alpha Deck, but the additional power from the reroute was just enough to protect us from catastrophic damage.

"Grids at zero," Ohno reported. "One more hit and we're dead!"

I looked down at my console and saw exactly what I was afraid of. The explosion had pushed us out of alignment with the *Delphinium*. Viv was going to crash right into us. She was too close and moving too fast.

"I can do this," Lorde loudly declared. And then once more, softly to himself, "I can do this."

I held my breath as Lorde rolled the *California* slightly starboard.

I checked the Blink Reactor on the other side of the split. Its lights still flashed sequentially, but their pattern had evolved into a beautiful kaleidoscope of fractals. It was as if it was speaking to me. Telling me it was alive. It was ready.

"Bix, stand by for Blink."

"Standing by."

Everyone turned toward the same thing I did. Both Destroyers coming at us at twelve o'clock, each flanked on either side by Strikers.

Viv was so close. I silently counted the time I estimated we had left.

Fifteen seconds.

More alarms blared.

"Kill that noise!"

Someone muted the alerts. The bridge fell silent.

Ten seconds.

I saw the launch combustion of countless missiles and torpedoes from every one of the Kastazi vessels.

Five seconds.

The *California* slightly shuddered, and the *Delphinium* disappeared from my console. I didn't know if she'd made it home safely or smashed fatally into our side.

Two seconds.

The deadly column of missiles and torpedoes sailed toward us through the empty void.

One second. Now or never.

"Commit to Blink!"

VIV

BLINDED INSIDE A CLOUD OF THICK BLACK smoke, I knew I was still alive only because of the burning pain of each labored breath. I struggled to push myself out of the pilot's nest, but my right arm was useless, dangling limply by my side and shooting inconceivable waves of agony up into my shoulder and neck. Totally disoriented, I had no idea which way was up, down, left, or right. I was slowly suffocating, helpless in the dark.

All I had left was the instinct to survive.

Got to get up.

Got to get out.

But there was nothing I could do. I was trapped.

The heat of an electrical fire singed my skin. Perspiration mixed with soot dripped down into my eyes, stinging them like acid. Desperate for oxygen, my heart raced uncontrollably. My spiking blood pressure only intensified my panic and shortened the intervals between stabbing rushes of pain. At least a Kastazi missile would've been quick and painless. Asphyxiating inside the *Delphinium's* smoldering carcass was torture.

A welcome sound suddenly joined the snapping and popping of the ship's melting components. The escape hatch being unlocked from the outside. As it fell open, smoke evacuated the compartment. Hoarding oxygen in desperate heaves, I could see two blurred silhouettes hurrying toward me through the dissipating haze.

The first silhouette to come into focus was Anatoly. I tried to warn him not to touch me but could only cough out the ashy phlegm clogging my throat. I cried out in pain as he lifted me from my seat. The other silhouette stepped forward to help him steady me. Julian.

"Where are you hurt?" Anatoly asked.

"My right arm."

Anatoly and Julian adjusted their grips, trying their best not to aggravate my injury.

"Slow. Slowly," Anatoly urged as they guided me through the hatch.

Gasping for clean air, I stepped down onto the hangar, bright light flooding my senses. JD and Ohno stood waiting. Bossa discontentedly hunched in a corner, cuffed to a heavy supply drum.

JD approached, barely managing to look me in the eye.

"Did we Blink?" I asked through gritted teeth.

Everyone exchanged loaded glances. Something strange was going on.

"Did we Blink?" I repeated.

"We don't know," JD finally answered.

"You don't know?"

"We're not in any danger. Scans show no Kastazi presence in any direction." He glanced down at my injury. "Let's get you to Medical so Toly can get a better look at that arm. Then I'll tell you what I know."

"I'm not going anywhere until someone tells me what is going on!"

JD hesitated and straightened his posture, as if bracing himself in anticipation of my reaction.

"We all lost consciousness the instant we activated the reactor," he said, an abrupt hardening of his expression telegraphing an obvious reluctance. "When we came to, the Kastazi were gone."

"They aren't gone," I replied. "We're gone. We Blinked."

"Yeah, that's what we all thought too. Until we got the Nav Array back online, and it told us we went nowhere."

"What do you mean we went *nowhere*?"

"I mean *nowhere*, as in we're in the same exact spot we were before we Blinked."

"The Array must be—"

"Broken? We checked it three times. It's working perfectly."

"So you're telling me we haven't moved an inch, and the Kastazi just disappeared?"

"That's what I'm telling you."

Distracted, I didn't notice Anatoly sneak up behind me. Before I could stop him, he placed something just above the break in my arm. I dropped to a knee and screamed at the top of my lungs. The pain was unlike anything I'd ever felt before.

"What did you do to me?" I shrieked.

Anatoly knelt beside me and gripped my hand tightly.

I felt like I was going to pass out.

"I attached a prototype Sanative Nanite Disk," he said in a calm, assertive voice. "It's releasing millions of microscopic nanites into your bloodstream."

"It feels like it's killing me!"

"It's not," he replied with the same assured manner. "The nanites are mimicking the path of your immune system's phagocytes, repairing your splintered bone fragments at an accelerated rate."

With my eyes closed he almost sounded like Dr. Green.

"The pain should almost be over," he continued. "Just another few seconds."

Right before my eyes, a thin, perfectly symmetrical scab formed over my wound. And the pain soon subsided, just as he promised.

"Bad magic," said Ohno, eyeing the nanites' handiwork with wonder.

"Good medicine," Anatoly replied, confidently snatching the disk off my arm.

JD tried to help me up, but I waved him off. "What about Earth?" I growled. "Have you been able to raise Alliance Command yet?"

"All secure channels still dead," he answered.

"What about the general bands?"

JD bowed his head. "Yes. Lit up with traffic. All of it Kastazi."

If every signal bouncing off Earth was Kastazi, it could mean only one thing. Total occupation.

My head was spinning.

What really happened when we Blinked?

How could Earth have been overrun so quickly?

Where was the enemy, and when would they come for us next?

"We'll get more answers soon," JD went on. "All that matters right now is that you're here and you're alive."

But I wasn't supposed to be. The only priority should have been giving the *California* the best odds. Nothing else should have mattered.

"Why did you come after me?" I railed at him. "How could you have put so many lives in danger?"

His eyes fell to his feet.

"Answer me!"

"He didn't," Julian interjected, breaking a short but uncomfortable quiet. "The rescue attempt was a collective decision, but not a unanimous one. John was in the minority."

I stood frozen in stunned silence. Leaving me behind would've been the right choice. It was what I had expected him to do. Still, it was almost impossible to believe.

JD really would have let me die.

And then, as painful as it was, I couldn't help but ask the next obvious question.

"Who else was in the minority?"

Out of breath and drenched in sweat, Bix ran into the hangar before anyone could answer.

"Guys, come quick," he begged. "It's Nick. He's dying."

———————

Nick lay supine on the reactor compartment floor, his dilated eyes staring off into nowhere. It was as though he were lost in a dream, his consciousness hopelessly adrift somewhere between our reality and something else. Suddenly he coughed out a long, wheezing breath, and the color in his face drained to a sallow, ghostlike pale.

While Nick's CPU should have been impossible to crash, it seemed the reactor had accomplished just that. And based on the underlying principles of how all Hybrids functioned, each of us understood the nature of the terrible catch-22 unfolding before us. Nick's body could not function without the systemic regulation of his CPU, and his CPU could not survive without the power source his body provided it.

JD turned to Bix. "What can you do?"

"I don't know."

"Think!"

"That's all I've been doing!" Bix nervously chewed on one of his cuticles. "One thing. Maybe. It's a shot in the dark."

"What?"

"He's still interfaced with the reactor. If I reboot the reactor, maybe it'll reboot his CPU. I need sixty seconds to cycle through startup sequence."

"Get started," JD answered. "Anatoly, do whatever you can to keep his body going until the sequence completes."

Anatoly didn't hesitate. Dropping to his knees, he began to push down on Nick's chest in even intervals with all his weight.

One. Two. Three. Four.

Nick's body jostled violently with each heavy compression.

One. Two. Three. Four.

Hours earlier I had been ready to kill Nick myself, yet now the sight of him dying was almost too much to take.

One. Two. Three. Four.

I tried to find some hope in JD's eyes, but he looked on mournfully as though Nick were already dead.

One. Two. Three. Four.

I turned to Julian next. Yet again, he wore the same distant, faraway gaze.

One. Two. Three. Four.

Ohno knelt down by Nick and lowered her head. It looked like she was praying.

One. Two. Three. Four.

Bossa made no attempt to take advantage of our unguarded moment. He stood there silently as Anatoly frantically persisted.

One. Two. Three. Four.

"Hurry, Bix!" JD hollered.

One. Two. Three. Four.

The mechanical hum of the reactor started to escalate. It didn't sound like it was rebooting.

It sounded like something was wrong.

One. Two. Three. Four.

"What's happening, Bix?" Ohno yelled over the noise.

One. Two. Three. Four.

"The reactor. It's melting down! I can't stop it!"

One. Two. Three. Four.

Then came a burst of sparks and a slow-rolling haze of gray smoke.

It was over.

One. Two. Three. Four.

One. Two. Three. Four.

"Stop," I gently urged Anatoly.

One. Two. Three. Four.

"Toly . . ."

I kept trying, but he refused to let go.

One. Two. Three. Four.

One. Two. Three. Four.

One. Two. Three. Four.

Finally, mercifully, JD rested his hand on Anatoly's shoulder. After a few more fruitless compressions, Toly slumped to the floor, exhausted.

As I watched my comrades gather around Nick, it occurred to me what he had showed us in dying. He was no monster. He was our friend.

It shouldn't have cost him his life to prove it.

I wanted to cry for him, but I had nothing left. With my mother, Captain Marshall, Safi, and so many others already lost, my capacity for grief was just about all used up. I was just . . . numb.

Ohno gently closed Nick's eyes.

"You had no idea he was a Hybrid, did you?" Bossa asked us.

"Not until today, no," Bix replied. "Before today, he was something else."

"And what was that?"

"One of us," I professed, coming full circle. "He was one of us."

For a while we stood in silent vigil, none of us wanting to be the first to move on.

"What do we do now?" Julian asked, finally breaking the silence.

"We triage," JD decisively answered. "Priorities are keeping the *California* out of harm's way, confirming the rest of the ship's complement is safe, and figuring out what really happened to us."

I jumped in. "Ohno, Bix, report to the bridge. Ohno, you'll make sure our immediate navigational perimeter is clear of any potential hostile activity. Bix, roll up your sleeves and analyze whatever Blink data Sentinel might have logged. We need you to get us some better answers."

"Aye," they both confirmed.

"Toly, you're with me and JD. We'll check on the students, verify they all came out of the other side of the Blink all right."

"If what happened to us happened to them, they're gonna have a lot of questions," Bix pointed out.

"And we'll answer them. We'll tell them the truth."

"What about me?" Julian inquired. "What am I supposed to do?"

"Your responsibility is Bossa."

"Return him to the brig?"

"No," I corrected. "Start by syncing his vitals into the biosig system. After that, cut off his signature's access to everything but the hangar."

"You've got your ship back, Bossa," added JD. "Until you can repair it or we come up with another way to cut you loose, that's where you live."

Like a mouse being invited out of its trap, Bossa looked at us with equal parts relief and suspicion. Whatever he was thinking, he lodged no protest.

Our immediate plan of action may have been settled on, but Julian's question still rang loudly in my ears. *What do we do now?* Without access to Earth or the support of the Alliance, we were alone, defenseless in the wilderness. The question of what to do next wasn't going to be confined to the next few minutes or even the next few hours. It was a question we'd be asking ourselves again and again until something beyond our control answered it for us once and for all.

What do we do now?

CHAPTER 32

JD

I SAT ALONE, STARING BLANKLY AT MY personal console. In the two weeks since the Blink, I had entered only two of the daily logs that were supposed to be standard emergency procedure when communication with Alliance Command was lost. I had countless excuses for not doing them, but bottom line was I just didn't have the intestinal fortitude to ritualize the litany of each day's new challenges.

The challenges themselves were more than enough for me to handle.

"Cadet Marshall, John Douglas. Explorers Class D27. UAS *California*. Emergency Log entry. Priority One. Record."

"Recording," came the automated voice.

"Per emergency procedure, we have maintained our position and are continuing scans in random intervals, but as of the time of this entry, we have been unable to locate or make contact with any Alliance vessel, outposts, or buoys. For all we know, we might be the only surviving Alliance vessel in the fleet."

I shouldn't have said that. Logs were for recitation of facts, not commentary.

"Correction," I said, rubbing my tired eyes. "Delete the last sentence."

"Last sentence deleted."

"Yesterday we were finally able to restore safe levels of atmosphere between Junctions 11 and 17 on Beta Deck, which allowed us to confirm what we had previously suspected. The bulk of the *California*'s PRM supply was lost during the attack on Gallipoli Station. Accordingly, we have been forced to reduce rations to one PRM per day to extend our remaining supplies for as long as possible. At our current rate of consumption, we will exhaust our food supply in approximately fourteen days. Stricter rationing will be instituted within the next seventy-two hours if we are unable to procure additional supplies or other means of nutrition."

I was already certain the next seventy-two hours would come and go without anything changing. Two weeks had already passed without the slightest indication anyone would be coming to help us.

"We have yet to locate the seven additional pulse pistols that were taken from the damaged small-arms repository at Beta Deck, Junction 4. Subsequent to my prior log entry, Cadet Bixby programmed an energy signature algorithm into Sentinel that should be able to detect the location of any pulse weapon if and when it is charged."

The missing weapons weighed heavily on my mind. Bossa had admitted to procuring his from the same cache, so we immediately searched the *Delphinium* for the others. When our search came up empty, the only remaining explanation was a student. Or, even more concerning, perhaps more than one.

"Searching the students' quarters remains an option, but we've determined it would be ill-advised to take such aggressive action at this time. Persistent challenges to our authority have only been exacerbated by our imposition of stricter rations, and any further encroachment on the students' privacy and personal liberties could quickly escalate what is already a very tenuous situation."

We had asked Lorde to keep us up to speed on the general state of discontent pervading the lower decks. Seemingly sympathetic to our efforts, he agreed. What he reported back to us came as no surprise. The students had always been distrustful of us, but our taking command of the *California* and the unexplainable result of the Blink had sent them over the edge. It had gotten to the point where the students' respect for our authority held by a dangerously thin thread, which in turn made maintaining order on the lower decks a near-constant struggle.

Their resistance to our command was understandable. No matter how justified we were, removing Gentry was mutiny. The only authority we had to act on was a moral one. Other than Lorde, none of the students had seen for themselves how close the ensign had brought us to destruction.

"At this time Ensign Gentry is still confined to his quarters. We will continue to evaluate his psychological condition and fitness for duty."

The students' questions relating to the Blink were equally understandable. Two weeks had passed, and so far Bix's only theory was that Nick's interface had somehow caused a Reverse Blink Field—essentially shielding the *California* from the reactor's disturbance of space-time, and instead transporting the Kastazi vessels to the other side of its rift. The only problem with his theory was that the Blink data logged in Sentinel seemed to indicate the opposite: that the *California* had, in fact, Blinked itself. It was confounding.

Disturbingly, a growing number of students had taken to actually believing we knew more than we were letting on. But considering how our circumstances had worsened their already-toxic feelings about us, nothing about it was particularly surprising.

"Despite our best efforts, we have not yet been able to determine what exactly occurred upon the Blink Reactor's activation. As previously noted, our location was not altered by its operation, and the Kastazi vessels that had been attacking the *California* have not yet returned or reappeared. Our forensic analysis of all available data is ongoing."

I leaned back in my chair and considered what else to report.

"We have granted Veen Bossa limited access to the bridge for the sole purpose of assisting us in partial restoration of the *California's* weapons systems. He believes he can restore functionality to our cannons by seeding them with plasma ore from the *Delphinium.*"

Annoyed at myself, I slapped my palm against the desk.

"Correction. Delete *Delphinium.* Replace with 'Interceptor.'"

I had fallen into the bad habit of referring to his ship by the name he had given it.

"'Delphinium' deleted. Replaced with 'Interceptor.'"

"Cadet Sousa is currently assisting him, and they are making incremental progress."

Bossa's assistance was transparently self-serving. Unable to repair his ship, he had been left in a position where his fortunes were tied to ours. It was in his own best interest to make sure the *California* was not entirely defenseless.

"As we have been unable to restore Medical Synths to functionality, Cadet Kuzycz has been tending to the injured students, all but two of whom have been discharged from Medical. Cadet Kuzycz has included more specific details in his daily medical logs. Cross-reference and attach, Cadet Kuzycz, Anatoly. Explorers Class D27. UAS *California.* Med-Logs."

"Med-Logs, Cadet Kuzycz, Anatoly. Cross-referenced and attached."

For the second time I considered expanding on my report on Nick. In my first log I had simply listed him as one of our casualties, and as a result, my reports remained materially incomplete, particularly as they pertained to the details surrounding the Blink. My dilemma was that Nick had obviously been a carefully guarded secret. Revealing the truth in the context of a log entry still felt too risky. Once again, I decided to exclude any further details.

"Open complement personnel file Cadet Diome, Safi. Explorers Class D27."

"Complement personnel file Cadet Diome, Safi accessed and available for cross-reference and attachment."

"Further review of supplemental sensor logs and damage reports confirm . . ."

My throat pinched hard as a torrent of emotion surged up from my gut. As the interior of Safi's quarters were undamaged, I knew she probably hadn't been killed by the blast that caused the breach. More likely she had been sucked out into the vacuum of space alive, with about ninety seconds of life left to suffer.

We'd been trained for a few seconds of exposure, so I knew all the grim details of what would happen to your body if you were left exposed any longer than that. The gas in your lungs and digestive tract rapidly expanding. The liquid on your eyes and tongue boiling. And then slowly suffocating into oblivion. From the instant I saw the gaping hole in the *California*'s hull, I had tried not to think of any of it, but anytime I heard her name the horror of her fate overwhelmed me.

"Correction. Delete the last sentence."

"Last sentence deleted."

I took in a deep breath, steeling myself to start again and push through.

"Further review of supplemental sensor logs and damage reports confirm our original assessment. The ship's emergency containment field did successfully activate, but Cadet Diome was lost during an activation lag of approximately one point six seconds between breach and containment."

Less than two seconds. That's all it took to claim her life. Had the Kastazi strike landed just a few meters off in any other direction, the lag might have been a fraction less. And that could've been enough to save her.

"As this report is intended as a final conclusion on the nature of Cadet Diome's death as a result of an enemy act of war, I formally submit her service for Alliance Golden Star consideration."

No one was ever supposed to get a medal on an Explorers mission. Certainly not a posthumous one. It was yet another painfully surreal layer of what was an already impossibly surreal situation.

"Cross-reference and attach personnel file. Encode log entry. Hold transmission pending confirmed secure Alliance com link."

"Personnel file Cadet Diome, Safi. Cross-referenced and attached. Log entry encoded. Transmission held pending secure Alliance link."

CHAPTER 33

LIKO

THE PAIN GNAWING AT MY STOMACH WAS becoming an all-too-familiar sensation. At first they allotted us two PRMs a day, and then, just the day before, they reduced our allotment to only one. The rationing had started two weeks earlier, the same day the cadets confirmed "the truth."

They told us the Kastazi had returned in overwhelming forces. That Earth was likely lost. That Captain Marshall and everyone on Gallipoli had perished. They also asked us to trust them, but how could we when we had already been told their initial story was filled with lies?

The *did we or didn't we* matter of the Blink and their so-called Reverse Blink Field theory was one of them. At first I was shocked they expected us to accept such an incredible explanation, but then I remembered something my father had once told me.

"Small lies are difficult to get away with. Big lies, the ones that appear too audacious to have been fabricated, those people will believe."

The cadets' *big lie* contributed to an almost absoluteness of uncertainty, leaving us to exhaust ourselves in a hamster wheel of nearly limitless circularity. We Blinked, but then we didn't. The enemy was all around us, but then they weren't. Its distracting effect was a feat of Machiavellian brilliance, no doubt inspired by all the tricky mind games that had been pounded into their heads during their training.

But if they intended to distract us, what was their ultimate objective? To me, the answer was clear. They were stacking the deck in their favor for an inevitable tipping point. The moment when survival came down to a question of us or them. Thankfully for us, we had someone who was already one step ahead of the cadets, and they had enlisted me to help ensure things never got that far.

While the cadets mostly cloistered themselves on the bridge, I made the rounds on the lower decks, just as I had been instructed. Armed with valuable intelligence, I knew which students to avoid and recruited only those who were inclined to rally behind our cause. In less than two weeks, I had grown our number of allies to eighteen, approximately a third of the ship's surviving students. And I knew I'd have more soon. It was just a matter of time.

Our list of ideas for taking back the *California* was long, but so far only one had been suggested that didn't rely on violence—seizing control of Sentinel. Pulling that off was going to require two things: gaining access to the mainframe compartment and somehow acquiring the Command Codes that were in the cadets' exclusive possession. Our plans to accomplish both had already been set in motion.

My eyes wandered to an old, dog-eared photo of my father resting on my desk. In the context of our new reality, my loyalties were as susceptible to perspective as his once were. Was I the traitor, or were the real traitors the cadets who had forced my hand?

I opened the supply trunk under my desk and prepared to return his photo to the place it had long been hidden. Resting above my books and other keepsakes was Miller's blood-soaked knapsack, bulging with the seven pistols I hoped we'd have no use for. If it came to that, however, we'd be ready. And by then it would be far too late for Cadet Bixby's algorithm to make any difference.

CHAPTER 34

JD

GENTRY SAT AT THE EDGE OF HIS bed, dejectedly peering down at his slippers as his jaw slogged through the chewy, unprocessed PRM I had brought him to eat. His matted hair, puffy eyes, and soiled clothing mingled to paint a disheartening picture. In removing him from command, we had deprived him of something more important than his authority. We had deprived him of his dignity. And it showed.

I wondered if it was time to consider having him confined to Medical instead. At least there he wouldn't be surrounded by so many reminders of the way things *should have been*.

"You don't need to watch me eat," he said without looking up, his neglected vocal cords struggling to push beyond a raspy whisper.

"It's not healthy to be alone in here all day."

Gentry gulped, his throat pushing down another dense lump of PRM. "I don't want your company."

"You've made that clear. Repeatedly."

He finally raised his head. Beneath all their puffiness, his eyes were glassy and empty. "Anything to report?"

"No."

"You still scanning for Alliance signals?"

"Yes. We're not getting anything."

"You've got to scan in random intervals. Scan too long on a single frequency, and the Kastazi will be able to track the *California*."

"I know."

"The Kastazi? Any noise at all?"

"Only from Earth. We haven't found anything that would indicate Kastazi patrols anywhere near us."

"And food?" he asked. "You told me that most of our PRM stock was lost. So what are you doing about finding more food?"

"We've been scanning for Alliance supply buoys. So far, nothing."

During the war the Alliance had dispersed thousands of interstellar supply buoys, each serving as an emergency lifeline for Alliance warships cut off from the primary supply chain. As no one bothered to collect them after the war, many well-stocked buoys were still floating freely through space.

"The buoys' location beacons probably aren't transmitting anymore. They're all too old. You need to scan for the radiation signature coming from their decaying power modules instead."

It was an idea that suddenly seemed obvious, but none of us had thought of it before.

"Noted," I replied.

Gentry took another pained bite of his PRM and looked up at the ceiling as if searching for something to say.

"You shouldn't worry," I said, doing my best to reassure him. "For now, we've got things under control."

Gentry chuckled with a light hint of condescension. "Really? I shouldn't worry? Let me ask you this—how are the students handling our situation?"

I could've accused Gentry of many unflattering things, but being stupid wasn't one of them. Despite being completely sequestered, he had already deduced what was going on outside his quarters.

"Some better than others," I replied.

"How bad is it really? You can tell me."

There was no reason for me to lie to him. "They don't trust us. They think we're hiding something from them."

"Are you?"

"The only thing we're hiding is that we're just as scared as they are."

Gentry nodded, subtly acknowledging my honesty. "And what are they doing? How is their distrust manifesting itself?"

"We've been trying to maintain normal routine, but not everyone is being cooperative. Small things mostly."

"But not all small things."

I hesitated for a moment before answering. I didn't want to admit the worst of it. "No, not all small things."

"Some panic?"

"A few students have struggled to cope, yes."

"Have they acted out?"

"There's been some combativeness in the lower decks."

"Fights?"

"Yes, fights."

"How have you addressed this?"

"The best we can," I replied, my body language no doubt conveying fatigue.

Gentry deliberately placed the remnants of his PRM on its serving tray. "It's time to let me out. I can help you, John."

We'd been through the same discussion multiple times already. He claimed he wouldn't interfere with our authority. That he'd concede—even support—that we should remain in command. Even if he was telling the truth, it was irrelevant. The real danger had nothing to do with his intentions.

If we had let Gentry walk free on the decks, how long would it have been before the students saw him as an alternative—or, worse yet, a savior? Even if he had no designs on retaking command, how quickly would that have changed if the discontented students rallied together and emboldened him with all their support? We had already seen firsthand what it looked like when the *California* was at the mercy of his authority, and there was no way we were going to let that happen again.

"We've covered this. Once we're able to stabilize our situation, we'll reconsider your arrangements."

"What exactly are you hoping to stabilize?" he responded, fighting through his own incredulous laughter. "And don't talk to me about arrangements. This isn't an arrangement. It's imprisonment."

As I had been doing all along, I tried my best to keep my cool with him. "So you keep telling me. And as I keep telling you, there is a good reason for everything we're doing. I don't expect you to see it or believe me, but the fact we're sitting here talking with the *California* still in one piece—that should tell you everything you need to know."

Gentry shook his head at me.

"What?" I indulged him.

"You still don't get it."

One of the reasons I visited Gentry every day was to give him someone to talk to and keep him from losing his mind. If allowing him to berate me did the trick, I was prepared to take it. "I'm listening."

"You relieved me from command and saved the ship. Then you managed to escape an entire Kastazi battalion. From there you made innumerable other decisions that have helped spare us from death and bring us to this moment. And for that I commend you. Bravo, John Douglas. Bravo."

I braced myself for the *but*, and Gentry did not disappoint.

"But you've only succeeded by taking the ultimate risk time and again. We always have the option of risking everything to win. If you're willing to risk everything, you'll often have the advantage. But what happens when you confront an enemy, one much more powerful than you, who is also prepared to risk everything? You haven't met that enemy yet, but it's possible you could soon. And guess what happens then, cadet?"

"What?" I answered curtly.

"That's when you die."

I let the silence linger. Let him feel like he'd exacted his pound of flesh from me. If that satisfaction sustained him for another twenty-four hours alone in his quarters, it was worth it.

"Are you done?" I asked.

"I'm done."

I patted my knees and stood up from the chair opposite his rack. "Well then. Lunch tomorrow? Same time, same place?"

Gentry didn't laugh. He didn't even smile. As I turned and walked away, I felt my body penetrate what felt like a thin wall of static. By this point I was accustomed to the sensation. It was the same feeling every time. From behind me I heard Gentry drop his serving tray to the deck and lunge in my direction. And then, once again, I heard the sound of him being repelled by the containment field Bix had jerry-rigged for me.

I had joined Gentry for lunch for nine consecutive days, and it was the fourth time he had tried this. No matter how many attempts he made, the field would only let my biosig through.

I turned to face him. He lay prone on the floor, looking up at me.

"You see, this is one of the reasons I don't trust you."

Gentry spit at me, his saliva crackling as it intersected the field.

"Go to hell!" he yelled.

"Yeah, you keep telling me that too."

CHAPTER 35

VIV

ALL I COULD SEE OF BOSSA AND Ohno were their legs protruding from an open junction panel beneath the bridge's Weapons console. Their bodies squirming against one another inside the cramped space was quite the visual. They had been working for more than three hours to bypass the plasma cannons' flow regulators, and the escalation in their bickering told me their frustration was starting to bubble over.

"Why can't you just do what I say and put your finger on that conduit?!" I heard Ohno say to Bossa.

"Because I'd like to keep my finger, that's why!" Bossa bit back.

"Do you think I'd actually open the flow valve while your finger was still on it?"

"I have no idea what you're thinking! And besides, what if your hand slips off the valve?"

"I. Don't. Slip."

How would Captain Marshall or my mother have reacted to scrapping on their bridge?

Three months KP duty?

Fifty laps around the track in full tactical gear?

Permanent suspension of Iso-Rec privileges?

Despite my best efforts to resist it, I smiled at that thought.

I shifted my attention to Julian's empty station. For the second day in a row, he was late to report for duty.

"Will you pull up Julian's biosig for me, please?" I called out to Bix.

"Aye," he answered, sweeping his fingers across his console. "Looks like he's on Beta Deck, Junction 6."

"Junction 6? What is he—"

An alert interrupted me.

"Report."

Bix consulted his console. "We've got another one," he said.

We had given the students the liberty to fraternize with friends, attend to their daily routines, and even use their Iso-Rec privileges. But because of scattered instances of disorderly conduct, we had also instituted some loose curfews and other modest limits on their freedom of movement.

"Who is it this time?" I asked.

"Liko Chen."

"Where's he going?"

"He's just outside—" Another alert cut Bix off. "Sorry, sorry. Looks like a biosig malfunction. Liko's in his quarters."

"And Julian?"

"I guess he never left his quarters either," he hesitantly replied. "The malfunction must be showing us an echo from earlier today."

Bix stared down at his console like it was spitting out readings in a foreign language.

"What?" I pressed him.

"I've just never seen a malfunction like this. Ever."

I'd witnessed Bix solve countless seemingly impossible riddles, but if he had a blind spot, it was sometimes missing the simple explanation right in front of his face.

"We've also never had entire decks decimated by a Kastazi Destroyer or Blinked while jerry-rigged to a Gen Two Hybrid," I reminded him. "Sentinel's going to keep having malfunctions. Let's just make sure we stay ahead of them."

"Yeah, sure," he replied, clearly not entirely sold. "But if I just power down Sentinel for fifteen, maybe twenty minutes, I can run a diagnostic and confirm—"

"Negative," I cut him off. "Until we have a better grip on what's out there waiting for us, we're not powering down Sentinel for twenty seconds."

"Aye," he reluctantly confirmed.

"Is Julian sleeping?" I asked, trying to move things along.

"That's definitely the biosig of someone who is out cold," Bix answered, tapping his finger on Julian's readings.

"Unbelievable."

"You want me to wake him up?"

Julian's faltering commitment was quickly becoming a serious concern.

"No. I'll deal with him later."

JD stepped out of the lift. "Where's Lorde?" he asked, annoyed.

"Sleeping," Bix volunteered, perhaps a little too eagerly.

I surrendered the captain's chair to JD. He stood close and spoke in a pointed whisper.

"Please. I need him to be your responsibility."

Looking into JD's eyes, I wondered if we'd ever talk about the moment between us in the hangar. Everything about my energy was inviting him to at least acknowledge it. I waited without responding, hoping he'd fill the space with what I wanted.

Say something, John.

Say anything.

Still, he gave me nothing.

He knows it could compromise our ability to keep the ship safe.

He's worried what the other cadets might think.

The Julian of it all is too much for him.

All the possible explanations running through my head were

perfectly reasonable, but there was only one that felt scary. That he wished it hadn't happened.

We couldn't just leave it untouched. One way or another, we needed to address it. In the midst of everything else, though, I worried the right time would never come.

"I think we could all use a day off from Julian, don't you agree?" I replied, moving on. "Myself included."

I watched JD's stiffness relent as he eased himself into the captain's chair.

As I returned to Piloting, he entered some calculations into his console.

"Whoa!" Bix exclaimed, reacting to a set of new readings. "How did you do that?"

"The reason we haven't found any supply buoys is because their power modules are exhausted. We needed to scan for their decaying radiation signature instead."

"Oh man, of course," Bix replied, all but slapping himself on the forehead. "I'm reading two Grade Alpha supply buoys only about a day's travel from our location!"

We all exchanged hopeful but measured glances. Grade Alpha buoys were stocked with enough PRMs to fill the comestible reserves of two Devastation-class ships. If there were two of them, they could provide enough sustenance to last us over a year.

JD entered another sequence into his console. "I've set a course. Autopilot disengaged. Viv, the *California* is at your ready. Take us there."

"Aye," I confirmed.

Bossa crawled out from under the Weapons console. No matter how much we needed his help, his presence on the bridge was a bitter pill for me to swallow. I hadn't forgotten a word of what he'd said to me in the brig. About my father. And the *New Jersey*. I promised myself he'd answer for that. One way or another. But this was not the time or the place.

Ohno emerged behind him, their sparring continuing uninterrupted.

"That would've gone faster if you hadn't felt the need to second-guess everything I did," Bossa spat as he dusted off his pants.

"It's not called second-guessing when I'm actually correcting your mistakes," Ohno shot back.

"There's your way, and there's my way."

"I'm not exactly sure what *your way* is, but it would have melted the entire plasma canopy."

"All right! Enough!" JD shouted. "Just tell me—are the cannons back online?"

"Sort of," Bossa replied.

"Basically," Ohno added.

JD rubbed his temples. "Brass tacks, please."

"The *California*'s weapons systems weren't designed to accept plasma ore from an Interceptor, so there's a compatibility issue," said Bossa.

"Of course. But what's the upshot?"

"Your automated targeting systems are gonna be impossible to calibrate. You'll need to have a human being at the trigger, not some Synth."

"That we can deal with. Is there anything else?"

"Yeah, there is," Ohno chimed in. "We won't be able to modulate the plasma cannons' yield."

Bossa scratched at his stubbly beard. "You know what that means, right?"

I did.

And considering what the Kastazi had taken from us, I didn't really care.

"It means we can only shoot to kill."

CHAPTER 36

LIKO

TWENTY-SEVEN STUDENTS WAITED EXPECTANTLY OPPOSITE ME IN the mess. Six more than the last time we had gathered. I was struck by how differently they looked at me. Gone was their contemptuousness, and in its place stood their implicit trust just waiting to be claimed. If only it hadn't required the threat of apocalypse.

"We need to get started," I said, breaking through their nervous chatter. "We can only ghost our biosigs for so long."

Having gained their attention, I continued. "We need to discuss some of the more difficult contingencies we might confront."

A soft murmur of voices billowed up from the crowd.

"Nothing has changed. Our priorities remain the same. Chief among them, avoiding violence. What we must prepare ourselves for, however, is the possibility the cadets won't be equally restrained in their response. If they resort to violence, we must stand ready to respond in kind."

"And what if it comes to that?" Annalisa called out. In the time since the attack, she had become one of my closest confidants and allies. She already knew the answer to her question, but we had agreed that a small measure of theater might be helpful in moving us along. "How do we respond in kind?"

My eyes found Cooper Lynch. After being reminded that the tall, often cantankerous student from Perth had played a big part in instigating the infamous Camp Penbrook brawl with the cadets, I had made him one of my first recruits. It was suggested to me that his "authority issues" made him more inclined to join our effort to unseat the cadets.

Cooper snapped a bedsheet off one of the dining tables, revealing the seven pulse pistols.

Jagdish Patel, who'd had two of his ribs unceremoniously cracked by Vivien Nixon in the same Penbrook incident, reached for one of them. Cooper grabbed his wrist. "Careful."

"We can't activate them unless and until it's necessary," I clarified. "The cadets have programmed an algorithm that can track the weapons as soon as they're charged."

Without our access to intel on what the cadets were up to, we never would have known about the algorithm. And then we would have walked right into their trap.

"I know what you're all thinking, but you have to understand who it is we're dealing with. John Marshall, Vivien Nixon, Iara Souza, Anatoly Kuzycz, Roger Bixby. We've grown too accustomed to thinking of them as unseasoned cadets. Make no mistake— they're already soldiers. That, above all else, is what they've been trained to be. And when you back a soldier into a corner, they don't give up easily or surrender. They fight. That's why we need to be ready for anything, even the worst-case scenario."

I scanned the faces of the crowd, trying to gauge their reactions. We had done everything possible to protect ourselves, approaching only those we had been given reason to trust or had been vouched for—but the potential for leaks persisted. Mindful that a single person could have exposed us, I remained vigilant.

"Anyone who objects to the defensive use of these weapons, please step forward and be heard."

If someone had stepped forward, it wouldn't have changed our plans. It only would've served to identify our weakest links and provided us with an occasion to deal with them. I had already been advised on how to safely sequester any such liabilities until after the *California* was under our control.

"Anyone?"

I waited, but no one accepted my invitation.

"A question," said Dominique Parry, one of Annalisa's vouches.

"Go ahead."

"Is it true? Did you really find a way to get Gentry out?"

"Yes," I acknowledged. "I did."

By necessity I was one of our movement's most visible lieutenants, but Gentry was our true leader. Using the HAT's backdoor channel to circumvent the cadets' watchful eyes, I first contacted him shortly after the attack on Gallipoli. He confirmed my suspicions: that the cadets had seized control of the ship without justification or authority, putting our lives in even more danger than they already were. After that there was never any other choice but to try to help him regain his command. Not only had he been guiding my recruitment efforts with his privileged knowledge of student behavioral profiles, he was also the architect of the endgame that would remove the cadets from command—seizing control of the ship by way of Sentinel.

But realizing our endgame still required surmounting two formidable obstacles, the first being access to the mainframe compartment, which required a facial-recognition ID and transdermal palm scan. The two security protocols were hardwired at the point of entry and nearly impossible to hack. Such impenetrability did, however, bring with it one very fortuitous silver lining. The cadets were as powerless as we were to make any modifications to the compartment's authorization roster. Whereas Gentry's facial ID and palm scan were still valid and active.

Consequently, and rather frustratingly, the challenge was not so much the compartment's security protocols as it was Gentry's confinement. We had been struggling to find a way to extricate him from his quarters, and finally, I thought I had stumbled upon the answer.

"We can try to ghost Gentry's biosig readings the same way we've been ghosting ours," I explained. "All the security protocols locking him in are keyed to his pattern. If we ghost his readings somewhere else—the bridge, for instance—Sentinel should interpret the readings as a malfunction and reset all the protocols. And if it resets the protocols—"

"It resets the lock," Cooper said, admiring the simplicity of my solution. "His door opens."

"Exactly."

Presuming my biosig hack worked, the second obstacle—getting our hands on Sentinel's Command Codes—still required its own solution. There was only one person capable of giving it to us. The same person Gentry had suggested as our first recruit. Julian Lorde.

"How close are you to getting the codes?" I asked him, my tone no doubt betraying some frustration with his lack of progress.

"The opportunity has yet to present itself," answered Lorde. "I need you to remain patient."

With the *California* listing in an ocean of uncertainty, I had no idea how much rope we really had to play with. The next catastrophic crisis could've been as little as minutes or hours away. Gentry needed to be returned to command immediately.

"Patience is a virtue we can ill afford right now, Julian. You need to stop being passive. Don't wait for an opportunity. Take the opportunity."

"That will require some risk."

"Everything is risk right now. We need to act."

Considering my words, his gaze floated to some unfocused point in the distance. By the time his eyes returned to meet mine, they had filled with a cold, detached resolve.

"I think I have a solution," he replied. "But for it to work, I'll need you to do more than just ghost a biosig. You'll need to make five of them disappear."

CHAPTER 37

VIV

WITH EVERY WAKING MOMENT OVERFLOWING WITH CONSTANT stress, the opportunity to close my eyes and grab a few stolen hours of sleep should've been welcome. But I dreaded the end of each day. Most nights I'd lie wide awake, staring at the ceiling, the low hum of the ship's oxygen regulators droning an accompaniment to the scattered thoughts rolling through my unsettled, sleepless mind.

My mother's fate.

The mystery of the Blink.

The Kastazi occupation of Earth.

The yet-unseen next lurking threat.

Julian lay next to me, just as he had every night since Gallipoli. I leaned in to the warmth of his body. But the closer we entwined, the deeper I sank into distraction. After a few more kisses at the nape of my neck, he stopped and pulled back.

"Are you all right?" he asked.

"I'm fine."

"Vivien. I know you too well. What's on your mind?"

"You don't have to read into everything, Jules. Things can just be off. There doesn't always have to be a reason."

"Things are off?" he replied, a tinge of insecurity creeping into his voice.

"Don't you feel it too? Everything is falling apart all around us, yet each night we come here and act like nothing's wrong. Why do we keep doing this?"

"We keep doing this because we love each other."

Because we love each other. His sentiment struck an uneasy chord with me. On top of everything else, kissing JD had left me in a state of near-constant confusion.

"This is what we're supposed to do," he continued. "We have no idea what tomorrow will bring. We don't even know what the next hour will bring. It could all be over in the snap of a finger. Every moment counts now."

The more he talked, the worse I felt.

"I'm sorry. I'm just . . . scared," I deflected.

"I'm scared too. In fact, I'm terrified," he said, gently taking my hand.

"Are you?"

"Of course I am!"

"You could've fooled me."

"It's all a deception, my dear," he replied with a disarming simper.

My stomach nervously stirring, I sat up and swung my legs off the bed.

"Where are you going?"

"I'm not going to be able to sleep. I might as well go back to the bridge and relieve JD."

Julian pulled me down on top of his chest and wrapped his arms around me. "Don't go. Talk to me. Tell me what's making you scared."

Our actions may have saved the ship, but from that point forward every soul on board had become our responsibility. Every day I woke up to the reality that a single mistake had the potential to cost everyone their lives. The pressure was unrelenting.

"That we won't be able to keep everyone safe," I lamented. "What about you? What scares you?"

"Losing you," he replied without a second's hesitation.

I sat back up. "Jules . . ."

Julian joined me at the edge of my rack. "It wasn't as singularly a romantic thought as you might presume."

"What do you mean?"

"What if something happened to you? What if something happened to both you and John? What then?"

"Ohno would take over, and if not her, then Bix, and if not him, then Anatoly. You know the chain of command just as well as I do."

"And then what? Gentry?"

"I don't know, Jules. I don't think any of us has thought that far ahead."

"It's time to," he asserted. "You can't leave everyone's lives in the hands of Gentry or a Command Synth. Not when there's already a better option."

His insinuation was clear. "And that better option would be you?"

"Is it such a crazy thought? I went through the same training as the rest of you. I even qualified for the command track. There's only one reason I'm not wearing a cadet uniform—because I was a statistical casualty of an ill-conceived, nonsensical Psych Ops bell curve."

"Julian, you know we can't just—"

"Don't quote protocol to me," he interrupted, slightly raising his voice. "You threw protocol out the window the moment you removed Gentry from command. Think about what's right. Listen to what your gut is telling you."

I did check my gut, and I didn't like what it was telling me. "You can't possibly be suggesting we give you your own set of Command Codes."

"Of course not."

"Then what?"

"Upgrade me to command-level clearance, but set my priority level below yours and the other cadets'. If heaven forbid all your biosigs ever went flat, Sentinel would recognize my signature as the next option in the chain of command and automatically transmit its Command Codes to me."

I racked my brain for all the reasons why it might be a bad idea, but his reasoning was undeniably sound. The Command Synth, intended for a limited array of crisis situations, was never going to be a workable long-term solution. That left Julian and Gentry as the *California*'s only viable alternatives. Regardless of who the right choice might have been if it ever came to that, a "post-cadet" contingency plan was certainly worth exploring.

"It's a reasonable thought, but I'll need to take it up with everyone else."

The tension in Julian's body spontaneously dissipated, and he leaned in to deliver an unexpectedly passionate kiss.

"What was that?"

"I don't know," he sighed. "I suppose I'm just relieved. I was worried you were going to be more resistant to the idea."

Finally, mercifully, I felt myself growing tired. I fell backward onto my pillow, pulling Julian down beside me. His anxious heart pounded against my back as we nestled together.

No more talking. No more thinking.

I just needed to sleep.

CHAPTER 38

JD

WHATEVER FOCUS I HAD LEFT WAS QUICKLY dissipating. Already an hour past the end of my graveyard shift, Viv's unscheduled priority meeting was still in full bloom.

"Maybe it will help if we take emotion out of the equation and go by the book," Anatoly said. "By the book, Gentry should already be in command. He's a commissioned Alliance officer. Maybe the answer is that simple."

"But it's not that simple, Toly," Ohno countered. "He had a nervous breakdown right in front of us. We can't just wipe that fact off the board and go 'by the book.' How do we know history won't repeat itself in a similar situation?"

"What do you think?" Bix asked me. "You're the only one who spends any time with him."

"I don't know," I replied. "He seems to have improved some, but I'm not going to sit here and tell you he's had an epiphany we can count on."

"It doesn't sound like any of you are ready to go by the book," Viv chimed in. "But if you throw out the book, let's understand what that means. It means you're throwing the case against Julian out the window with it too. He's technically qualified for command and has already proven himself capable under fire. 'The book' is probably the only thing stopping you from making him the perfunctory choice."

"It's not helping that you keep arguing both sides of the issue," Ohno responded in frustration.

"I'm arguing both sides because I'm trying to be dispassionate. You know I'm compromised."

Losing patience, I slapped my hand on my console. "If something kills all five of us, it's probably taking the ship with it anyway. So let's stop overthinking it and just make a judgment call here. Call it out. Anatoly?"

"Gentry," he answered, albeit reluctantly.

"Bix?"

He nervously pushed his glasses up the bridge of his nose. "Julian."

"Ohno?"

"Julian. Definitely Julian."

"Julian it is, then," I volunteered, bringing our debate to a conclusion.

My vote carried the decision into majority without having to put Viv on the spot.

"Should I install his priority key now?" Bix asked.

"Wait," Viv interjected. "Biosigs have been going haywire for the last two weeks. What if a malfunction pushed all of our signatures offline? That would give Julian command priority, wouldn't it?"

"No. Not possible," Ohno answered, shaking her head with definitive confidence. "Biosigs are synced to life support and have more redundant safeguards than any other system on the ship. The sigs might ghost, but they aren't going to disappear. Unless . . ."

"Unless what?"

"Unless we're dead."

"Or if someone with command authorization accessed the system," added Bix. "They couldn't change priority, but they could unlink tracking to our sigs. That'd take us offline."

"Only we have command authorization," I reminded him.

"Gentry," replied Viv. "He still has command authorization."

"One of the many reasons he's locked in his quarters. He has zero access to any of the ship's systems or any means of communication with anyone who would."

"Bix, is there anything we're missing. Anything at all?" Viv asked.

He rolled his eyes upward, as if searching his brain for any stone left unturned.

"No. Not that I can think of."

If Bix couldn't come up with anything for us to worry about, that was good enough for me.

"Fine, then. It's done. Go ahead."

Bix swiveled back to his console and began the update to add Julian to the Command Priority Roster.

Responding to a message at his station, Anatoly got up and tiredly shuffled off into the lift. "Looks like I have a broken nose to attend to in Medical."

"Another fight?"

"Either that or he repeatedly fell on something fist-shaped," he quipped just before disappearing behind the closing doors.

My console chimed.

"Command authorization required for Command Priority Roster modification."

I entered my Command Code, authenticating Bix's update.

"Command Priority Roster successfully modified. Lorde, Julian C., confirmed Command Priority Six."

Exhausted, I pushed myself to my feet. "See you at 1900."

"Why don't you relieve me at 2100 instead?" Viv offered. "Looks like you could use a couple extra hours of shut-eye."

I was more than happy to take her up on her offer, but I didn't make it more than three steps before long-range proximity alarms rang out over the bridge. So much for sleep.

"Report."

Bix hastily shuffled his feet.

"Come on. Talk to me, Bix."

He activated the Holoview's stellar-cartographic overlay. Its crisscrossing lattice divided the immediate navigable sector into equally apportioned zones. "Q-Five-A."

My attention narrowed to Quadrant Five Alpha, where a small red blip was approaching the supply buoys from the opposite direction of the *California*'s trajectory. Its yellow pulsing perimeter indicated a very familiar energy signature.

Viv leaned forward, squinting. "It's the Grays!"

Ohno's ink retreated under the cuffs of her uniform jacket. "If they're as desperate for supplies as we are, that's not a good sign."

"No, it's not," I agreed.

Bix zoomed out the overlay to a wider perspective. "The Grays aren't the whole story. Check out Q-Seven-D."

A second red blip appeared, its perimeter pulsing blue. The color of the Alliance.

"Are those readings confirmed?" Viv asked.

"Yes," Bix acknowledged. "It's definitely an Alliance vessel, and it's on an intercept course with the Grays."

"What ship is it?"

"I can't tell. Its transponder isn't throwing off a signal."

"Should I com them?"

"No," I cautioned him. "We don't know who else is out there listening."

"We can't risk missing them," said Viv.

"We won't. Activating Nav Synth," I replied, entering its activation sequence. The avatar materialized at Navigation.

"Plot an intercept course with unidentified Alliance vessel at Quadrant Six Gamma."

Intercept at Six Gamma would get us to the Alliance ship before it reached the Grays.

The Synth paused. "Warning. Intercept at Six Gamma requires propulsion to exceed acceptable parameters."

"Disregard warning. Ohno?"

"Got it. Rerouting available power from grids to propulsion."

"Course plotted," the Synth confirmed. "Intercept with unidentified Alliance vessel at Six Gamma in thirty-nine minutes."

As the *California*'s autopilot adjusted its course and hurtled us toward Six Gamma, it occurred to me that something other than a happy reunion was likely waiting for us aboard the Alliance ship. We were mutineers. There was undoubtedly going to be a reckoning for what we had done.

Bix inspected his console as if it were malfunctioning.

"What is it?"

"I don't understand," he answered, looking uncharacteristically befuddled. "We're . . . dead."

"Excuse me?"

"I mean our biosigs went flat. Look."

It was the exact contingency we had just determined impossible.

"Reboot the system, quickly!" I shouted.

"I can't. Biosig reboot is a command function. You need to reboot from your console."

"Stand by." I entered my command code.

"Command authorization invalid."

"It rejected my code."

Viv slowly rose from her station, the color evaporating from her face. "Refresh the Command Priority Roster."

"Why?"

"Just do it!"

Confused, I did as she asked.

The Command Priority Roster instantly repopulated with only one name.

Lorde, Julian C. Command Priority One.

I looked up from my console in shock.

"Julian."

Viv pounded her fist hard against her console. "They were

waiting to pounce," she said, her wide, disbelieving eyes signaling the weight of her realization.

"*They?*"

I wasn't sure she heard me. It was like she was a thousand miles away.

"I don't know how, but they found a way to communicate," she continued, eyes vacant.

An unfamiliar alert sounded.

"It's Gentry," Viv said, not even bothering to consult her console.

Bix, however, consulted his.

"She's right. The lock on his quarters. I don't know how, but it's been reset."

"Isolate his biosig. Tell me where he's going."

"Gentry *and* Lorde both located on Delta Deck, port side," Bix confirmed, pausing in stunned disbelief before delivering the rest. "Headed straight for the mainframe compartment."

"Gentry has authorization to get into the compartment," Viv groaned.

Ohno swiveled around from her console to face us, her pained expression telegraphing how dire the situation was about to become. "Julian's command priority gives him the Command Keys for Sentinel. As soon as those codes are ingested, the ship is Gentry's."

Rushes of anger and panic competed against my focus.

"All right, let's stop and think this through. How long will it take for Sentinel to ingest the codes?"

"Sentinel throws up a multitude of automatic failsafes anytime new Command Codes are entered," Bix answered. "But it's nothing Gentry won't be able to work his way through. We've got thirty minutes tops. Maybe twenty if he works fast," Bix answered.

A new alert sounded. Then one more. And then another.

"I've got unauthorized movement all over the ship," Ohno reported. "Over thirty students on Beta Deck. Transferring biosigs to the Holoview."

The Holoview revealed a dense cluster of bodies heading straight past Medical. I tried to raise Anatoly on both visual and audio coms. Neither worked.

A few seconds later Anatoly's biosig was moving inside the cluster, his heart rate skyrocketing. They had taken him.

"Freeze the nearest lift!" Viv called out.

"Can't access lift controls!" Ohno thundered. Another alert sounded. "All the missing pulse pistols just went active!"

Then, one by one, the interfaces on my command console shut down. With our biosigs no longer active, Sentinel was purging every authorization it didn't recognize and waiting for Julian to enter his.

"All systems failing!"

Then the Holoview went dark, and the ship lost propulsion.

I sank into my chair.

"We've got to do something!" Viv shouted at me.

"Like what? They've completely outflanked us. We're boxed in, locked out of every system, and there's an armed insurrection waiting for us on the lower decks."

"There has to be something. What can we use? What's still working?"

"Barely anything," Bix said. "I might be able to squeeze some functionality out of basic infrastructure systems. Lifts. Emergency power routing."

"Emergency power?" Ohno queried. "How much of it do you think you can grab for me?"

"I don't know. Most of it? All of it, probably. Why? What can you do with it?"

Ohno doffed her uniform jacket and pulled the utility panel off the back of her console. "Something unpleasant."

I had no idea what she meant, but it inspired a very familiar reaction.

Bix beat me to saying it out loud. "Oh no."

CHAPTER 39

VIV

A COLUMN OF STUDENTS STOOD IN TIGHT formation guarding the mainframe compartment as JD and I approached. Seven of them were armed with the missing pulse pistols. The weapons looked like toys in their unsure hands. My eyes almost couldn't believe what they were seeing.

Cooper Lynch stepped forward, pointing his pistol at us. His beady brown eyes amplified his sinister intensity. "Looks like we have ourselves a Devastation Class reunion," he sniped.

"Be careful with that, Cooper," JD warned. "The trigger is extremely sensitive."

Cooper smirked. "I know how it works."

Kemi Abioye and Hamid Jahan frisked us.

"No weapons," Hamid confirmed.

"We didn't come looking for a fight. We can resolve this peacefully. Find a way to work together," I said.

"Is that so? Where was this team spirit before?"

JD tried to step forward, but Cooper stopped him with a cautionary wave of his pistol.

"You need to listen to me," JD beseeched him. "We've isolated the signal of an Alliance vessel two sectors from here. They're the lifeline we've been waiting for, and if propulsion isn't restored soon, we could lose them."

"Propulsion will be restored soon enough. Under Gentry's command."

"By the time Sentinel ingests the new Command Codes, it might be too late."

Cooper smirked. "How convenient."

"Why would I lie to you?"

"Because you can't help yourself," another voice called out from behind the students guarding the entrance.

Gentry exited the mainframe compartment, his unearned cocky swagger reclaimed. Wearing a fresh uniform, he had taken the time to shave and neatly coif his hair.

He snatched the pistol from Cooper and swung it right between JD's eyes. "You know how serious a mutiny is, don't you, cadet?"

"I do," JD answered, unable to restrain the nervous quiver in his chin.

"Alliance Uniform Code of Military Justice. Article Four, Section Two. 'The ranking officer aboard an Alliance vessel may carry out any of the authorized penalties for acts of treason. Including summary execution.'"

"In times of war," JD defiantly countered.

"Is this not war?" Gentry scoffed.

JD cringed as Gentry's finger flinched against the trigger.

"Don't!" I shouted.

I could see flecks of sweat beading at Gentry's temples. He was completely locked in, feeding off JD's fear.

JD closed his eyes.

"Please, no!" I implored Gentry.

"Move her back!" he shouted at Cooper.

Cooper grabbed me from behind, dragging me away from JD.

I'd been powerless to stop what happened to my mother. To Safi. To everyone on Gallipoli. But all that had happened at a distance.

Now I was powerless to stop what was happening right in front of me. I felt like I was being ripped in half.

Gentry cocked the pistol's plasma chamber, and it squealed through its power cycle. "You brought this on yourself."

JD offered no response.

The world around me began to spin.

Not like this.

I can't lose him like this.

"Do you have anything you want to say before I carry out your sentence?"

JD looked Gentry squarely in the eyes. "Yes. We did what we had to."

Gentry shook his head in disgust. "That's all?"

"That's all."

With a sickening crack, Gentry pistol-whipped JD across the face. He crumbled to the floor, blood spilling from his nose and mouth.

Rage overwhelmed me. I executed a reverse head butt against Cooper's chin and rushed Gentry, knocking the pistol from his grip with a roundhouse kick. Caught off guard, he staggered a step to his right. Pouncing, I landed an uppercut to his solar plexus and followed with a stabbing jab to the ribs. Belching out a groan, he set his feet and struck my collarbone with a sharp left chop. Adrenaline dulled the pain radiating down my arm as I fell into a backward roll and leapt back to my feet, keeping my stance low.

Gentry furiously charged me. Dodging his stomping kick, I surprised him with a martelo do chão to the knee. He cried out in agony and dropped to the deck.

Just as I readied a finishing axe kick, I heard JD shout, "Behind you!"

Cooper was already aiming his pulse pistol at my head by the time I spun around.

"Don't even twitch," he warned me.

Protected by Cooper's cover, Gentry rose and grabbed me by the throat. It felt as though he was crushing my larynx as he locked his elbow and held me at a distance. I tried to scream, but all I could muster was a squeal. Then, right before I passed out, someone pushed between us to free me from his grip.

As soon as my eyes came back into focus, I saw that it was Julian. "What do you think you're doing?" he scolded Gentry.

Gentry straightened his uniform. "She's dangerous. They're all dangerous!"

Julian offered JD a hand. JD reluctantly took it and struggled to stand.

"No violence unless necessary. That's what you promised," Julian railed at Gentry before turning his attention to me. "Are you okay?"

It gutted me to look at him.

"How could you do this?" I seethed.

Julian stood silent, either without an answer or unwilling to give me one.

JD burst into laughter. Looking at his face broke my heart. His gentle features were swollen and disfigured. "What did Gentry promise you, Julian? That he'd tell High Command you saved the *California* from treacherous mutineers? That he'd find a way to get you a commission?"

"Is that how little you think of me, John?" he indignantly replied.

"Then why?" I demanded.

"Because you were going to lose!" Julian shouted, momentarily losing his composure. "Look around you. You're surrounded by those who resent you. Don't trust you. Want you gone. Even if I never lifted a finger, how long did you think you would've lasted before you found yourself here, in this very same inevitable moment?"

"So this is about winning?"

"What was it that you said to me in Iso-Rec not so long ago?" he answered, turning his focus to JD. "Perhaps if I concentrated more on winning, I wouldn't be languishing on the lower decks? Well, thank you for your guidance, but this was always about much more than winning. I chose the side I knew would prevail. It was about *survival*."

My anger dissolved to pity. I didn't need to see his Psych Ops results to know what they must have said.

That he was a coward.

JD spit a clot of blood right at Julian's feet. "If you want to survive, I promise you've picked the wrong side."

Annalisa Vaccaro peeked out from the compartment. "Liko needs you," she called out to Gentry.

"Bring them inside," ordered Gentry, turning to follow Annalisa back into the compartment.

With Cooper's pistol at our backs, we followed a procession of students through the entrance. Liko was inside, working away at Sentinel's control panel. About a dozen more students surrounded him. The condition of JD's face made it clear they had gone past the point of no return.

As we walked farther inside, we came upon Anatoly. Seated on the ground under the guard of two armed students, he appeared to be unharmed.

"You okay Toly?" JD asked.

"Better than you," he answered.

I held my breath as JD reached into his pocket and stealthily dropped a Magnetic Field Generator band by Anatoly's side. It was the same kind JD and I already had concealed on our wrists. MFGs were originally intended to function as energy-shielding safety accessories for engineers working inside the ship's propulsion systems. I had never worn one before—let alone successfully charged one. I prayed the five minutes we had to grab them from Engineering and follow Ohno's instructions were enough.

Liko swiveled away from the control panel to address Gentry. "I made it through Sentinel's second failsafe. What do I do now?"

"Initialize the boot sequence. It's ready to accept the Command Codes."

"Initializing now."

Julian produced a microdrive and handed it to Gentry. "They're fully rendered and ready to be input."

JD and I stayed focused on Anatoly. He still hadn't noticed the MFG band lying beside him. If he didn't catch on soon, we were going to have a problem.

"It's too late," I blurted out, trying to stall.

"Yep, definitely past the point of return," JD joined in, wiping more blood from his nose.

Gentry looked at me, amused. "Too late, is it?"

"That's right. You've already lost. It's over."

Unconcerned, he returned his attention to Sentinel.

"Wait," Julian warned. "That look on her face. She's up to something."

Cooper pushed his pistol's barrel against my cheek. "Speak."

"He's right. I am up to something. But there's no way for me to stop it now."

"Why hasn't it happened yet?" JD asked me, a tinge of perverse satisfaction creeping into his voice. He was enjoying toying with them. "She did say ten minutes, right?"

"Yeah. Ten minutes. That's what I heard too."

JD darted his eyes at the MFG band, hoping to draw Anatoly's attention to it. He still wasn't catching on.

Julian looked me up and down. His eyes stopped at my wrist when he saw it. "MFG?" he muttered, perplexed.

Liko's ears pricked up. "What did you just say?"

"An MFG band. She's wearing one."

"Any second now," JD alerted me, this time legitimately.

Liko tilted his head back and his eyes traced the vast, twisted maze of power conduits feeding downward from the ceiling into Sentinel's core.

There was no time left for subtlety. "Anatoly! Beside you!" I hollered.

First he looked the wrong way, to the left, then back to the right.

"No!" Liko shouted. "Evacuate the compartment now!"

The students barely even moved. They were all too confused. Undeterred by Liko's warning, Gentry slipped Julian's microdrive into Sentinel's control panel.

Finally, Anatoly saw the MFG. He quickly put on the band and cringed in anticipation of what was coming next.

An instant later, from the bridge, Ohno released a concentrated surge of emergency power through Sentinel's power conduit matrix, sending a massive electrostatic wave across the compartment. White arcs of electricity viciously stabbed at everyone in their path.

I braced myself, my eyes locked on my MFG.

Please work.

Please work!

A bolt of energy sliced toward me but was intercepted by my MFG's protective bubble. JD's and Anatoly's MFGs shielded them as well. After a few short seconds, we were the only ones left conscious.

My MFG disengaged, releasing a wave of static electricity that made every hair on my body stand on end.

Anatoly ran in front of me to check on Julian.

"It's okay," I assured him. "Ohno modulated the surge ceiling. They're only in bad headache territory."

Obviously not entirely trusting Ohno's calibrations, he waited for a pulse anyway.

With a nod, he confirmed Julian was okay.

"Is it too late for me to complain that this was a very crazy, stupid, and dangerous idea?"

"Crazy, stupid, and dangerous was all we had left."

JD hustled to Sentinel and entered his Command Code into its control panel. After what seemed like an eternity, Sentinel finally returned its confirmation.

"Marshall, John Douglas. Command Priority One."

Sentinel had done just what we thought it would do. After Julian lost consciousness, it had automatically sought out the next person in the chain of command. Finding no one and presuming a malfunction, it then instructed the biosig system to reboot. The reboot refreshed our biosigs, which in turn restored the Command Priority Roster we had reprogrammed after relieving Gentry of command.

"All bridge authorizations reestablished," JD reported into the compartment's com. "Ohno, do you copy?"

"Go for Ohno. It worked?"

"It did."

"And you're all okay?"

"We are. Recalculate our navigational trajectory and restore propulsion immediately. We can't lose that ship."

"Aye."

Anatoly crawled from body to body, checking everyone's vitals.

"What's their condition?" I asked.

"Pulses all strong and steady."

"We've got to get back to the bridge," JD urged us. "Let's go, Toly."

"I can't. These people are going to require medical attention."

JD hesitated.

"Don't worry. No one is going to be in any condition to fight with me. I can promise you that," Anatoly assured him. "Take their pistols, and I can handle myself from here."

Acquiescing to Anatoly, we rushed to collect the weapons strewn all about the compartment. One pistol hung limply from Gentry's loose grip. Julian lay unconscious beside him, an oddly peaceful look on his face.

"Guys, we're T minus twelve minutes away from Quadrant Six Gamma," Ohno's voice echoed from the com. "I need you up here."

"Copy that," JD replied. "We're on our way."

"Alliance Emergency Directive Four," I said as he approached me, his arms filled with pulse pistols. "'In the event of war or any prolonged campaign of enemy engagement, all unidentified vessels shall be presumed hostile unless and until confirmed otherwise.'"

"We're talking about an Alliance vessel here, though."

"An unidentified one."

"What exactly are you suggesting?"

"I'm suggesting we be prepared for anything."

CHAPTER 40

JD

THE WHINE OF THE UPWARD-CLIMBING LIFT PERVADED the close confines as Viv gently blotted the blood still seeping from my nose. Across from us stood Bossa, wearing a skeptical expression.

"So what's it going to be?" I asked him. "It's either you or a Synth."

"Like I already said, never trust a Synth to do a human's job."

"Thus your presence in this lift."

He leaned in to inspect my damage. "Man, they really did a number on you."

The lift jerked to a stop.

"I need an answer."

"I'm still thinking about it," he replied, clearly relishing his leverage.

We stepped onto the bridge.

"What did they do to you?" Ohno blurted out.

"Don't worry, I'm fine," I said, relieving her from the captain's chair. "Stations, everyone."

Bossa lingered by the lift.

"What do I have to do? Ask nicely?"

"How about you start by telling me what I'd be shooting at," he tossed back.

"Nothing, hopefully."

"And if hope disappoints you?"

I gestured to Bix. "Let's see it."

He activated the Holoview's stellar-cartographic display, and the two blips—one pulsing blue and one pulsing yellow—hovered opposite each other in Quadrant Five Alpha. The Alliance vessel had already intercepted the Grays.

A superimposed timer counted down to visual contact.

00:01:45

Bossa shrugged his shoulders. "Looks like the good guys to me."

"That certainly appears to be the case, but—"

"Alliance Emergency Directive Four," he said, finishing my sentence.

"How do you know that?" Viv questioned him.

Bossa nonchalantly took his position at Weapons and cracked his knuckles. "Not really in a sharing mood."

"I don't care what kind of mood you're in. Answer my question."

An alert sounded. An instant later the Grays' blip disappeared.

"Please tell me that was a malfunction."

Bix scanned his readings. "I can't find their signature. It's . . . gone."

"Grids to maximum," I ordered.

"Aye," Ohno confirmed.

Another alert sounded. An incoming com.

"Alliance vessel comming us," Bix reported.

"Ignore them until we have a visual."

00:00:37

Then we saw it. A debris field of flaming wreckage, unmistakably the remains of the obliterated Genuvian ship.

"They fired on the Grays?" Bix exclaimed.

Ohno shook her head. "That's impossible. There's no way—"

"What else could it have been?" Viv retorted.

As unthinkable as it was, we had to assume the worst-case scenario.

"Weapons status?"

"Ready if you are," Bossa answered.

The *California*'s bow pushed through the smoldering remnants of the Grays' ship.

00:00:10

"There!" Bix pointed.

It was just a tiny speck in the distance.

"Magnify."

The Holoview zoomed in to reveal an Alliance Patrol Scouter.

00:00:00

Sentinel confirmed the ship's identity and displayed it on the Holoview.

The UAS *Kyoto.*

The *Kyoto* was Captain Marta Aviles's ship.

"Open visual com."

"Opening com."

Soft, evenly dispersed ping tones signaled our invitation, but no one answered. The *Kyoto* had gone quiet.

"What's happening?"

"They're trying to scan us," Bix called back. "Should I jam?"

"The way we jerry-rigged our plasma cannons—am I correct in thinking they won't read active?"

"They shouldn't."

"Let them scan."

After another thirty seconds of unanswered pings, a visual com finally came through. I expected to see Captain Aviles on the Holoview but instead was greeted by a middle-aged male officer I did not recognize.

"The *California*," he said. Genuinely perplexed, his eyes surveyed our bridge. "How?"

"Excuse me?"

He took a step closer, his confusion bending toward suspicion. "How have you managed to stay hidden all this time?"

"Where is Captain Aviles, and why did you fire on—"

"Where is the Resistance base?" he demanded, rolling right over me.

"Resistance base?"

"Answer me!"

Viv and I exchanged befuddled glances.

"I have no idea what you're talking about."

A bridge officer whispered something in the captain's ear. A moment later the com went dark, the Holoview returning to a full image of the *Kyoto*. She stood still at twelve o'clock, menacingly staring back at us.

"They cut the com on their end," Bix said.

"You wanna tell me who that is and what is going on?" Bossa groused.

I flinched as an alarm shrieked.

"Target lock!" Bix yelled.

"Viv, evasive now!"

"Aye!" Viv slammed down her throttle, and the *California* leapt forward from a dead stop.

The *Kyoto* pursued us from behind, firing two pulse missiles at our turbines. Their incendiary halos flooded the Holoview with warm orange light.

"Reroute all available power to aft grids!"

Ohno made the adjustment, bulwarking our aft defenses, just before the *California* absorbed an unexpectedly powerful wallop. She pounded her first on her console and swore in Portuguese.

"What happened?"

"Power-flow overload in the Primary Grid Generator."

"Upshot?"

"We can take one more hit. Maybe two."

Bix jerked his head back in disbelief, reacting to the readings on his console. "Their weapons yield is forty percent higher than it should be. Doesn't make sense."

"Bossa, get your finger on that trigger."

"I'm ready," he acknowledged, his eyes trained on the hard-charging *Kyoto*.

"Try to get them back on com."

"They're not receiving," Bix replied.

Ohno swung around from her console. "She's firing again!"

Seconds later, multiple waves of concussion rocked the *California*. The bridge's lighting fluttered and dimmed.

"Grids at ten percent!" Ohno reported.

Viv looked at me. "You can't wait any longer."

"We shoot, they die."

"And if we don't?"

"She's right, cookie," Bossa squawked. "It's us or them."

Backed into a corner, I had no other choice. "Plasma cannons armed and at your ready, Bossa. Fire at will."

Straightaway he unleashed a torrent of unmodulated plasma fire on the *Kyoto*, but somehow, inexplicably, she held together.

"Keep firing!"

The target lock shrieked again.

"She's got us!" Ohno yelled.

Fixated on his console, Bix held up his hand. "There's a small integrity gap in her grids. Just below secondary thrusters."

Bossa stopped firing and searched his targeting screen for the vulnerability. "Keep us steady. Keep us steady for just two bloody seconds."

Viv precisely stabilized her yoke. "This is as steady as she's gonna get. If you've got a shot, take it!"

Bossa flicked his finger against the trigger, and a single plasma stream burst from our cannons. It landed right below the *Kyoto*'s secondary thrusters, threading the needle of her grids' razor-thin fallibility. The surgical strike's small blast expanded outward, setting off a cascade of massive explosions that quickly devoured the ship in a circle of fire.

"All stop," I ordered.

Viv popped the *California*'s reverse thrusters, bringing us to a halt.

"What have we done?" Bix wailed as the flotsam of the *Kyoto*'s obliterated carcass ticked harmlessly against our hull.

Bossa angrily pushed away from Weapons. "Whatever it is you're not telling me . . ."

My adrenaline still surged, sending my pulse pounding into my ears. I ignored him and turned my attention to Bix.

"You still with me, buddy?"

"Yes, I'm all right," he replied, wiping the wetness from his eyes. "I'm okay."

"Can you scan the supply buoys from here?"

"I think so."

"Try."

Of all the possible perils waiting for us in the darkness, starvation was the most immediate. We barely had any food left.

Bix's shoulders dropped. "They're empty," he said. "The Grays must've raided them before they got hit."

"What now?" Ohno asked, her body almost writhing with palpable anxiety.

"We work with what we know," I asserted.

"That's the problem. We don't know anything."

"Not true," Viv corrected. "We know the *Kyoto* was looking for a base. We find that base, maybe we find ourselves another lifeline."

Bossa dispiritedly raised his hand. "Question, folks. Presuming this base exists, and presuming it's even a place where this ship would be welcome, what makes you think you'll be able to find it when the *Kyoto* couldn't?"

"We can find it because we have something they didn't," I answered.

It took a second before Bix realized I was looking at him.

"What? *Me?*"

CHAPTER 41

VIV

WHAT DO YOU DO WHEN FACED WITH the impossible? You give Roger Bixby an extra twenty minutes to find a solution. That was the bon mot I had come up with shortly after befriending him. By the time we'd graduated from boot camp, I'd realized it wasn't so much a joke as it was a statement of fact. Bix wasn't just a genius—he was an absolute freak of nature.

"Almost there," he said as the echoing feedback of his tracking algorithm grew louder and more frequent.

Extrapolating from Sentinel's detailed logs of the Grays' propulsion signature, Bix had isolated the unique subspace imprint of their dissipated ionic turbulence. That had allowed him to create an algorithm that enabled our sensors to retrace their footsteps— hopefully leading us back to wherever they had come from.

The way Bix had explained it made it sound like common sense. The reality, however, was quite the contrary. It was something that had never been done before.

What do you do when faced with the impossible? You give Roger Bixby an extra twenty minutes to find a solution.

This time it had taken him fifteen.

JD activated his com.

"Toly, report."

"Put it to you this way—I wouldn't lift the lockdown anytime soon," he responded after a short delay.

With the biosig system back up and secured against infiltration, we had every member of Gentry's insurrection boxed in on Beta Deck. As temporary a solution as it was, it at least had the benefit of buying us time to find a more permanent one.

The problem was I had no idea what a permanent solution might look like. We had always been aware of the dangerously escalating tensions on the lower decks but had totally underestimated its risks. Gentry wasn't going away, nor were the students who had thrown their support behind him. And our severe solution for protecting Sentinel from them had almost certainly made a bad problem worse.

"Copy that. How about their conditions?"

"I've discharged most back to their quarters," Anatoly responded. "I've still got two with me in Medical. They'll be fine, but they've suffered minor electrical burns that still need treatment."

Part of me hoped one of them was Julian. After everything he had done to deceive and manipulate me, the thought of him suffering was disquietingly pleasing.

"Understood. Keep me posted."

"Don't worry, they'll be fine," said JD, noticing the uneasy look on my face.

"I'm not worried about their health," I replied. "I'm worried about what they might do next."

"Don't be. They're not getting off Beta Deck."

"Just like Gentry wasn't getting out of his quarters?"

"We got caught with our pants down," JD answered, scrolling through his console's readout to avoid eye contact. "We'll figure out how he managed that and make sure it doesn't happen again."

"You're missing the point."

"Which is?"

"There's fifty-eight of them and five of us. Whether we control Sentinel or not, we can't keep this up forever. If they want us out, eventually they'll find a way."

JD angrily snapped his head up from his console.

"So you're agreeing with Julian now?"

"I'm not agreeing with what he did. But what he said . . . he's not wrong."

I braced myself for a snippy retort, but it didn't come. Instead he just stared ahead blankly.

"We beat them," he finally replied after a long pause. "We can beat them again."

"Beating them isn't a solution. A solution is not having to beat them. That means finding a way to come together."

"Good luck with that," said Bossa, gesturing toward JD's bloodied, swollen face.

Eager to change the subject, JD turned to Bix. "How's the ionic footprint integrity holding up?"

"It's dissipating rapidly, but I'm still getting readings."

I massaged my neck, listening to the monotonous droning of the tracking algorithm's feedback. "What if we lose it entirely?"

"We won't," Bix answered. "Taking into account the average range of a Genuvian ship and the dissipation rate of their wake, we have to be drawing close to their point of origin."

"I'll say it one more time," Bossa said while comfortably splayed out on the floor, his bundled-up jacket serving as a makeshift pillow. "I'm not so sure you should be counting on it as a sanctuary."

"Noted yet again," I replied.

The algorithm's feedback suddenly accelerated toward a fever pitch. The sound instantly made me feel exhausted. My adrenaline had already peaked and subsided too many times for one day.

"Grids to full," JD ordered.

"Aye," Ohno confirmed.

"Holoview, forward perspective."

"Aye, forward perspective," Bix acknowledged.

No more surprises.

Please let this be what we need it to be.

The Holoview flickered to life to reveal a jagged, pockmarked planetoid in the distance. Gray and lifeless, its surface was littered with seemingly endless crevasses and shadowy abysses.

Bossa approached the Holoview. "Congratulations. It's a rock."

My heart sank, but I wasn't ready to admit defeat. If Bix said there was something there, there had to be something there.

I squinted my eyes at the display. "Are you sure your algorithm is functioning properly, Bix?"

"Yes. This is where the Grays started from. I'm positive."

"Ohno, scan the surface. Look for anything out of the ordinary."

"Way ahead of you," she replied. "All I'm seeing is background radiation."

Ohno's report didn't shake my confidence in Bix.

Something's here.

There's got to be.

"What kind of background radiation?"

"Sensors are having trouble isolating its wavelength."

Bix suspiciously cocked an eyebrow. "Transfer those readings to my station."

Ohno swiped her fingers across her console. "Transferring now."

It took about three seconds for Bix to start laughing.

"What?" I asked.

"Our sensors are confused because it's just a bit too clean."

"Too clean as in . . ."

"Something inside that rock is trying to fool us," he said excitedly as he swiveled to face us. "It wants us to see normal background radiation. But it's too perfect. An all too human reproduction of something only nature could create."

"So not a dead rock?"

A wide grin split Bix's face. "It's alive inside."

"Alive with . . . ?"

"This camouflage has Fuller's fingerprints all over it. Well, maybe not him, but definitely his tech."

"Which means whatever's inside that rock has to be Alliance."

"Considering recent events, I'm not sure that's good news," Bossa weighed in.

Good point.

A proximity alarm sounded almost on cue.

Two spherical drones, each no larger than a transport shuttle, emerged from the inky blackness of one of the planetoid's abounding caverns.

"They're arming!" Ohno yelled.

The drones manipulated their structures, collapsing inward before reconstituting into self-propelled turrets, each brandishing four hyper-phasing rail guns.

I had seen drones like them before, but only in schematics for advanced theoretical weaponry.

"Those aren't supposed to exist," JD sputtered in disbelief.

Bossa ran back to Weapons and booted up its targeting screen. "We're the ones who aren't going to exist if you don't move fast. Bring the plasma cannons back online now!"

JD raised his hand. "Stand by."

"Are you crazy? Let me take them out!"

"Drones in firing range," Bix reported.

JD stared intently at the Holoview as the drones swiftly descended on our position.

"Drop grids," he ordered.

Ohno hesitated, waiting to see if I would object.

"Delay that order," I instructed her. "Tell us what you're thinking, JD. Quickly."

"If this is where the Grays came from, we need to send a message to whoever's in there," he implored. "We need to let them know we're on their side."

I nodded to Ohno. "Do it."

"Dropping grids," she reluctantly confirmed.

JD anxiously drummed his fingers on his armrests. "Come on. Come on." After a precarious silence, an alert sounded.

"Incoming com," Bix announced. "Alliance priority band."

"Open com," JD replied, the tension slowly abating from his posture.

"Aye. Opening com."

The visual was corrupted with interference, but we could see the shape of someone lurking beneath the static.

"Clean up that visual!" JD demanded.

Working his console, Bix brought the image into focus. Staring back at us was none other than General Aldridge Staxx, second in command of the Alliance forces. His close-cropped hair was grayer than I remembered, and his skin seemed to have sunken more tightly against his cheekbones. It was as if the events of the past few weeks had aged him years.

As his penetrating eyes moved across our faces, I sensed a myriad of emotions emanating from him. But, above all else, I sensed surprise.

"John Marshall?"

JD had tears in his eyes. "Yes, it's me, General."

Staxx paused to collect himself. "Son, where have you been all this time?"

"With all due respect, sir, I don't even know where to begin. Request permission to be debriefed in person."

Another alert sounded as the drones began to scan the *California*.

"Permission granted," the general commented, his eyes pointing downward as he reviewed the data being fed to him by the drones. "The Gatekeepers will guide you inside."

As soon as the com link closed, the drones reverted to their original configuration and circled back toward the cavern from which they had emerged.

"On to sanctuary?" Bossa skeptically remarked.

"Let's hope so," JD replied. "Take us in, Viv."

"Aye," I confirmed, pushing the throttle forward.

Gliding ahead in pursuit, we followed the drones in through the cavern's mouth, and the Holoview faded to black as we plunged ourselves headfirst into the planetoid's murky depths.

"Forward arc lamps," JD ordered.

"Aye. Engaging forward lamps," Ohno confirmed.

The space around us illuminated bright as day, revealing our narrow, craggy environs. Pushing deeper, I pitched the *California* upward, following the drones over a vast palisade of what seemed to be selenite crystal.

As soon as we crested the palisade's peak, I saw the base. Carved into the reddish-brown bedrock, it boasted an intricate array of walkways and observation decks overlooking an enormous horseshoe-shaped docking platform. A smattering of vessels— Alliance, Aeson, Xax, and Genuvian—were moored all along its circumference. Battered and battle-scarred, they looked like tragic artifacts from an already-lost war.

The lights on the centermost berth flashed in progressive sequence, inviting our arrival. I eased us into its mooring, and the bridge shuddered slightly as the *California* gently came to rest.

"So what do we do now?" I wondered aloud, expressing the same thought that had to be going through everyone's mind.

"What we said we were going to do all along," JD responded as he slowly pushed himself up out of the captain's chair. "We turn ourselves in."

CHAPTER 42

JD

THE CONTENTS OF THE MEAL TRAY RESTING on the table had long since gone cold. Its three compartments held something resembling beans, something resembling rice, and something resembling nothing I recognized as edible. At least I wasn't hungry. General Staxx had managed to deprive me of my appetite.

We had gone over the same details again and again. The attack on Gallipoli. Our engagements with the Kastazi. Nick. The Blink. Even our mutiny. I told him everything that happened honestly and truthfully, but nothing I said seemed to have satisfied him. Eventually he had grown frustrated enough to throw up his hands and move on to the others. Exhausted from his questioning, I was just glad to be left alone.

Confined to a small, dimly lit chamber, it didn't take long for the shadows to start playing tricks on me. They seemed to crawl across the mineral-encrusted walls, giving menacing form to all the unanswered questions festering in my mind. After a while I had resorted to staring at a long, jagged crack in the pebbly ceiling just to avoid the unsettling sight of them.

Finally, the door opened. Flanked by two soldiers, one Xax and one Aeson, Staxx returned and reclaimed the chair opposite mine.

"You haven't touched your food."

Sitting up straight, I took my elbows off the table. "No, sir. I'm not very hungry."

Staxx motioned to the Xax soldier, who briskly cleared my untouched meal.

"I spent the last two hours with your fellow cadets," Staxx said. "Their version of events is exactly the same as yours. Chapter and verse."

"That's because we're telling you the truth."

He folded his arms, looking at me with indifference. Something about our story still wasn't adding up for him.

"I also spoke to Ensign Gentry."

I braced myself, expecting the worst. "If he told you we're lying—"

"He didn't," Staxx cut in. "Accounting for some embellishments related to his opinion of you, I'd say the ensign's recitation of facts was ostensibly consistent with yours."

"If he gave you the same information we did, doesn't that tell you something?"

"To the contrary—it's only made me more confused."

Until that moment I had presumed Staxx's suspicions were rooted in something we had told him. Suddenly it occurred to me they were more likely rooted in something we hadn't.

"What else can I tell you, sir? What do you need to hear?"

"You honestly don't know, do you?" he asked, a hint of empathy breaking through his cold veneer.

"Know what, sir?"

Staxx gestured to the soldiers. "Leave us." Following his order, they retreated to the corridor and secured the door behind them.

Locked in, just the two of us, the air took on an ominous weight.

"Why do you think the *Kyoto* attacked you?"

"I was hoping you'd be able to tell me."

Staxx leaned in, narrowing his eyes. "They attacked you because you're an enemy of the Alliance."

The words came out of his mouth as clear as day, but I tried to convince myself I had misheard him.

"Excuse me, sir?"

"You are an enemy of the Alliance. As am I, and everyone on this base."

"That's ridiculous. We are the Alliance."

"No. The Alliance belongs to the Kastazi now."

As absurd as it sounded, Staxx's sober tone imbued his words with an undeniable sincerity. He believed what he was saying.

"Everything you think you know is wrong," he continued. "The world you remember is gone."

Acid pooled in my gut in anticipation of where he was leading me. "I don't understand."

"This is going to be very difficult for you to believe. I won't be able to provide you with an explanation. I don't have one."

"Tell me."

Waiting for his response, I almost expected someone to wake me from a dream.

"Son, you haven't been out there for three weeks," he said. "The *California* has been missing for five years."

CHAPTER 43

VIV

FIVE DAYS HAD PASSED SINCE GENERAL STAXX left us to our own devices in temporary barracks within the base's sparsely appointed armory, which I estimated was about the size of the *California*'s gymnasium. Its perimeter was lined with barren weapons lockers, and enormous crates, already depleted of larger armaments of torpedoes and missiles, were scattered and stacked wherever there was room.

Perched high up atop one of them, Bossa watched us. He couldn't possibly have looked any more bored, and I certainly couldn't blame him. We were, yet again, behaving like children.

Caught in the middle of a scrum, I took an inadvertent elbow to the cheek from JD. I shook it off and yanked him backward while Anatoly pulled Cooper in the opposite direction.

"I'll end you, Marshall!" Cooper yelled as he struggled against Anatoly's powerful restraint.

"Let him go," JD barked. "If he wants to do this, we'll do this."

"Enough!" I shouted.

Their fight, like all the others, wasn't instigated simply by what had already happened between us. It was just as much about the stress of our impossible new reality, a nightmare where in the blink of an eye, almost everyone you knew and loved had already died.

Earth had fallen. As had Aeson, Xax, and Genuvia. The Alliance itself hadn't been destroyed. It had been taken. Our bases. Our ships. Even our people. The traitors aboard the *Kyoto* were no aberration. Faced with extinction or submission, many of the survivors of the Kastazi second wave had made the same traitorous choice.

Gentry approached Anatoly from behind and rested a hand on his shoulder. "It's all right," he said. "It's over."

Initially assigned to soldiers' barracks elsewhere inside the base, Gentry had returned to us only three days later. He had claimed Staxx sent him back to get things under control, but I didn't believe it. Walking around among the Resistance's rank and file, he must've felt like an outcast. They carried the wounds of having fought a losing five-year war while he had leapfrogged all but a few weeks of it. As strange a thought as it was, he was much more one of us than one of them. If I were him, I probably would've wanted to come back to the armory too.

Released by Anatoly, Cooper stood his ground and stared JD down.

"What's this about?" Gentry asked.

"Does it matter?" JD angrily fired back before walking away.

I watched Gentry's eyes follow JD and didn't see the familiar anger I was expecting to find.

More one of us than one of them.

I couldn't get the thought out of my head.

The same sentiment applied to Julian, Liko, Cooper, and everyone else we had so recently pitted ourselves against. In the future we had arrived in, we all faced the same existential threat, and it was far worse than anything we had ever done to each other. Staxx's shocking decision to hold no one to account for what had transpired aboard the *California* should have made that point clear.

Yet we were still at each other's throats. Were our differences that severe? Did we really hate each other *that much*? Backed into a corner, up against an insurmountable enemy, it all suddenly felt so needlessly petty. Maybe that's why neither side was letting go. Because it required admitting how foolish we had been.

Anatoly and I followed JD back toward the encampment we had built at the far end of the armory. Composed of an assortment of empty PRM pallets and the few scratchy wool blankets we had been provided, its exterior had the appearance of a child's makeshift fort. Inside we rested on the flimsy mattresses we had pulled from our racks, and bided our time playing cards and reading old books from the *California*'s library.

The monotony was mind-numbing, but there was nothing else for us to do. Capable as we were, to Staxx we were a burden. Sixty-five liabilities who inconveniently required his feeding and watering.

Ducking inside the encampment, JD kicked an empty meal tray across the floor.

Ohno and Bix, busy tinkering with some contraption, flinched as the tray crashed against the wall.

"I know that look," Bix asserted while Ohno grumbled. "Who was it this time?"

"Cooper," I answered, massaging my still-throbbing jaw. "Again."

JD plopped down on the nearest mattress. "We need to get out of here."

I sat down beside him and inspected a little swelling over his eye. "Maybe we talk to Staxx again. Find some small job he'll let us do."

"Mop the floors? Hand out PRMs to the soldiers?"

Bix held up the contraption he and Ohno had been working on. "Or make repairs."

"What is that?" I asked.

Bix tossed it back to Ohno.

"Fuse cartridge from a flash grenade," she replied, catching it with one hand. "We found one smashed to pieces at the bottom of one of those munitions crates."

"Do me a favor and don't play with that."

"Why not?"

"Because I don't want it going off in my face."

Ohno playfully spun the cartridge in her fingers. "Hilarious."

"What's hilarious?" Bossa called out from behind me, poking his head inside.

JD threw up his hands at the intrusion. "What do you need, Bossa?"

"Someone out here looking for you, cookie."

"One of Staxx's goons?"

"Yup. Grumpy fella. Not very talkative."

"Guess it's my turn today," JD quipped as he got to his feet and grudgingly made his way back out into the armory.

The dread in him was obvious. Since establishing we had in fact Blinked into the future, every day Staxx randomly summoned one of us to rehash every last detail of our experience since Gallipoli.

As tiring as his interrogations were, I understood what he was doing. Somewhere inside the mystery of our Blink, he was hoping to find the only thing that could save our already-lost cause: the power to manipulate the hands of time.

Following JD out into the open, my eyes were drawn to where the students had cobbled together their own haphazard enclave. A few had taken to etching graffiti onto the chalky stone wall behind it. All their different, indecipherable doodles were beginning to merge into something more singular. In its own strange way, it was kind of beautiful.

I noticed Julian crouched beneath the mural, uncomfortably nestled between two students with whom he had nothing in common. His regretful eyes followed us as we walked toward the soldier.

For all my well-earned anger and resentment toward him, the same thought floated up yet again.

More one of us than one of them.

JD took close measure of the hulking visitor as we approached. I saw the same thing he did. Something about the soldier looked conspicuously annoyed. "Off to see the general, are we?" JD asked.

"No," the soldier deadpanned. "Someone else wants to see you."

CHAPTER 44

LIKO

FROM MY POSITION, HUNCHED AGAINST A CRATE inside the student encampment, I watched from a distance as Gentry tried to calm Cooper down near the back of the armory. I couldn't hear what was being said, but no doubt it was about his latest quarrel with Marshall. It was the third time in two days Cooper had instigated trouble with one of the cadets. And also the third time Gentry had played the unlikely role of peacemaker.

"There is very little space between men," my father once told me. *"Within it there is neither good nor evil. Nor is there right or wrong. There is only circumstance."*

He had used those words to convey a simple sentiment—that he did what he had to do for us to survive the war. As I grew older, I realized he was also speaking to something else: the fine line between allies and enemies.

I didn't know what happened in Gentry's few days away from us, but something about him had changed by the time of his return. My only guess was that the same fine line my father saw may have started to reveal itself to him.

There had been no consequence for anything. Not for Gentry's alleged failure at Gallipoli. Not for the cadets' mutinous response.

Not for the measures we had taken to remove them from command. Regardless of any possible defense or arguable justification, we should've all been brought before an Alliance military tribunal, yet Staxx did nothing other than deposit us in the armory to stew in a cauldron of mutual animosity.

I asked myself why. How could it be that the general would have such little concern for actions so abhorrent to the laws and codes of conduct of the Alliance? I could only conceive of one possible answer.

It didn't matter.

Not anymore.

With the world collapsing around him and the entire accumulated history of humankind hanging in the balance, the events that transpired aboard the *California*—no matter how grievous or repugnant—paled in comparison to the existential threat of the Kastazi.

Thinking of things in those terms, it was becoming harder and harder to remain faithful to the identities that divided us. *Cadets. Students. Explorers. Soldiers.* With the Kastazi threatening our extinction, was there anything left other than *us* and *them*?

The fine line between enemies and allies.

Inside the Resistance base, was it possible for us to be on anything but the same side of it?

We were all orphans of a world that no longer existed, clinging to survival in a time in which we did not belong, battling an enemy for which we had no answer.

Watching Gentry go about his business, it seemed clear he was beginning to operate under a similar awareness. No longer preoccupied with a vendetta toward the cadets, he concentrated on keeping order and calm among our ranks—moving quickly to reintegrate us with those who hadn't joined his insurrection.

Gentry also took it upon himself to tend to the fragile psyches inside our encampment. Some cried day and night. Others had stopped eating. A few had even become physically ill. It didn't seem like something he was particularly well equipped to deal with—nevertheless, he was doing the best he could.

In our second day in the armory, I observed him consoling Jagdish Patel. Gentry spoke to him softly, never wavering in his steady, reassuring eye contact. A few minutes later, Jag picked up a discarded PRM lid and scratched the words *Devastation Class* onto the wall. I wondered what Gentry might have said to inspire him to do that.

I wondered if Gentry'd go so far as to try to integrate us with the cadets next. Even if he wanted to, I wasn't sure where he'd even begin. There were still plenty of students like Cooper. Those who insisted on blaming everything that happened to us on the cadets, as if their actions alone had caused the Kastazi invasion and all that had followed in its wake.

It was irrational, but I thought I understood the psychology of it. They needed to point their angry daggers at something, and the cadets offered a far more immediate target than the Kastazi.

"One by one, they leave and come back," Cooper grumbled, stomping back into our encampment with Gentry in tow. "Where do they go? What are they planning?"

"They're not planning anything," Gentry calmly replied. "They're being debriefed."

"Debriefed? They mutinied and Blinked us into oblivion. That's all there is to it."

"Some think they saved our lives," I interjected almost reflexively, surprising myself.

"No, Liko. They stole them."

"How? By Blinking us past an apocalypse?"

"By Blinking us into one!"

"Gentlemen, let's move on," Gentry admonished.

"Are you serious? To where? To what?" Cooper snapped at him.

Gentry crouched down, wearily resting his back against the crate beside me.

"We're still here," he said, looking up at Cooper. "And as long as we're alive, we've got a fighting chance."

"Does this feel like a fighting chance to you?" Cooper asked, gesturing at the walls surrounding us.

"What does it feel like to you?"

"Hopelessness."

"Is that how you feel?" Gentry asked, tapping my knee. "Hopeless?"

Even after three days with little else to do but sit with my thoughts, I didn't have a clear answer.

"I'm feeling a lot of things." ·

Gentry closed his eyes and nodded to himself. "Lima Station."

"What did you just say?" Cooper indignantly replied.

"Lima Station. The first civilian outpost attacked in the war. Your mother refused to evacuate and held off an entire Kastazi platoon for two days. By herself. No weapons, no reinforcements. Just her wits."

"And then she died. Just like she would have if she'd done nothing," Cooper spat.

"Ju-long Chen," Gentry said, turning to me. "Your father was the highest-ranking Axis operative ever captured by the Alliance."

"That's no secret."

"His infiltration went all the way to the High Command, entirely undetected. He never made a mistake. Not one."

"Yet he was discovered nonetheless."

"Only because the Alliance turned another Axis operative against him."

"If you've got a point, why don't you just go ahead and make it?" Cooper complained.

Gentry pulled down the creases in his uniform.

"When we were prepping for launch, Captain Marshall briefed me on every single one of you. Prelaunch briefings are standard operating procedure, but this was something different. He wanted me to know everything there was to know about every student and cadet in the Explorers Program. Not just test scores, special skills, and disciplinary histories. Your families. Where you came from. What made you who you are. When I asked him why, he said it was because each of you was on the *California* for a reason. I thought he was just making a point. Telling me that there was a method to his madness, because some of you weren't even close to meeting the Explorers candidate profile. Now I'm beginning to think maybe he was trying to tell me something else. That he knew something was coming, and he was putting everything in its right place to be ready for it."

As crazy as it sounded, jumping five years into the future had left me ready to consider almost any possibility.

"You think Captain Marshall knew all of this was predestined? That somehow we were meant to be here?"

"Maybe."

"That's ridiculous!" Cooper scoffed.

"Is it? Even after everything you've seen?"

"If it were true, it wouldn't make any difference."

"If it's true, you wouldn't need to feel hopeless."

"Why?"

"Because Captain Marshall never would have set all this in motion just to have us die here."

CHAPTER 45

JD

I MADE SURE TO TAKE EVERYTHING IN as the soldier escorted me toward my unknown destination. Along our path I recognized the docking platform from our arrival, various guard posts and staging areas, as well as a mess and an infirmary. Each looked conspicuously vacant, undoubtedly the result of the Resistance's mounting losses.

We turned another corner and walked past what appeared to be a provisional chapel. Inside, four rows of hastily constructed pews faced an ornately dressed icon of an Aeson goddess. A few Aeson knelt quietly before it, their heads solemnly bowed.

"Do they pray every day?" I asked.

"They're not praying," he stoically replied. "They're asking for permission to die."

"Bavmat?"

"Yes, I think that's what they call it."

Bavmat, the Aeson death rite, was no perfunctory ritual. It was said to be practiced only at the imminent intersection of life and death. Whatever threat had put the Aeson on their knees had to be grave. It also had to be close at hand.

At the end of one more long corridor, there were no more

corners for us to turn. All that remained was the heavy alloy door. Affixed to it was a handwritten note.

Must you disturb me?

Annoyed, the soldier snatched the note and tossed it to the floor.

"Weirdo," he muttered to himself as he placed his hand on an adjacent scanner. With a clang and hiss, the lock disengaged and the door fell ajar.

"What is this place?"

Ignoring my question, the soldier ushered me inside and retreated in the opposite direction.

I immediately recognized I was inside a laboratory. In addition to the sophisticated analytical equipment I expected to see, its space was littered with antiquated accoutrements, such as funnels, test tubes, stir rods, pipets, and volumetric flasks. At the center of the space, a body lay on a long steel examining table, obscured by a sheet. It appeared to be humanoid.

At the far end of the lab, an observation window overlooked the docking platform. From my vantage point many of the ships were hard to make out, but I could clearly see the mighty *California*. Dwarfing every vessel around her, she was front and center and prominently in view. The repair drones blanketing the fuselage made her appear like a dog infested with thousands of tiny, spark-throwing fleas. The *Delphinium* was tethered to an adjacent berth, her damage being attended to as well.

"Welcome," a voice called out from behind me.

A figure lurked in the shadows, watching.

"Who are you?"

"A tired old man," he answered, striding into the light.

With each step forward his features came more clearly into focus. His shoulder-length black hair and carefully manicured beard. A small, jagged scar just beneath the right eye. I knew exactly who he was.

"Fuller," I whispered.

"Hello, John."

"But, you're . . ."

"Dead?" he spiritlessly answered. "Reports of my death . . . well, you know the rest."

A sharp chill ran down my spine. To see Fuller standing before me, in the living flesh, was almost impossible to process.

Despite his pronouncement to the contrary, he didn't look very old. If memory served me, he was somewhere in his late forties when he disappeared, and his appearance had barely changed at all. The question of his age aside, he did look tired.

"I've read your debriefing reports," he said, sluggishly lowering himself onto a chair by the examining table. "You claim the Hybrid—"

"Nicholas," I corrected him, my ears thumping with the pressure of my skyrocketing pulse. "His name was Nicholas."

The doctor reacted with a winsome tilt of his head. He seemed pleased I had referred to Nicholas by name.

"Nicholas," he cordially repeated. "You claim his self-termination protocol malfunctioned."

Still in shock, I struggled to articulate a response.

"This is important, John," he prodded me, assuming a more reassuring tone. "I need you to focus."

I tried to calm myself as best I could. "No, that's not what I said. I said he disregarded the protocol."

Fuller pensively massaged his temples.

"Tell me what you think the difference is."

"It was a choice. Not a malfunction."

"What makes you so sure?"

I paused, not sure how to express what I perceived in Nick to be the nuance of sentience.

"A malfunction is mechanical. It occurs, and its consequence inescapably manifests."

"And that's not what you observed?"

"No. There was an awareness. And a struggle."

Fuller's impassive expression suddenly bloomed into a full-blown smile.

"Come. Sit," he invited, gesturing to an adjacent chair.

My adrenaline finally regulating, I cautiously approached and sat facing opposite him. It was hard not to stare. I was looking into the eyes of not just a legend, but a ghost.

"You cared about him."

"We all did. He was one of us."

Clasping and unclasping his fingers, the doctor silently regarded me. It seemed clear he was engaging in some manner of internal deliberation, carefully considering what to say next.

"You should know your father risked his commission to help me bring Nicholas into being," he finally said. "If not for him, Nicholas would never have existed."

Whatever anxiety I was feeling was abruptly joined by indignation.

"You can't possibly expect me to believe that."

"Why not?"

"Because if you knew anything about my father, you'd know he'd never willingly subvert Alliance law."

"So says his son the mutineer," Fuller scoffed. "Your father was my friend, and I can assure you your apple didn't fall very far from his tree."

"If you want me to believe you, you need to do better than that," I shot back, recoiling at the unearned tone of familiarity he was addressing me with.

The doctor nodded, perhaps acknowledging for himself that he was moving too fast.

"I can tell you he did what he did because the Kastazi revealed an undeniable truth to him. That our existence is little more than a fragile metamorphic mutation. An evolutionary aberration waiting to be culled by the universal laws of natural selection. It could be a hundred years or a thousand, but, absent extraordinary intervention, our extinction is inevitable."

"And Hybrids were supposed to be that extraordinary intervention?" I skeptically retorted.

"No, it needed to be something more than that. Your father tasked me to engineer a second-generation Hybrid. One that would be entirely self-determinate. Capable of inheriting our civilization and carrying it forward long after we fade away."

It took a moment for the full impact of his revelation to hit me.

"Are you telling me he wanted them to replace us?"

"Not to replace us. To succeed us. By the operation of nature, humanity will eventually end. It is inevitable. So it was intended for them to continue on as the children of our civilization when that time comes, and for some vestige of us to live on within them."

"And that's what Nick was. The first Gen Two."

"Not the first. The first was barely distinguishable from a human being, possessing almost none of a Hybrid's special abilities. I thought self-determination might be more easily realized under the constant, existential threat of mortality. When that experiment bore no fruit, I abandoned it and created Nicholas. And then I waited."

"Waited for what?"

"Sentience. He could not have defeated his termination directive without it. What transpired aboard the *California* is proof of it. I have finally succeeded in endowing something born from lifelessness with life."

"You make it sound like you gave him a soul."

"I didn't give him one. It was there for the taking. The marrow of sentience and essence of life, it is inextricable from the fabric of space and time. It is material. It has form and substance. It can be captured. Harnessed. Directed."

As I had so often experienced with Bix, Fuller seemed to have no awareness of the complexity of the ideas he was trying to relate.

Yet, despite the unwieldiness of the metaphysical brain twister he had sent tumbling through my head, I still managed to deduce my way to the next step on the path he was leading me down.

"The marrow of sentience and the essence of life, it is inextricable from the fabric of space and time," I repeated, contemplating his words as I recited them out loud. "Whatever it is you found, you didn't just put it in Nick. You also put it in the reactor."

"Precisely," he conceded. "Properly channeled, it can transform the reactor into a disruptor of not just space, but also time. In interfacing Nicholas with the *California*'s reactor, you unwittingly unlocked its temporal displacement capacity."

For all the pernicious weapons created by the hands of men, none had ever held the potential to be as cataclysmically destructive as what Fuller had created. Bizarrely, his disaffected manner revealed no obvious concern for its terrifying implications.

"Why would you ever open the door to something so dangerous?"

Fuller looked away as if consulting the shadows for guidance.

"I knew your mother too. She was very kind. And quite beautiful."

His non sequitur landed like a punch to the gut.

"Yes, she was," I answered, trying not to let on he had rattled me.

"May I ask you something personal?"

A sense of dread billowed up inside me. "Go ahead."

The doctor leaned in and locked his eyes on mine.

"Do you dream of her?"

His query felt somehow rhetorical. It was as if he was more interested in gauging my reaction than actually procuring an answer.

"Yes," I replied, barely mustering a whisper. "Almost every night."

"And where do you go? What is it that you see?"

"The end. The way she died. I can't escape it."

"It haunts you."

"Yes."

Fuller wearily raised himself out of his chair and looked forlornly out the observation window.

"What if you could go back and stop it?" he asked, his eyes trained on my reflection in the glass. "Would you?"

All at once, I understood. "That's what happened to you. There wasn't any accident. You were trying to go back."

"I tried, yes," he confessed, turning to face me. "I wanted to go back far enough to build a new, indefatigable fleet of warships. Raise an army of Hybrids that would be impervious to enemy corruption. All the suffering. All the lives that were lost. I could have prevented it."

"But you didn't."

"But I couldn't," he corrected me. "There's a quantum barrier protecting the timeline. It cannot be penetrated. Any attempt to do so will deflect everything inside the reactor's temporal displacement field into the future—approximately five years into the future if we are to presume the misadventures of the *California* and the *Tripoli* represent a constant."

I quickly calculated the math of Fuller's time jump in my head.

"That would've landed you right into the heart of the Kastazi second wave."

"Correct. I spent nearly a year hiding and scavenging before I found the Resistance, and this sanctuary is where I have remained ever since. I can't even remember what it feels like to see the stars with my own eyes."

As Staxx was still searching for an explanation for what had happened to the *California*, I knew Fuller couldn't have confided in him what the Blink Reactor was really capable of.

"And in all your time here, why did you never tell Staxx the truth?"

"What good would it have done other than to inspire him with the same false hope I had so foolishly indulged? Fate delivered me to this base to attend to the practical, everyday needs of the Resistance's survival, not to chase the impossible."

"So that's all that's left for us to do now? Survive?"

"A week ago, I probably would've said yes. But then you brought me the *California*."

"The *California* can't save the Alliance, Doctor."

Fuller ambled clumsily toward the examining table.

"No, she can't. But what she was carrying just might."

He ripped the sheet off the body.

My stomach lurched, instigating a heaving retch.

Nick lay on the table, his torso open and cross-sectioned like a dissected cadaver.

"I'm sorry," Fuller apologized. "I should've warned you. But rest assured I can restore him to functionality."

Dizzy, I braced myself against the table. Had Nick been an android, his insides a tangle of wires, hydraulics, and power relays, he would have been easier to look at. But there was nothing about him that seemed any different from me.

"Sentient or not, one Hybrid can't save us either," I replied, covering my mouth to suppress the indelicate culmination of yet another gag.

"A forest starts with but one seed," Fuller replied while carefully folding a hemisected flap of skin back over Nick's sternum. "What exists in him can be shared. Populated forward."

"Populated forward to what?"

"The first-generation Hybrids, of course," he answered as if it were a self-evident conclusion. "Finally woken from their sleep."

Despite the hopeful gleam I noticed in Fuller's eyes, rousing one of the greatest threats humanity had ever known and endowing them with the power to do as they pleased sounded like a resoundingly bad idea.

"You can't be serious."

"Considering our lack of viable alternatives, I don't think it would be possible for me to be any more serious."

"Think this through," I urged him. "If you give them free will, what's stopping them from siding with the Kastazi?"

"Nothing," he replied, almost smugly.

"Then why would you ever trust them?"

"You trusted Nicholas, did you not?"

"He's one individual," I countered, not buying into his wild leap of extrapolation. "You can't predict what all of them will do."

"To the contrary. I believe I can."

"Why?"

Fuller ran his fingers through Nick's hair, gently straightening its tangled waves.

"Because to me they're not Hybrids. They are my children."

CHAPTER 46

VIV

I WASN'T SURE IF IT WAS HIS stiffness or his cold, disaffected eyes, but something about the soldier who had come calling for JD told me he was Shadow Ops. Shadow Ops were a small cadre of covert agents who reported only to the High Command. Recruited to undertake clandestine operations that could not be lawfully authorized, their ranks were populated by operatives with a predisposition for the kind of work that left a thick layer of dirt under their fingernails.

Why would someone have dispatched a Shadow Ops goon to retrieve JD?

And why was such a foreboding escort suddenly necessary when it hadn't been before?

Those were the questions I kept asking myself as I rested with my back against Bossa's munitions crate. The moment I sat there I realized why he had chosen its perch as his personal squat. Even from my lower vantage point I could see everyone and everything happening in the armory.

Deep in thought, I peered between the loitering bodies and focused on the tall shale wall behind the student encampment, where someone had scrawled *Devastation Class* in big block letters.

It seemed the students had taken ownership of the nickname that had been intended to mock us, transforming it into something of an ironic but proud identity.

"Hey!" Bossa called out as he jumped down, startling me.

"Thanks for the heart attack."

"For you," he said, holding out a piece of paper intricately folded into the shape of a rose. "Origami. It's a flower."

"Yes, I can see that," I answered, inspecting the meticulousness of its many layers. "You must really spend a lot of time alone."

I waited for a snappy comeback, but Bossa just stood there awkwardly.

"Did you expect me to trade you my PRM ration for this thing?" I said, offering his paper flower back to him.

"No, I just . . ."

"What?"

"It's nothing."

"Whatever's on your mind . . ."

"It's just a question."

"Ask it."

"What I told you in the brig," he said, his fingers twitching nervously. "About the *New Jersey*. Why haven't you asked me any more about it?"

"Because there's no point. You were lying. Trying to get under my skin."

Bossa's dancing fingers fell still.

"It was the truth."

"No. You couldn't have been any older than—"

"Sixteen," he softly uttered. "I was sixteen."

"That makes no sense."

"I can explain."

"What are you trying to do, Bossa? What's your angle?"

"I know it's hard for you to believe anything I say, but if you just listen to—"

A sudden rumble of commotion interrupted him.

It was JD marching back into the armory, making a beeline for the student encampment. Confused, I watched as he collected Gentry, Julian, and Liko and led them toward Bossa and me. Bix, Ohno, and Anatoly noticed what was happening and rushed toward us from the opposite direction.

I sprang to my feet as our two factions converged. My attention was irresistibly drawn to Julian. It was the closest I had been to him since we had arrived at the base. He noticed my scrutiny and dropped his gaze.

"All right," Gentry said. "We're listening."

"The past is written, but our future is not," JD proclaimed, briefly hesitating when he noticed the *Devastation Class* graffiti on the opposite wall. "If we're going to survive this nightmare, it's all going to come down to one question. Are we going to keep fighting each other, or can we come together to start fighting back?"

"Fight back how?" Liko replied with more than a hint of resignation. "This isn't a war. It's the aftermath of one. We've already lost."

"No, we haven't. Not yet."

"Do I sense a forthcoming rousing speech?" offered Bossa.

"If the cadet has something to say, let him say it," Gentry surprisingly interjected.

Acknowledging Gentry with a slight, respectful bow of his head, JD proceeded to debrief us. As his narrative unfolded, each new detail was more shocking than the last. Fuller. The secret of the Blink Reactor. Nick, and the plan to revive the dormant Hybrids. Likely because conceptions of the impossible were already almost entirely eroded, no one challenged a word of it.

"We told Staxx everything, and he's all in," JD continued. "He's recalling every remaining Resistance vessel to this sector. Once those ships are in position, a twenty-four-hour mission countdown will begin."

Apparently the general's conceptions of the impossible had

been similarly eroded. Or maybe he was just so desperate, he had no choice but to believe.

"And then what happens to us?" I asked.

"We've been given field commissions. The general is taking the *California*'s captain's chair. We won't be on the bridge, but we'll serve under his command however he can use us."

If there was going to be a fight, I wanted to be part of it. A "demotion" back to the lower decks wasn't what I had in mind, but I was relieved we weren't being left behind.

"And we stay here?" Liko lamented. "Waiting in the dark, praying you can pull off a miracle?"

"No," JD replied. "We all go. Live or die, we're going to do it together."

"Staxx authorized this?"

"To pull this mission off, he's going to need every able body he can get."

"Most of the students have no training," Julian interjected. "They're not prepared for battle."

"They may not be cadets, but they are Explorers," Gentry retorted. "The best and the brightest the Alliance had to offer. We can help them."

Ohno pounded her fist into her palm, her tattoos bursting with luminescent color. "So where do we begin?"

JD opened his mouth to reply but was preempted by a blaring siren. Not five seconds later there was an explosion, and the entire armory rumbled as if it were at the epicenter of an earthquake. Through the exit I could see Resistance infantry running in every direction. Two soldiers, one human and one Aeson, broke from their ranks and hurried inside.

"Listen up!" the human soldier yelled.

Disoriented by the frenzied chaos, few students paid him any heed.

The Aeson fired a short, controlled burst from his pulse rifle into the deck. That immediately got everyone's attention.

"We're going to secure you inside," the soldier resumed yelling. "Whatever you do, once we lock the doors, do not open them for any reason."

"You can't leave us," one student cried out.

"What's happening?" shouted another.

In the distance, I heard an echo.

As it drew closer, screeching like a wounded animal, it became hauntingly familiar.

In a few more seconds, it was unmistakable.

No.

Not now.

Not yet.

It was the sound of Kastazi Strikers.

JD ran out ahead of us. "Let us help you."

The soldier defensively raised his weapon. "Back off!"

I took JD's hand and slowly pulled him toward me, careful not to agitate the panicking soldier.

The Aeson swiftly gathered his comrade, leading him back out into the passageway. A moment later the armory's two heavy steel doors swung closed and locked themselves in place. Outside we could hear the muffled sounds of a pitched small-arms firefight. With each passing second its calamitous din drew closer.

His fingers still entwined with mine, JD tightened his grip and looked me in the eye. "Do you understand why I would've Blinked without you?"

His words hung in the air alongside the sound of howling weapons fire just on the other side of the armory door. I had struggled with the very same question, but in time an answer revealed itself to me.

In taking the *Delphinium* I had decided to give my life for what

I believed was more important than anything else—my duty to the Alliance and the souls aboard the *California*. But my choice was about far more than sacrifice. In a world upside down, where a meaningless fate like Safi's could come at any moment, I had chosen a destiny few ever get to touch. One of *true purpose*.

JD understood this.

And he loved me too much to take it away from me.

"Yes," I answered, squeezing his hand back twice as hard. "I do."

CHAPTER 47

JD

I CROUCHED ON MY KNEES, WAITING FOR the inevitable. Behind me, everyone else did the same. The sound of discharging pulse rifles had stopped. All that remained were intermittent shrieks of Kastazi Eradicator fire.

"All right. Get ready," I said. "Hands behind your heads."

The sound of students restraining their whimpers and cries was starting to rattle me. I just needed them to keep it together a few minutes more.

It took a little longer than I expected, but the Kastazi soon turned their attention to the armory. First I heard their muffled voices filtering through the doors. Next came the faint beeping of a timer. I translated its escalating frequency into a rough countdown.

"They've set a charge. Five seconds."

Trying to slow the flow of endorphins dumping into my bloodstream, I drew in short, even breaths through my nose.

"Four."

Behind me, someone softly cried.

"Three."

I looked over my shoulder at Viv. She was ready.

"Two."

I clenched my stomach in anticipation of the blast.

"One."

A small, controlled explosion flung the doors wide open, and a scout team of three Kastazi soldiers rolled in as if born from the soft white smoke that accompanied their intrusion. Each wore matte black body armor with distinct honeycomb-shaped, blast-resistant scales. Ghoulish, sharply angled helmets obscured their faces.

As they descended upon us in a tight, triangular formation, I focused on the lead soldier. His shoulders bore jagged, blood-red stripes signifying the rank of Rapax, a Kastazi platoon leader. As was the macabre tradition of the Rapax, his helmet boasted hundreds of clumsily etched hash marks—one for each of his confirmed kills.

A cold bead of sweat trickled down my nose as he slowly turned his head from left to right.

"*Ket al,*" the Rapax called out to his men.

Sixty-four. His head count was correct. Not including Bossa, there were exactly sixty-four of us. My Kastazi wasn't very good, but I knew enough to count to a hundred.

"*Obas han,*" one of the flanking soldiers called back to him.

Han was *no.* I was almost certain *obas* meant "prisoners."

I cautiously separated my fingers clasped behind my head. Taking my signal, Bossa lobbed Bix and Ohno's repaired flash grenade down from his perch behind us. It bounced once and harmlessly rolled to a stop at the Rapax's feet.

I held my breath, waiting.

The Rapax tapped at the sorry-looking contraption with the toe of his boot. Two tense seconds passed before the grenade finally exploded, consuming the Rapax and his men inside a blast of brilliant yellow light. A concurrent sound wave pounded my eardrums with a thunderous, stabbing concussion.

"Go!" yelled Viv, rallying us to charge the disoriented soldiers before they could gain their bearings. All three went down hard and fast under the weight of our swarming bodies, but not before the Rapax squeezed his Eradicator's trigger.

Cooper clutched a gaping wound in the meat of his thigh.

Despite the chaos, everything around me seemed to slow in anticipation of the horror I knew would come next.

Almost instantaneously, the gruesome damage to his leg festered outward in an unstoppable chain reaction of cellular necrosis, devouring every molecule of organic tissue in its path until there was nothing left to feed its progress.

I whipped my head toward the open entryway, afraid more Kastazi would respond to the students' horrified screams. One step ahead of me, Bossa leapt down to the deck and secured the armory's blast-warped doors as best he could.

"Him," I said to Anatoly, pointing to the Rapax lying faceup on the floor. "Quickly."

Anatoly grabbed the soldier's feet and dragged him toward me. I jammed my boot up under his chin, pinning him to the floor.

"Show me his face."

A whoosh of pressurized oxygen escaped as Anatoly removed the Rapax's helmet.

With his bald, narrow, sloping head and thickly husked, oyster-gray skin, the Kastazi's humanoid appearance was infused with all the same predatory efficiency as a great white shark. Even after so many years, their menacing appearance still managed to unsettle me.

"How many ships? How many infantry?" I demanded.

He offered no response, but his gleaming silver pupils darted back and forth, regarding me with a rabid intensity.

I squeezed my boot harder under his chin, choking off his airway.

"How many?"

Just as his lips parted to speak, a voice called out from his helmet. It repeated the same Kastazi refrain again and again.

Mar'eh Gral, bak. Mar'eh Gral, bak.

"What are they saying?"

"It's his name," Liko told me. *"Mar'eh Gral.* They're asking him to report."

I could hear the same queries broadcasting from inside the helmets of the other two soldiers. Each frantically barked responses back into their coms. A moment later their voices went quiet, abruptly replaced by an escalating, high-pitched frequency. I knew what was coming, and there was nothing I could do to stop it.

The earsplitting noise crescendoed to a barely perceptible *pop.* An instant later the Rapax and his men synchronously stiffened and then fell limp.

"Widowmakers," Anatoly confirmed, referring to the tiny charges embedded deep inside the brain of every Kastazi soldier. The remotely detonatable implants ensured they could never be taken prisoner.

My ears still ringing from the grenade's bang, I fixated on the dead Rapax's empty stare. Blood seeped into the whites of his eyes, encircling the dilated silver crescents peeking out from under his lazy, drooping eyelids.

"Don't touch that!" Bix screamed at someone standing behind me.

Startled, I spun around to see Annalisa holding an Eradicator. The weapon recognized her human biosig and automatically began to squeal toward overload. She looked more confused than frightened as it detonated in her hands and sent its virulent energy surging through her body. In the span of little more than a heartbeat, she was gone.

Liko dropped to his knees, hovering over her smoldering biomass in a state of shock.

Julian yanked him right back to his feet. "We have to go!"

Overwhelmed by the nauseating smell of Annalisa's melted flesh, I stood frozen.

Viv shook me. "John!"

Her voice was like a distant echo.

"John!" she shouted again. "Let's go!"

I staggered back a step, a sudden dizziness washing over me.

"John?"

My head filled with intense pressure.

"Anatoly, help! Something's wrong with him!"

White noise clogged my ears. Viv yelled something else, but I couldn't hear her.

I held up my hand, urging her to stay back.

Then, just as quickly as the feeling came, it was gone—leaving in its wake a powerful presence. And it spoke to me.

John, come now.

The voice's intrusion into my head was unsettling, but I wasn't afraid. I wasn't afraid because of who it belonged to.

Fuller.

Anatoly took hold of my chin and loudly snapped his fingers in my face.

"Are you all right? Can you hear me?"

There's very little time.

You know what to do.

Since Fuller was the architect of countless technologies that defied our understanding of nature, his figuring out how to broadcast right into my skull wasn't so much difficult to accept. It was more difficult *to explain*. Nonetheless, I made an attempt.

"It's Fuller," I began. "He's . . . talking to me."

Noticing the concerned expressions staring back at me, I quickly abandoned any notion of explaining. We didn't have the time.

"Forget it. I'm fine," I said abruptly, pulling away from Anatoly's hand. "The docking platform is only about two hundred meters from here. We need to get everyone to the *California*. Right now."

Gentry looked at me like I was out of my mind. "We have no idea how many Kastazi infantry are between us and that platform!"

"Try, or wait to die," I stoically replied. "Those are our options."

Gentry craned his neck around the armory. "Do you all understand what he's suggesting?"

No one answered, but their terrified expressions told me they understood.

"If we're going to do this, we need to do it right," Gentry said, reluctantly conceding we had no other choice. "Let's get our people into skirmish formation."

The others waited for me to move first.

"Go," I ordered them. "Do what he says."

"What about you?" Ohno asked.

"You're going for Nick," said Bix, his face growing pale with dread. "Aren't you?"

"I have to. Without him, Fuller's plan won't work."

Viv stepped beside me. "I'm coming with you."

"No," I insisted, steering her back toward the others.

"You need my help!" she protested, grabbing me by the wrist and stubbornly pushing back.

"So do they."

Consulting the students' desperate faces, Viv loosened her grip.

"Get them through. I'll meet you at the ship. I promise."

She looked at me, crestfallen, like I was saying goodbye.

Hurry.

You must hurry.

Bix nervously blinked his eyes. "And how are you going to get past the Kastazi?"

I picked up the Rapax's empty helmet and held it in my hands. Its many pointed, sharp edges pricked at my fingertips.

"Ruse de guerre," I answered. "They'll never see me coming."

It took a thousand meters or so before I felt comfortable inside the Rapax's armor. A persistent electrical charge supported its heavy exoskeleton, assisting each of my steps toward an awkwardly light and powerful gait. A muddled array of readouts projected inside the helmet clouded my field of vision. I did my best to tune them out and concentrate on taking smooth, even strides.

Straight ahead.

I nearly stumbled as I approached a small unit of Kastazi soldiers, but none of them seemed to notice. They were too fixated on the Aeson they had pushed down onto his knees. He looked up at me as I passed, his eyes bulging with fear. I wanted to stop, but I couldn't.

Don't look back.

Behind me I heard the sound of Eradicator fire and the Aeson's screams. The two horrible noises melded together and bounced from the corridor walls like a demonic howl. I cringed, half expecting a second blast to hit me in the back. It was another twenty paces before I exhaled.

Keep going.

With each additional turn I happened upon more remnants of the Resistance's dead, and the revolting smell of death grew thicker and more pungent. I kept pushing forward, focusing on arbitrary spots in the distance to prevent my senses from ramping into overload.

Focus.

You're getting closer.

Amid the carnage I had lost my bearings, but the voice continued to guide my path. Summoning me toward it.

Over the gangway.

Crossing over a long, metal-girded gangway, I could see the movement of Kastazi troops in the corridor just beneath me. Sparsely dispersed, they methodically prowled forward in the same direction. It wasn't what I would have expected from a coordinated infiltration. Their numbers were too few. Their movements too passive.

Into the lift.

An open lift waited at the end of the gangway. I recognized it from before and stepped inside.

Level 3.

My helmet broadcasted constant Kastazi chatter into my ears as the lift shot up three levels. Almost all of it was gibberish to me. Except for one thing they kept repeating. *Ampla'ras.* I knew that word. It meant "reinforcements."

The Kastazi's call for support confirmed my suspicion that their incursion had been precipitously launched, presumably acting upon a sudden and unexpected piece of intelligence.

The lift doors opened to reveal a long, empty corridor, its lights flickering on and off.

Run.

I burst forward, each of my strides landing with a thud. A few hundred meters in, the lighting failed completely, automatically activating bright green–hued night vision inside my visor. I quickly adjusted to the artificial illumination and ran even faster.

Finally turning the corner to Fuller's laboratory, I stopped dead in my tracks. Two Kastazi soldiers were standing guard outside its open doorway. My adrenaline peaked and sweat oozed from every pore in my body.

"*Ahk bak al,*" one of them called out to me, light emanating from the lab silhouetting his formidable stature.

I didn't understand what he was saying.

Don't stop.

I ignored him and proceeded forward.

Both Kastazi stepped in front of me, blocking my path.

"*Ahk bak al,*" the soldier repeated.

Don't stop.

I tilted my head toward the red stripes on my shoulder, invoking my "superior rank."

"*Dach!*" I barked, confident that was their word for *move.*

"*Ahk bak al!*" he demanded once again.

I wanted to turn and run the other way, but it was far too late for that.

Don't stop.

"*Ahk bak al,*" I repeated, wrongly guessing it was some kind of salutation.

"*Ertu!*"

I knew *ertu*. It meant "human."

The soldiers drew their Eradicators and straightened their arms to fire.

I stood frozen in terror, but a guttural voice boomed from Fuller's laboratory before they could pull their triggers.

"*Pral!*" it shouted.

Pral meant "stop."

A thickset Kastazi soldier lumbered through the laboratory's doorway, each of his armor-clad thighs nearly as wide as a tree trunk. The three white stripes on each of his shoulders told me he was an Apexus, the rank of a Kastazi battalion commander. He wore neither a helmet nor gloves.

"*Tak za ras,*" he said.

His men detached my helmet and threw it to the ground.

I could see my reflection in the Apexus's eyes. His silver pupils eerily distorted my image like a funhouse mirror.

"The son of the Butcher of Titan Moon," he said in perfect English as he ran his hand back along his head. His fingers, wet with fresh blood, left dark-red stains inside the bald, wrinkly folds of his scalp. "Fortune has smiled upon me today."

Following their commander back through the doorway, the soldiers ushered me inside with a few swift jabs to my ribs. The first thing I saw was Nicholas's pale, lifeless body lying prone on the table. A thick umbilical wire connected him to a tall, black obelisk I hadn't seen before. Fuller sat slumped in a chair beside it, his head slung low against his chest.

"He said you'd come for him," the Apexus said, loitering between us, his swollen hand still dripping with Fuller's blood.

The obelisk looked inert, but like a magnet, something about it beckoned me.

"And he said you'd bring me the key."

"Key to what?" I hazily replied, forcing myself to break free from the enchanting power of the obelisk.

"To the source code of that abomination on the table," he replied, perfunctorily gesturing toward Nick's body.

I had no such key.

"I'm afraid the doctor lied to you," I answered, settling back into my center.

The Apexus dismissively smirked at me. "He would not be so foolish."

"You're the fool if you thought torturing him would get you what you want."

Angered, he stepped close and inspected the contours of my placid expression. His moist breath wafted against my nose, its sour odor burning my nostrils.

Vexed by my calm, he cocked his head to the side. "You are not afraid?"

"No," I lied, mustering everything I had to maintain the illusion of fearlessness.

"You should be," he hissed, leveling his Eradicator at my head. I could feel the weapon's radiant energy pulsing against my skull. "Without the key, your life has no purpose."

I ignored him, knowing that no matter what I said or did, he was still going to kill me.

"Speak!" he shouted, spraying me with a fine mist of his vile spit.

My mind ranged back to the Code of the Alliance Fighting Force. In combat, it was every soldier's duty to evade capture, resist while a prisoner, or escape from the enemy. Resistance was the only option left at my disposal.

"My name is John Douglas Marshall," I defiantly responded, "senior cadet aboard the UAS *California*. Service designation mark X1A26-Alpha."

The Code required us to provide our name, rank, and SD mark, and nothing else. After that we were supposed to evade any and all questioning to the utmost of our ability.

"The key!"

I was absolutely terrified, and with each passing second it grew more and more difficult to hide.

I looked to Fuller. He was drifting in and out of consciousness, perhaps not even aware of my presence.

"My name is John Douglas Marshall, senior cadet aboard the UAS *California*. Service designation mark X1A26-Alpha."

The Apexus pressed his Eradicator against my forehead. Its vibration rattled down into my teeth.

The Kastazi's finger tensed against the trigger.

An overwhelming sadness began to swallow my fear. Not because I was going to die. Because I had failed.

"My name is John Douglas Marshall," I repeated one last time before closing my eyes.

And then I waited.

When nothing came, I wondered if I was already dead. That perhaps fate had mercifully spared me from the pain.

"Very well," the Apexus sighed.

Holstering his weapon, he stepped behind Fuller and snatched his head up by the hair. "If you don't fear for yourself, perhaps you'll fear for him."

The doctor's eyes rolled forward as the Apexus unsheathed a short, serrated dagger from his belt and slipped it under Fuller's chin.

"Don't," Fuller pleaded, blood drooling over his lips.

"You can save him."

I stood silent, knowing I could not.

His attention focused on me, the Apexus began to cut. I watched helplessly as blood spilled down Fuller's neck.

"Stop!" the doctor shouted just before the blade sliced his jugular.

The Apexus paused. "You know how to end this, Doctor."

Fuller meekly wiped his mouth with his sleeve.

"He doesn't have the key," he gurgled. "He is the key."

I didn't react. I recognized Fuller's fantastical lie for what it was. A futile attempt to buy us more time.

"Explain," the Apexus replied, bending his ear close to Fuller's mouth.

Exhausted and broken, the doctor pressed his quivering hand against his open, seeping wound. "It's inside him," he weakly uttered. "A biometric interface. If he touches the Hybrid, its source code will export to the obelisk."

The Apexus looked at me skeptically, searching my face for any hint of complicity with Fuller.

There was nothing for him to find. Fuller's desperate rambling was nothing but nonsense.

"Bring him to the table," he ordered his men while impressively twirling his dagger back into its sheath.

The soldiers pushed me toward Nick. His pallid body lay rigidly on the cold slab.

"Go ahead, then," the Apexus instructed me. "Touch him."

It made no difference, but adhering to the Code, I refused.

With a perfunctory nod from their commander, the soldiers forced my hand down upon Nick's chest. As soon as my fingers rested on his flesh, a sharp spike of pain rushed up through my arm. It felt like acid coursing through my veins.

The Apexus tapped his sharp, yellowed fingernails against the still-inert obelisk.

"More lies?"

"No more lies," Fuller replied, flashing his blood-soaked teeth with a wide, wily smile.

Just then the obelisk came alive, strobing thousands of images. They were, inexplicably, my memories. My life, all at once flashing before my eyes.

The arrival of Kastazi Destroyers to Earth before the war.

My father and Commander Nixon wishing Viv and me goodbye before shipping off to join the fight.

Lying in a hospital bed, writhing in agony from my burns.

Charlie.

My mother's murder.

Striker fire raining down upon Farragut.

The first time I met Bix.

The Crucible.

Our prelaunch fight with the students in the Camp Penbrook canteen.

My father sitting across from me, confessing his own fear.

Sigma 547-T's pink ocean waves breaking against its beach's blue silicon sand.

Gallipoli ravaged.

Settling into the captain's chair for the first time.

The gaping hole in the California *that sucked Safi into space.*

Nick standing in his doorway without a scratch.

Viv's gentle kiss.

The obelisk froze on that final memory, a cosmically cruel reminder of how much I had left unsaid. I should have told Viv how her kiss made me feel. That I didn't want it to be the last time.

Filled with regret, my eyes fell down to Nick. It actually brought me solace to think that I'd soon be like him. At peace.

Then his eyes snapped open. Still flat on his back, he snatched the Apexus's Eradicator and squeezed off three quick blasts with exacting precision. By the time I'd gained my wits, each of the

Kastazi had collapsed to the floor, their skin and bones already catabolizing toward liquescence.

Nick slowly pushed himself up and watched them die. Light from crisscrossing Strikers beamed through the observation window, setting his eyes ablaze. His chest angrily heaved, pulling in deep, gulping breaths of air.

His name spilled from my lips in a faint, disbelieving whisper. "Nick."

Fuller, not nearly as weak as he had led the Apexus to believe, stepped over the soldiers' hollow, flesh-leaking armor and helped Nick off the table. "His speech index is still repopulating. He can't speak."

Standing before me naked, the scars of his vivisection completely healed, Nick smiled at me reassuringly.

"What is that thing, Doctor?" I asked, looking at the obelisk over Nick's shoulder. "And how did it get in my head?"

Fuller laid his hands on both of us and bowed his head. Blood slowly trickled from his shattered nose and oozed from the deep laceration across his neck.

"We need to get Nicholas to the *California*. Once we're there, I can explain everything."

CHAPTER 48

VIV

THE HAIR ON THE BACK OF MY neck stood on end as Gentry, Bossa, and I cautiously led everyone down the corridor. Liko and Julian followed right on our heels while Bix, Anatoly, and Ohno evenly dispersed inside our tightly packed procession.

It was five corridors from the armory to the docking platform, and we had made it four without encountering a single Kastazi. With their numbers so few, I knew their raid was likely spontaneous. Maybe a roving patrol responding to anomalous sensor readings, or, more distressingly, a traitorous leak from inside the base.

A bead of sweat dripped off the tip of my nose. I was so tense that I literally flinched when it hit the floor, as if the sound of the tiny bead of moisture hitting stone would be loud enough to expose us.

Breathe, Nixon.

Breathe.

I raised my fist, giving our group the signal to stop as we approached the final turn. "Probably a choke point around the corner," I whispered.

The fourth corridor was a hard ninety degrees off the fifth, and a thick emergency bulkhead sat recessed in the rock above the perpendicular intersection.

"How many you thinking?" Gentry whispered back.

"If we're only up against a rover unit, most of them are probably sweeping the interior. That would mean maybe a handful stayed behind to guard the platform."

"Agreed."

"A handful?" Julian asked. "Doesn't that change things?"

"Still only one way onto the platform. If I'm right, it just gives us a better chance of getting through."

"You really believe the students are going to run into the line of fire?" he skeptically replied, perhaps more concerned for himself than for them.

I turned to Liko, inviting his response.

"Some will," he answered. "But when the first Eradicator blast goes whizzing by their heads . . ."

Glancing away, I noticed Bix's and Ohno fiddling with a small junction box mounted on the wall. Anatoly stood apprehensively beside them.

"Keep everyone settled. I'll be right back," I told Liko. "Gentry, Julian, with me."

Breaking from the line, we hustled to the wall, where Bix's and Ohno's hands were deep inside the box, picking through a tangled mess of wires.

Bix pulled up a thin red one. "Emergency bulkhead?"

Ohno inspected it closely. "I think so, yes."

Reaching behind the morass, Ohno pinched a thick-gauged yellow cable. "Primary power coupling?"

"Looks like it," Bix responded.

"Talk to me, guys."

Ohno tugged the yellow cable to the limit of its slack. "Shorting this will throw off an electromagnetic pulse. However many Kastazi are waiting around that corner, it should power down their Eradicators and fry the support charge in their exoskeletons. They'd have to jettison their armor off just to move."

"What's the catch?" Gentry asked.

"Catch is, the only way to get a strong enough pulse is to concentrate it in a confined space," Bix replied, massaging the red wire between his fingers. "We'd have to send a few people into the next corridor and drop the emergency bulkheads on either side of them."

"So they can take out the Kastazi soldiers guarding the choke?"

"Yes. Exactly."

Julian shook his head. "That's not an idea. It's a Hail Mary."

"The odds would be evened," I responded. "No weapons. No armor. They'd have to take us on hand to hand."

"What if there are ten of them? Or twenty?"

"If there's twenty, we're dead already."

"We're not talking about a bunch of sparring Synths here," Julian protested. "We're talking about combat-ready Kastazi soldiers. They're trained to fight. And kill."

"So are we," Gentry answered, unbuttoning his uniform jacket.

Taking his cue, I did the same. "Can I count on you in there, Evan?"

"I won't let you down again."

Dropping our jackets to the floor, we turned to Julian.

"Are you with us?" I asked.

Julian looked past me, peering at the corner's break. "Watch your low block."

"What?"

"When you low block, you drop your head. Almost every time we spar. I never exploited it. When we're in there, the Kastazi won't be so kind."

"Noted."

———

We positioned ourselves at the very end of the corridor, our backs flat against the wall's jagged rocks. So close to the edge, I could hear Kastazi soldiers talking just out of view. I just couldn't pick out how many.

Bix stood by the junction box, at the ready.

Prayer was little more than ritualized superstition to me, but I found myself praying nonetheless.

Please don't let there be any more than we can handle.

Please, no more than three of them.

Julian exhaled deeply. "Ready?"

"I am," I answered, brushing my fingers across the smooth stones of Safi's bracelet.

"Remember, their Eradicators will reset themselves in three minutes," Gentry warned us. "So that's all the time we've got."

I raised my fist in the air. As soon as Bix nodded back, I began my silent countdown. Three fingers. Two. One.

The bulkheads dropped faster than I expected, and Gentry narrowly missed having his legs crushed as we rolled underneath.

I quickly counted five Kastazi. So much for prayer.

Bix released the pulse just as the soldiers turned to face us, freezing them where they stood. I charged before they could eject from their armor, smashing one in the chest with a leaping tiger kick. He crashed against the wall and bounced back into my waiting shoulder check. The second blow sent him flying off his feet.

As soon as he hit the deck, his helmet and exoskeleton jettisoned with a powerful hydraulic burst. I dropped my knees on either side of his unprotected neck. Pinned, he looked up at me in fear. Confronted by his mirrored eyes, I broke his neck with a single, sharp twist of my hips. The sickening crack lapsed me into a momentary stupor. It was intoxicating and revolting all at once, unlocking a capacity I never knew I possessed, let alone ever wanted.

Hearing footsteps behind me, I snapped up and spun around, but stepped right into a punch to the throat from another Kastazi. As I fell, he caught me by the hair. Dangling over the floor, I could see Julian fighting for his life just behind me. Ducking a sloppy haymaker, he bounced up to land a vicious uppercut under his opponent's chin. His Kastazi fell backward into mine, jostling him just enough for my fingertips to touch the ground. I locked my elbow and spun on my hand's axis to deliver a sweeping leg kick. The blow took out my opponent's feet and sent him crashing to the floor.

Both our opponents were flat on their backs. His lay still while mine slowly rose back to his feet. A few paces ahead of us, Gentry flailed against two soldiers at once.

"Help him—I've got this."

"Vivien . . ."

"Go!"

Julian ran to Gentry, and I bent my knees, readying for attack. I threw my best exploding jab, but the Kastazi caught my wrist and nearly twisted my arm out of its socket. Helpless, restrained in his armlock, I winced as he lifted me into the air by my neck. I instinctively clawed at his hands, but his grip was unrelenting.

Sucking in a labored breath, I mustered the strength to box the Kastazi's ears with a rocking wallop. Stunned, he lowered me to eye level, allowing me to drop a devastating head butt on his orbital bone. A bleeding red halo expanded around his pupil as he stumbled backward in agony.

Taking back my wind, I followed until his back was against the wall. Steadying him by the collar, I finished him with a swift elbow strike to the skull. His blood spattered on my face like war paint.

I promptly spun to orient myself. Julian was still engaged in combat, but Gentry lay prone, a soldier ferociously pummeling his face. With each blow, her sweaty black hair whipped violently about her head. It was only then I realized that she was human.

"Hey!" I yelled, getting her attention.

She stiffened and looked over her shoulder at me as I marched toward her.

"You look at me like I'm a traitor," she said, slowly rising off of Gentry. "I'm not."

"No? Then what are you?"

"A survivor."

I crouched into snake position, bending my body backward and raising my head up to strike.

She lunged at me as if shot out of a cannon. I was ready with a Wing Chun punch, but she adroitly evaded and hit me with a spinning backfist to the temple. It was no arbitrary strike. She intentionally targeted my trigeminal nerve to disrupt the blood flow to my brain. Right out of the Alliance Field Combat Manual.

Disoriented, I dropped my hands, leaving myself vulnerable. I took two palm heel strikes to the chest and one to the chin. I struggled to stay on my feet as blood spilled over my lips.

She came at me again. I blocked high and center mass, directing her blows to where I knew I could take the most punishment. Playing into my hands, she adjusted to pound the meatiest parts of my torso with a series of stinging left and right crosses. Excruciating as it was, it kept my damage to a minimum. Stumbling back, I drooled a string of bloody mucus and doubled over in exaggerated pain.

"Is that all you've got?" I taunted her.

Anticipating a cut kick to the stomach, I focused on her midsection. At the first twinge of her hips, I tensed my abdominals slightly. The jolt to my gut pushed me three meters back, more than enough runway for her to think she could finish me.

I swayed on my feet and drooped my eyelids for effect. Sprinting toward me, she dropped her head slightly. It was only a split second of vulnerability, but that was all I needed. I knew what was coming next. She was cocky, and that made her predictable.

Springing forward, I grabbed her arm and used the force of her own acceleration to vault myself up onto her shoulders. Locking my knees under her chin, I leaned back with all my weight. Like a tall tree severed from its roots, she fell over backward, sending us crashing to the floor together.

She tried to right herself, but I smashed my elbow down upon the bridge of her nose. Even in the heat of the moment, the cracking sound made me gag. Her head fell limply to one side, a foamy white residue leaking from the corner of her mouth.

Pushing myself off her, I saw Julian in the final throes of asphyxiation, the last standing soldier choking him from behind. I limped three or four steps toward them before the Kastazi buckled and fell. Gentry stood over him, a long, jagged fragment of armor in his hands.

The corridor fell eerily quiet absent the sounds of mortal combat. Exhausted, Gentry let the armor slip through his fingers onto the unconscious soldier's chest.

Julian ran to me, seemingly numb to the damage he had taken.

"I'm sorry," he said, gently caressing the stinging edges of a deep gash above my eye.

I pushed his hand away. "Please don't do that."

Gentry pulled the manual release lever on the first bulkhead, and it began to gradually recede.

"If anything ever happened to you . . ." Julian said to me, his lips quivering.

Just then he noticed something and froze. Well over three minutes had passed since Bix unleashed the pulse. Enough time for the Kastazi's Eradicators to charge back through their power cycles.

In the open, a sitting duck, I pivoted to see what was waiting for me.

It was the human. I should've finished her.

Before she could fire, a powerful jolt threw her onto her back. Behind her, a Kastazi soldier walked under the still-receding bulkhead, throwing a long, exaggerated shadow over her fast-disintegrating remains. On either side of the soldier were two more.

The Kastazi made no allowances for failure. Summarily

executing their human confederate for letting us get this far came as no surprise.

I set my feet and raised my fists to fight. Taking my cue, Gentry and Julian followed suit. As futile as it was, it offered a more digni-fied alternative to dying on our knees.

With the docking platform and the *California* just on the other side of the bulkhead, it felt like fate was delighting in cruelly toying with me.

So close.

We were so close.

Having reached the center of the corridor, the soldiers removed their helmets, sending a hydraulic hiss echoing off the walls. And then came their faces.

"I don't believe it," gasped Julian.

I didn't say it out loud, but I had the same exact thought.

Left and right were JD and Fuller. In the center, Nick, holding an Eradicator. Like all of Fuller's Hybrids, he possessed the ability to replicate a Kastazi biosig.

Every tightly spasmed muscle in my body relented all at once and my knees buckled as JD ran over and embraced me. The sharp edges of his Kastazi armor stabbed at my skin, but his touch still felt perfect.

He was alive. He was next to me. That's all that mattered.

Over his shoulder, I stared in wonder at Nick's face. To see him alive, literally resurrected, took my breath away. "Nick. Thank you."

He smiled but didn't speak as our full contingent spilled under-neath the bulkhead.

"He can't talk. His speech index is repopulating," Fuller said.

"Vivien Nixon, Doctor Samuel Fuller. Doctor Fuller, Vivien Nixon," said JD, providing us our battlefield introduction.

"And now?" Liko asked as everyone circled around us.

JD pointed to the bulkhead separating us from the docking platform. "Now we open it and go through."

Gentry wearily ran his fingers through his bloody hair. "Let's not and say we did."

"Was that a joke?"

"I think it was."

"I've been waiting three months to hear you say something funny."

"Everything you hoped for?"

Indulging a moment's gallows humor, JD cracked a smile.

"Listen up," I announced. "We don't know what's waiting for us on the other side. Whatever you're thinking, presume it will be worse. You have one mission. Run to the *California*. Run as fast as you can. If you fall, do not cry out for help. If a friend falls, leave them. Whatever happens, do not stop."

"I'll open the bulkhead on your mark," said Gentry.

"Copy," I answered. "Everyone line up and get ready."

"C'mon, let's go, let's go," Liko barked, urging the students forward.

"Where's the *Delphinium*?" Bossa called out to us, splitting through the mass of bodies falling in toward the bulkhead.

"One berth past the *California*," Fuller volunteered.

"Thank you, Doctor."

"So that's it?" JD asked Bossa.

"You expected me to stick around?"

"Our world's falling apart, Bossa. We're in this together now."

"Your world had already fallen apart, cookie. You just had the blinds drawn."

"Forget it," I interrupted, pulling JD away. "He's a lost cause."

Bossa's eyes tracked us as we walked away. I saw something different in them. Something far more vulnerable than anything they'd revealed before.

Settling in at the center of the line, I positioned myself between JD and Julian. "Ten seconds!" I shouted.

Unbeknownst to each other, they both rested a hand on my back.

"Five seconds!"

I surveyed our ranks one last time. Beside us one student placed her trembling fingers against the bulkhead.

"Now!"

Gentry pulled the release lever, and the bulkhead began to retract. The first thing I saw were armor-clad boots. Dozens of them. And then, as the bulkhead retracted farther, I saw the rest. Two full battalions of Kastazi reinforcements surrounding a unit of Resistance soldiers—at least forty human, Aeson, and Xax— submitted on their knees. Staxx stood defiantly before them, a live phasing grenade peeking out from either side of his grip. Both ends pulsated with bright-blue swells of light.

The general acknowledged our arrival, nodded to himself, and squeezed. The blue swells immediately faded to yellow.

"Your end begins today," he called out to the Kastazi, squeezing again. Then the swells went dark red.

A second later the grenade exploded, releasing concentric circles of energy pulsing sequentially outward. The first wave instantly ran through Staxx and his men. The second incinerated more than half of the Kastazi. The third blew anyone left standing off their feet.

"Run!" I screamed.

We ran through the smoke like a herd of stampeding cattle. My ears still ringing from the blast, I heard the muted sound of Eradicator fire all around me, but couldn't tell where it was coming from. Disoriented, I tripped and fell over the body of a dead Xax soldier. Nobody stopped to help. Before I could get up another body fell beside me. It was one of our own, but I couldn't make out who. An Eradicator blast had already devoured them beyond recognition.

I jumped up and resumed sprinting. My feet nearly slipped out from under me as I ran through another puddle of decimated remains. My lungs burned as I pumped my legs harder and harder. An awful feeling of dread knotted in my stomach. Lost in the smoke, I didn't know if I was even running in the right direction.

Finally, I saw the *California* in the murky distance. I shook my head to convince myself it wasn't an illusion spawned by my panic-stricken mind. JD and Julian were already there, shepherding our people up the gangplank. Ohno, Bix, Anatoly, Nick, Fuller. Even Liko. They had all made it.

JD reached out for me as I ran up the gangplank's steep incline. Completely out of gas, I stumbled and fell off the side. JD leapt to the platform and offered me his hand. I took it and looked up into his eyes.

JD shuddered and let go of my hand. A black ring spontaneously consumed the skin around his neck and grew outward from there. He never once stopped looking into my eyes until he was . . . gone.

Gone!

I lived inside that moment for what felt like an eternity.

There was no sound.

No light.

Just him and me, in a bubble, vanishing from existence together.

I closed my eyes and stood alone in the darkness. The ringing in my ears returned. Beneath that were layers of shouting voices and the shrill, piercing noise of Eradicator blasts firing from every direction. Then I felt something tugging at my arm.

"Vivien!" a voice cried out, piercing the wall of commotion.

It was Anatoly, trying to pull me up the plank.

"Get her up here! We've got to go!" Gentry shouted from inside the ship.

"I'm trying!" Anatoly yelled back to him.

Liko jumped to the platform to help.

I was only a shell. An empty vessel, incapable of putting one foot in front of the other. As the smoke cleared, I saw two students, Jagdish Patel and Dominique Parry, pinned down behind a supply drum. Completely defenseless, their eyes were filled with terror. I broke free from Anatoly, but Liko grabbed my shirt.

"Let me go!" I demanded.

Liko pulled me close. "It's too late! You can't help them!"

A hand reached between us and pried me free. It was Julian. He looked at me sorrowfully. "Let her go," he told Liko. "She's gone already."

He understood. JD was part of me. Without him I didn't exist either.

As soon as I ran, I felt the tingling energy of an Eradicator beam against my face. It was a near miss, but the radiant heat of the blast was enough to bubble a small patch of skin running along my jaw line. I evasively tumbled into a diving roll and came to rest at the feet of two dead Aeson. Both still clutched their Stingers.

The Aeson sidearms were almost as powerful as Eradicators, but not nearly as cruel. One blast, maybe two, were sufficient to breach the Kastazi's armor, bringing death instantly and without pain.

I took their Stingers in each hand and fired wildly as I ran. The farther I made it, the more things slowed down. I was adapting to the adrenaline. Regaining my focus. At the last possible second, I clocked a Kastazi firing at me from three o'clock. Ducking under his blast, I slid behind the supply drum.

"Get ready!" I shouted at Jagdish and Dominique. "When I say go, you run behind me!"

Panicked, they vigorously nodded.

I popped up and sprayed cover fire.

"Go!"

We ran back out into the open as I showered the Kastazi with Stinger blasts from all angles. A few meters from the gangplank, I stopped and covered Jagdish's and Dominique's backs. Once Gentry and Julian pulled them safely inside the ship, I dropped my Stingers and waited.

I was ready to die. I wanted to.

Ten meters to my left, a Rapax took aim at my chest, but someone took him out before he could fire. In the distance I saw Bossa lowering the barrel of a dead soldier's pulse rifle. Then he disappeared into the *Delphinium* like a phantom.

No more than three minutes could have passed since we had spilled under the bulkhead, but it felt like time had nearly stopped ten times in that space. Now, once again, every second felt like an eternity.

I wanted to let go. Just let it be over. But then my emptiness began to fill with the memory of all I had lost.

My father.

My mother.

Now JD.

No.

Not me.

You don't get me.

My anguish giving way to fury, I sprinted up the gangplank into Gentry's and Julian's waiting arms. They pulled me inside, and we took cover behind the *California*'s closing hatch.

Fuller took hold of my face and held it in his hands. "Everything in its right place. Everything as it's supposed to be."

I didn't understand, but his words brought on a strange feeling of déjà vu.

"What does that mean, Doctor?"

"Sentinel has everything you need," he answered, sliding out the hatch just as it closed.

Julian reached for its controls, but Gentry stopped him. "We can't. He's gone."

"We need him!"

"He gave us what we need. Nick."

The *California* rattled as she took fire from the Strikers hovering all around her. Each impact felt strangely muted.

Ohno craned her neck, trying to make sense of the soft hits reverberating off the hull. "At this range the Strikers should be tearing us apart!"

I pulled a command control module from its mount beside the hatch. As soon as I touched it, Sentinel gave me access to every one of the ship's systems without prompting me for a Command Key.

"It recognized your biosig," Bix observed. "It's not supposed to do that."

"No, it's not," I answered, holding the module out toward Gentry.

"What are you doing?"

"Restoring you to command. You're the ranking officer. This is your ship."

Gentry hesitantly took the module and peered at the survivors standing behind me. Nodding in unspoken agreement with whatever their faces were telling him, he handed the module right back to me.

"Your orders?"

Stunned, I didn't know how to react.

Another series of soft impacts landed against the *California*.

Liko stepped forward and repeated Gentry's gesture. "Your orders?"

Then Jagdish and Dominique. "Your orders?"

One by one, like a chorus of echoes, every student did the same.

Finally, Nicholas stepped forward. "Good to see you again, Vivien," he said, his voice finally returned. "Your orders, please."

The Holoview lit up to display countless Strikers raining fire on us, but their plasma tracers bounced off the *California* as harmlessly as rain.

"Grids?"

"Ninety-five percent and holding," Bix reported. "The grids' energy matrix is entirely different. It's like nothing I've ever seen before."

"Staxx made some upgrades."

Bix scanned his console. I could see a raging torrent of data reflecting in his glasses. "Not Staxx. This is Fuller's work. And it's not just the grids. It's everything."

I leaned back, settling into the captain's chair. "Blow the moorings and take us out of the berth at quarter speed."

"Aye," Julian confirmed while reversing throttle.

Our bodies jerked slightly as the ship pushed back from the platform.

"Go, no go for shipwide vitals?"

"Go for vitals," Anatoly replied.

"Go, no go for Navigation?"

Gentry consulted his console. "Go for Navigation."

"Rotate at one-hundred eighty degrees."

Julian adjusted his yoke. "Aye. Rotating one-hundred eighty degrees."

"Go, no go for propulsion on full?"

"No go," Liko reported from an auxiliary console. "Stand by. Checking on Ohno's progress."

Cold starting the *California* required a hands-on jump start. It wasn't a job that could be done remotely or alone, so Ohno enlisted a contingent of students to help her seed antimatter plasma into the ship's engines. Anything less than exacting precision had the potential to blow the ship to kingdom come.

"Talk to me, Liko. What's going on down there?"

Bix swiveled to face me. I recognized a familiar excitement peeking out from under his otherwise distressed posture.

"I can show you."

"No time for riddles, Bix."

"No time to explain."

Bix swiped his console, activating a flash of blinding light. As my eyes came back into focus, I saw everything. Not just what was in front of me, but literally *everything* on the ship. A fierce wave of nausea nearly sent me tumbling from my chair as images streaked through my mind faster than I could process them.

"Breathe. You're going to be okay," said Bix. "Fuller gave you a direct cortical interface. Every camera on the ship. They're your eyes."

The engine compartment. Medical. The hangar. Every one of the decks. Visuals of each flew past me as if rotating on the fast-spinning blades of a pinwheel. "It's too much! I can't handle it!"

"Breathe. Let your brain adapt."

I inhaled and exhaled in deep, even breaths. The pinwheel began to slow, just like Bix said it would.

"Concentrate. Use your mind. Tell Sentinel what you want to see."

I thought of Ohno and everything else fell away, leaving only the engine compartment and bridge. I saw both at the same time without any confusion or disorientation.

My nausea subsiding, I observed Ohno shouting orders. Students scrambled around the compartment with surprising syn-chronicity and purpose, manipulating the engines' many controls at her strict direction.

"She did it! Propulsion at the ready and standing by," Liko announced, telling me what I had already seen for myself.

"Commence countdown for full propulsion."

"Commencing countdown."

I turned my mind to Weapons Control, Delta Deck's manual-targeting theater. As fast as I summoned the thought, I could see inside its pitch-black confines. Six students stood in a V-shaped pattern, with Nick positioned at their head. Each wore blue glowing Holovisors that provided them a 360-degree view of the ship's outer perimeter.

"Ten seconds to full propulsion."

I hit my com, broadcasting wide to the ship.

"Attention all decks. This is the captain."

A full squadron of Strikers circled off our bow, regrouping in a coordinated attack pattern.

"None of you are soldiers, but you all know how to fight."

Nick and his team slowly raised their hands, revealing the motion-sensitive gloves that were their targeting controls for our full weapons arsenal.

"Five seconds to propulsion," Liko called.

"Together we are stronger than the enemy."

The Strikers dove and unleashed plasma fire at us. The flaming bolts bounced impotently off our grids.

"One second," Liko said.

"We are not the Resistance . . ."

My vision expanded, showing me the face of every living soul on the *California* all at once.

"We are Devastation Class."

"Go for full propulsion!" Liko exclaimed.

"Now let's show the Kastazi what that means!"

The *California* darted forward like a missile—piercing through the first line of Strikers like a razor-sharp bayonet. Bouncing off our grids like flies, the Kastazi ships plummeted down upon the planetoid's rocky palisades in flames.

Nick and his team waved their arms, together choreographing a devastating attack on the next wave charging at us from a distance. With every turn of their wrists and twitch of their fingers, a barrage of plasma rained down on the hostiles like a hurricane. The Holoview danced with light and fire while the weapons console incessantly chirped confirmations of their kills.

Beyond the chaotic symphony of destruction, a Kastazi War Cruiser coasted through the planetoid's narrow passage to block our escape. Before we could engage her, the *Delphinium* shot out from underneath us like a bullet. Firing supercharged plasma from her forward guns, she opened a gaping hole in the Cruiser's starboard hull. A half rotation of Nick's fist sent a phasing torpedo right through it. Another half rotation detonated it, obliterating the Cruiser in a bluish-white ring of flames. Bossa twisted the *Delphinium* through the blazing wreckage, punching his engines to their limit.

We barreled through the passage after him, but just as we surfaced, an oversized Striker closed on us, maneuvering more dynamically than the rest.

"RAF," I said, recognizing the hostile as a Rapax Attack Fighter. "Kill it, Nick."

He and his team immediately took aim.

"Wait! Hold fire! Hold fire!" Bix shouted.

"Hold fire!" I repeated into my com, trusting his call.

Bix pointed to a biosig on his console. "It's Fuller!"

"Are you sure?"

"Yes. He's at the controls."

"Open a—"

Before I could finish my sentence, the RAF vanished like a ghost.

Gentry squinted his eyes at the Holoview. "What just happened?"

"I think he . . ." Bix trailed off.

"Think he what?"

"Blinked."

"How can that be possible? The Kastazi aren't Blink-capable."

I gawked at the barren Holoview, dumbfounded.

"What do you want me to do?" Julian asked.

"Point us back toward the base," I answered, shaking off my distraction.

"Aye, bringing us around."

The *California* rotated to face the crater leading to the planetoid's interior.

The base lost, my call was clear. Still, I looked to Gentry to push me across the line.

"Finish it," he said.

I said a silent prayer for any Resistance fighters left alive. Nothing about it felt superstitious that time.

"Fire Fusion Package."

Nicholas and his team clasped their hands in front of their chests in unison, launching seven torpedoes in the same V-shaped configuration—one at the bow, three port side, and three starboard. Meeting five hundred meters in front of the *California*, they assembled into one and disappeared inside the crater.

"Detonate package."

Nicholas separated his hands, triggering a chain reaction of nuclear annihilation. The planetoid burned like a cinder, its many crevasses and canyons erupting with incandescent molten rock.

Together, we watched in silence.

"What do we do now?" Bix asked, violent, spitting flares of magma filling the Holoview just beside him.

"What JD told us to do. Get Nick home."

"Home? How are we supposed to get home without help?"

"Search Sentinel's registry for anything new or out of the ordinary," I answered, thinking back to Fuller's last words to me. "Tell me what you find."

CHAPTER 49

VIV

"IT DOESN'T MATTER WHO YOU REALLY ARE. What matters is who you were supposed to be. You can still be that person. Help is out there. Find it. Then follow the Beacon. If you don't, it's over. Not just for me. Not just for this ship. For all of us."

Standing in pitch black, I couldn't see a thing, but the peaceful beauty of Sigma 547-T wasn't very difficult for me to imagine. Just as it had in my time at Farragut, my mind often drifted to its distant paradise to find comfort.

"I never got a chance to soak this place in. How about you get me back here so I can."

Of all the files Staxx had uploaded to Sentinel, the one pertaining to Bossa was perhaps the hardest to believe. If the intel was accurate, it meant everything he'd tried to tell me about the *New Jersey* was true. It also meant he was much more than just another Outer Perimeter scavenger.

A pop of static flitted past my ears.

"Is that it?" Bix's voice descended upon me from the darkness.

If I hadn't gotten my message right yet, it was unlikely I ever would.

"That's it. Overwrite file Nixon Delta One, save, and export to Sentinel."

"Copy. Saved and exporting program update to Iso-Rec file registry."

The lights came on, revealing a barren compartment. Bix sat behind a soundproof glass partition. Arranged around me in a circular configuration was an array of heat-sensing cameras that had been tracking my every movement and linking them to my pre-ingested avatar.

"All right, let's go."

Making my way out the door, I couldn't shake the feeling that leaving behind a message meant I wasn't entirely confident in what we were about to do.

Waiting for us inside Sentinel had been something far more difficult to grapple with than anything Staxx had left behind—a file packet we had taken to calling *Mindbomb*. Authored by Fuller, its encryption was so complex that not even Bix could crack it. Liko had no better luck, but did eventually stumble upon something else. A not-very-well-hidden message in the packet's metadata:

*V_Nixon_eyes_only_*

Fuller wouldn't have locked his message in a box with no key, so I knew there had to be an answer. After days of fruitless brainstorming, it finally occurred to me that it might just be the most obvious one.

*V_Nixon_eyes_only_*
What if it meant exactly what it said?
My eyes only.

Following my hunch, Bix linked the file packet to the bridge's new cortical interface. With a swipe of his console and a flash of blinding light, Fuller's message was revealed to me. And then, just as quickly, it was gone.

Well, *almost* gone.

Despite his message being wiped from my memory, I was

somehow certain the amnesic effect was intentional and necessary to protect our mission.

I remembered Fuller's instructions for Phase One, the first steps of a plan that would get us to Earth safely and draw the Kastazi into the beginnings of a trap.

I also knew there would be three phases in all—the details of the other two buried somewhere deep inside my mind and set to be triggered by my intersection with certain unknown future events. Sort of like a "mindbomb" waiting to go off.

An echo of a larger understanding remained as well, its remnant giving me the confidence to believe that Fuller's puzzle pieces would eventually fit together—allowing us to breach the Kastazi's defenses and fulfill our mission of resurrecting the Gen One Hybrids. Everyone else, however, was left in the unenviable position of having to take their confidence from me on faith.

Bix stepped out from the adjacent control room, a frustrated look on his face.

"Third time you've recorded that message?" he asked as we began walking toward the lift. He was already struggling to trust the life-and-death plan I had relayed, with two-thirds missing, so the distraction of my message in a bottle to Bossa was clearly rubbing him the wrong way.

"Fourth," I replied.

"I still don't understand the point of this. If he ever gets your message, it means our plan failed."

"Which is exactly why we'd need his help."

"And you really think he's the right guy to be our last-hope Hail Mary?"

"You saw Staxx's files same as I did. If they're accurate—"

"*If* they're accurate," Bix cut me off. "Everything in those files is conjecture, pieced together from dribs and drabs of disparate intel. There could be ten other explanations for who he is and where he came from."

"He's obviously had extensive Alliance training. You saw how much he knew about this ship and all of our protocols."

Bix stopped in his tracks and looked at me as though insulted. "What?"

"Don't patronize me," he replied. "This isn't about who Bossa really is or how much he knew about this ship. You want to believe what's in those files because it'll finally give you your answer about what happened to the *New Jersey*."

"You think I've lost my objectivity?"

"I think that's definitely a question worth asking," he answered just as the Command Synth materialized before us.

"Yes, Joseph."

In the fourteen weeks since we'd escaped the Resistance base, the Command Synth had become a ubiquitous presence and constant resource to us all. Giving it a name helped everyone feel more comfortable engaging with it. Particularly the students.

Joseph hesitated before responding, as if considering the gravity of what he was about to say. Command Synths were programmed to mimic human behaviors, but something about his countenance felt uncannily real. Perhaps too much time in his company had started to blur the lines for me.

"You're needed on the bridge," he finally answered. "It's time."

Bix and I stood in the quiet as the lift whooshed us up to the bridge. Even after all our preparation, I still didn't feel ready. I wasn't sure I ever would.

"Tell me the Beacon is going to work. No matter what."

"It will," Bix replied. "I followed Fuller's specs to a tee."

In addition to Mindbomb, Fuller had left cache upon cache of specifications for new technologies inside Sentinel for us. Like the stealthing field generator that had allowed us to traverse the expanse undetected behind a phasing particle field.

"You're absolutely sure there's no way they'll be able to detect it?"

"No shot. Not even if they cut Nick in half."

The lift opened to the bridge, and, as was often the case, I almost expected to find JD waiting there for me. It was like a nightmare I hadn't yet woken from.

Gentry, now serving as my first officer, sat at Communications. Our chemistry wasn't perfect, but over time we had forged a mutual respect. Together we had decided to assign Nick to Weapons and also slotted Liko at Safi's vacant Navigation station, where, with a little help from us, he quickly got up to speed. As usual, Ohno and Anatoly occupied their posts at Engineering and Medical.

I missed having my hands on the controls, but Julian was a capable replacement for me at Piloting. Each day I'd stare at the back of his head, trying to make sense of his truth. In the days after Gallipoli, he had both loved and betrayed me and displayed the best and worst parts of himself. As much as I tried, I still couldn't understand him—let alone trust him. Regardless, survival required us to cooperate without enmity. So that's what we did.

"Report," I called out, easing into my chair.

"Confirmed sensor hit," Gentry responded, swiveling to face me. "UAS *Vanguard* patrolling Sector Delta Six One."

"Farther out than we expected."

"But still inside Earth Corridor. Exactly what we needed."

"How is it that we're only seeing them now?"

"Our sensors were looking for the wrong thing," Bix answered, settling himself into Analytics. "I'm seeing signatures similar to Alliance and Kastazi, but not quite either. Very strange."

A proximity alarm sounded as the *California* entered the *Vanguard*'s estimated sensor range.

"Bring it up on the Holoview."

"Activating Holoview."

The *Vanguard* flickered to life in front of us, its fuselage retrofitted in bizarre patterns of hexagonal scaling.

Julian leaned over his controls, gawking at the sight. "What is that?"

"Some kind of reactive shielding," Bix posited. "Their entire hull is energized."

"Instead of grids?"

"In addition to grids."

"Focus, people," I said. "This is it."

The alert grew louder and more frequent.

"We've run through this a million times," I continued. "Now we do it for real."

"Five thousand meters," Liko announced. "We've crossed the threshold."

"Drop stealthing field integrity by four percent."

"Aye," Ohno confirmed. "Dropping stealthing field integrity by four percent."

"Do it slow. Make it look like we're damaged and bleeding ions."

"Copy that."

Another alert sounded.

"They can see us," Gentry reported.

"Good," I replied. "Grids?"

"Stable. Holding at one hundred percent."

"Everyone on Beta Deck in their safety positions?"

"Affirmative."

"Dampening matrix?"

"Active."

"Nick, the Beacon?"

"Cycling pattern initiated per Doctor Fuller's instructions."

A new alert chimed from Communications.

"It's the *Vanguard*," Gentry confirmed.

"Knock, knock," Anatoly pondered aloud.

"All right," I responded. "Let's open the door."

"Aye, opening com."

As soon as the link went live, I recognized who it was.

"Identify yourself." It felt surreal to be staring at the face of Mathias Strauss on my Holoview. Captain of the UAS *Vanguard*, he was a legend of the Nine-Year War.

I paused to consider everything I knew about him. It came as no surprise to see him as a traitor. Even when he was "one of us," he had earned himself something of an ugly, bloodthirsty reputation.

"Identify yourself," Strauss insisted a second time.

"My name is Vivien Nixon. Captain of the UAS *California*."

Strauss took two steps forward, his face filling the Holoview. "No. You are a child playing a dangerous game."

"Let's just get on with it, shall we?" I baited him, staying on plan.

Strauss angrily punched his fingers against his command module, and a three-dimensional identification photo appeared on the Holoview alongside him. *John Douglas Marshall: Age 18.* My heart broke all over again as JD's image rotated on a 360-degree axis.

"John Marshall—where is he?" he demanded.

"KIA," I replied.

Strauss's angry expression gave way to something that looked a whole lot more like anxiety, as if JD's demise had some greater consequence than I could have known. "I am placing you and your crew under arrest as enemy combatants of the Alliance. Lower your grids and prepare to be boarded."

Not yet. I had to take it further. Make him believe we were ready to die.

"I'm afraid you have it backward," I answered. "We're all that's left of the Alliance. You and your crew are treasonous cowards and Kastazi sympathizers. So just in case it isn't clear . . . no, I will not be lowering my grids."

Gentry anxiously glanced over his shoulder at me, concerned I was overplaying things.

"Then you leave us no choice but to destroy you," Strauss replied, looking suddenly more emboldened.

"Give us your best shot," I countered, knowing we had to take a beating in order to draw him in.

"We will," Strauss glibly replied as six hulking hostiles materialized from behind stealthing fields, three on either side of the *Vanguard*. The sight of the ships took my breath away. A peculiar amalgam of both Alliance and Kastazi technology, each was twice the size of the *California*.

One ship or seven, it made no difference. We still had to take it all the way to the brink.

I faced Strauss, narrowed my eyes at him, and issued the command I knew could very well be my last if everything didn't go according to plan.

"Fire all weapons!"

We bombarded the hostiles with everything we had, but nothing in the *California*'s arsenal came close to penetrating any of the ships' defenses.

"They're absorbing our plasma fire!" Bix shouted. "Phasing torpedoes aren't getting through either!"

The *Vanguard* returned a volley of plasma fire at us. The streaming flares' incendiary radiance saturated the bridge in bright orange light.

"Incoming!" Gentry yelled.

Absorbing a thunderous impact, the *California* rattled down to its substructure.

"Their weapons' yield is off the charts!" Bix hollered.

"Grids falling fast. Down to forty percent," Ohno reported right after him.

"Now?" Gentry anxiously urged me.

"No, not yet," I asserted, holding firm. "Maintain position, keep firing."

The *Vanguard* launched another sortie at us, sending a wave of electromagnetic interference sizzling through our coms system.

"Brace for impact!" Anatoly shouted.

The *Vanguard's* strike landed like a punch to the gut, its concussive force slamming my head back against my chair.

"Grids at ten percent!"

"Now?" Gentry asked again, shouting above the *California's* creaking hull.

I nodded. "Now," I confirmed. "Show them our cards."

"Aye. Deactivating dampening matrix."

The *Vanguard's* plasma cannons glowed hot, charging for another barrage.

"We can't take another hit," Ohno warned.

Hovering menacingly before us, the *Vanguard* edged closer but did not fire.

"What's happening?"

"They're scanning us again," Bix reported.

"Anything?"

"Not yet."

"Come on . . . Come on . . . You should be able to see him by now."

Bix's shoulders slumped in relief at the sounding of an alert.

"That's it," he said, acknowledging what we had all been waiting for. "They've locked onto Nick's signature."

The *Vanguard* powered down its weapons, and one hostile broke from formation, aligning her nose only a few hundred meters off ours.

Then the Holoview abruptly dropped to static.

Gentry pushed away from his console. "That ship. It's overriding our coms system."

A silhouette gradually bled its way through the nebulous soup of gray-and-white fuzz. At first I thought my mind was playing tricks on me, but as the shadowy figure came into clear view, there was no denying it was real.

"Mother?"

"I've targeted forty-seven biosignatures on Beta Deck. Surrender or I will kill them all. You have five seconds to comply."

"Mom, no! It can't be . . . You can't . . ."

"Three seconds."

Another figure stepped into view just beside her. *Captain Philip Marshall.*

"They're arming weapons again!" Bix shouted.

"What is this? What are you—?"

"One second."

I felt like I was about to crumble, but I had to finish the last piece of our plan.

"We surrender," I said, setting Phase One into full motion.

LOCKED IN AN EMPTY DARKNESS, THERE WERE no memories to fill my dreams. I possessed no identity or purpose. There was only pure existence. Then came flashes of experience. I recognized them as my own, but they neither pleased nor disturbed me. That was because emotion came last, traumatically invading the peace of my blissful nothingness. As I opened my eyes, it wasn't like waking up. It was like being born.

I could feel a bed beneath me, its frame rattling with the familiar vibration of a slow-moving ship. A small beam of starlight filtered in from a porthole above, dimly illuminating the cramped quarters of what looked like an old Alliance science vessel. I slid my feet to the floor and stood.

"Welcome back," a voice called out from the shadows.

My brain still searching for focus, I couldn't quite place it.

"What happened to me?"

"You died. Do you feel rested?"

I felt more than rested. I felt perfect. I ran my hands down my torso. My skin was smooth and pristine. I lifted my shirt to see if it was real. The ugly burns from my childhood were gone.

My unseen companion stepped into the starlight. It was Dr. Samuel Fuller. "I decided not to restore your scarring," he said. "It seemed . . . unnecessary . . . this time."

Fear and confusion infested my mind. Succumbing to dizzying panic, I braced myself against the wall. My hand came to rest next to a small com unit. Its display read UAS *Tripoli*. "What have you done to me? What do you mean, *this time*?"

"I made a promise to your father. You were never supposed to know."

"Know what?!"

"The truth."

Somehow I already knew. But I needed to hear him say the words. "Tell me!"

"This isn't the first time you've died. In the Kastazi attack on Camp Jemison, you weren't just injured. You were killed. But I brought you back. I made you . . ."

"A Hybrid? Are you telling me that I'm a Hybrid?"

Fuller smiled at me. "No, John Douglas. *I made you something more.*"

ACKNOWLEDGMENTS

We are thankful to all our incredible friends, family, and colleagues who encouraged and supported us on our journey to bring the world of *Devastation Class* to life. While there are many who endured our constant creative anxieties and all too often cancelled plans, we want to thank those people without whom *Devastation Class* would still be confined to our imaginations.

FROM GLEN

My brother, Ralph Zipper, for telling me it was okay to stop being a lawyer, and promising to catch me if I fell. My mother, Dorothy Golaine, for bringing me into this world, and never delivering on the threat to take me back out of it when I misbehaved.

FROM ELAINE

My mother, Joanne Parnell Mongeon, for encouraging me to be a writer and creator for as long as I can remember, seeing the story-teller in me when I didn't, and providing infinite love and support. My siblings, Daniel Mongeon and Deborah Mongeon, for igniting my love of sci-fi and cheering me on. My chosen families—my women, my dudes, my people, my cheerleaders—for inspiring me, filling me up, and holding me up.

FROM BOTH OF US

Tom Forget, for being the first person to read the beginnings of our idea—then called "California"—and insisting it had to be written as a novel.

Charlie Olsen, our friend and agent, for believing in us from day one and fighting for our vision ever since.

Hannah VanVels and Jacque Alberta, our editors who helped make our good ideas better and our bad ones die peaceful, dignified deaths.

Amy Nickin, Erica Barmash, Lee Goldberg, Ellen Goldsmith-Vein, Richard Heller, Mark Merriman, University of Pennsylvania professor Mbacke Thioune, Lindsay Williams, and Thom Zimny, whose guidance and counsel steered us through so many storms that otherwise surely would have sunk us.

Michelle Holme, who captured so much of the essence of the *Devastation Class* world in a single, striking image.

And, again, to our fathers and Anthony the dog. It breaks our hearts that we cannot share this time with you, but they are still filled with endless love and gratitude because you made it possible.

CONNECT WITH GLEN ZIPPER AND ELAINE MONGEON!

GLEN

Twitter: @Zipper

Instagram: @glenzipper

ELAINE

Twitter: @E_Mongeon

Instagram: @elainemongeon

ABOUT THE AUTHORS

GLEN ZIPPER PRODUCED THE OSCAR-WINNING DOCUMENTARY *UNDEFEATED,* and the hit Netflix series *Dogs*. Born in New York City and raised in Fort Lee, NJ, Glen currently resides in Los Angeles, where he enjoys motorcycle riding and stopping to pet every dog he sees.

AWARD-WINNING FILMMAKER ELAINE MONGEON WROTE AND DIRECTED the short films *Good Morning* for Warner Bros. Pictures and *Swiped to Death* for Hulu and the Sundance Institute. She also served as an associate producer on *Magic Mike XXL*. Elaine has a love for the outdoors and has been known to spend her time traversing glaciers in Canada and precision motorcycle riding.

BLINK